Wake a
Sleeping Tiger

Wake a Sleeping Tiger

Lora Leigh

BERKLEY
NEW YORK

BERKLEY
An imprint of Penguin Random House LLC
375 Hudson Street, New York, New York 10014

Copyright © 2017 by Lora Leigh

ISBN: 9780425265475

An application to register this book for cataloging has been submitted to the Library of Congress.

First Edition: March 2017

Printed in the United States of America
1   3   5   7   9   10   8   6   4   2

Cover photo by Claudio Marinesco
Cover design by Rita Frangie

Yesterday's dreams . . .
Today's reality . . .
Tomorrow's hope . . .

· THE WORLD · OF THE BREEDS

They were created; they weren't born.

They were trained; they weren't raised.

They were genetic creations. Human DNA merged with that of the animal. The perfect soldier, a disposable creature.

They were created to die, often in the most horrible experiments that the human mind could ever imagine.

Their lives were a horror story from the moment of their births.

Babes that knew no tender care, no sweet lullabies nor a mother's love. They cried until hoarse, until they learned no one was coming unless they required feeding. And many times, they were allowed to go hungry until they lay weak and in pain.

Only the most basic of service was given to the babes. Creations that millions, billions of dollars had gone into in more than a century of scientific experiments and genetic engineering. "Cubs," they were called, never "babes," but they were living beings that, in terms of the cost of their creation, were nearly priceless.

Yet in the eyes of those who made them, they were worth no more than the young women who died giving birth to one after another of the creations implanted in their wombs.

Human and animal. Determined and far stronger in both spirit and body than the scientists could have ever envisioned.

Despite the cruelties heaped upon their young bodies, the experiments, the demented training exercises designed to ensure their success in any mission they were given, many of them survived. The strength of their hatred, of their hunger for freedom, refused to allow them to pass quietly from the world they'd been brought into.

Those creations are free now.

They're triumphing against all efforts to see them back in the labs from where they came.

Their intelligence is far greater than any could ever comprehend. Their strength is more primal than any could ever suspect.

And they're living on the fragile, desperate hope that the world never learns the secrets they fight to hide.

· THE BREEDS ·

From the journal of
Dr. Ambrose,
Geneticist,
Genetic Theorist

Science.

The ultimate good or the ultimate evil?

In this, I say, we have become the ultimate evil.

Two hundred years before, a vision came into being, one that began with the purest of intentions, yet turned to the darkest of perversions.

The creation of an altered being, one that began with the mutation of the most base genetic code even before conception. Those first scientists had a vision for their creations. A mix of human and animal, stronger, faster, more enduring and impervious to the illnesses or wounds that kill and maim. *If such a species of man could be created, they argued, then they could be studied, their talents used to strengthen the human race.*

Arrogance.

There is such arrogance in science.

What began with such innocent intentions became darker, more perverted, with the first surviving human/animal creation that took breath and grew strong. Stronger than any of them imagined. The animal strength and power merged with the human spirit and gave birth to such determined will, such preternatural beauty and grace that those scientists could not bear to admit they could not control what they believed they had created.

The spirit, the heart and soul of life, cannot be created. Man cannot breathe life into a being, and he cannot sustain that life against the worst of odds.

And they hated the beings they envisioned for the very fact that they knew and understood that what they altered, a superior being, was refining, strengthening.

Man. Born to such innocence, so easily corrupted by such black evil. Soon, they tortured the beings they birthed. They created such horrendous experiments—in the name of science, they were eager to argue—but it was in the name of their own greed and corrupt natures.

For over a century and a half they gave birth to one after another of those they called Breeds. Hundreds, perhaps thousands. They were soldiers sent to assassinate, to spy, to gain riches and power for the organization that funded the research program. Then they were experimented upon, to see how much pain they could endure, how deeply they could be wounded and still survive.

The babes, to ensure only the strong survived, weren't cuddled or given affection. They weren't nurtured or raised. From the moment they drew their first breath, each moment of their lives was an exercise in training.

In horror.

Such horrors.

So many babes left to die, to wither to a final breath when but a gentle touch would have brought about untold strength.

They were Breeds. Less than human, less than animal as far as those scientists were concerned, and they spilled the blood of the Breeds, took life after life, as though such atrocities would never be found out.

But they were found out.

Found out, proof given, the creations then turned on those who believed themselves to be their creators, and each day they're free is the greatest insult to the organization that funded them, gave birth to them, tortured, maimed and committed such evil against them.

Each day they're free is a miracle, a gift I pray they appreciate each moment of. Because the Breeds hold many secrets of their creation and many more will arise. Man may believe he created them, but a much higher power breathed life into them, and that power is refining them and re-defining them, daily.

And that redefinition could end up being the very weapon that destroys each and every Breed walking free.

· P R O L O G U E ·

From Graeme's Journal
The Recessed Primal Breed

Recessive, Primal Breed genetics, after age five, begins with an animal's awareness of its own strength and the danger surrounding it. It can also be the child's primal response to protecting itself and the creature lurking inside.

Continued recession after age eighteen to twenty can be blamed solely on the Breed and the dictates of his human genetics. The animal refuses to go against its nature, and the human refuses to acknowledge what the animal knows. At its base, the stubbornness of the two natures is in conflict, both refusing to relent.

In the end, the awakening of those recessed abilities comes when the animal grows tired of the human's obstinate nature and surges forward to take control in ways that prove false the belief that the human controls the predator within.

———————

Five in the morning was too damned early for a knock on his front door. He was barely out of bed and showered. His coffee was still dripping into the cup and he hadn't even had a chance to strap his weapon on.

Cullen Maverick liked things in order whenever possible. It made life a hell of a lot easier.

Pulling his weapon from his side holster, he made his way to the front door, confident that if a threat awaited outside, then it wasn't directed by forces other than a normal workday upheaval. As commander of the Navajo Covert Law Enforcement Agency, he'd made a few enemies over the years.

Those enemies weren't the ones he watched out for, though. It was the enemies he'd made as a teenager that worried him.

The knock came again, firm though not masculine in the least. Recognizing the sound, a direct knock without pounding, he knew instantly who it was without questioning how he knew. His lips almost quirked into a smile.

A quick look outside the narrow window next to the door showed a slender feminine figure dressed in jeans and a light jacket. One of the junior members of the force, she'd been on a few operations, though he'd refused to give the go-ahead to move her higher.

Chelsea Martinez, with her black hair, brown eyes and dusky skin of combined Navajo and Caucasian parents, stared at the door as though she could will it open. She was a force to be reckoned with when she wanted to be.

He should know; he was usually the one butting heads with her.

Swinging the door open as he leaned against the side of the wall, he stared down at her somber, implacable expression with a slight smile.

Dawn was barely lighting the land outside, giving it an otherworldly, quiet sense of solitude belied by the homes along the side of and facing his own.

"You didn't call, so I assume this isn't life or death," he remarked when she just stared up at him silently.

She'd been doing that a lot in the past few months, just staring at him as though she expected something from him, as though he'd forgotten something.

She cleared her throat, lips thinning, her gaze sliding from his for just a second before jerking back.

"I need to talk to you." Quiet, intense, her demeanor wasn't threatening, just too damned serious.

"Come on, I'll give you the first cup of coffee," he sighed heavily.

No doubt she was there to argue over her place in the Agency again. She'd been pushing for some of the more dangerous assignments in the past months. Covert Ops agents were kept quiet. They had no official uniforms, didn't call attention to themselves. Chelsea was one of their more covert agents, though she mainly worked in an assistant capacity at the office. She could streamline files and people like nobody's business. Hell, her name wasn't even officially listed with the Agency and he liked it that way. It lessened any danger she might face and ensured he didn't have to worry about losing a damned good friend because someone else blinked.

She was too young to be part of operations, he'd tried to explain to her, to make her understand that he couldn't put her in the line of fire until her training was far more seasoned.

"Here you go." Stepping into the kitchen, he removed that first cup of coffee and placed it on the round table that sat in the middle of the darkened room. "Flip a light on if you need to."

He rarely turned the lights on in the place simply because he spent the least amount of time there as possible. It was a place to sleep and keep the few possessions he owned. Mainly, his clothes.

Sometimes, the television screen set in the fridge door was on, but not this morning. He hadn't had time yet to turn it on, and music would get on his nerves after an hour or so.

"I'm fine," she assured him.

His night vision had improved over the past years. At first, he'd questioned the change until realizing his twin, Gideon, was in the area. For some reason the appearance of the Primal Bengal sibling had sharpened a few of the recessed Breed traits Cullen possessed, but not enough to change his life. Not enough to worry him.

"Let me get my coffee before we start, minx." He shot her a grin. That solemn, sad expression was beginning to bother him in ways he couldn't put a finger on.

"Of course." The answer wasn't exactly what he wanted to hear. "I know how you are without that first cup."

There was no amusement in her tone, no teasing.

What the hell was up with her?

Leaning back against the counter and crossing his arms over his chest, he frowned at her. Damn, she looked so sad, not angry or upset. There was a sense of loss emanating from her, and he couldn't find a reason for it.

Pulling the cup free of the coffeemaker when it finished, he lifted it, sipped and continued to regard her. She wasn't fidgeting in front of him, wasn't acting in the least nervous as she usually did whenever she was ready to put forth yet another position she could hold on an operation. Anything to get her out of the office and to put her training to work, she'd demand.

She was a member of the Breed Underground, she'd pointed out the last time. She'd helped move juvenile and adult Breeds more than half a dozen times, keeping them just ahead of the Genetics Council or pure blood fanatics searching for them.

And yes, she had done that, but he didn't command the Breed Underground. He couldn't disqualify her as a member of the forces that aided hidden Breeds or mates, so he ground his teeth each time she went out and argued with her cousins over it on a constant basis.

She was too innocent for covert work, too innocent to be scarred by the crazies in the world.

"Spit it out," he sighed, lowering the cup and facing her quiet, intense expression. "What have you come up with this time? What argument do you think will sway me?"

She blinked a few times and if he wasn't mistaken her eyes actually looked as though—were those tears?

What the hell had happened? Setting his coffee aside, he prepared to act, to fix whatever had been done to bring tears to her eyes.

"Chelsea?" he questioned gently. "What's going on, honey?"

Cullen watched as she pulled back the front of her jacket, removed a folded piece of white paper from inside it and slowly laid it on the table.

Cullen swore he felt the need to growl. One of those deep, dark rumbles of dangerous warning he'd heard come from his twin's throat more than once.

Every muscle in his body tensed and he knew, knew to the soles of his damned feet what that simple piece of paper represented.

9

His gaze lifted to hers once again.

"You don't want to do this, Chelsea," he sighed. "Come on, honey, we can talk about this."

They had to talk about it.

They were going to talk about it.

He'd be damned if he'd let her—

"It's my resignation from the Agency," she told him, her tone soft but firm, determined.

She'd made her mind up. By God, she actually thought she'd made her mind up to leave him—to leave the Agency. That she could just walk away.

He stared at it, glared at it.

If he had his way it would burst into flames and the memory of it would dissipate along with the paper.

"The hell you are." Lifting his head, he directed that glare at her.

And she met it.

Not once did she flinch or look away. Not one time did she even pretend to acknowledge his dominance. Hell, she didn't even consider it.

"The Agency isn't going to work for me, Cullen—"

"Because I don't let you run it?" he snapped. "You don't make the decisions there, girl. If you did, 'Commander' would be sitting in front of your name instead of mine."

There were times, few though they had been, that standing firm would encourage her to back down. She had to back down on this.

She nodded sharply. "Agreed. But I never wanted to run it. I just wanted to be a part of it, not a glorified running girl for you and the other agents. That's not happening, so it's time I leave."

His jaw tightened with a surge of anger at once confusing and filled with frustration.

"You won't give it time," he began, his back teeth grinding.

"I don't have any more time to give it, Cullen." Her lips tilted in remorse as she lifted one hand out to him before dropping it just as quickly. "It's just time, okay?"

"Time for what?" He stepped closer, though she chose that moment to look away from him, unaware he was coming closer, that his refusal to accept this was about to get up close and personal.

"Grandfather agrees it's time I go. That I find my own way . . . Cullen?" She turned back, her gaze going first to where he was supposed to be, then to the shadow suddenly at her side.

"Cullen?" Breathless, a woman's sound, one filled with surprise, a bit of shock and a hint of apprehension as he swung her around, pulling her against him, letting her feel the erection he had no intention of hiding from her any longer.

And damn her. Her lips parted; her eyes, like soft melted chocolate, stared up at him, widening, then turning slumberous as her breathing escalated, her breasts rising and falling faster as he held her to him.

What the hell was wrong with him?

That distant thought wasn't enough to stop him, it wasn't enough to pull back, to free her and let her walk away. He'd known for years, far too many years that this was coming. And when it happened, letting her go wouldn't be an option. All that wild independence and pure energy she possessed would have to be tamed. The thought of the danger she'd face otherwise was more than he could contemplate.

"This is why," he snarled, his lips lowering to her ear, his own breathing harder, hunger driving a stake straight to his balls as he fought the need to take her then and there. To back her against the wall, get her hot and ready for him before taking her. He'd take her from behind, pushing inside the sweet heat between her thighs as his teeth gripped her neck—

They were already there, raking over the tender flesh at the bend of her neck and shoulder, gripping, releasing, his tongue laving the sharp bite. Her nails were gripping his shoulders, her head resting against his arm as he held her, the little cry that left her throat one of pleasure and shock. Sharp, sweet pleasure struck at his senses, the reaction so strong, so deep he felt it awaken something inside him that he knew he couldn't allow free.

Something dark.

Something hungry—

"Fuck!" As quick as he'd pulled her to him, Cullen released her and all but jumped back from her.

God, the scent of her, the taste of her skin, so sweet and soft. Giving his head a hard shake and turning his back on her, he raked his fingers through his hair and fought to get a grip on himself.

Lust had never controlled him. He'd never let his hungers free like that, even during his marriage, before his wife's painful death; he'd never felt that deep, dark hunger, like another presence coming alive inside him.

"God, Chelsea, I'm sorry." What more could he say? He couldn't explain it, even to himself.

"Good-bye, Cullen."

He turned as she raced from the kitchen to the living room. He'd taken two running steps to stop her before pulling back, forcing himself to stop, to let her go. His lips pulled back in fury, a snarl ripped from him seconds before he turned and plowed his fist into the wall, burying it in the suddenly crumbling drywall.

Jerking back, he stared at his knuckles, his fingers. They ached, but not from the strike. And it wasn't just the fist that slammed into the wall that was aching; his other hand was balled so tight he swore his nails were pricking the flesh of his palm.

"Damn her!" he bit out, forcing himself back to the kitchen and that damned letter on the table.

Before he could stop himself, he ripped it to shreds and let the pieces fall to the floor, watching them flutter with a slow, gliding grace.

She'd be back.

It was just another damned way to show him how serious she was. He'd put her on one of the less dangerous operations when she came back, he promised himself. Hell, he should have done it already but he liked having her with him in the office. She was funny, insightful. She smelled good—

And she'd run from him.

He must have scared her, though Chelsea wasn't the type to get scared over a kiss. He knew her better than that. And she knew him better than to think he'd hurt her. He'd give her a day or two, let both of them calm down, and then she'd be back.

She couldn't have been serious.

He wouldn't allow it.

He couldn't allow it.

· C H A P T E R   I ·

From Graeme's Journal
The Recessed Primal Breed

The Primal Breed will know his mate, sensing her even without the benefit of Mating Heat. The recessed Primal will sense his mate, know her and find comfort and calm in her presence. Only Mating Heat will release his Breed genetics, though, and allow the Primal free of its cage—

NAVAJO NATION
PINON, ARIZONA

Oh God!

  Oh God!

  She was just a baby.

Tiny, delicate, a mop of tangled black hair and wide, shock-filled eyes.

Rage clenched Chelsea's guts, formed a layer of ice around her emotions and stilled her racing heart. Logic and training snapped in and she forced herself to move into position slowly.

Horror. Terror.

Those distant, primal warnings of evil were pushed quickly to the back of her mind as the child stumbled forward.

Oh God, she had to get just a little bit closer. If this wasn't timed just right, if Chelsea didn't calculate everything perfectly, then she knew that baby wouldn't be the only one who died in this lonely desert tonight.

Night vision glasses allowed her to pick up even the most minute detail in the deepening night. The sight of huge bite marks over the child's body would live in Chelsea's nightmares. If she survived. Deep, jaggedly torn flesh still seeped blood, spilling more down the already bloodstained little body.

Long, tangled black hair fell to the child's shoulders and covered the side of her heavily bruised and swollen face. She was weak, far too cold and suffering blood loss definitely, possibly hypothermal shock. If she didn't get that child out of there fast, then she was going to die.

Come here, baby. I'm right here. Come on, let me take you to your momma . . .

The plea was soundless, no doubt useless, but still, she urged the child to the edge of the rising tower of rock that hid her presence from the Coyote soldiers.

She didn't dare show herself. If they saw her, then she'd never have time to get the baby into the Desert Runner she'd taken out that night on patrol.

She was in the middle of a nightmare she couldn't have imagined. Even her deepest, darkest fears didn't hold anything this horrific.

Demonic yips and howls filled the night with terrifying sounds.

They were merely tormenting the little baby, keeping her little heart beating fast and hard, her blood seeping steadily from her wounds.

So much evil. The creatures pushing the child through the night were hellish. Only hell could conceive monsters such as the ones trailing after the child.

Right here, baby. Come on, Louisa, you're almost safe. Let's go find Momma . . . She kept her eyes on the child, willing her to come to her, to sense her waiting in the shadows, ready to scoop her up and race her away from this nightmare.

"Momma, help me." The night carried the hoarse, dazed little voice clearly to where Chelsea hid. "Momma, help me." Over and over the ragged plea filled Chelsea's soul with agony and threatened to pierce the layer of ice covering her emotions.

If she let the fear free now, then she'd lose her mind, Chelsea knew. There would be no way to function, to think.

She took her eyes off the child only long enough to check the distance between the enemy and the little girl stumbling through the dark.

The Coyote soldiers were keeping Louisa in sight. If Chelsea just waited, remained out of their field of vision, then she'd have Louisa and be gone before they could get close enough to stop her. Then it would just be a matter of staying ahead of them until she got to safety.

She'd glimpsed their Runner, but she knew hers would be lighter, the motor modified to get an edge on the ones being used by the soldiers. The Breed Underground modified their vehicles for speed rather than defense or heavy weapons. Still, the Coyotes' Runner would be hard to get away from without a good head start.

It wouldn't be easy.

Watching the little girl, Chelsea gritted her teeth and made herself wait. Just a little more.

That's it, Louisa. Come this way. I'm right here, baby.

"Momma. Help me, Momma." The little voice was so weak, the night so cold, and time was running out.

Holding the blanket she carried ready, Chelsea kept a wary eye on the Coyotes and waited, still, silent. The body-warming technology of the covering would hopefully keep the little girl warm enough and protect her from further chill as they raced through the cold night; the open design of the Runner would do little to stave off the chill.

The Coyotes paused, yips and laughter filling the desert as Louisa headed straight for Chelsea, her dazed eyes staring unseeing into Chelsea through the darkness of night.

She could do this. Louisa was almost in place. Just a little closer.

The kids' parents were about thirty minutes away, their desert estate well armed as they waited for word of their daughter. Search efforts were being concentrated in the opposite direction; the report of Coyote soldiers closer to Window Rock had drawn searchers there.

It was that odd piece of information Chelsea had collected the day before that placed these creatures closer to Pinon and already had her in the area when the report went out. She was turning around and heading toward Window Rock when she'd heard the Coyotes.

The child stumbled to her knees and Chelsea felt her breath catch. She was so close.

"Come to me, Louisa," she whispered, a breath of sound she prayed the Coyotes didn't catch.

Louisa made it to her feet, jerky, uncoordinated, but she made it to the edge of the rock.

Chelsea moved.

Snapping forward, she wrapped the dark blanket around Louisa's slight body, lifted her into her arms and ran the ten feet to the Runner she'd left on standby. Before she could jump into the Runner, the night went silent. Totally, completely silent. There was no time to secure the little girl into the opposite seat now.

No time.

It had just run out.

As she latched the restraining harness around both of them, the feel of Louisa shuddering and the sound of her gasping breaths filled Chelsea with dread.

Enraged howls filled the night as Chelsea slammed the Runner into gear and the desert vehicle shot forward. The deep tread of the tires bit into dirt, sand and gravel, then all but picked up and flew through the night.

Thirty minutes.

Thirty minutes to the Cerves estate, and she was on her own until she got there. The radio had gone out, refusing to work, but there was also a chance the Coyotes' Runner was equipped with a jammer. And she wasn't far enough away from them for her radio to work yet.

The Runner's back cameras and radar were working great, though. Good enough to see that those bastards were gaining on her.

She should have never come out alone.

Under no circumstances.

She should have called in backup when she first heard the Coyotes' howls. But her cousin Linc was manning communications and he would have ordered her back.

She'd already been in the area when she picked up the radio transmissions earlier that night that the Cerveses' young daughter had been taken from the compound by suspected Council Breeds.

How the Coyotes managed that, she couldn't imagine.

Checking radar and cameras again, she calculated the distance to the compound and saw a glimmer of hope. She was actually closer than she'd thought she'd be. Not much farther.

Not that she would be exactly safe once she arrived at their compound—if she arrived. The Cerves family had brutal reputations. The Cerves criminal cartel didn't wait to ask questions. They killed first.

As she checked the monitor again, her jaw tightened. Shifting gears with fierce, quick movements, she heard power build in the motor as she pushed it for more speed, gritting her teeth and restraining a curse as the first bullet struck the side of the Runner.

The desert vehicle wasn't bullet resistant and the Coyotes knew it.

Fire flashed in the cameras and the sound of automatic gunfire behind her, pelting over the Runner, had her using every trick she knew to push the motor harder, faster.

Gunfire still erupted behind her, but the pinging had stopped. She estimated she was staying just out of reach of them. But she and little Louisa weren't home free yet, and she was running straight into an armed force that would already be prepared to shoot at the first sign of a threat. A Runner crashing the gates would definitely be seen as a sign.

The night sped by as adrenaline pumped fast and hard through her body and the Runner raced through the desert.

She had to keep both hands on the steering wheel. At the speeds she was pushing the Runner to, she didn't dare take one off to comfort the baby.

Louisa was only eight years old, though, and Chelsea knew that comfort was something the child could have used.

Eight years old.

If she survived, would her young mind ever pull free of what had happened tonight?

Twenty minutes.

She'd been racing through the night for twenty minutes.

The temperature gauge on the Runner was edging higher. It wasn't meant to run this hard, this fast, for this distance.

She was close, though. Any minute she should see the glow of the lights that lit the estate like a damned airport runway.

Guards had surrounded it earlier in the day before Louisa's disappearance. Surely they were still there.

What if they weren't?

What if the estate was deserted?

As she flew over the next rise, those lights glowed in the distance. Rather than pulling back, the Coyotes were firing again, and another ping to the side of the Runner had Chelsea quickly twisting the wheel, fighting to keep the Coyotes behind her. The chance of a bullet hitting her was slighter there. There was no protection to the side.

As she drew closer to the estate, she could see men running, automatic weapons in their hands. The gates weren't opening and there was no time to stop. If she stopped, her side would be exposed as the Coyotes raced past her. She'd be easy to pick off.

Praying the reinforced metal of the Runner's front guard held up, she pointed the Runner toward the gates, her teeth locked tight, her eyes narrowing on that point. If she could just make it to those gates and crash through . . .

As long as the Cerves guards didn't shoot her first.

She prayed they glimpsed the Breed Underground insignia she hurried to flip on. The bright red BU on the front guard was all she'd have to alert them that she wasn't some dumbass just hoping to break through and cause murder and mayhem.

No, she was bringing the murder and mayhem.

"Hang on, baby," she screamed above the sound of the Runner's motor.

Louisa's arms and legs tightened around her, but not by much. Chelsea could feel the dampness of her night suit from the little girl's blood and the child's cold flesh.

"Momma's waiting for you, baby."

She prayed that Samara Cerves—the Blood Queen, she was called—was waiting for the little girl who still whimpered for her, and that the savagery she was reported to have wasn't something her child knew.

Chances were slim, though.

Still, the Cerves compound was the little girl's only hope. And God help the family if anything happened to Chelsea because her own family wouldn't play nice.

Automatic weapons were turned on her as a dozen or more soldiers and security personnel braced to fire on her. Faces brutally hard, determined . . . murderous.

Her life flashed before her eyes and one image held in her mind.

"Cullen." She whispered his name as the gates loomed, coming closer, faster. "I'm sorry . . ."

Metal hit metal, the Runner reducing speed with a force that had the safety seat and harness reacting with the same speed to hold them in place. The collision rippled around the powerful vehicle, the frame taking the brunt of the force, the seat reacting to the still-strong shock wave that hit the interior.

Automatic gunfire ruptured the night as the gates were pushed open, and the Runner came to a stop several feet inside the interior of the compound.

Chelsea was confident the child hadn't sustained further injuries, though for some reason, her own arm was burning like hell.

"Wait! Wait!" she screamed, fighting the hard hands that reached in, tore at the harness and tried to jerk her from the seat. "Louisa. I have Louisa."

She scrambled to release the restraint, trying to be gentle, to hold the child securely as she whimpered, crying for her momma.

"I have her," she cried out, suddenly staring down the barrel of a gun, eyes wide, the certainty of death filling her mind. "I have Louisa."

Hands shaking, she let the blanket fall back, her eyes lifting to the cold, stark blue gaze of the Blood Queen herself. In those crystal-hard eyes Chelsea saw a mother's torment and a killer's need for blood.

"Momma." Weak, fear and terror worn, the little girl was suddenly trying to struggle against Chelsea, ragged nails dragging against the shoulder of Chelsea's black top.

Frantic, hysterical desperation filled the child now; those wide, dazed eyes flickering with horror would forever be seared into Chelsea's memories.

The gun barrel jerked back and the woman was reaching for the girl, screaming for the doctor, and in Samara Cerves's face Chelsea saw such misery, such pale, terror-filled pain, that she had no doubt little Louisa was safe now.

The question was, was Chelsea safe?

"Move." She was hauled out of the Runner with a suddenness she found shocking.

The hands that jerked her from the vehicle were rough and bruising as she was dropped to her feet, then dragged through the courtyard toward the side of the mansion. Stumbling, she had only a moment to glimpse the chaotic activity of soldiers and security personnel rushing behind the woman known as the Blood Queen and the blood-soaked body she cradled in her arms.

"Where are you taking me?" Desperation sliced through her as they disappeared around the side of the house.

She couldn't die here.

Struggling against the powerful grip, she tried to dig her heels into the dirt and loose stones beneath her feet, only to risk falling and being dragged along the ground.

Furious cries were falling from her lips, the need to escape frantic when he suddenly stopped, all but throwing her against the side of the house, his hand pressing over her mouth and his face only inches from hers.

Green eyes flecked with amber rioting through the irises. Rage burned in his gaze, in his expression, along with steely, uncontrolled demand.

Cullen?

Shock blazed through her mind, froze all her senses.

"Shut the fuck up and follow me. Now." Turning, he had her wrist again, dragging her behind him once more, uncaring of the fact that her knees were suddenly jelly.

What was Cullen doing here? Covert Law Enforcement didn't have an op with the cartel. If they did, she would have known. Wouldn't she have? It had just been three days since her resignation, not months or years.

And since when did Cullen do ops himself? He was usually in command or logistics only. As commander of the Agency, he oversaw the assignments; he didn't take them himself.

In the four years she'd been with the Covert Law Enforcement Agency, she'd never known him to go undercover himself.

"Get in." She was lifted and all but tossed into the passenger seat of another Runner before Cullen went over the hood of the desert vehicle and slid into the driver's seat with an ease that amazed her.

As he jerked the vehicle into gear, the Runner raced for the back wall that surrounded the estate. No one tried to stop them. As they neared the gates the heavy metal barriers opened smoothly, giving Cullen just enough room as he shot past them.

She didn't dare look at him. She could feel the fury rolling off him in waves, see it in the hard grip he had on the gear shift as he accelerated through the night.

The Runner was in lights-off, full covert mode, a model only the Bureau of Breed Affairs possessed. It was a little heavier than the one Chelsea had crashed into the estate with, but the motor was far more powerful and it was equipped with defensive features the others didn't have. They'd have no problem if the Coyote soldiers happened to see them.

She was going to have a problem once Cullen stopped this Runner, though, and she knew it. She could feel it.

◆ ◆ ◆

Decelerating the Runner, Cullen eased the desert vehicle along the back entrance of his property, then into the dark silence of the garage. Activating standby mode again, he let his hands grip the steering wheel, his hold so tight even the tips of his fingers ached.

"What the bloody, insane fuck were you doing out there?" The words ripped from his mouth, a harsh, guttural growl filling them. "You were not scheduled out there. You weren't even supposed to be out tonight."

He snapped his mouth shut, his teeth clenched hard, jaw locked. The memory of that fucking gun the Blood Queen had in Chelsea's face, her finger on the trigger, still had his blood boiling.

There wouldn't have been a chance in hell for him to jerk that murderous bitch away from Chelsea before she pulled the trigger. As fast as he'd been moving, as desperate as he'd been, he wouldn't have made it in time.

He knew, had known for years, that her work with the Breed Underground would get her killed. He'd argued with her cousin Linc over it, fought her grandfather over it, and none of it had mattered.

"It's my choice if I decide to go out at any given time," she reminded him, that cool, distant tone she sometimes got scraping over his nerves like nails on a chalkboard. "I need to call a ride . . ."

"I'm your fucking ride." Vaulting from the low vehicle, he stomped around the back of the Runner, just making the opposite side as Chelsea jumped to the ground and stared around warily.

"I lost my glasses," she said tonelessly, reaching up to touch her face. "I don't remember when they came off."

"Probably when that fucking bullet hit your arm," he snapped. "You have a flesh wound at your shoulder. Come on and I'll check it out."

He gripped her opposite arm, pulling her after him to the kitchen door. The biometrics on the door had it unlocking at his touch, swinging wide easily.

"What were you doing there?" Her voice was low and thready as he pushed her into a kitchen chair before moving to the cabinet over the refrigerator and retrieving the medical kit he kept there.

"The Agency wasn't involved with ops on the cartel." She stared up at him, her dark eyes fathomless, her face pale.

"The op wasn't listed on the books." He slapped the kit to the table. "Take off your shirt. Let me see your arm."

He didn't wait for her to take it off herself. Gripping the hem of the snug shirt, he lifted it, teeth grinding, and eased it off her.

The exercise bra she wore covered her more than adequately but still had his mouth drying at the sight of the rounded tops of soft, tan-dark flesh, her breasts rising and falling with each breath she took.

She took the shirt from him and held it on her lap, remaining silent as he checked the slice across her arm before cleaning it. After smearing antibiotic salve over the shallow wound, Cullen bandaged it, then gave his head a clearing shake.

"Sit still. I'll get you one of my shirts to wear. You're probably hurting by now."

He could sense the pain she was actually ignoring. The damned woman was so stubborn she should have been born a Breed.

Stepping into the connecting washroom, he pulled one of the short-sleeved shirts from a hanger and returned to her, helping her into it.

"I can button it," she assured him, pushing his hands away and doing just that as she looked around. "Don't you ever turn any lights on?"

"Why? I can see perfectly well in the dark." His voice was harsher than he meant it to be as he stared down at her.

The braid in her hair was coming undone, heavy strands falling from it to frame her tense features and emphasize her dark eyes. Fragile and so damned pretty, she made him ache like a teenager. She didn't look strong enough, durable enough to accomplish what he knew she'd accomplished that night. The physical endurance it would have taken to race through the desert at the speed he knew she'd pushed that Runner to was something men he knew didn't have.

"If you're my ride, then take me home." She rose to her feet, looking around the dark kitchen without expression before meeting his gaze.

He saw something flicker in her eyes then, something feminine and hungry, and just as quickly it was gone.

"Chelsea . . ." he began warningly.

"If you hear anything about Louisa, could you let me know as well?" The concern in her voice assured him that if he didn't, she'd stick her damned nose into it herself.

He nodded abruptly, frowning down at her. "How did you find her?" he asked, wondering how she'd done what three teams of Breed Enforcers hadn't been able to do.

"Right place, right time." She looked like a little waif in his too-big shirt, her hair tangling around her face and those big eyes. "I heard the radio transmission of the abduction but wasn't in the area searchers had been sent to." She gave another of those little sighs. "I heard their hunting yips, followed the sounds, and when I saw they were hunting the kid I got in as close as possible in the direction they were pushing her, managed to snag her and race to the compound. End of story."

End of story his ass.

"Now, I'd really like to go home, Cullen . . ."

"You can stay here tonight," he informed her briskly. "I want to be certain you weren't recognized and that Samara doesn't send any of her men to collect you. She's even more insane than normal when it comes to her kid. She could come after you, consider you easier prey than those Coyotes."

She shook her head. "She won't come after me."

"You don't know that," he bit out, his fingers curling into fists to keep from touching her, from jerking her against him, and aching to still the fires that burned in him for her.

"I won't have to worry unless Louisa dies." Somber knowledge filled her expression as she lifted her gaze to him then, her lips trembling just a second before she stilled them. "It'll take a miracle to keep her alive. It was bad." She swallowed against the ragged pain in her voice. "I'll make sure Linc sends you my report when I turn it in."

Hearing the sound of a vehicle slowing in front of the house, its headlights piercing the front window, Cullen turned back to her slowly, glaring at her furiously.

"That should be my ride," she said on an inhale, as a scent of relief reached his senses. "I activated the alert when we arrived." She plucked at the shirt. "Thanks for something to wear. I'll make sure you get it back."

She turned and started for the door.

"This isn't over, Chelsea," he warned her, watching her pause, feeling her resolve.

"Yeah, it is," she said softly. "It was over before it ever started."

◆　　◆　　◆

The message came three days later from her cousin Linc and sent agony tearing through Chelsea's chest.

Re: Requested information

The child didn't survive her injuries. She passed at 8:04.

If you need me, call.

Sitting down slowly on her bed, her arm wrapped around her stomach, Chelsea lost her battle with the grief that exploded inside her.

Louisa Cerves was gone. That sweet, beautiful little baby was gone, and no doubt the Coyotes that inflicted the damage were hunting again.

The unfairness of it shattered her and left her sobbing alone, her pillow catching the tears and the cries, just as it always had.

· C H A P T E R 2 ·

From Graeme's Journal
The Recessed Primal Breed

Recessed Primal genetics and Mating Heat is a combination guaranteed to drive any sane Breed to psychological mayhem. For the Primal Breed, Mating Heat is a time bomb ready to detonate with a force that will reshape that Breed's life forever.

The Primal Breed, more cunning and predatory than any other, will not stay hidden indefinitely—as those without the Primal designations may do—once free, the animal may be impossible to control.

The female that loves such a creature must be not just strong, but in possession of a chair and whip long enough to force the Primal Breed to some semblance of at least the appearance of humanity—

THREE WEEKS LATER

There it was again.

Cullen stilled the moment his senses sharpened, aligned until scent, sight, his very pores began pulling in information around him. It lasted only a second. Only long enough for his head to jerk up, awareness slamming into him before it stopped.

He would have blamed it on an overactive imagination if it hadn't happened more and more often in the past weeks.

In the weeks since he'd last seen Chelsea. Since she'd awakened a hunger inside him that refused to be pushed back to nothingness again.

Three weeks since he'd seen her, a month since she'd resigned.

He'd told himself she'd be back. When she hadn't come back that second week, he'd given it another week. Somewhere around the third week, he'd finally admitted it might take a while longer. But she would be back. He just had to wait her out.

Chelsea could be stubborn; that steel will inside her often took a while to relent and allow emotion to rule her once again. If he hadn't known that, he would have learned it after her report on Louisa had come in and he'd realized the horror she'd faced that night.

His head jerked up, some sixth sense warned him there was a slight difference in the air outside his office now. Someone was coming, but it wasn't her.

It wasn't Chelsea.

The office door pushed open without a knock. The tall, broad form that stepped inside closed the panel silently behind him and then grinned mockingly.

Graeme. Or Gideon, as he had once been called. He had a new

identity now, much as Cullen had created one for himself, leaving his previous one as Judd behind.

The crazy twin. Madness was an old and familiar friend, he'd told Cullen. And his brother wore it like an intimate, well-molded garment.

Though in the months since Graeme had found his mate, there were days his brother actually seemed close to sane.

Days.

Not all the time, and he had a feeling this might not be one of those times.

He was six and a half feet tall, and the primal stripes that sometimes bisected Graeme's face were absent. They only came out during moments of extreme worry now, rather than the animalistic rages he'd once experienced. As the Primal, as Graeme called the transformation, the animal side his brother possessed revealed itself in striking, physical characteristics that could cause grown men to whimper.

They'd been identical twins at birth, but over the thirty-some years of their lives, life, scars and the monster Graeme possessed inside himself had left them with only a resemblance to each other. The resemblance could be stronger if Cullen allowed it.

"What the hell do you want?" Cullen snapped. It never failed that where his brother went, trouble tried to follow. Though the trouble, he admitted, wasn't as severe as it had once been—or it just wasn't trying as hard.

Graeme arched one sandy blond brow, that mocking smile that tugged at his lips becoming deeper.

He was amused. Almost playful.

That never failed to bode ill for Cullen.

"Just thought I'd stop by and visit with my favorite sibling," Gideon drawled. "What's wrong with that?"

"I'm your only sibling," Cullen grunted. "Alive, that is."

For a moment, his brother's gaze glittered with that wild promise of madness.

"That's still debatable," Graeme stated then, as enigmatic as always.

That was Graeme, always playing games.

"Gideon . . ." He used the one name guaranteed to piss his brother off, and he didn't even want to know why he was so determined to arouse the insanity his brother possessed.

"Eh, that's not my name, remember? It's Graeme. You should re-member that, *Judd*." There was an edge of warning to his voice now.

Cullen had grown tired of the warnings when they were no more than teenagers confined in hidden cells beneath dirt, cement and steel and experimented on daily.

"Get out of my office and leave me the hell alone," he ordered, trying to turn his attention back to the files he should be going over.

His concentration was shot since the night he'd pulled Chelsea out of the Cerves desert compound.

He kept expecting to hear from her or to see her walk through his office door, a wry smile on her lips asking for her position back. And he'd give it to her.

He'd frown, berate her a bit, but he'd make certain she was re-instated and perhaps begin working her into some less dangerous assignments.

If she'd just walk through that damned door.

Gideon, Graeme, whatever the hell he was calling himself this week walked to the chair in front of Cullen's desk and sat down casually, as though he had every right to be there. Except that was where Chelsea was supposed to be sitting and Cullen wasn't in the mood to deal with Graeme's dramatics.

"You have that irritated look on your face, but the scent of rage is like wildfire." Gideon tilted his head to the side, a thoughtful look on his face. "What's going on, Cullen? I haven't seen you for weeks. I could use some help in the labs."

Use some help in the labs?

That Dr. Jekyll and Mr. Hyde personality of his held an instinct for Breed genetics and an intelligence that could be damned scary.

Graeme watched him in silence, his hands resting calmly on the arms of the chair, his savage features far too perceptive.

Genetics wasn't the only instinct his brother possessed. Graeme could get into a person's head with frightening ease. And once he did, he'd turn order into chaos.

"Go home," Cullen ordered, feeling as disagreeable and put out as he knew he looked. "Torment Cat."

Dammit, he was getting tired of waiting for Chelsea to come back, and he was getting real damned tired of everyone he met talking about everything and anything but her. As though she had never worked in these offices, never made herself a part of their lives. Even the agents never spoke of her, as though waiting for him to ask if they'd seen her, talked to her.

The only one he gave that satisfaction was his second in command, Ranger. They'd been friends since Cullen had been brought to the Navajo Nation.

"Cat is actually the reason I'm here." Gideon smiled then. It wasn't a comforting look. "She asked me to come check on you. It seems few people have seen you except your agents. When asked about you they get this wary look on their faces, as though to speak is to court the wrath of demons." Gideon gave him a brooding look. "You're encroaching on my territory. Only I'm allowed to produce such reactions, not a recessed little snot such as yourself."

A recessed little snot?

One of these days, he was going to kill Graeme. It was coming. Cullen could feel it.

"Go home, spend some time with your woman, give her my condolences for when I kill your sorry ass. I'll send your hide back to her for the memories," Cullen promised, his fists clenching, hands aching with the effort to hold his fists back. He'd been after a good fistfight for weeks and no one seemed willing to give him one.

Gideon would give him a fight, though, surely—

His brother watched him suspiciously for a moment before grinning.

"Oh, Cullen, brother," he chuckled, his tone berating. "You've surely not lost your senses to the point that you'd actually believe you can direct all that aggression toward me? Have you?"

Cullen came up from his chair.

Enough of this bullshit.

"Get out of my office," he snarled. "Or I'll not just get aggressive, *Graeme*." He sneered the name. "I'll make damned sure you don't make the same mistake again."

◆　◆　◆

Graeme stared at his brother and almost snickered.

Cullen—or Judd, as he'd once been known—was so ready to fight he'd forgotten who he was dealing with. Not that Graeme would actually go primal during a fistfight with his brother, but Cullen wasn't aware of that. Graeme would never let him in on that little secret. Until Cullen released the animal prowling inside him, desperate to be free, then Graeme had to play nice. His own animal demanded it. No claws unless claws were bared, or so his mate made him promise. He couldn't think of any way to break that promise without pissing her off.

35

Or actually hurting Cullen.

Graeme didn't want to do either.

He actually felt sorry for his brother.

Almost.

He looked around the office as though backing down to Cullen's demand.

His brother was a man, not a kid, he reminded himself. Not a teenager who needed to be watched over, or a young man grieving the loss of a wife.

A wife, not a mate, Graeme reminded himself. Cullen hadn't lost his mate, but if he didn't get his head out of his ass fairly fast, then he just might end up doing that now.

Cullen sat down slowly. "Don't you ever listen?" he growled, pushing his fingers through the overly long dark hair that was already fading to the more natural dark brown and blond strands.

"Listen to who?" Graeme smirked. "You? Why would I do that? You never say anything I actually agree with."

✦   ✦   ✦

Cullen doubted anyone said anything his brother agreed with.

Running his hand along the back of his neck, he tried to tell himself that fighting with Graeme never accomplished anything. Even as children Graeme had inevitably won their disagreements.

"Tell me why you're here or get out," Cullen breathed out roughly.

The last thing he wanted to deal with was another of his brother's little games.

Graeme's disagreeable grunt only irritated Cullen further.

"As I said, Cat's worried and asked me to check up on you," Graeme stated then, a small frown appearing between his brows for no more than a second, as though he was not exactly certain why Cat's request mattered.

Everything about Cat mattered, though. From the moment Graeme had stared into the face of the four-day-old infant Cat had been when they were no more than eleven, nothing had mattered to Graeme but Cat. Her existence was everything. It had driven the far-too-intelligent, too-animalistic Graeme to actually find enough sanity to survive.

Though Cullen doubted the meaning of survival some days when it came to Graeme's life in the years before he'd returned to find the woman he'd given up when she was no more than twelve years old. Survival these days was looking pretty good for the too-calculating, beyond-genius-level Bengal Breed Cullen knew as his brother.

"She shouldn't worry. Is that all you wanted?" he gritted out when Graeme said nothing more.

Settling back more comfortably in Chelsea's chair, his twin let a small, amused smile curl his lips.

"Well, Cat did want to have friends over for dinner, and she does consider you a friend," he grunted, as though he couldn't figure out why. "I came to extend the invitation. Be there tonight around seven." With that order in place, Graeme rose from the chair as though preparing to leave. So certain Cullen would just follow his orders that he didn't even pretend to ask a damned thing.

"I'm busy." Seven this evening his ass. "You should have tried a little advance notice."

Graeme's eyes narrowed, his powerful body easing back into the chair.

"That would have only given you an advance warning and allowed you to simply not show up with only the flimsiest of reasons," Graeme pointed out logically. "I checked your schedule. You have nothing planned for this evening other than returning home as you usually do after leaving the office." Mockery filled his expression again. "That is, if you leave the office. Tonight you can show up for a decent meal and a little social chitchat." The last was a primal growl. "If I have to do it, so can you."

For a moment, Cullen stared at his brother in amazement.

"Since when do you indulge in social chitchat?" he asked, wondering if the guests had any clue about the monster they were actually chatting with, if such a thing happened.

Graeme's expression became a glare. "I am no longer a monster, brother," he informed him. "Cat has tamed the beast."

And he actually sounded proud of that, Cullen noticed.

"That's all well and good for you. I'm excessively proud," Cullen sneered. "But like I said, I'm fucking busy."

If anything, Graeme's glare darkened. "If you aren't there and on time, I will find you before the night's out and make you wish you were there." The green of his eyes darkened, nearly overtaking the pupil before Graeme pulled back the monster he claimed was tame. "This is for Cat. I will not have her hurt because you didn't show up. Are we understood?" Strong canines flashed in Graeme's savage smile as he came slowly to his feet, his gaze never leaving Cullen's.

It was almost amusing. The creature Graeme had become during those years of unbridled fury was so much a part of his twin that there was no hiding it. The fact that it was indeed under control now amazed Cullen.

"Forget it. I'm busy," Cullen reminded him, really not fazed by the beast. Graeme wasn't dangerous yet, just a little put out.

Graeme's nostrils flared in displeasure. "Very well." He gave in so easily that Cullen's gaze narrowed on him. "I'll inform Cat so she can take your name off the invitation list. She can find another damned dinner partner for her friend Chelsea Martinez. Miss Martinez will probably thank her for it."

Cullen froze for a single heartbeat, a flash of something akin to horror racing through his mind. People, Breeds and humans alike, who associated with Graeme usually ended up in harm's way. Many had been known to die.

He came slowly from his seat in the next heartbeat.

"What the hell are you up to?" Rage began licking the edges of his control, fraying it with a flame that threatened to engulf him. "And don't bother lying to me. I know you too damned well."

Graeme tipped his head to the side at a curiously thoughtful angle. "I believe I'll offer her the position of Cat's assistant. I know her, her training." His lips tilted into a smug grin. "And her trainer. I'm rather leaning her way; there are just a few things to consider first. I had hoped to get to know her better by inviting her to Cat's little dinner party."

Cullen had trained her for the most part. For four years he'd invested more hours than he cared to calculate in her training. And he knew she was good. Good enough to steal Coyote prey from beneath their noses and get her to safety. But that was far different from working for Graeme.

"No," he snapped, furious. "What the hell do you think you're doing even considering putting her in the line of fire? She'll have a price on her head within a week if she goes to work for you or Cat."

Graeme's brow arched. That superior, arrogant calculation that was so much a part of his brother was readily apparent now.

"I'm considering her because no one would expect her to be the fighter she truly is, and the fact that she managed to work for you for four years means she has plenty of patience," Graeme countered softly, with no small amount of menace. "She'd be a good fit for the position.

And her training means she'd be prepared should anything happen. I like to be prepared."

He liked to be prepared? Graeme was never prepared. He flew by the seat of his pants, his arrogance refusing to accept that he could lose. There was no preparation, only bloodshed.

"Chelsea is not bulletproof." Cullen came around the desk before he considered the move. Nearly nose to nose with a creature even the hardest soldiers, the most fanatical killers flinched in the face of. "You know hiring her is out of the question."

Graeme actually had the temerity to laugh. "Being a friend of yours does not automatically disqualify someone from working with me. On the contrary, her training is excellent . . ."

"She belongs here. Keep your damned nose out of it and she'll be back," he argued, furious.

His brother only laughed. "After a month? Is that what you really believe, brother?" The grin that curled his lips was more a smirk. It was going to be a bloody smirk soon.

"You will not hire her." Cullen's tone lowered to a deliberate, roughened warning that would have had every man under his command paling if they had been in the room.

Graeme merely stared back at him without so much as a blink.

"Or what?" his twin asked knowingly. "How will you enforce that order? When you're strong enough to survive the animal I hold back, then you can make such demands. Just because you wish it doesn't mean she'll return. And just because she's a woman isn't reason enough to refuse her a job she's perfectly qualified for." He flashed a deadly smile. "Or did you forget? A woman will kill an enemy faster than any male simply because it's unexpected. Besides, Cat likes her."

Cullen's fury was completely ignored. He could feel it. The knowledge of it was pumping through his bloodstream, burning at his mind. The rage that enveloped him consumed him.

Uncaring of the strength of the monster he'd set loose by enraging his brother, Cullen's fist flew out and connected with Graeme's face, and to both their amazement, the blow threw the Breed back with a force that put him on his ass.

For about a heartbeat.

With an agile flip Graeme was back on his feet, crouching, waiting, as a chuckle slipped past the amused smile on his face and he slowly straightened.

His smirk was now tinged with blood, not that the sight of it satisfied Cullen in the least.

"That was rather surprising," Graeme stated, one broad hand lifting to work his jaw as he stared back at Cullen, eyes narrowing, his expression flashing with a hint of calculating knowledge. "You're still invited to dinner, though I suspect Cat will have words with you for the bruise that will no doubt mar my handsome profile."

Egotistical, snide, arrogant bastard . . .

"Go to hell, you mangy, black-hearted fucker. I told you I'm busy," Cullen muttered, turning his back on his brother as he pushed his fingers through his hair and fought the need to push Graeme into a full-fledged fight.

Not that Cullen thought he'd survive, but at least he could expend the fury raging through him.

"I'll be sure to inform Cat that she needs to find another male to fill your seat next to Ms. Martinez." Graeme only laughed at the rage.

Moving behind his desk once again, Cullen stared back at his brother, jaw clenched, fighting back the need to tear something, anything, apart.

"Why?" he bit out furiously. "Why stick your nose in this? If I wanted her in the line of fire I'd have given her operational status here. You know that."

He hadn't even been able to make that offer to her after pulling her out of the desert, fully cognizant of the fact that if she hadn't been fully trained, she would have never survived that.

Surprisingly, Graeme nodded, his expression losing its amusement, though the calculation burned fierce and bright in his green eyes.

"You don't have that right, Cullen, that's why," his brother stated softly. "She's intuitive, smart and willing to train to be the best operative you could possibly have at this place. Instead, you turned her into a glorified personal assistant." He shook his head as though amazed. "Though working for me can't possibly be more dangerous than the job she's taken chasing down rumors of Breeds and Council misfits." His head tilted thoughtfully. "I believe she was nearly knifed in her latest skirmish. I'd have never allowed such a thing, of course, but until I learn who she's working for, I can't exactly discuss it with them. Can I?" He gave a light shrug and another of those knowing smirks. "Enjoy your evening, brother."

With that, he turned his back and left the office.

Chelsea, nearly knifed? Even the insulting maneuver Graeme made by turning his back on him during a confrontation didn't register as that information exploded in his head.

Chasing down rumors of hidden Breeds and Council misfits?

Were her cousins fucking insane to allow such a thing, especially after what had happened weeks before?

If his Breed genetics weren't still comatose, he'd show all of them the error of their ways.

But they *were* comatose, Cullen reminded himself, fingers curling, aching with the need to hit something, that burning, hollow rage still beating a fierce tattoo through his brain. A recessed little snot—wasn't that what Graeme had called him?

The bastard.

And he was right. His Breed genetics had become recessed when he was no more than ten and hadn't reemerged. There were the odd moments of scent sensitivity, intuition and advanced strength, especially when he was angered. For the most part, he was no more Breed than any human walking down the street.

That didn't mean he couldn't show the members of the Breed Underground Network the risks in placing Chelsea in a position of danger.

Jerking his keys from his desk, he left the Underground offices, enduring the elevator ride to the parking garage, all the while his teeth grinding so tight his jaw ached.

No wonder he hadn't heard anything about Chelsea in the past weeks. No fucking wonder no one dared give him the chance to ask about her. They knew he'd probably throw a punch at the messenger.

Not that he'd done that in a damned long time.

Unlike some Breeds—his brother, namely—he'd learned control in the past decade.

At least, until it came to Chelsea.

CHAPTER 3

From Graeme's Journal
The Recessed Primal Breed

At its base, the male, whether human, animal or Breed, has a core nature equal to that of a sullen child denied a favored treat.
And the male can react accordingly—

The last thing Chelsea wanted to do was have dinner with Graeme Parker and his fiancée, her cousin Claire—or Cat, as she was now called.

Especially after her employer, Cassie Sinclair, texted with the night's job.

The other woman had sent another list of locations for pictures, along with the best possible times to be in place.

What Cassie was searching for, Chelsea didn't have a clue. She had to admit, though, the job was far more interesting than working as her father's legal receptionist. She'd been bored to tears when she'd taken that particular job at sixteen. She simply couldn't imagine taking it again.

Cassie's offer of a job had been just what she needed. Especially in light of the fact that the other woman wanted to keep it completely secret that Chelsea was working for her. It was really going to look good on her résumé once the job was over.

"Dinner with Cullen's brother, or work?" she muttered, staring at the addresses and lists of times on her e-pad.

She knew why Graeme had invited her to dinner; he was still trying to convince her to take the job as Cat's personal assistant.

That was a job guaranteed to get her killed. Graeme and Cat weren't exactly homebodies. They lived dangerous lives, especially Graeme if rumors were to be believed. And those particular rumors, Chelsea guessed, didn't even come close to how dangerous Graeme actually was.

Still, not showing up for dinner would no doubt have him finding her and questioning why. The man was so damned nosy it amazed her. The fact that he seemed to be taking some kind of interest in her after she left the Covert Law Enforcement Agency worried her. Graeme wasn't known for his concern for anyone but Chelsea's cousin Cat. How Claire had ended up with that nickname, Chelsea hadn't figured out yet.

Padding naked from the shower to the attached walk-in closet, she considered not just what to wear, but also what to do.

Dinner at Graeme's would require at least a dress, while heading out to the clubs and various underground bars on the reservation required an entirely different sort of attire.

Jeans and boots worked. There were plenty of underground clubs, but they were often dangerous, raided and not always easy to get into. Still, Cassie had managed to list several of the more popular and harder-to-access locations.

Those establishments were frequented by a high number of Breeds, despite the clubs' illegal status. Having Breed members made them harder to raid as well. The Enforcers always seemed to have advance warning of any raid being made, unless Cullen's Agency made the raids. And it was rare that Cullen could be convinced to do so.

Cullen.

God, she missed him.

Missed working with him, arguing with him, and sometimes he even laughed with her. Not that he laughed much after his wife's death a decade ago. He'd retreated from everyone then, closing himself off and concentrating on his rise up the ranks of the Covert Law Enforcement Agency instead.

Would he be at Graeme's? she wondered. He usually showed up at his brother's dinner parties. Several times, they'd actually ridden in together whenever Chelsea had been invited as well. Graeme's attempts to befriend her since his relationship with Cat never failed to confound her, but she was certain he had the best chef in the world.

The question remained, though. Dinner where Cullen would no doubt be in attendance, or another night staking out illegal bars and photographing Breeds and whoever they were with?

Decisions, decisions.

Seeing Cullen would definitely hurt after all this time. For some reason she'd expected him to make more of an effort to call or at least check on her after the night he'd pulled her out of the Cerves compound.

And he hadn't kissed her before she left, either. She had hoped that maybe he would. Amid the crashing adrenaline and fight to stay in control of the resulting devastation of tears and emotions returning with a rush, she'd hoped he'd kiss her.

Her lips tingled with the need; her neck ached where his teeth had scraped the skin the morning she resigned from the Agency.

Sleeping was impossible some nights if she dared let herself think of it, and most nights, she dared. She'd lie awake, reliving it, torturing herself with a need that she knew he wasn't about to slake for her.

Asshole.

Going to dinner at Graeme's and risking having to actually socialize with Cullen was more than she could deal with.

Pulling dark pants and a T-shirt from the closet, Chelsea stomped to her bedroom and threw them on the bed mutinously. She might as well work. At least then, she might actually become too immersed in finding Breeds to think about Cullen. That or she'd be attacked again.

She pushed that memory back. She wasn't going to let it spook her. The Coyote her Wolf Breed Enforcers had taken down was a verified Genetics Council soldier, not part of the Breed society. He was one of the monsters the Council had first envisioned, merciless killers that followed their creators' orders, nothing more. He must have somehow caught her snapping those pictures of him from her truck and taken offense. Or worried he'd be identified. There couldn't possibly be another explanation.

Pulling on lacy black panties, she frowned at the uneasiness she could feel at the rationalization. No matter how many times she tried to be logical about it, the possible reason for the attack didn't sit well with her. And she might tell herself she wasn't going to let it spook her, but Chelsea knew she was spooked.

Not simply because she could have died. She should never have been attacked to begin with.

Dressing quickly, she fought back the hint of nerves that came with thinking about it, concentrating on the job instead. She was familiar with the list of locations Cassie had sent. A few of them she could actually get into on her own; for the others, she might need to get her handy-dandy Wolf Breed shadows to get her entrance.

She pulled on her boots and was just picking up the small pack she kept her equipment and other necessities in when the sound of the doorbell had a grimace twisting her lips.

Hopefully, it wasn't her sister, Isabelle, making a quick little visit to make certain Chelsea was attending Graeme's dinner. Isabelle and her husband, Malachi, were often invited to the dinner parties Graeme hosted, and Isabelle would guilt the hell out of her if she learned Chelsea wasn't going.

Family dynamics—good grief.

Gripping the doorknob, she gave a quick turn of the lock and swung the door open, not bothering to check to see who her visitor was first.

She should have checked.

Her breath caught. Something hot and achy tightened in her chest and for just a split second, her heart seemed to pause before it jump-started and began racing in her chest.

"Cullen." It seemed like it had been forever since she'd seen him. Since his green eyes had sparked with that hint of warmth while staring back at her and his far-too-somber expression made her ache to bring a smile to it.

"Hello, Chelsea," he greeted her, his voice low. "Can I come in for a minute?"

Dressed in dark slacks and a long-sleeved white shirt, the sleeves of which were rolled back, he looked far too handsome in a rough, rugged sort of way. Those Breed genetics he possessed might be recessed, but the unique handsomeness Breed males possessed was in full force.

From his amber-flecked green eyes, to the longish, once black, now dark blond hair streaked with darker brown hues, to the tall, muscular form of his body, he was the very essence of a woman's most sexual dream. And like all the other women who lusted after his arrogant ass, she couldn't help but want to pull him straight into her bed and just have her way with him.

"Why?" The question popped out of her mouth before she could stop it.

Those devilish lips quirked into a hint of an amused grin as he scratched at the closely cropped beard he was now sporting. When had he decided to wear a beard?

"Because I wanted to see how you were doing?" he quipped, the dark timbre of his voice sending a thrill of sensation racing down her spine. "See if you were still mad at me."

Mad at him? She was still furious with him, but she stepped back and waved him in, despite the feeling that she should have just closed the door in his face.

She knew Cullen. He didn't just make friendly visits to anyone's house. He always had a reason, an agenda.

"I still think you're an ass," she informed him, turning for the kitchen. "But I have time for a cup of coffee before I have to leave."

Work, she reminded herself. She had a job to do, and doing it didn't include entertaining her former boss or lusting over him for the evening.

"You're going to Graeme's dressed in jeans?" There was a hint of surprise in his voice.

"I'm not going to Graeme's." She kept her back to him as she spoke and busied herself with the coffeemaker.

Looking at him just made her feel way too conflicted.

Not to mention too damned aroused. Thank God he didn't have the normal senses a Breed possessed. Like that pesky sense of smell that alerted them whenever a woman was aroused by them. That was just wrong as far as she was concerned. On so many levels.

"So what's more important tonight than making certain my brother doesn't involve himself in your life?" he asked, the mockery not in the least subtle. "Missing one of his dinner parties is guaranteed to make him suspicious, you know?"

Finishing the coffee, she picked up both cups, turned and moved to the table. Her gaze lifted to his as he stood in the doorway, his shoulder resting against the frame as he crossed his arms over his chest. Placing his cup on the table, Chelsea stepped back, leaned against the counter and sipped at the hot brew, all the while holding his gaze.

Graeme had no reason to involve himself in her life. Missing a dinner party wasn't exactly a crime.

"I'm certain Graeme and I both will survive me missing one of my cousin's little get-togethers," she assured him.

Cullen's lips quirked knowingly. It wasn't a smile, it wasn't a grimace. It was a look of certainty and pure confidence.

"You don't know my brother very well, Chelsea." The chastisement in his voice was more than a little mocking. "He seems to be fond of you, and after catching wind of that Coyote attack the other night, he's concerned." His voice lowered, hardened as his expression turned downright dangerous. "You could say I'm a bit concerned myself."

Chelsea placed her cup of coffee on the counter more as an excuse to break his gaze and gather her thoughts than to keep from throwing the cup at him.

"Concerned, are you?" she scoffed, turning back to him. "I haven't seen or heard from you in weeks, and now you're supposedly so concerned for me?" Her brows lifted in disbelief at the very thought of it. "Sorry, Cullen, not buying it, and I don't have time to stand here discussing it with you."

Maybe if he'd shown a little interest in the past weeks, then he might have been able to fool her. If he had been the one to tell her Louisa hadn't survived, if he'd at least been there to share her sorrow.

His eyes narrowed on her, dark green glittering between heavy gold-tipped dark brown lashes. She didn't like that look either. It was one she'd only seen rarely, and then only during interrogations of some low-life suspect as she watched from behind a two-way mirror. Until now, he had never turned that look on her, though.

It was a bit unsettling.

"What are you up to, Chelsea?" He questioned her softly, the tension in the room rising by the second. "And who are you working for? I'd have thought that night in the desert would have caused you to at least show some caution for a little while."

Chelsea lifted her brow, disgust surging inside her as anger threatened to get the better of her.

"You need a ladder to climb out of my business?" She tried for sarcasm, but even she heard the hurt in her voice. "What I'm doing and whoever I may be doing it for doesn't concern you in the least. I resigned from the Agency. Remember?"

There was a predatory grace in the way he straightened from the door frame. His head lifted, his expression tightening until for a moment, it would have been easy to believe that those Breed genetics he possessed were anything but recessed.

"And you think resigning from the Agency meant I'd stand aside and let you get yourself killed?" His lips peeled back in a snarl, prominent canines flashing dangerously. "Chelsea, sweetheart, you should know better after that night in the desert."

Gentle, caressing . . . warning. That tone of voice made her ache with arousal even as she tensed at the dark undertone and the fact that he was moving closer.

"And I should have known better—why?" she asked, gripping the counter as she watched him warily. "I haven't heard from you once since I returned that baby to her mother." She swallowed tightly, the memory of the child a torment she couldn't seem to escape.

"Because I spent the past four years doing everything I could to protect you? To make certain you were trained before throwing you into the field?" His jaw clenched as he bit out the words angrily. "And now you're pushing your way into it as though it's a Sunday picnic?"

Her brow lifted despite the fact that he was less than six inches from her and glaring down at her while his eyes flickered with amber fire within the green.

Hell, she'd never seen the color in someone's eyes flicker like that. She'd definitely never seen his eyes do it. And if he was pissed now, God help her if he learned exactly what she was doing and who she was working for now.

"You have no idea what I'm doing, Cullen, and if I considered it any of your business, I would have contacted you myself and explained it all to you," she informed him, narrowing her eyes back at him as she gave a dismissive wave of her hand. "And you don't get to butt into my life now just because you decided you want to. I don't work for you any longer."

"Does that cancel out friendship?" he asked, tilting his head to the side, a decidedly calculating gleam entering his eyes.

He was trying to manipulate her. She knew Cullen when he was like this; he'd used just such tactics almost every time she'd lobbied for fieldwork.

"Friendship implies at least a small amount of respect. Something you don't have for me, so let's not pretend you do." She didn't like games, especially not the type that kept her in that carefully constructed box her family as well as Cullen seemed determined to keep her within.

◆　◆　◆

Confusion raced through the anger and protectiveness Cullen couldn't seem to push back.

"Where do you get the idea that I have no respect for you, Chelsea?" Bracing his hands on the counter on each side of her, he stared into her eyes, wondering if he could become lost in the dark depths of liquid emotion there. Not that he could often decipher the shadows of deeper emotion hiding beneath whatever she showed the world at any given time. He had often tried, though.

"Are you serious?" Her hands lifted, pushing against his chest, then remaining when he refused to move.

"Really, Chelsea," he assured her. "What would make you think such a thing?"

It was inconceivable to him that she would believe something so ridiculous. They'd spent four years working together. She'd been closer to him than anyone else, even his closest friend, and she believed he felt no respect for her?

The laugh that left her lips was filled with hurt and anger. He hadn't just made her angry; he'd hurt her, something he hadn't meant to do. Something he hadn't wanted to do.

"I trained for four years for the field." She pushed at his chest again. "Four years and you wouldn't even let me be a part of tech support. What is that if not a lack of respect for me and the training I busted my ass to learn?"

"You weren't ready—"

"And as far you're concerned, I'll never be ready." The cry broke from her as she pushed at his chest again, the sudden, wild scent of her slamming into his senses, taking him unaware. Enough so that he pulled back, giving her the opportunity to push past him.

She would have escaped. Hell, he should let her escape and he knew it. Instead, before the impulse was even thought, he caught her arm, pulling her back and trapping her against his chest.

That scent. It was like a summer rainfall in the Virginia mountains, pure and clean. And sweet. So sweet and fraught with a hidden kiss of heat that he found himself nearly dizzy. The scent of her wrapped around his head and sank inside him until he swore he could taste her against his tongue.

"What are you doing?" The whispered gasp barely registered as a myriad of scents twisted through him. "Dammit, Cullen, you can't just kiss me whenever I piss you off."

Whenever she pissed him off?

"Darlin', I don't just kiss you whenever I'm pissed off with you," he assured her. "If I did, I'd have been kissing you every day for the past four years. Because I think you live to piss me off."

And then he did kiss her.

As he covered her surprised lips, his tongue pushed past them and he sank into the sweetest living taste a man could ever know. She didn't taste of another male, another's kiss or passion. Her lips parted in surprise, her tongue stroking over his even as he slipped it past. Cool and sweet, a summer rain over desert heat, and he loved it, ached for more of it.

This woman and her taste had kept him awake night after night for the past month. The memory of her, of this need, was one he couldn't push away, couldn't forget, no matter how hard he tried.

She could become addictive.

One hand tightened on her hip, at first in protest. The sound of a subtle feminine moan pierced whatever reason might have risen to the surface at the moment. That sweet murmur of pleasure swept away any thought of letting her go. Any thought of releasing the sweet taste of her.

Cupping the side of her neck with his free hand to hold her in place, he deepened the kiss, his lips slanting over hers, a rough groan tearing from him as her arms wrapped around his neck, her fingers spearing into his hair, blunt little nails scraping against his scalp.

Pleasure coursed through him like a drug. Her tongue stroked over his, rubbed against it, fought for supremacy of the kiss, and the resulting pleasure sent a wave of heat rushing through his body.

His cock was so damned hard it was nearly agony. The need to release it from his jeans, to strip her bare and take her right there in her kitchen, rode him hard. His hand slid from her neck to the hem of her T-shirt. Gripping the material, he pulled it up with a desperation he couldn't remember ever feeling. Lust burned through his system, wiping away caution, finesse and reason, pushing him to take her, to mark her.

As he slid his lips from hers, her protesting cry barely registered before he had his lips at her neck, tasting her, licking against the satiny flesh before his teeth raked against it.

She bucked in his arms, lifted closer, her head tilting to the side to allow him access to the sensitive skin as he bit and licked at it demandingly, needing every nuance of taste, every cry of pleasure she released.

And he wanted nothing more, needed nothing more than to taste more of her, to pull more of those heated little cries from her lips and strengthen the scent of her arousal.

As his lips reached the bend of her neck where it met her shoulder, his hand found the curve of her breast, the warmth of her flesh, the pebble hardness of her nipple barely covered by the thin lace of her bra. That fragile barrier was more than he could bear, though. He wanted to feel her skin to skin. He wanted the swollen bud of her nipple between his fingers, his lips.

The thought of the taste of her nipple against his tongue had his hands sliding back to her hips, gripping, lifting her to the counter and pushing between her thighs as he pulled the cup of her bra beneath her breasts.

The lace frame was damned pretty, but he wasn't about to waste time admiring the sight of it, not when he needed the taste of her with a hunger he found himself powerless against. The need for her was killing him. All of her. He wanted to taste every inch of her. No, he *needed* to taste every inch of her.

"Cullen—" Whether protest or a cry of pleasure, he wasn't certain, and he wasn't asking as his lips covered the taut, cherry-flushed tip and drew it firmly against his tongue.

❖   ❖   ❖

Chelsea couldn't hold back the sharp cry or the sensation that rushed through her senses with a strength she couldn't fight against.

She told herself she could hold some part of her response back, that she could return to reality whenever she wanted to.

And she was fooling herself. She had been fooling herself all along. Each stroke of his tongue against hers was so hot, so good—the feel of his lips and teeth against her neck burned through her flesh straight to her nerve endings, where explosions of incredible pleasure detonated with devastating results.

But when he lifted her to the counter, pushed between her thighs, and his lips surrounded her nipple, any molecule of common sense or reality she might have possessed disintegrated.

"Cullen—" She couldn't hold back the cry as his tongue licked over her nipple, sending fingers of sensation racing straight to her womb.

Lips, teeth, tongue, he devoured the nerve-laden point until she was shaking with need. Between her thighs the engorged length of his cock pressed against her sex, their clothing a hated barrier between them as he rubbed against her, inciting the needy heat seizing her vagina.

Panting for breath, locked in an inferno of arousal she had no intention of resisting, Chelsea could only hold on to him and pray she survived it. Because there was no escaping it. She didn't want to escape him. She wanted nothing more than the feel of his touch, his kiss, over every part of her body.

Each deep draw of his mouth on her nipple sent heat rushing through her system. His tongue stroked over it each time he sucked at her and rubbed over nerve endings linked to her womb.

When he moved to her other nipple, the fingers of one hand captured the tip he'd abandoned, keeping it on the edge of ecstasy as his lips surrounded the other and drew it into the heat of his mouth.

Each draw of his mouth, each tug of his fingers, sent waves of sensation coursing through her, arrowing between her thighs, heating her vagina and striking at the swollen bud of her clit. Rolling his hips between her thighs, Cullen stroked the agonized knot of nerves with each press of his engorged cock, amplifying each pulse of pleasure tearing through her.

"Oh God, yes," she whispered, her voice strangled as his teeth grazed over her nipple before delivering a quick little nip and sucking it into his mouth once again.

His tongue stroked and rubbed over it. It was incredible, so good, so hot she could barely stand the heat. She could barely stand it, but she wanted more.

Her breasts were swollen, the mounds tight and aching. Each suckling caress, each stroke of his tongue against her nipples only increased the need for more. The roughened touch of his tongue against it sent shudders tearing through her, flames racing over her nerve endings.

"Don't stop," she whispered as his head lifted, the blinding pleasure still suffusing her even as her body demanded more.

"Stop? I have no intentions of stop—" His head jerked up, nostrils flaring.

Before Chelsea could process what was happening, her shirt was jerked over her breasts and Cullen had turned, a furious snarl sounding from his chest as he braced himself in front of her.

In the doorway, two Wolf Breeds watched them curiously as they leaned against the door frame, their faces hard, gazes locked on Cullen.

"You told us to be here on time, Chelsea," the taller of the two reminded her as he crossed his arms over his black T-shirt, his gray eyes mocking. "Did you forget?"

Forget? Her brain was mush.

But she could feel the tension in the room; it radiated from Cullen in waves. And no matter how Draeger and Tobias appeared to be, they were anything but relaxed.

Chelsea cleared her throat nervously, slid from the counter and wondered if she'd ever lose the shakiness in her legs. She could still feel the arousal, the need racing through her. The impulse to order the two Wolf Breeds from the house and drag Cullen to her bed was almost impossible to resist.

Almost.

"I have to go." Her voice sounded far too weak, too desperate as she moved to go around Cullen.

"Go where?" Reaching out, his fingers gripped her arm, pulling her to a stop as the hoarse growl in his voice had her staring up at him in surprise.

The tone was rough, grating, animalistic. A sound she'd never heard in all the years she'd known him. It was the question that jerked her fully back to reality, though. The possessive demand tore through her, reminding her of everything she was fighting to escape.

Jerking her arm from his grip, Chelsea flicked him a glare; hurt pride and the fear of surrendering forced her to step farther away from him and away from the pleasure and the need she'd felt for this man for far too long.

"It's time you leave, Cullen." She forced the words past her lips, forced herself to put more distance between them.

"The hell I will." The amber in his green eyes seemed to burn. "What are you up to with these two, Chelsea?"

What was she up to? She didn't dare tell him.

She shrugged, fighting to ignore the nervousness, the needs clashing inside her.

"Lock up when you leave, then," she told him, heading for the door. "I have things to do, and explaining my actions to you isn't one of those things."

At least not today. Later, she had no doubt.

Hurrying from the house to her truck, she could feel her hands shaking, her stomach roiling with the need to go back into the house, to go back to a man who couldn't love her and damned sure didn't know how to work with her.

His heart had died with his wife, he'd once claimed; he had nothing left to give another woman but whatever lust he felt for her. And as much as she wanted the lust, it was the heart she'd always dreamed of.

✦ CHAPTER 4 ✦

From Graeme's Journal
The Recessed Primal Breed

Once awakened, Primal Breed genetics can and will play havoc upon a Breed's mental, emotional and psychological balance. The animal, for a while, may act independently of the human he resides within, in essence taking control of the human psyche without the Breed realizing exactly what he's lost control to. At this point, a Breed is at his most dangerous.

Especially if the animal genetics have awakened for Mating Heat—

What the hell was she up to?

Cullen stood at the bar of yet another underground club, his eyes narrowed, tension raging through him as he watched Chelsea from where she stood talking to several Coyote Breed females on the other side of the room.

It wasn't just those females around her, though. At least a half dozen Coyote Breed males, the females' security detail, stood, arms crossed, expressions interested as they listened to Chelsea talk. If he wasn't mistaken, every damned one of them had checked out her ass. And those rounded curves looked real damned good in the snug jeans she wore. So good that it was hard to keep his eyes off her himself. Still, watching those Coyotes check her out made him want to plant his fist in their faces. They had no business staring at her ass, not when he knew for a fact that the smell of his touch, his lust, covered her like an invisible cloak.

Now, that thought brought an edge of smug satisfaction.

He knew the animals he was dealing with, and there was a silent code among most Breeds. No Breed would touch her as long as his scent lay on her like that. The animal inside them wouldn't allow it, even if Chelsea invited it.

Not that she had invited any man or Breed to touch her. He had no doubt that if his scent hadn't covered her, many would be offering, though. Just as those at the other clubs she'd visited.

This particular club was located beneath a warehouse outside Gallup, New Mexico. Each illegal club she'd chosen was in the same area, within ten to twenty miles of one another.

Though this was the only club she'd been to that was located underground.

The cavernous room throbbed with the sound of the latest dance music and an abundance of alcohol. Humans and Breeds alike filled the dance floor and congregated in small groups.

Chelsea seemed to have made her rounds of all those groups and then some. The three Coyote females she now stood with had shadowed her, seemingly without her knowing it. Ashley, Emma and Sharone were regulars at many of the underground bars. Like most Breeds they never became drunk, but enjoyed the music, dancing and socializing.

Cullen had followed her through three different highly illegal establishments over the course of the night. She stayed an hour or so at each one, nursing a single drink as she moved through them, and if he wasn't mistaken she chatted with every damned Breed she could find, with the exception of him.

She didn't talk to any one Breed or human with more interest than the other, and she only danced with the human males. A few male Breeds showed some interest in her, watched her with a surfeit of it, but none approached her. If she approached them they talked with her but watched her with suspicion and a hint of question. A few actually glanced over at him disapprovingly as they talked to her.

His jaw tightened in satisfaction that it was his scent that stopped them. He'd made certain she carried it as he kissed and tasted every inch of flesh he could get to before she left with those two damned Wolf Breeds earlier.

Draeger and Tobias had been far too smug, too satisfied as they left the house with her. Something about their expressions and the gleam of knowledge in their eyes as they glanced back at him had set his teeth on edge.

The two Breeds in question were currently making their way to where he stood at the bar, their hard, savage expressions drawing looks of wary interest from the women they passed.

Draeger, black haired, his dark blue eyes intense, didn't draw the gazes his partner Tobias did, though. Red hair, carefully cropped beard and mustache and grayish green eyes were rare enough in a man. In a Breed, when combined with the rough-hewn features, years of savage training and an innate determined force, it ensured he'd never be overlooked.

Both men wore jeans, dark T-shirts and boots, similar attire to everyone else at the club. Still, like every other Breed there, they stood out, drew notice.

"Maverick." Draeger nodded as he slid up to the bar on one side of Cullen while Tobias slid in on the other side. He didn't miss the fact that they were attempting to close him in, to make him feel hemmed in, restrained.

Most Breeds would have instinctively felt that way about two others they were uncertain of. Cullen wasn't uncertain of the Wolf Breeds, though. He knew why they were with Chelsea, he just couldn't figure out what the hell she was doing that caused her to need them.

"Took the two of you long enough to visit," Cullen murmured, lifting his beer to his lips as his gaze sought out Chelsea again.

She gave Draeger and Tobias a long, probing look, met his gaze, then turned away as he tipped his beer in her direction.

She wasn't happy with his presence there any more than her Wolf Breed shadows were. And he hated that. There was a time that she would have smiled at him, her dark eyes filled with warmth and a subtle invitation. An invitation he hadn't allowed himself to accept while she was with the Agency. Now, in the weeks since she'd left, that invitation had been replaced with a gleam of hurt and no small amount of anger.

"You going to make a habit of following her everywhere she goes?" Tobias cut straight to the point. "That's not very smart. You're just going to call more attention to her."

No one had ever accused the Breed of being tactful, Cullen guessed.

"Looks that way," he drawled, keeping his eyes on Chelsea. God only knew what kind of trouble she'd get into if he actually took his eyes off her. "And from what I understand, it would be hard to draw more attention to her. Wasn't she just attacked a few nights ago?" His fist clenched at the thought of the knife-wielding Coyote the two Wolf Breeds had been forced to kill to defend her.

"Anomaly." Draeger shrugged. "She's not in any danger, unless you make an issue of this. Is that what you want to do?"

The warning tone of the Breed's voice didn't sit real well with him. If the Wolf thought Cullen was going to back down in the face of it, then he'd better think again.

"If making an issue of it becomes a problem, then I'll be here to take care of it, now won't I?" he informed them coldly. "The two of you are wasting your time. If you don't have anything constructive to say, then go back to your corners and become shadows again."

The two Breeds glanced at each other, their expressions closed, revealing little but the wariness he knew he was causing them.

Assholes. Unless they wanted to tell him what the hell was going on, then he had no use for them.

"You're becoming a problem, Commander," Draeger commented. "You ignore her for weeks, then think you can step in and play white knight? Stay the hell way from her. Your scent is becoming a deterrent to other Breeds and placing her off-limits. And we both know you have no intentions of keeping her."

And what exactly was Chelsea up to that required her to associate so closely with male Breeds? He wanted to ask that question so bad his back teeth ached as he locked them tight to hold it back. Asking wouldn't get him anywhere, and he knew it.

"Pest control." Cullen grinned. "I'll have to remember that. As for keeping her, last I heard, she wasn't a possession."

The two Breeds were silent for long moments, obviously debating their next words, wondering the best way to get rid of him, short of killing him. And killing him could prove difficult for them. Perhaps not impossible, but difficult.

From what he'd gathered on the two over the past hours through several sources he'd contacted, Draeger and Tobias were supposedly not aligned with any particular pack or alpha leader. They weren't associated with the Bureau of Breed Affairs or any of the smaller task forces working to identify and control the Breeds still working for the elusive Genetics Council.

Who the two Breeds were working for, Cullen hadn't been able to learn. The fact that they were indeed employed wasn't in doubt. Just as Chelsea's employment now wasn't in doubt. But if anyone knew who had retained their services, they weren't saying.

"Four weeks since she parted ways with your Agency and you're only now becoming curious in regard to how she's using the training you gave her while she was with you?" Tobias asked as Chelsea and Ashley moved to join a small group of feline Breed males and their human dates. "Why now?"

It was obvious they were unaware it was Chelsea who'd rescued the little girl in the desert weeks before, then disappeared.

The attack had no reason or explanation. Council Coyotes didn't just attack for the hell of it. If she'd somehow been identified as Louisa's rescuer, now, that would be a reason for an attack. Or someone knew what she was involved in with these two.

"She wasn't in danger until now." He shot Tobias a look of promised retribution. And he would repay the two Breeds just as soon as he figured out what they had drawn Chelsea into. "I'll put a stop to who-ever sent those Coyotes after her the other night, and when I do, then I'll come looking for the two of you," he promised.

He wanted answers and he wanted Chelsea safe before making any moves against the two Breeds reported to have saved her from the knife-wielding Coyotes that came after her.

Draeger grunted at the promise, his gaze gleaming in amusement as he leaned back against the bar. "You don't scare me, Maverick."

"That's your first mistake, Draeger," Cullen stated coolly. "I'm not a good enemy to make. I'd remember that if I were you."

The day was coming that he'd prove it to them. They didn't want that. As much as he hated it, loathed it, by becoming a thorn in his side, the two were ensuring that if Graeme learned of the problem, he'd make certain that the two Breeds were excised quickly.

Merciless and efficient, that was the twin he was saddled with. Graeme rarely gave Cullen a chance to deal with his own thorns if he knew of them. Cullen had learned years ago to make certain Graeme never learned of them.

"You're no different than any other human in this place," Tobias stated, his gaze taunting as Maverick glanced over at him. "Stronger than a few, perhaps, but no match for a true Breed. Recessed genetics don't count in a fight."

Recessed little snot, Graeme liked to call him. Cullen snorted at the insult.

"Keep it up, boys," he invited the two men, not in the least intimidated as they no doubt expected him to be. "You'll learn the hard way not to keep fucking with me."

His animal genetics might be recessed, but the strength, coordination and sheer cunning savagery bred into his genetics weren't. They never had been. And lately, they'd increased in power. He simply refused to put them on display.

Finding Chelsea within the crowd once again, he met the displeasure in her gaze and arched his brow with mocking inquiry. She seemed more put out with him than usual.

Shooting her a slow grin and another tip of his beer, he then lifted the bottle for another drink. The anger that snapped in her dark gaze was almost funny. It would have been highly amusing if not for the disapproval in the gazes of the male Breeds she was with as they looked in his direction as well.

Bastards, what the hell was their problem? He wasn't the reason she was here risking her ass in whatever the hell she was doing. He couldn't even figure out what it was she was doing. And no one else seemed to know either. That, or they just weren't talking. And the fact that they weren't talking indicated a loyalty to a Breed far more powerful than any Cullen was aware of.

Except perhaps Graeme.

Normally, the very fact that he could claim kinship with the monster Graeme was enough to get any answers he needed.

Until now.

Whatever Chelsea was working on and whoever had hired her was such a closely guarded secret that all he'd found were more questions when he'd gone looking for answers.

And these two were becoming useless where answers were concerned.

A moue of disgust pursed Chelsea's lips before her gaze turned from the Breeds she was chatting with to the two standing on each side of him. Her brow lifted and a second later she was moving purposely through the crowd to the exit.

That little arch of the brow was a clear signal to her shadows, he'd learned. She was ready to leave this particular club and head to the next. Or home.

Glancing at his watch, he noted the hour, timed it to the schedule he'd put together of her activities and guessed she was heading home. Whatever she was there for, he was going to assume it hadn't panned out and she wasn't happy about it.

And that was just too damned bad. He'd keep interfering until she deigned to tell him exactly what the hell she was doing and who she was doing it for. He'd be more than happy to take care of whatever job she'd been given, after he made certain she was safe.

Reaching the elevator leading to the upper floor of the warehouse just behind Draeger, Cullen executed a quick jab to the Wolf Breed's side when he tried to block the entrance, then slid quickly around him to stand next to Chelsea.

"Bitch," Draeger growled, one hand pressed to his kidney as he slapped the control panel.

The doors slid closed as Draeger glared back at him with a gleam of retribution in his dark blue eyes.

"Call your guard dog off, Chelsea," Cullen advised her, catching a glimpse of her concerned expression from his periphery. "I don't think you want to see the fight that's coming if you don't."

She lifted her gaze to him and narrowed her eyes, the dark depths of her brown eyes snapping with ire.

"I know how to look the other way." The grip she kept on the pack slung over her shoulder turned her knuckles white.

Cullen chuckled at the response.

"But we both know you won't. And once I get finished with your Boy Scouts here, then you and I might have words." He stared down at her, his expression and his tone warning her to remember the years they'd worked together and exactly how determined he could be.

Her lips thinned, her gaze holding his, she crossed her arms over her breasts as her delicate little nostrils flared furiously.

"He's bluffing, Chelsea," Tobias chuckled. "He can't take me and Draeger both and he knows it. Even one at a time. He's recessed and untrained. He doesn't stand a chance."

It was the "untrained" comment that got her.

Cullen watched her gaze flare, glimpsed the knowledge in her eyes and just managed to keep a smug grin from his face.

He was recessed, but he wasn't untrained and she knew it. She'd been there the few times he'd sparred with the Breeds in the area, knew exactly how well trained he was and how powerful he was.

Graeme had trained him as a boy and as a man. The monster his brother had been for years had shown up, taunting Cullen, pushing him to fight, to pit his strength and cunning against a creature born of murderous skill and well-honed insanity. Cullen knew he'd leave Draeger and Tobias both bleeding, and she knew it as well.

If he didn't triumph over the Wolves, Cullen knew that Graeme would turn the monster loose and start training exercises all over again. That was incentive enough to win the fight.

"Let it go," she muttered.

Draeger gave a low growl. "Like hell . . ."

"I said let it go," Chelsea snapped then. "This is childish and I'll be damned if I'll put up with it. All three of you can stop now or I'll make damned sure you wish you had."

Cullen's brow arched. That might work with Breeds who had a boss, but Cullen hadn't had a boss in his life. There was no one she could go over his head to.

"Excellent threat, sugar," he told her softly, grinning down at her in approval. "I'll be sure to show my approval later."

Her eyes narrowed back at him, a flush working over the sun-kissed flesh of her face as her lips pursed in an expression he knew well.

"Remember what happened the last time you pissed me off, Cullen?" she asked, her voice as sweet as candy, her expression promising her own brand of vengeance.

At that question, he couldn't control the little wince that crossed his face.

The last time he'd pissed her off, as she called it? He'd given his agents orders to keep her at the offices when her sister had been attacked. He'd had no idea the danger she would face if she went rushing headlong to her sister's side. When he'd returned, she'd curled that little fist and planted it square in his eye. That bitch had smarted for days.

"Vengeful wench," he muttered.

"Remember it." The elevator doors slid open. "Because I promise you. It can happen again."

With a toss of her head she lifted that cute little nose of hers, waited for Tobias to give her the okay, then left the elevator to step into the warehouse and stalk to her truck. Once again she stood aside as Tobias and Draeger checked her vehicle, presumably for explosives.

What the fuck was she up to?

Once the two Breeds cleared the truck, Cullen moved around the back of the vehicle, and before Chelsea lifted herself into the driver's seat, he had the passenger door open and slid in as well.

He knew there were no explosives; he'd come with backup himself. He had no idea what she was involved with or who might want to get rid of her, and he wasn't taking chances. Ranger was still sitting in his car within sight of the truck, just as he had been since their arrival.

"I wouldn't leave my vehicle here if I were you," she bit out, anger pulsing in her tone. "It may be gone when you return for it."

"No problem. I caught a ride with someone else," he replied without inflection, watching her mutinous expression closely. "Looks like you're stuck with me."

Chelsea couldn't believe those words had actually crossed his lips. Damn him.

She was stuck with him?

No, she wasn't stuck with him. Cullen wasn't the kind of guy to stick around, and she had to remember it. Forgetting it could break her heart more than he already had. He'd already given his heart away and he didn't want to heal from the loss. No, Cullen wanted to wallow in it, remain mired in the hopelessness of loving a woman who couldn't come back from the dead.

"I'll take you home." He wasn't going home with her.

She had enough problems; she didn't need to add an affair with him to the mix. His affairs were always short, uncomplicated and uncommitted. She'd always known that it wasn't something she could handle.

Starting the truck, she pulled from her parking spot and drove from the warehouse, glaring into the darkness. She'd just take him to his house, drop him off, then go home. She was tired, irritable and still aroused—damn his hide.

"If you take me to my place, then you'll be staying there with me, whether those two yahoos behind us agree with it or not," he warned her, his tone curt. "We're going to talk, Chelsea, and we're going to do it tonight."

Clenching her hands on the steering wheel, she fought the anger building inside her. It had been building ever since he'd shown up that afternoon.

"We don't have anything to talk about." Bristling with indignation, she shot him a hard glare. "And if we did, the time to discuss it was, ohh"—she waved her hand with a mocking exclamation—"four or five weeks ago. All the kisses in the world, demands and irritable-commander looks are not going to change that." She shot him a furious look. "Ready to go to your place now?"

Because that was damned sure where she intended to take him. Taking him home with her was out of the question. She simply had no willpower where he was concerned.

"Chelsea," he began warningly.

"I mean it, Cullen," she snapped. "You can go home."

He growled at her, a low, deep, feline rumble that so shocked her that it had her foot releasing the gas pedal and her eyes widening in confusion.

He growled at her?

Seriously?

"What the hell was that?" she exclaimed, finally recovering and hitting the gas harder. "Oh my God, I thought you couldn't do that. I never heard you do that before. Are you like going freaky cat on me or something? I thought you were—recessed?"

She'd seen Cullen absolutely enraged before, but she'd never heard that sound coming from his chest.

"I am." His voice was deeper, rougher than normal. "But I *am* still a Breed and you're driving me fucking crazy. Now, let's wait till we get to your place before you make me crazier."

Had he lost his ever-lovin' mind?

He had to have done just that.

"Sounds to me like it would be hard for you to get any crazier," she muttered, glancing over at him warily as she took the turn toward Window Rock. "How long have you been making that crazy sound anyway? Should you see a Breed specialist or something? Maybe those recessed genetics are going all wacky."

She glanced over in time to catch the glare he shot her.

"Wacky?" he questioned her carefully. "Breed genetics don't go wacky."

"Course they do." She shrugged, frowning. "Malachi's go wacky on Isabelle all the time. Growling and acting all possessive and crap. He even bites her." She rolled her eyes before frowning again. "Come to think of it, you bit me."

Chelsea reached up and rubbed at the sensitive area at the bend of her neck and shoulder. At her touch, the spot tingled with sensation, reminding her of the pleasure she'd felt at the bite. That sensation became a subtle wave of pleasure that washed through her and reminded her that the arousal she'd felt that afternoon hadn't abated.

A lower, possibly deeper growl sounded from the passenger seat.

"What now?" she demanded irritably. "Stop that growling stuff, Cullen. It makes me nervous."

It made her nervous?

Cullen fought to block the sounds. He could count on one hand how many times he'd actually growled in the past thirteen years.

Maybe she was right—he needed to see a Breed specialist. The only problem was, Bengal genetics were even odder than Coyote genetics and Cullen only knew one specialist.

Graeme.

No way in hell was he going to tell his brother how his normally silent Breed responses had become more active in the past weeks. Graeme would pull out his needles and sensors, demand blood and tests—he almost shuddered at the thought of it. Graeme had shown up periodically over the years, the monster even Cullen had been uncomfortable in the presence of, and demanded blood, genetic tests and a chance to study the recessed genetics Cullen possessed.

Cullen had given in not because he feared the monster; he hadn't. He'd feared his brother slipping so deep into the monster that resided within him that Cullen had given in and allowed the tests simply because Graeme seemed saner while he was conducting them.

His brother was obsessed with recessed Breed genetics for some reason. During those years that research had seemed to center Graeme, though, and that had made it worth that aggravation.

As Chelsea drove, perhaps faster than the speed limit suggested, he sat back in the passenger seat and focused on rebuilding his control. He'd had to do that a lot in the past weeks since Chelsea had left the Agency. Irritability and a lack of patience plagued him constantly, and taking care of the various details of the Agency that Chelsea had always taken care of flat pissed him off.

Hiring anyone else was out of the question. Even before Chelsea had come into the Covert Law Enforcement Agency, he'd found it hard to work with anyone on a daily basis. For some reason, rather than grating on his nerves, Chelsea had actually calmed them with her presence. She took care of complaints, made certain paperwork was filed and saw to the hundreds of details that irked the hell out of him.

And then she'd left.

After her resignation his temper had become even more unpredictable, and he couldn't even explain why. He had no idea why the lack of her presence affected him as it had.

It had become so bad in the last week that his men avoided him whenever possible. At this rate, the Navajo Council would end up asking for his resignation before much longer.

Forcing himself to remain silent, to keep his questions to himself during the drive, Cullen was relieved when she finally turned onto her street and seconds later pulled into her driveway. Her shadows pulled into the driveway next to her house and before she shut the truck off, the two Breeds were moving to the front door of her home.

Their caution and foresight where her protection was concerned only irritated him further. The fact that they were wary enough, on guard to such an extent, led him to suspect that the danger she was facing was far more severe than Draeger and Tobias let on.

And that, Cullen knew, he simply couldn't tolerate.

Nothing could happen to Chelsea. No matter what it took, no matter the blood he would have to shed, he couldn't lose her.

· C H A P T E R   5 ·

From Graeme's Journal
The Recessed Primal Breed

It is a good thing a woman's heart was created to nurture and to forgive—
for a Breed, whether recessed, active or anything in between, will tempt his
mate to murder.

Chelsea stared through the darkness to the small house she rented,
wondering at what point Cullen had decided he could master her life
in this way. That he could master her.

What disturbed her the most was that she was letting him get away
with it. He was running roughshod over her objections and doing what
he wanted to do. And rather than retaining control, she was letting
him do it.

If she let him into the house, then he'd end up in her bed. She knew it and he knew it.

"Are we sitting here all night?" The question was low, the roughened quality of his voice sending a flush of need racing through her.

How many years had she fantasized about him? Ached for him? Even as a young girl Cullen had drawn her. His close association with her family, the tormented depths of his dark eyes and quiet strength had always made her hurt for whatever pain he'd known. When he'd married her distant cousin, Chelsea had only been twelve, but she remembered sensing that Cullen cared far more for her cousin than Lauren felt for him. To her knowledge, Cullen had never learned that his wife had known about her cancer before they married. That their relationship was instigated in the hopes that the stories in the tabloids about Mating Heat were at least partially true.

Lauren hadn't loved him; she'd wanted to live and believed Mating Heat would cure the cancer and extend her life.

✦   ✦   ✦

"Chelsea, you don't want to have this conversation sitting in your driveway," he warned her, his voice oddly gentle.

"Why?" She licked her lips, uncertain how to proceed. "Because you intend for your discussion to end up in my bed?"

She turned to look at him then, her fingers clenched tight on the steering wheel, her body humming with tension.

"It's going to happen," he sighed heavily. "Tonight, tomorrow night, but it's coming."

A sharp, incredulous laugh left her lips.

"I worked for you for four years and not once did you even hint at any desire for me. And now, a month after I resign, you've decided you just can't wait to get into my bed? Really, Cullen?"

"Really, Chelsea," he mocked her, though gently. "And I think we both know it didn't just happen. I just stopped fighting it."

"And just like your determination to ride home with me, your sudden determination to sleep with me is all that matters." She couldn't believe what she was hearing. "Why don't you just take my truck and leave. You're just making me crazy, and I was tired of crazy when I resigned."

◆   ◆   ◆

Turning in her seat to stare back at him, Chelsea was caught by the somber intensity in his expression and in his gaze. His green eyes gleamed back at her with savage fierceness while his tall, well-honed body appeared as tense as she felt.

"You didn't resign because I made you crazy. You resigned because you weren't getting your way," he retorted, his tone cool, almost unemotional. "You think you were ready for Ops. You weren't."

His statement infuriated her. Every time he made that argument she wanted to scream in frustration.

"I was twelve when Dad put me in self-defense and firearms courses," she reminded him, her voice low but furious. "At fourteen Claire's brother, Lincoln, who was in Special Forces at the time, took over my training whenever he was home. At eighteen I was considered well qualified to work with the Breed Underground. Two weeks ago I did something well-trained agents would have had a hard time doing, and you think I'm not qualified to even oversee operations with you in the command van. All you wanted me to do was file your damned paperwork."

A grimace pulled at his expression, but he knew he couldn't argue her qualifications. He had never been able to argue them. In the past he'd shut her down by walking out of the office or simply staring back at her silently no matter what she said.

He turned his head away from her then, staring back at the house, tension radiating from him though he maintained the appearance of casual relaxation. He wasn't relaxed in the least. She knew him, knew the signs of his tension—

Then he growled again. A low, dangerous sound that had her rolling her eyes in exasperation.

"The growl isn't going to change anything, Cullen. I trained my ass off to be a part of the Agency. I trained after I came into the Agency. Everyone there knew I had the qualifications to join Ops or Command, and you refused to hear it." She gave a weary shake of her head. "And now it doesn't matter. This is my life; you can't order me out of it no matter how much you might want to."

He turned back to her slowly, the gleam of his eyes more intense now, the shadows filling the truck actually giving him the appearance of stripes across his face.

"Tell me what you're doing and who you're working for. I'll take care of it, finish the job, and then I'll bring you into Command at the Agency," he offered. "You'll work directly with me."

At first she was certain she couldn't have heard him correctly.

"Are you serious?" He couldn't have meant it. Even Cullen wouldn't go that far to get what he wanted.

"I'll train you to take over Ranger's position within two years. He wants to step into admin." He continued with the promise. "You'll be my second, Chelsea. You'll oversee all ops with me and be an integral part of the planning. That was what you wanted. You can have it."

She turned away from him; she had to.

"I'll finish this job for you personally," he continued. "You'll go straight to Ops and begin training while I do it."

He was that desperate to close her in, to put her in a box and join her family in keeping her locked away from the life she wanted to live.

Her father had seen to her training in the interests of self-protection, he always argued. His beloved sister had been kidnapped by the Genetics Council when she was only sixteen. He'd been terrified of losing one of his daughters.

He hadn't intended for her to use the training as a career. It had been to keep her safe, and he complained often that he would have less gray hair if he'd just hired bodyguards.

"You need to go home, Cullen." God, it hurt. He was dangling a carrot in front of her that she had worked toward for years.

She would have enjoyed Ops, but Command would have suited her so much better. Being in on each operation from planning to completion, overseeing it, working with each agent and coordinating their reports after they went undercover. Working with Cullen on a daily basis, sharing every phase of the work they both loved.

The price he was demanding was far too high, though.

"I have a job now." She forced the words out, forced the denial past her lips. "What I'm doing and who I'm doing it for is none of your business. Just as the operations that went through the Agency weren't considered my business. Just go home and stop trying to protect me. It was never your protection that I wanted."

♦   ♦   ♦

At the last moment, Cullen pulled back the harsh, brutal growl that would have escaped his chest. The scent of her pain was like wildfire racing out of control, and what it was doing to his self-control was shocking.

Flexing his fingers, he stared at them for a moment, wondering at the ache he could feel in them and the anger rising inside him.

"You're important to me, Chelsea." He'd tried to make sense of why his Breed genetics were suddenly rearing their sullen heads and making his life hell since Chelsea had left the Agency.

"We're friends," she agreed, and he wanted to latch onto that excuse so bad he couldn't stand it. "I get that. But friends don't get to tell friends how to live their lives."

Cullen breathed out heavily as that scent of pain increased. And determination. Damn, she had to be the most stubborn woman he'd ever known. She even had Breed females beat.

"We're more than friends," he acknowledged, silencing her, surprising her. "Letting you leave the Agency was the hardest thing I've ever done. This is the right thing to do, you know it is."

She was shaking her head the whole time he was talking, with her hands latched onto the steering wheel like a lifeline. He could feel the denial racing through her, sense it moving on the air around him.

"It's my job," she whispered, the scent of tears raking over his senses now, almost pulling a snarl from his lips. "And it's just not realistic to assume that I can do it on my own or aid in any op you could come up with, is it?" Scorn filled her voice. "God, Cullen, I already have one overprotective father, I don't need another one."

Father? He'd be damned if he felt anything fatherly toward her.

"And if you die doing this your way? What about the grief you leave behind? The loss?" he demanded.

What could he say or do to make her understand how much it would hurt to lose her in such a way?

"And what about *my* grief?" Her question had his eyes narrowing on her in confusion.

Her eyes were filled with that grief, with a tormented hurt and longing whose cause he didn't understand.

"You want me to deny who I am, what lives inside me." One hand lifted from the steering wheel to press between her breasts. "You want me to deny the dreams I've had all my life. Deny who and what I am. It's no different than imprisoning me while you ride off into the sunset to do it all yourself. Why don't you spend the next two years doing my filing while I do your job, and see how well you like it?"

His jaw clenched to the point that his teeth ached. She was right, and he knew she was right. She had been right for years, yet each time he'd considered giving her a place on Ops or Command, he'd forced himself to pull back. Neither position was secure enough to make him feel confident that she was safe.

"It's what you wanted," he growled instead. "Command is what you wanted, Chelsea."

"Not at the price you're asking," she cried out. "It was what I wanted when I was with the Agency. What I wanted before I left and learned how much I enjoy working with people who actually consider the possibility that I might know what I'm doing."

As his lips parted to reply, lights cut through the back window of the truck and Cullen recognized the Agency Dragoon pulling in behind them. Dammit, he didn't need this. This wasn't finished. He hadn't touched her, tasted her again. He hadn't found a way to convince her to drop whatever she was doing until he could figure out why some damned Council-bred Coyote had come after her with a knife.

With a muttered curse he stepped from the truck and strode to the

Dragoon as Ranger stepped from the powerful desert-capable law enforcement vehicle.

"What?" he snarled.

Ranger's dark brow lifted in surprise. "The Peterson op is heating up. We need to get Command in place and get ready for that buy, Cullen. Our window in is limited. We're going to have to roll."

"Fuck!" They'd been working that op for six months. A small Coyote Breed unit they were working with was setting up a drug buy with one of the bigger movers in the West. He couldn't afford to drop the ball on this one. "Give me a minute. Have the unit ready to roll and get Dog on the radio. I'll be right back."

The Coyote, Dog, was their eyes and ears in the small group of Genetics Council Coyotes selling the drugs. Working with the other Breed had made this operation move incredibly fast. Cullen knew if they lost this opportunity, then the Genetics Council would receive an influx of cash that would fund more operations against free Breeds than Cullen wanted to contemplate.

Chelsea was stepping from the truck as he turned back and strode to her. Her expression, despite the mutinous set, was disillusioned, though, the hurt still lingering.

"This isn't over," he assured her, reaching out to grip her upper arm and pull her to him. His arm went around her waist, his head lowered and before she could resist he let his tongue taste her lips, then pushed between the curves and claimed her mouth with a kiss he was craving.

There was no time to sate himself, no time to claim her, but he'd be damned if he'd let her forget what was burning between them.

Forcing himself to pull back, he glared down at her for a moment before releasing her. Turning, he stalked back to the Dragoon, waved Ranger to the passenger side and slid into the driver's seat.

God only knew how long this was going to take.

As they reversed from the driveway and accelerated away from the house, he pulled his sat phone from the clip at his belt and hit speed dial.

"Do you know what fucking time it is?" his brother snapped as he answered the call.

"You're obviously still awake," he pointed out in annoyance. "Don't worry, I'll make it quick."

"You're getting too uppity for those recessed genetics of yours," Graeme groused. "What the hell do you want?"

Cullen ground his teeth before once again smothering a growl.

"I'm going to be out of town for a while. I'm not certain how long," he informed the other man. "Put a shadow on Chelsea for me."

"She has two," Graeme reminded him irritably. "And you told me to keep my nose out of it."

"Then make it three, dammit," he snarled. "Keep her safe, Graeme; it's no less than I did for you."

Silence filled the line for long seconds before he heard a heavy sigh.

"I did that when I heard of the attack," Graeme finally admitted. "And if you want to know what she's doing, check with Rule Breaker, the new director of the Western Division of the Bureau of Breed Affairs. According to my informant she's working with his Covert Breed Management Division, currently headed by that little witch Cassandra Sinclair. And I just received that information a few hours ago, before you start snarling your displeasure that I might have been holding back on you."

The Covert Breed Management Division?

Fuck, she was looking for Council-held Breeds; no wonder she was attacked. And the attacks wouldn't stop either.

"I have two men shadowing her, out of sight of the two Breeds assigned as her backup. Just let me know when you return." Graeme breathed out heavily. "And I wouldn't be gone long if I were you, Cullen. That girl's stubborn, and she knows her directive. She won't wait for you to return before heading into trouble."

No, she wouldn't.

Disconnecting the call, he tossed the phone to the console as he glowered into the darkness, the silence in the Dragoon becoming heavier by the second.

"Don't say it," he finally warned the agent riding with him. "I don't want to hear it."

"Of course you don't," Ranger scoffed mockingly. "Sucks knowing you fucked up, doesn't it? I told you to talk to her and get her back at the Agency when she first resigned. That damned pride of yours gets you in trouble every time."

"Shut the fuck up," Cullen ordered, hating the truth of his friend's words.

"Admit it, Cullen." Ranger sighed. "That girl's been important to you since you first came to Window Rock. Lauren might have been paranoid, but she wasn't wrong about you and Chelsea being close. She's important to you. She always has been."

More important than Ranger guessed. More important than even Cullen had realized at the time.

"She was a friend. She's still a friend." He sighed wearily. "How that's changed since Lauren's death isn't the point, Ranger. I wasn't unfaithful to my wife." No matter the fact that she had been.

"If anyone knows that, it's me," Ranger stated quietly. "But now, Cullen, you're going to have to make up your mind what you're going to do where she's concerned. Because she's not one of those one-night stands you keep insisting on having. You break her heart, and you'll make enemies."

Sliding him a sidelong look, Cullen only grunted at the warning. It wasn't the enemies he would make that bothered him. The thought of breaking Chelsea's heart wasn't the problem. If he took her to his bed, he'd keep her. He wouldn't have a choice in the matter. It was that wild courage that was so much a part of her that held him back. A wild courage that terrified him on a good day. Chelsea would insist on fighting by his side and he'd go crazy worrying about her safety and losing her.

He was starting to realize that was all he was doing now, though.

Chelsea had proven she wasn't going to be restrained with her rescue of the Cerves daughter that night in the desert. The memory of that still had the power to send fear crawling up his back. She could have died out there, alone, tortured by the monsters that had such a lack of mercy they'd killed a child with the physical and mental wounds they'd inflicted.

And making enemies wasn't the greatest risk he was taking. Losing her was his greatest fear, but losing himself if anything ever happened to her was a certainty.

CHAPTER 6

From Graeme's Journal
The Recessed Primal Breed

The recessed Primal Breed will deny Mating Heat only as long as his animal genetics will allow—

Two days later Chelsea stepped into the office of the Director of the Western Division of the Bureau of Breed Affairs, where Rule Breaker and his assistant director, Lawe Justice, and her handler, Cassie Sinclair, waited.

Cassie looked as cool and composed as ever dressed in gray tailored slacks, a white silk blouse and four-inch heels. Her long black hair was drawn back into a low ponytail and secured with a white silk ribbon.

She appeared both innocent and confident and it was a look she did well.

Rule and Lawe, on the other hand, despite their expensive suits and smooth manners, were still the hard, savagely trained Breeds they were when they'd first come to the Nation several years ago. The rougher edges were smoother now, but they hadn't lost anything in strength or the wary caution in their eyes.

"Chelsea. It's good to see you again." Rule rose from his seat behind the long executive desk at the other side of the room. A smile tipped his lips and amusement filled his dark blue gaze, but she was certain that could change as quickly as any threat could rear its head.

"Yes, it is," Lawe agreed. "Though we expected to see you at Graeme's dinner party the other night."

Her brow lifted as she shook their hands, appreciating the light firmness that didn't pinch her hand.

"I should have just attended," she grimaced, taking her seat next to Cassie in front of Rule's desk. "Our friendly commander of the Covert Law Enforcement Agency made things a little difficult while we were in the field."

Rule grimaced at her comment as he took his seat as well and pulled a file up on the holo-screen he used at his desk.

"So your report noted," he sighed. "I wanted you to come in to let you know in person that your cover has likely been blown with the commander, and definitely with his brother, Graeme. It's rather difficult to keep Graeme out of our files whenever he decides to plunder them."

She nodded at that. "It lasted longer than I anticipated. Cullen, I know, is rather good at getting the answers he wants. I suspected he'd request Graeme's help in getting those answers after he showed up at the house the other day."

She'd worked with him long enough to know exactly how good he was at it. She'd simply assumed after a month of no contact that he really didn't give a damn what she was doing.

"I should tell you Grandfather contacted me as well," Rule sighed. "He wasn't happy with me for offering you the position."

Sometimes, it was damned hard to remember that this forceful Breed and his brother were actually her first cousins. When her aunt, Morningstar, had been kidnapped by the Council, she'd been impregnated with Breeds. Rule and Lawe were just two of them. And through them they'd learned that Morningstar's brother, Raymond, had actually been working with the Council at the time. He'd betrayed his sister to them.

"Did Cullen call him?" she asked him warily then.

If he'd been carrying tales to her grandfather, she might end up taking her grandmother's black cast-iron skillet to his head.

Rule's lips twisted with wry amusement. "Grandfather claims less conventional means in acquiring his information."

"He told Rule he wasn't pleased that the winds were forced to come to him rather than his own grandsons to inform him of the dangers said grandsons had drawn his granddaughter into," Lawe smirked. "He was a little put out."

Chelsea let her fingers tighten on the arm of the chair for a second before giving a heavy sigh. Her grandfather could be temperamental at times. And if the "winds"—the breezes that whispered over the Nation—tattled on his grandchildren, then he could become extremely irate. He claimed his family should keep him in the loop no matter the trouble they were about to get into.

She should have known she couldn't keep what she was doing away from him. She was thankful the winds had remained quiet as long as they had.

"I'm glad he called you rather than me," she finally said with a little grin as her gaze met Rule's. "He must be waiting for you to take care of the problem."

Lawe grunted at that. "He demanded we fire you immediately."

Her eyes widened in surprise and wariness. "Fire me?"

Rule leaned back in his chair, his gaze never leaving hers. "He claimed this position would endanger you because you were too stubborn to accept help."

Her brows lifted at the accusation.

"Hmm," she muttered, restraining a smile. "And here I thought the winds knew me better than that."

Lawe chuckled from her side as Cassie's silent laughter sparkled in her blue eyes.

"Cute." Rule nodded, his lips quirking with amusement at her response. "But I'm curious to know why he'd think you'd refuse help?"

She didn't have a clue.

Unless . . .

Lips pursing thoughtfully, she breathed a short sigh before shaking her head in resignation.

"Cullen," she stated, pushing her fingers across the fringe of bangs that fell over her brow. "When I refused to tell him what I was doing or who I was working for, he offered me a place on Command at the Agency if I'd let him finish whatever job I'd taken. Without my help, of course."

Rule's brow lifted with a hint of surprise as he reached up to scratch at his cheek lightly. "Interesting," he finally commented. "Cullen was rather determined to keep you in the office, wasn't he?"

"A bit," she agreed. He'd been fanatical about it; she'd often accused him of that.

"Hell of a concession to make just for some information," Lawe pointed out.

"Oh, he didn't just want the particulars." Shifting in her chair, she could feel the remembered anger returning. "He wanted me to allow him to finish the job himself while I returned to the office and waited for him. It didn't seem like a fair trade to me."

"Yeah, I bet his filing has piled up a bit," Cassie commented with a hint of laughter.

She had no doubt in her mind that his filing had piled up. When she'd first gone to work for him, it had taken her two months to clear up his filing system.

"In an age of complete digital filing and retrieving, for some reason, law enforcement still loves its paper," she sighed, glancing at the folders and files stacked on one side of Rule's desk.

"Can't hack hard copy," Lawe drawled.

"You can't forward it either," Rule grunted.

"I'd burn his files if I had to return to that office," Chelsea informed them. "And I'm sure he's completely destroyed my filing system by now."

She'd taken a week for vacation once; when she'd returned, the filing system was a disaster, not to mention the files strewn from one office to the other. What was it about men and their files?

"I don't intend to send you back to filing hell," Rule promised with a quirk of his lips. "I wanted to apprise you of the situation, let you know that he's likely aware of the operation you're a part of."

Well, at least she didn't have to worry about explaining it to him now.

"Maybe he'll let it go now." She shrugged. "His curiosity has been assuaged and he can go back to his own job and leave mine alone."

She had to admit, knowing he was at the clubs the night he'd followed her had given her a sense of security she hadn't known in the weeks before, or the past two nights. For some reason, the knowledge that Cullen was there meant far more than knowing Draeger and Tobias were shadowing her.

"I wouldn't bet on it if I were you," Cassie whispered, her voice almost too low to hear.

Chelsea refrained from shooting the other woman a warning look. Cullen hadn't cared one way or the other what she was doing until that responsibility complex of his had kicked in at the news of her attack. Then he'd felt he had to protect her. He'd never considered the thought that protection wasn't what she needed.

"I'm betting on it." Chelsea gave a firm nod, determined she was right.

She knew Cullen. She'd worked with him for four years; she knew how deep his sense of responsibility went. He felt responsible for her. Felt he had to protect her. That was the reason he hadn't wanted her in Command or in Ops. He could keep her safe in the office.

Cassie snickered beside her while Lawe and Rule cast the other woman a hooded look. No one had ever accused Breeds of not being weird.

"If that's everything?" She rose slowly to her feet, her gaze encompassing the three Breeds currently seeming to have some joke at her expense. "I'd like to get to the operations center and go over the pictures and video that's come in over the past week so I'll to know where to concentrate my interest when I head back out."

Rule nodded as he and Lawe rose to their feet once again.

"Draeger and Tobias are waiting for you outside the office," Lawe stated, nodding to the door.

"I'll be down to join you in a bit," Cassie informed her as she headed for the door. "Give me about thirty minutes."

"You know where I'll be," she called back to the other woman.

Leaving the office, she was aware of the two Wolf Breeds waiting for her as they rose to their feet and trailed behind her.

Cassie seemed certain Cullen wasn't going to let this go so easily. Chelsea sincerely hoped the other woman was wrong. She knew Cullen. Working with him on this would be impossible, and she wasn't about to quit and turn it over to him or anyone else.

◆　◆　◆

As the door closed behind Chelsea, Cassie lifted her gaze from where she'd been concentrating on a chip in the polish on her nail. As advanced as technology had become, one would think nail polish wouldn't chip. Especially professionally applied polish.

Her gaze locked with Rule's concerned one, and she knew what worried him; it was the same thing worrying her now.

"I had no warning of the attack on her," she told them, though she knew they were aware of that. "She shouldn't have been attacked."

It made no sense. There was no reason Chelsea should have been in any danger whatsoever. There was nothing there to tell her why Chelsea had been attacked, or to lead her in the right direction. All Cassie could see was the shadow of a Coyote, ragged, worn, watching her from her periphery. That Coyote had been a steady companion for years now.

"Do you think it has anything to do with her rescue of the Cerves daughter? Those Coyotes as well as the Cerveses have been hunting for the girl that rescued her," Rule pointed out, his hard expression concerned.

"That's definitely not it," Cassie assured them. It was one of the few things she was actually certain of. "Samara and her family are back in New Mexico. They took their daughter there for burial. Samara's determined to learn Chelsea's identity, but her reasons aren't clear. As for the three Coyotes . . ." She grimaced with the memory of the terror they'd inflicted on a child. "Samara Cerves is damned intelligent. She had the doctors at the estate swab for DNA as they tried to close the bite marks on her daughter's body." She covered her lips, her hand shaking as she turned away from the brothers and fought to hide her own emotions and the sickening horror of what that baby had suffered. When she turned back, she could at least speak. "Samara turned those swabs over to Jonas and told him if he could prove he had the Breeds responsible for her death as well as the young woman that returned Louisa, then they'd align with the Breed Underground and begin legitimizing their operations. He took them up on it."

"Not because he believes them," Lawe snorted. "Still, keeping them from aligning with the Council is what matters."

No, Jonas believed the cartel leaders. It had been in his eyes, in his stark expression, when Cassie had accompanied him to see what those animals had done to Samara's child.

"Samara loved her daughter, Lawe," Cassie stated, absolutely certain of that. "I met with her when Jonas was called in. She was inconsolable, broken. And so desperate to get her hands on those Coyotes she would have promised anything, and because of her child, she'll never break that vow. But I have no doubt the Cerves cartel will never align with the Council whether Jonas agreed or not. As for Chelsea, I think

Samara wants the girl who rescued her daughter so she can express her gratitude, though, not to harm her."

Samara Cerves wasn't the woman she had been before the night her daughter was taken from her bedroom and brutalized by the three Coyotes. The Blood Queen wasn't dead, but the blood she wanted had nothing to do with criminal activities now. She wanted the Genetics Council. Not just their soldiers, but the Council itself. And Cassie knew she'd be unstoppable.

"Graeme has three Breeds trailing Chelsea and the Wolf Breeds we assigned her." Rule pushed his fingers through his hair, his expression tightening in irritation. "We have no idea what designation they are, or who they are. We haven't been able to identify them."

"Draeger and Tobias have sensed them." She nodded. "They've tried to draw them in close enough to scent them, but they've not exactly been cooperative." She stared down at her fingers, smoothing one finger over the chipped polish again. "I believe one of them is female, but I have no confirmation." And no matter how hard she tried, she couldn't sense the answers to her questions.

"The attack outside the club was a singular attack, and Draeger and Tobias got to her in time," Lawe pointed out. "According to their reports she was holding her own, though. She's well trained and knows how to watch out for herself."

And all that was true, but Cassie couldn't discount Chelsea's grandfather's words either. She was in danger because she was too stubborn to accept help. Too stubborn to accept Cullen's offer? But that offer hadn't been an offer of help. Cullen wanted her out of it, period.

"Cullen won't let this go." Cassie breathed out heavily at that inner knowledge. "His recessed genetics are either emerging or going through some transition, but whatever's coming awake inside him is incredibly powerful. More powerful than even Graeme suspects, I believe. Possibly even as Primal as his brother. Bengal Breeds are unknown variables the way it is; their genetics are far more wild than most other Breeds. Cullen is but one of a few that we're aware of, and according to his files, he's the twin to one of the most dangerous Breeds we know of. If he's Primal as well, and his genetics are becoming active, then his focus on her could be more than just that of a protector."

"You think it's Mating Heat?" Rule asked. "There was no scent of Heat."

No, there was no scent of Mating Heat; but then, Mating Heat had its anomalies from couple to couple. They couldn't rule it out, and Cassie knew it.

"But her scent has changed over the past few weeks," she said thoughtfully. "Sometimes she shows signs of the Heat, and then they disappear, as though the spark needed hasn't fully awakened his Breed side." She shook her head at the thought. "I'm still trying to figure it out."

"So we could have a possible Bengal mating? A recessed Primal beginning to emerge?" The concern in Lawe's voice wasn't misplaced. Primals were highly unpredictable, just as their four-legged cousins were known to be. Secretive, powerful, savage when they erupted and so mysterious that even the few that had been tested rarely showed reliable readings from one test to the next.

"I just don't know yet." She shook her head, confusion threatening to turn to irritability.

Lawe and Rule exchanged looks, their silent communication not unknown to her.

"I'd have them tested for mating but we learned with Tanner and

Cabal that even fully mated, their tests aren't always conclusive." Rule shook his head.

Tanner and Cabal were, for many years, the only Bengal Breeds known to exist. Tanner was part of the original feline Breed Pride that revealed itself to the world, and he'd been the head of Breed public relations for more than a decade. His mate was the daughter of a now-deceased general who had worked with the Council, trained and killed dozens of Breeds and nearly killed his own daughter as well.

"Ask Graeme for help," Cassie suggested. "I believe he's done extensive research on Bengal genetics. Perhaps he's aware of something we're not, or at least could give us a good guess as to what's going on."

Rule's gaze jerked back to her. "How do you know that?"

Cassie shrugged at the question. "Graeme actually mentioned it to me at the dinner party the other night." Now it made sense why he'd mentioned it. "I believe he'll be expecting you to call."

Evidently, like all Breeds considered less than sane, Graeme was just as manipulating as those she'd been raised among, if not more so, Cassie thought.

"I'll contact Graeme," Rule stated, his expression becoming thoughtful, cunning as he stared back at her. "You'll stay on the operation as her handler and when Cullen comes demanding answers, I'll give him the option of joining her. He can work with her or we'll find a way to keep him away from her while she's on it."

That could work.

Cullen wouldn't want to go against Rule, and he wouldn't want to deal with the pressure Rule could put on the Covert Law Enforcement Agency.

"We'll see how that works out for us." She sighed heavily. "Let me know when you've discussed it with him. Once we know his answer, then I'll let Chelsea know the plan."

Rising to her feet, she left the room; the disquiet she could feel moving through her was more bothersome than she wanted to admit. She wasn't used to handling this part of her life without the ghostly images that had aided her for so long.

They had been coming more rarely over the past years, replaced by that war-torn Coyote that never let her fully see him. If she could stare into the eyes of the image, then she would know the Breed he belonged to. She would know then if he was the Breed that haunted her nightmares and her fears.

The image trailed just behind her, though, shifting if she turned her head, if she tried to see him more fully, always just out of sight.

Was he the reason those who had helped her before didn't appear any longer? Was the Coyote somehow keeping them away? And if so, why? The haunting presence could cause her to endanger the plan she'd had in place for years, and the delicate rescue operation she was working on. That operation depended on Cullen and Chelsea, as well as Samara Cerves and her husband and brother-in-law.

This had to work. It wasn't just her own survival that depended upon the plans she'd been laying in place so covertly over the last years. There were others just as important. And one of them, one of those she was carefully drawing from hiding, wasn't just important to her; she was Cassie's only hope of survival.

Her only chance at freedom . . .

◆   ◆   ◆

The operations center of the Western Division of the Bureau of Breed Affairs was as high-tech as it came and a much larger version of the mobile command Cullen used for the operations he oversaw.

Chelsea stood at the digital information table next to the Russian

Coyote Breed female Ashley, watching as the other woman arranged and rearranged the photo and video files they'd taken over the week. With those files were the written reports of the Bureau agents involved in identifying the Breeds they encountered as well as the rumors and information they'd picked up in the weeks they'd been working the operation.

"This Breed." Chelsea pointed to a hard-eyed, scarred Breed they'd seen only twice in the four weeks she'd been working with them. "He hasn't shown up in any of the other files we have. We still haven't uncovered his name or anyone else he associates with."

Ashley pulled the digital file to the middle of the interactive table and, with one finger from both delicate hands, enlarged it before tapping it twice. The informational file included with the photo popped up next to it.

"No name," Ashley agreed, her Russian accent emphasizing the somber quality of her voice as she tapped a link included with the information.

Instantly another picture popped up. "Emma and Sharone caught him again meeting with Dane Vanderale when he was in the area last week. It seems he disappeared with Dane as well. He could be part of the South African contingent that often shadows our luscious Mr. Vanderale. His father worries, you know," she added drolly, repeating the reason they'd heard for the hard-eyed security force that sometimes shadowed Dane.

Dane Vanderale was the heir to a massive fortune. Known as an international playboy as well as a corporate shark, he was one of the Breeds' greatest supporters, and his father's company contributed heavily to the Breeds' coffers.

"From what I've gathered, Dane and his bodyguard, Rhys, are now in Somalia on business for his father, though. If he's one of the South

African Breeds, then he'd be with the heir apparent rather than lurking in our desert." Ashley input that information into the text file.

Moving more files into several groupings, Chelsea tapped one that held half a dozen other unidentified Breeds along with pictures of those Breeds with several known Wolf Breeds. "These I suspect are part of Lobo Reever's pack."

"Reever hasn't notified us of any new pack members, but all alphas are amazingly reticent when it comes to identifying any Breeds who request anonymity. I'll mark them for facial rec, though, and we'll see if we can't verify it."

There were few packs or Prides outside the main four. Two Wolf Breed packs in Colorado, as well as the Coyote Breeds. The only feline Breed Pride so far was based in Virginia.

"My alpha, Del Rey, has petitioned Director Breaker and the Navajo Nation to allow an official Coyote presence in the Window Rock area," Ashley told her. "He's considering alphas for the pack. I've sent him the pictures of the Coyotes we haven't ID'd yet for verification. Though I haven't seen them myself at Citadel."

Citadel was the Coyote stronghold overlooking the valley where the major Wolf Breed pack was based.

"There are a lot of Breeds in the area who aren't verified," Chelsea murmured.

Unverified meant they weren't registered and no alpha claimed them. The Bureau didn't request names or designations, only verification that they were part of the packs or Pride and indeed friendlies.

"Too many," Ashley agreed. "If our information is correct, the Council is using known gathering places of pack and Pride members in the area to gather their own intel."

There were no new packs, other than Del Rey's request to begin one, and no new alphas had stepped forward to notify the Bureau of their presence.

"I checked with a friend at the Navajo Council and she has no information of Breeds requesting land to settle on either," Chelsea said as the door opened and Cassie strolled into the room. "Before they can settle in the Nation, they have to request permission from the Council and submit DNA to prove their ties to the People."

"Wouldn't it be so much nicer if the Breeds aligned with the Council would just identify themselves?" Cassie grinned wryly as she stepped to the table. "It would make our job much easier, wouldn't it?"

It would at that.

"And it would make Chelsea's job easier if one bad-assed recessed Bengal Breed wasn't so nosy," Ashley drawled.

Chelsea covered her face in exasperation. "What is his problem? That man is driving me crazy."

"Maybe he wants to mate you like all those juicy tabloids are writing about," Ashley teased with a mock shiver. "Let me know if you become all hysterically horny and start fucking like rabbits. The tabloids pay prime cash for the details, you know." Lifting one hand, she checked her nails with exaggerated care. "And my nails are due a little work."

Cassie chuckled at the little Russian's antics. Ashley was simply her favorite Breed, period. Even a near miss with death hadn't brought her down from her quirky antics.

"He probably wants to turn me into one of those insipid little secretaries he had before me. I was such a disappointment to him," Chelsea scoffed. "Those wide-eyed little debutantes made me want to lobby the Nation for stupidity tests before hiring."

A low laugh spilled from Ashley's lips. "Yeah, I hear he went through a lot of those before you came around. All vying for a place in the hotshot commander's bed. They didn't last long, I heard."

Working through the pictures, Chelsea frowned at the statement.

"The longest was two months," she finally sighed, taking a moment to glance up at them. "They all quit, most in tears."

Ashley began moving pictures again as well, adding some to Chelsea's piles and using some to make her own.

"Jonas Wyatt had the same problem until Merinus Lyons hired his wife, Rachel, as his assistant," Cassie told them. "Jonas was a goner the second he laid eyes on her."

"Maybe Cullen has the same problem with you," Ashley chimed in, the laughter still filling her voice. "Breed men have such a hard time admitting when they've met their match. Would it not be simply fitting if all those protective, alpha instincts toward you were all caused because he is crazy in love with you?"

Chelsea snorted at that one despite the ache she felt that it wasn't possible. "I rather doubt that's the problem. Cullen's still in love with the wife he lost almost ten years ago. He became so distant after her death that I rarely saw him until I went to work for the Agency."

She met Cassie's incredibly bright blue eyes as the other woman watched her closely.

"Breeds can be very difficult and very stubborn," Cassie said softly. "But he is a Breed, recessed or not. I don't get the sense that Cullen loved his wife as deeply as you suspect, though. Not to say he didn't love her, just not with the depth that a Breed can experience."

Chelsea shrugged at that. Abandoning the pictures, she propped her hip against the digital table and crossed her arms beneath her breasts as she glanced between Cassie's and Ashley's somber expressions.

"Lauren was his first relationship after he was placed within the protection of the Breed Underground. They married six months after his arrival. It was just a few months later that she told him she had a particularly virulent form of cancer. She died just before their second anniversary."

"How did he meet her?" Ashley asked, the compassion in her tone thickening her accent.

"She was Ray Martinez's assistant." Chelsea grimaced. Her uncle Ray had betrayed her entire family for most of his life, especially his daughter Claire, or Cat as everyone called her.

"She was your cousin as well, was she not?" Ashley asked.

Chelsea nodded. "Fourth cousin, actually. Though we weren't very close."

Lauren's father had come from a very well-to-do family until that family had gone bankrupt and her parents had moved into her grand-parents' home. Even then, her father, an attorney, had done quite well for himself, and Lauren had always felt as though she were better than the rest of the family.

Her parents had left after Lauren's death and, as far as Chelsea knew, didn't even visit.

"A man as strong as Cullen would feel he had failed her," Cassie stated cryptically. "And the tabloid stories may be far-fetched, but the bonding between Breeds and their mates is well-known. Cullen didn't have that bond with his wife, I don't believe."

Lauren wasn't one for bonds, though, Chelsea remembered.

"Before she died Lauren blamed everything and everyone in those last months," she remembered. "Especially Cullen. Just before she died she accused him of not loving her enough. That his love could have saved her. Dad was there when she said it. He was shocked by her cruelty."

Terran Martinez had been so shocked by Lauren's accusations that he hadn't even attended her funeral.

"She sounds much like Claire's father, Ray," Ashley pointed out.

"They were very close." Chelsea shrugged, staring down at the table once again for long moments. "Dad once commented that they were very much alike. But Cullen loved her. He was devastated when she died."

"No wonder," Cassie sighed heavily. "Such guilt to put on any husband, especially a Breed."

The looks Chelsea caught Ashley and Cassie exchanging brought a frown to her face, but she refused to ask about it.

"But now all his Breed instincts are going crazy because you were attacked," Ashley pointed out. "That Breed is a goner for you, my friend." She gave a quick little flip of her hand for emphasis. "Breed males are so weird with it too. You will see."

No, she wouldn't, Chelsea knew, though she kept that to herself. Cullen had loved Lauren so deeply that no other woman would ever compare. Especially not her.

She wasn't super girly, she rarely wore makeup and she had no idea how to simper and charm. She didn't want to keep home and hearth while he fought the battles alone. She wanted to fight at his side, at least for a while. She wanted to be his partner, not his secretary.

She would have settled for working Command, overseeing each operation with him. She was good at communications and logistics, but he wanted her filing and answering his phones instead. And she had hated every moment of it. Hated it so much that she'd begun resenting him for it. That was when she'd known it was time to leave.

"Draeger and Tobias's report of the night Cullen followed you to the clubs included the information that they could smell his anger coming from him in waves," Cassie said.

Chelsea sighed at the description. "I think *I* could smell it, and I'm not even a Breed."

"Oh, trust me," Ashley drawled in amusement. "The scent of it rolled off him. That was one jealous Breed glaring at every male you spoke to, my friend."

She highly doubted the jealous part, but he had made it impossible to do her job.

"Every Breed there kept glancing at him as though asking his permission to speak to me." She rolled her eyes in disgust.

"Because they could smell his lust covering you like a blanket." Ashley laughed. "They are animals, you forget. They would not tempt another Breed's rage by showing interest in the woman he had so marked."

A blush worked over her face at Ashley's teasing comment.

"I hate those pesky noses the lot of you possess," she assured them. "Every one of you."

Their laughter was good-natured and teasing, but Chelsea caught the thoughtful look on Cassie's face before it was quickly replaced by amusement. There was something the other two weren't telling her, some secret they all seemed to share where Cullen was concerned.

If they believed that deeply that he somehow cared for her as more than a friend, then they were wrong. He'd had four years to figure it out if he did. The fact that he hadn't proved her suspicions. Cullen might desire her, definitely wanted to protect her. But he didn't love her and his lust wasn't enough—

Unfortunately it was all he was willing to give her.

· C H A P T E R 7 ·

From Graeme's Journal
Recessed Primal Genetics and Mating Heat

Wild and unpredictable, the recessed Primal genetics are like the animal
itself—waiting, stalking and ready to pounce with deadly force—

Four weeks into the operation to identify any unknown Breeds and
their target, and still she and her team hadn't been able to narrow the
list of possibilities. Cassie of course headed the list of targets; the price
on her head was highest. Ashley ran a close second. After that, Alpha
Reever, Cullen's brother, the Western Division's director, and the
highest-profile Breeds in the area brought the list to over a dozen.

Until she could find a parameter, a name—hell, she'd love to find
a loose-lipped Genetics Council puppet willing to spill a few secrets.

That was just her favorite scenario. Finding the Genetics Council Breeds or their potential abduction targets wasn't coming easy at all.

There were suspected Council Breeds in the area, but anywhere Breeds congregated, there were suspected spies, especially if Coyote Breeds were among them.

Tracking down the source of the information had proven impossible, and actually identifying a Council spy and getting him to talk was even more so.

Entering the house a week later, Chelsea headed to the shower, hoping to clear her head. If she didn't manage to find the answers soon, Director Breaker would shut her down as quickly as he'd given her the go-ahead on it.

The attack the week before hadn't helped matters in the least. Now her team as well as the director seemed suspicious that she'd somehow given herself away as she navigated within the underground world of contacts and information. Chasing down rumors of Breeds. That had been her primary focus in the Breed Underground. Though she'd been searching for Breeds seeking safety rather than spies, she admitted.

She'd been part of the Breed Underground since she was sixteen years old and still worked with them occasionally. Going covert was just about a requirement for the job.

She hadn't given herself away.

So why had she been targeted that night? And why was it suddenly impossible for her to gain information that she'd been accessing easily in the ten years prior?

She'd begun working with the Breed Underground just after Cullen's wife, Lauren, had died from the cancerous tumors they'd found in her brain. Cullen had worked with the Breed Underground only rarely at that point, though if needed, the few Breed agents he had were assigned to aid certain Breed Underground cases.

He'd worked one of the cases when she first joined, and she remembered being sent home immediately when she'd arrived at the meeting. When she protested, he told her he didn't think her family needed to lose another of its daughters. Especially because of foolish courage.

Because he had lost Lauren, he thought it was perfectly okay to shatter her dream of working with him and send her home as though she were a child. Her knowledge that Lauren had only tried to use his love, she had kept to herself. He'd been hurt enough, she'd told herself painfully. No matter how angry she was, she wouldn't hurt him more.

Her cousin had always been a bit superior, a little smug, but in the year before her death, she'd become cruel and cutting, seeking to hurt everyone and anyone she could focus on.

Especially her husband.

Unknown to her father, Chelsea had learned Cullen was a Breed before he'd ever married Lauren. It had been that first night Cullen had arrived in the Nation. She'd overheard them talking as she watched from the darkness in the other room, and her father had called him a Breed.

A year or so later she'd been practicing the survival skills she'd been learning, when she followed her father one night into the desert. There, he'd met with several Navajo, their faces obscured by shadowed markings, and Cullen.

"I may be recessed, but I'm still a Breed," Cullen had stated in reply to her father's doubt that Council Breeds were in the area searching for someone. *"They can't sense me, but I can damned sure sense them."*

Chelsea had remained silent, a shadow within a shadow as her grandfather had been teaching her. When the meeting concluded and her father returned to the house, Chelsea had remained hidden, sensing that perhaps all the men he'd met with hadn't left the area.

She remembered the feeling of another presence, not a danger, but watching, waiting. And someone had been. They'd outwaited her, so still and silent in the night that after two hours she was certain she had been wrong.

Still, she'd been careful creeping back to the house and into her room. Two days later, her father and her cousin Lincoln Martinez had been waiting when she came home from school, aware of the meeting she'd overheard. And from that day, her cousins had taken over her training.

Her father had worried; he still worried. Her grandfather railed at her constantly for putting herself in the slightest danger, while her sister, Isabelle, always remained quiet but concerned.

The phone calls and visits she'd received from her family after Cullen learned of the attack just pissed her off. Her grandfather's mutterings that the winds were failing him because he hadn't known of it, her father's angry demands that she stop whatever she was doing and her sister's quiet concern had gotten on her nerves fast.

Stepping from the shower, she quickly dried her body and then her hair before staring into the mirror silently. She was twenty-six years old and her family thought she was wasting her life chasing danger. But it wasn't danger she was chasing.

She'd never forget the night Cullen and two young women had come to her father's house. Bloody and bruised after an attack by Council soldiers. The girls hadn't been crying; they'd been stoic, their eyes filled with nightmares. And Cullen's eyes had burned with rage, with determination despite the blood that marred his hair and his clothes.

She'd been so angry, furious as she overheard her father and the warriors standing in the shadows discussing the attack of the Council soldiers against the three. A Breed and two young girls he was trying so desperately to protect. The Council Breeds chasing them were intent on recapturing them, torturing them.

And Cullen had stood silently, the two girls huddled behind him, uncertain of the men who had saved them and clearly willing to go to battle again. She'd wanted nothing more than to be at his side and help him.

Reaching up, she touched a single tear that drifted from her eyes at the memory. She'd shed a lot of tears as a teenager for Cullen. And she'd trained, worked her ass off just to fight beside him to make certain other Breeds were protected. Such fierce determination to survive should have never been threatened in such a way.

He didn't want her working by his side, though. He wanted her in the office, away from him.

Breathing out heavily, she swiped the nearly dry strands of straight hair back from her face, her gaze critical now. She wasn't nearly as beautiful as Lauren had been.

Her shoulder-length black hair wasn't the rich, textured black ribbon that Lauren's had been. Her brown eyes were flecked with hints of green. Her skin was much lighter than Lauren's. She didn't have the dark Navajo bronze skin; rather hers was the color of a good suntan, closer to that of her Caucasian mother.

She was short, her breasts fuller, and she was rounder than her cousin had been. She wasn't girly, a debutante or fragile and she'd never wanted to be. At best, she could only claim pretty, maybe.

Damn sure she couldn't claim the man she often wondered if she'd fallen in love with when she was no more than a young girl staring through the darkness and seeing that fierce will burning in his eyes.

It was still there. That determination to survive, to fight, to protect those he took responsibility for. And she still wanted nothing more than to fight by his side.

Shaking her head, Chelsea tucked the towel tighter at her breasts and strode into her bedroom, where she came to a hard, shocked stop.

As though conjured there by thoughts alone, Cullen stood leaning in the door frame between her bedroom and the short hall leading into the living room.

Dressed in a short-sleeved khaki shirt, jeans and boots, arms crossed over his broad chest, his gold-flecked green eyes hooded and brooding, he watched her with silent intensity.

Her fingers tightened at the tuck of the towel as her heart fluttered with sudden nerves.

"Forget how to knock or call?" she asked as she strode across the bedroom to her dresser. Pulling out drawers, she collected a pair of panties and a bra and tucked them between a pair of yoga pants and a loose gray T-shirt.

"And give you warning that I was coming? You might have left," he told her, his tone querulous.

The sound of his voice had remembered pleasure washing through her senses. Reaching up, she rubbed at the reddened area between her neck and shoulder, her eyes closing with the subtle sensations that shot through her body.

"I would have still been here." Chelsea shrugged, turning back to him. "Give me a minute and I'll get dressed."

She was not getting involved in one of their irate discussions dressed in only a towel.

"Why?" He tilted his head to the side, his expression appearing darker somehow, sexier. "I'll just have to take the clothes back off you soon. Why go to the trouble?"

She almost dropped her clothes. Eyes widening, she stared back at him, unable to believe the words that had just come out of his mouth.

"Why make it easy for you?" Casting him a narrow-eyed look, she hurried back to the bathroom, dressed and, for a moment, actually considered texting Draeger to see if he and Tobias wanted to play cards for a few hours.

Wouldn't that put a crimp in Cullen's little plan?

Asshole.

She didn't need another Breed to fight her battles, though, she finally decided. She might have waited far too many years for him to show more interest than it took for him to hand her a file.

Returning to the bedroom, fully dressed but no less nervous, Chelsea found him in the same position she'd left him in. He hadn't shifted an inch, nor had his expression changed.

Smoothing her hands over her hips, she drew in a deep breath and steeled herself for the coming confrontation. She could see the storm brewing in his eyes, feel it brewing in herself.

"I hope you aren't expecting to tear my clothes off anytime soon," she told him sweetly as she stalked across the bedroom to the doorway. "I'd at least like a cup of coffee first."

Brushing past him, she almost let out a silent breath of relief when he caught her arm, drawing her quickly to a stop.

Staring up at him, she was caught by the flecks of amber fire in the jungle green as they seemed brightened by the anger that narrowed his gaze.

"Why didn't you tell me what you were doing for the Bureau?" His lips pulled back from his teeth and she swore his incisors looked just a little more prominent than she remembered them being. "Why didn't you come to me first?"

Lifting her eyes, Chelsea stared back at him and forced herself to breathe slowly, evenly.

"Would you like a cup of coffee before we begin this argument? Or do you just want to start now?" she asked, her lip curling in disgust. "Because I find it highly distasteful arguing in my bedroom. And I'm sure as hell not doing it while you're holding on to me as though I were a suspect in need of detaining."

His gaze flickered, then dropped to where he was holding her firmly. He released her slowly, almost finger by finger, until she was free. "Answer my question."

"Not until I've had my coffee," she informed him, her voice sharper than she intended. "Hell, maybe a drink too. Dealing with you is becoming harder by the day."

Of course, it would help if she didn't allow herself to get drawn into conversations about his former marriage or her own doubts about her ability to measure up to the femininity his deceased wife had once possessed. That was always guaranteed to put her in a bad mood.

Add the instant arousal the minute she caught sight of him into the equation and there probably wasn't enough coffee or alcohol to settle her nerves.

Stalking through the dimly lit living room and into the spacious kitchen, Chelsea raked her fingers through her hair and told herself she was not going to become distracted by his touch or that gleam of lust she'd glimpsed in his eyes as she moved past him.

If she didn't keep her wits about her, then Cullen would end up destroying any chance she had of proving herself as a dependable agent. She wasn't going to allow that.

Sliding two cups beneath the dual spouts of the coffeemaker, she programmed in the strength of the brew and waited the five seconds or so it took to fill them. When she turned back to him, she placed his cup on the table before cradling her own and leaning against the counter.

And if he started toward her as he had the last time he was in her kitchen, then she was going to run. She was not letting him touch her. For some reason, his touch just fried her brain synapses.

The fact that they were facing off in the kitchen once more wasn't lost on her, though. The irony of it was really kind of amusing.

Every discussion her family had ever had that was of any importance had taken place in a kitchen over coffee or alcoholic drinks. Hell, it was here where she'd met with Ashley and Cassie just after her contact, an employee for a desert tourist guide business, had called her and given her a lead on the Genetics Council's upcoming plans.

A week after she'd resigned from the Agency and walked away from Cullen. A week of questioning herself and her decision, and the answer to what she was going to do after Cullen, had come in the form of that phone call.

Taking the information she'd gotten from her contact, she'd contacted Ashley and Cassie, asked them over for coffee, then proposed the operation she was currently conducting. Cassie had immediately called Director Breaker, and within the hour he and his brother,

Operations Commander of the Western Division, had been on her doorstep. From there, the operation had become her baby.

She didn't appreciate Cullen's desire to take it away from her.

"I'm waiting on that answer." His voice rumbled with demand. "Why didn't you come to me if you suspected the Genetics Council was up to something?"

She shrugged with a tight, tension-filled movement. "I didn't suspect crap, Cullen. A close friend of mine, a contact I've used when working with the Underground, contacted me. He overheard a Coyote and one of the other guides discussing the Genetics Council sending a team into the area to abduct a high-profile Breed target as well as placing double agents within the Breed community being established here. I took that information to the Bureau, and Director Breaker gave me lead on the operation. That Coyote and guide disappeared before enforcers could get to them, but we still have a chance to save their target."

His eyes narrowed on her, brooding and not in the least pleased. "How did you verify this information?" he demanded, suspicion flickering in his gaze. "For all you know it could just be some story your contact concocted for you. You know exactly how unreliable information like that can be."

She shook her head, incredulity filling her now. "I'm sure that's what you want me to believe, Cullen." She scoffed at the accusation. "This wasn't some carefully designed fairy tale, I promise you that. Within days the Bureau had taps on several known Council associates, and the information was verified and reverified before we ever finalized the parameters of the operation. We've been trying to identify the Council Breeds and the target the team is coming after. The targeted window of the attempt is within two to four weeks. And we're getting closer, I can feel it."

The phone taps as well as the listening devices she and Ashley managed to place in areas where suspected Council associates were talking in those clubs had brought in several clues. Nothing concrete, nothing they could act on. It was more questions than answers, but they knew they were on the right track.

"And the attack against you last week?" he bit out then, anger brewing in his eyes. "Did you consider that your status on this operation has been compromised? Or worse, they identified you as Louisa Cerves's rescuer?" Frustrated outrage filled his tone. "For God's sake, Chelsea, you should have never taken this assignment after you snatched that child from those Coyotes. You needed to stay low for just a little while."

She'd considered that the operation might have been compromised. She, Ashley and Cassie had actually discussed it several times. It wasn't possible, though. She knew she hadn't given herself away and neither had anyone she was working with.

As for being identified by Louisa's rescuer, that one she didn't worry about as much. Had it happened, Samara Cerves would have already had her executed, no doubt.

"Only the director, the operations commander, Ashley, Cassie, Draeger and Tobias are aware that it's even an operation. And I trust them as well as you trust Ranger. That attack had nothing to do with the operation, and it definitely doesn't have anything to do with Louisa," she argued calmly, refusing to let her rage and anger over that baby free.

She wasn't going to let herself become angry, and she damned sure wasn't going to let him draw her into another of those fights where she was made to feel that every word she said only made her appear weaker.

"Then why attack you?" Skepticism filled his voice and his expression. "Why else would a Council Coyote attack you? Your cover had to have been blown one way or the other. There's no other reason to come after you with a blade."

Her lips thinned at the certainty in his voice. Of course he believed every word that passed his lips. And once he decided he knew the answer, there was no convincing him otherwise without proof in black and white, or in blood.

His lack of faith in her abilities was enough to completely piss her off, even on a good day.

"Raymond Martinez was my uncle," she reminded him caustically. "He was working for the Genetics Council since he was a young man, remember, Cullen? My whole family became targets once they knew we learned what he had been doing and unveiled many of his contacts. He put a price on our heads himself when we helped the Breeds gather that evidence. I was just in the wrong place at the wrong time, and one of them realized who I was. That simple."

◆　　◆　　◆

He didn't know whether to turn her over his knee and paddle her ass or throw her over his shoulder, cart her to the bedroom and fuck her until neither of them could move. The terrifying part was the fact that both options were working in his head at this point.

She had herself convinced of the bullshit that fell from her lips. And it was bullshit. He knew it. The minute the words tumbled out, his newly awakening instincts reared up in furious denial.

"Nothing is ever that damned simple with the Genetics Council," he barked out, pointing a finger in her direction as he fought back the need to do a little abducting himself and locking her away for her own safety. Not to mention his sanity. "And the Breeds they control do not just attack because they deem the opportunity appropriate. It's carefully planned and the target quickly executed. And the Council didn't give a damn about Ray Martinez after his association with them was revealed."

Neither the Genetics Council nor their trainers, soldiers or fanatical Breeds operated that way. If they did, then it would have been far easier to bring the entire organization down a decade ago. Hell, Callan Lyons would have destroyed the twelve members controlling the Council himself rather than being forced to reveal the existence of the Breeds if it were that easy.

Chelsea was so damned stubborn she refused to see that.

"My status hasn't been compromised, nor has my identity as the person who rescued Louisa Cerves been revealed," she repeated, determination straightening her spine even as he glared at her. "It's not possible, Cullen. And if it had been, there would have been some warning, no matter how slight, before that attack."

His lips thinned as he fought back a curse. Stalking from the doorway to the back door, he stared out at the night for a moment to consider his options.

"Who's your contact?" he asked, turning back to her and crossing his arms over his chest as he stared at her, determined to get the answer.

He'd follow up on this himself, find out what the hell was going on and make certain she wasn't endangered.

For a moment, her eyes simply widened, shocked anger filling her gaze just before she laughed mockingly and propped her hands on her hips, anger flushing her face.

"Really, Cullen? You think I'm that naive where you're concerned? I know you far too well for that," she assured him.

She shook her head before pushing her fingers through her hair, gripping the strands at the back of her neck for a moment, then letting her hands fall to the back of a kitchen chair as she moved to it.

Cullen watched her silently, gauging her determination. It didn't take him long to realize she was stubborn enough to refuse him the answers he needed at the moment.

"You know," she finally said, her voice trembling with the hurt and anger he could scent filling the room. "I really appreciate the concern and the need to protect me," she offered, her tone sincere. "But I left the Agency for a reason. You take this from me and I'll make damned sure you never do it again."

His brow lifted in surprise. "And you'll do that how?"

He'd be damned if he'd allow her to continue risking herself this way.

"I'll leave the Nation if you do what I think you're getting ready to do." Her shoulders squared, her eyes narrowing on him warningly. "You have no influence with the Breed Underground on the East or West Coast, and I'm sure I'd have no problem whatsoever working in a covert capacity with them. Do this, and that's exactly what I'll do."

The Breed Underground in either area would be ecstatic if they acquired her. And he'd go crazy worrying about her, imagining her hurt, without help.

And she wasn't bluffing. His sense of smell was sharper, his instincts stronger tonight than they'd ever been. If she were bluffing, he would have known it the second the words passed her lips. Pure determination filled her voice instead. And he knew just how stubborn she could get.

"Chelsea," he sighed, fighting to find a way to try to make her understand. "We're the same as family—"

"The hell we are," she snapped out, her anger exploding through the room now, intensifying with a force he couldn't have expected. "Number one." She ticked off a single, graceful finger. "We so are not related, no matter how many distant cousins you marry. Number two." She ticked off another finger. "My family members do not shove their tongues halfway down my throat every chance they get. You can take those arguments and kiss my ass, Cullen Maverick, because there's not a chance in hell I'm letting you direct my life for me. Not now, not ever." Disgust filled her expression. "You can leave now. Right now. Because I'll be damned if I'm not finished with you and this argument."

She was what?

Something snapped through his senses. She was finished with him and their argument? The hell she said. Incredulity flared through him. Never in all the years they'd worked together had she attempted to blow him off or turned her back on him during one of their confrontations. And he wasn't about to let her get away with it now.

The careful control exploded. Suddenly, his sense of smell was magnified tenfold, and it wasn't just anger he could scent pouring from the woman determined to drive him past insanity.

Beneath the feminine fury and emotional distress was the sweet, hot scent of female challenge and arousal. Strong and determined, she'd found a way to push past the guards in place that had kept the animal sleeping inside him and awakened him with a vengeance.

The dark dominance Cullen had always kept carefully in control had been strained where she was concerned for years, with each confrontation they had. The few times she had actually challenged him, it had jerked at the leash he kept around it and had threatened to come to full consciousness. And now it awakened with a vengeance. The animal, already pacing restlessly, leapt past his control now, determined to meet her challenge and to show her the consequences of making it.

He'd be damned if she would face this danger alone. It was bad enough that she'd already deliberately courted it, but if she thought she could push him away from her now, order him from her, then by God, he was about to show her the error of her ways.

⋄ C H A P T E R   8 ⋄

From Graeme's Journal
Recessed Primal Genetics and Mating Heat

The recessed Primal Breed in Mating Heat is like an animal with a thorn stuck in his paw. And he'll bite the head off anyone daring to attempt to remove the object of his pain—

Cullen had always wondered how an active Breed felt, having both animal and human genetics merged inside them and working as one. There were times he'd actually imagined living with all his instincts intact.

This feeling was like nothing he'd ever imagined, though.

One arm went around Chelsea's waist as she dared to turn her back on him. As though he were of no consequence. As though he weren't man enough, Breed enough, to pull her anger into submission with his touch.

She was waiting for him.

As though the anger and pride burning in her spilled into the arousal simmering just beneath the surface, she didn't fight him. The scent of her hunger speared through his senses instead, igniting what was already a combustible need burning through him.

She was already reaching for him as his lips ground over hers, parted them, and his tongue thrust into the sweet depths he found there. The taste of her kiss was hotter, sweeter than he remembered, burning through him like a flame. As her arms went around his neck, Cullen pulled her closer, reveling in the way her body arched to him, in the low feminine groan of hunger and pleasure that filled the air around him.

He'd dreamed of that sound while he'd been away. Ached for it. Ached for her.

The taste of her, the feel of her in his arms, against his body, made him more desperate, wilder to take her.

Beneath his jeans his already engorged cock swelled thicker, harder, his balls aching with the need for release. The need to fuck her, to bury inside her balls deep was a fever searing his senses.

Never had he needed a woman with the desperation he needed this one. And the knowledge that his hunger for her had only been growing over the past four years fed that need.

God knew he'd tried to stay away from her, to ensure she was protected, even from him. Especially from this wild, unbidden hunger he'd always fought to control. A hunger he had no idea if he could control once he loosed it.

And now it was loose.

Pushing one hand beneath the hem of her shirt, he let his fingers trail over the soft flesh of her side until they reached the full curve of her breast. Beneath the lace of her bra, her nipple was peaked, pebble hard and tempting.

Stroking his thumb over her nipple, Cullen growled as a shudder worked through her and the scent of her need intensified. Wild, all female, demanding and hot, that scent spurred his own hunger, his lust. And he knew he was hooked on that scent now, addicted and uncaring of the implications.

With each touch, that subtle sweet-and-spice scent went to his head and made his mouth water for a taste of her. She'd be hot and wet, silky and syrupy sweet against his tongue. And waiting any longer for the taste of her was a hell he didn't want to visit.

Lifting her against him, Callan meant to carry her to the bedroom, to her bed. He had every intention of laying her down and at least trying to take her slow and easy. Then her legs lifted, her thighs gripping his hips, pelvis tilting forward until she was riding the ridge of his cock with little stroking motions that threatened to take him to his knees.

Making it to the bedroom just wasn't going to happen.

He made it as far as the couch, where he laid her back against the cushions before stripping the T-shirt and bra from her and tossing it to the floor. And he thought he'd explode. The sight of her breasts arching to him, nipples hard and reddened, her expression dazed with pleasure, was killing him. God, she was beautiful.

Hunger glowed in her dark eyes, flushed her face and had her breasts rising and falling in quick little motions as she fought to breathe.

When her tongue licked over her lips and her gaze met his, he couldn't resist another taste of those lips. A deep, drugging taste that had his senses spinning with the intoxicating sensations tearing through him.

Awakening Breed instincts were kicking through him with a vengeance now, and every damned one of those instincts was screaming at him to take her. Take her hard and deep, until all she knew was his touch, his hunger.

As each kiss deepened he palmed her breasts, shaped them, let his fingers pluck at her tight nipples as each little feminine moan pulled him deeper into the hunger tormenting him.

She met each kiss with demands of her own as well, then slid her hands between their bodies, her delicate fingers working desperately at the buttons of his shirt until each one was released and she was spreading the edges apart.

Her nails raked over his chest. He could swear he felt the caress through the fine hairs beneath her hands arrowing straight to his balls. The tiny, almost invisible hairs along his skin felt as sensitive as his flesh. Each touch sent pleasure racing through him like flames burning a path through his senses.

Trailing kisses from her lips to her neck, Cullen raked the sensitive skin there with his teeth, licked it, loved the taste of her. He couldn't get enough of her. With each kiss, each taste, his hunger for her only grew.

◆　◆　◆

Chelsea wasn't a virgin. She had known sensuality and pleasure at a man's hands before. She might have only had a few lovers, but those lovers had been considerate and experienced. She hadn't left their beds feeling cheated. But she knew that if there was ever another man after Cullen, she wouldn't feel that way ever again.

His kisses were potent. With each drugging caress of his lips over hers, his tongue plunging forcibly into her mouth, the sexual intensity moving through her only became stronger.

The taste of his kiss kept her reaching for more. A mix of heated male with a hint of cinnamon. Just enough that she began craving the taste of it, desperate for more when his lips moved from hers to stroke down her neck.

She stilled as his teeth raked over her throbbing pulse, shocked by the sensitivity of her flesh as he drew at it lightly before giving the area a firm little nip.

Flames arced along her nerve endings as pleasure exploded through her senses. Clenching her fingers against his chest, Chelsea turned her head, baring more of her flesh for his lips, teeth and tongue to raze.

Her senses were dazed, drugged as each rake of his teeth and stroke of his tongue burned against her flesh, made her desperate for more.

Moving her hands from his chest, she pushed them to his back beneath the material of his shirt. She raked her nails over his tough flesh, arching against him until her nipples pressed into his chest.

The sensitive points rioted with pleasure. Electric trails of sensation tore from the tender tips, joined with those caused by his lips at her throat before racing to the swollen bud of her clit. Damp heat spilled from her aching sex, slick, sensitizing her further.

Chelsea felt feverish, desperate. She'd never known a touch like Cullen's or her response to it. As though her body had been waiting for his touch, anticipating it, and now every synapse it possessed was coming alive for it.

This need wasn't normal, it couldn't be normal. Sexual hunger clawed at her pussy, pulsed through it and had her clit so swollen and painfully sensitive she couldn't help but whimper. Her juices spilled along her sex, slickening the folds between her thighs, preparing her for him.

She clutched at him as his lips came down on hers once again, his kiss holding her captive as he worked the band of her cotton pants over her hips before stripping them down her legs along with her lacy panties.

"Cullen . . ." she cried out as his lips jerked back from hers, stealing the subtle flavor of cinnamon spice she'd found there. "What are you doing to me?"

Her hips arched as she shuddered in reaction to his callused fingers sliding through her swollen slit.

"Oh God, Cullen—"

His thumb found her clit, raked over it, caressing it with devastating results.

"It's okay, baby, I have you," he whispered, his lips moving along her jaw, trailing along her neck and burning a path to her breasts as his hands stroked and caressed her with burning heat. A blaze she couldn't combat, one that couldn't be fought back.

The need for him was so out of control, so desperate she wanted only one thing.

"Please, Cullen, now," she moaned, arching against him as his tongue stroked over one painfully erect nipple, then another.

His fingers stroked, played, teased the saturated folds of her pussy.

"Soon." The growl in his voice was deeper, more arousing than ever. "Let me touch you first, sweetheart, taste you."

His lips settled over a nipple then, sucked it into his mouth, rasped it with his tongue until she was writhing beneath him and only barely aware that he was stripping his own clothes from his body.

Chelsea was shaking with the driving need to be taken, to feel him moving inside her, hard and hot. Her hands moved from his shoulders to his hair, tangling in the rough strands, her nails pricking his scalp as she tried to pull his mouth closer, convince him to suck at her nipple harder.

Instead, he released the peak, licked over it a final time. Looking up at her, his gaze hooded and heavy with lust, he began kissing down the middle of her stomach in a burning path to the aching flesh between her thighs.

She had never known such pleasure. She'd never burned like this, never felt this need raging through her with such painful intensity. And when he breathed over the sensitive bud of her clit, that need became a wildfire racing out of control.

As he stretched out between her thighs, one hand tucking beneath her to lift her leg, resting it over the back of the couch, his lips lowered, his tongue stroking through the quivering folds of her pussy with devastating results.

Pressing her thighs farther apart, he worked his tongue through the folds with a rough, growling sound of pleasure.

"Fuck, you taste sweet," he groaned. "Sweet and hot, burning through me like a flame."

She strained against him, whimpering as he rimmed the entrance to her vagina, his tongue flickering over it, pushing her higher.

Fighting to breathe, gasping with each sensation, Chelsea strained against him, desperate now for orgasm.

His tongue tormented, teased, pushed her into a storm of sensations where pleasure was but a paltry word for the exquisitely painful bliss raging through her. Waves of it tore through her, shuddering through her body as she cried out for him again.

His lips returned to her clit as one hand moved between her thighs, his fingers finding the entrance of her pussy where he stroked her, his finger dipping in marginally, then pulling back to stroke again.

"Cullen . . . Please . . ." The gasp was involuntary as her head twisted against the cushions, her fingers fisting in the edge of the one beneath her.

Spasms were rippling through the tender inner flesh as her womb clenched with the need for release. Then another finger joined the first, a pinching, heated pressure as he worked both inside her. Her hips jerked up, slick moisture spilling to meet his fingers as his tongue flickered over and around her tormented clit.

She couldn't stand it. He was killing her. The pleasure was so extreme, so intense it was overwhelming.

The sensations tearing through her came in rolling, blistering waves, building steadily, racing through her with each thrust of his fingers as they pushed steadily deeper inside her; she wasn't certain she'd survive it.

The last wave exploded in an orgasm that powered through her senses with such force she tried to scream his name. It tore through her body as she thrashed against it, crying out at the pure pleasure.

Violent tremors jerked through her body, the devastating release unlike any she'd had before. And still, it wasn't enough. She needed more, burned for more.

"Look at me, Chelsea." The demand didn't make sense at first. "Look at me. Now."

She forced her eyes open, staring up into the brilliance of his gaze as he knelt before her, the thick, heavy stalk of his cock gripped in one hand.

"What have you done to me?" she gasped, her breathing shallow, her pussy rippling with the demand to be taken. "What have you done, Cullen?"

"What have you done to *me*?" he groaned.

Coming over her, he tucked the wide crest of his erection between the swollen folds, a heavy grimace of pleasure tightening his expression. His eyes were brighter, his face sweat dampened. A single bead of perspiration trailed down his hard jaw, drawing her gaze for a second.

Just a second.

Her eyes jerked back to his as he began working his cock inside her, stretching her, burning her. Her head tossed, her hands jerking to his arms, desperately needing something to hold on to as brutal, fiery pleasure began pouring through her.

Her knees bent, lifting to grip his hips as her nails bit into his biceps, her eyes staring up at him in dazed, agonizing pleasure.

"Don't—" A groan whispered past her lips. "Oh God, don't play with—" A sob shuddered through her. "Don't play with me— Take me now . . . Now . . ."

His hands clenched at her hips then, a snarl pulling at his lips as he drew back, his muscles bunching just before his hips moved, impaling her with several hard, throbbing inches of his cock.

He didn't pause after that first thrust.

His mouth slammed down on hers, his tongue pushing past her lips as he pushed deeper, harder inside her, burying the hardened flesh to the hilt.

She couldn't take more. His cock filled her, overfilled her, throbbed and burned inside delicate flesh stretched around him. With each hard stroke her juices spilled from her, coating his cock with a heavy layer of slick heat and aiding each impalement.

His kiss was spicy hot now, that taste of cinnamon heat intensified, sinking inside her senses and making her crave more of it. The heavy thrusts between her thighs began gaining in speed, jackhammering inside her pussy, each stroke vibrating into her clit and intensifying the swelling, burning pleasure raging through it.

She couldn't bear it. She was racked by so many sensations, each one brutal on its own; combined they razed her senses. Wild and tumultuous, she tried to fight it, fought to pull back, only to be dragged deeper into the maelstrom. Deeper, higher, until she stiffened, jerking as a harder series of orgasms began tearing through her, exploding with such power, such force, she swore she was losing herself in him. Giving him a part of herself even she didn't know existed inside her.

As the first waves of ecstasy invaded her, she felt his thrusts change, become harder, shorter, and then he jerked above her, an animalistic growl rumbling in his throat a second before the first pulse of semen spurted inside her, just before she felt the impossible.

The tabloid stories—she hadn't imagined they were true. But she felt it. Felt an added erection emerge from beneath the head of his cock, lock inside her, pulsing with each hot spurt of his release as it filled the snug confines of her vagina.

It was all true.

Oh God, what had she gotten herself into?

· C H A P T E R   9 ·

From Graeme's Journal
The Recessed Primal Breed

Recessed genetics make the Primal Breed a wild card. Because the animal,
predatory and cunning, will not stay hidden for long.

She was sleeping.

A deep, hard sleep of exhaustion.

Standing in the doorway to the bedroom, Cullen watched her silently. She was curled beneath the sheets, her expression relaxed, breathing deep and even.

He'd taken her again and again until she'd collapsed against his chest, falling asleep before the barb released its grip on her. Perspiration had soaked both their bodies and dampened the sheets. But when he'd eased her off him to the pillows, she hadn't even blinked.

Hell, she'd done no more than mumble sleepily when he'd taken a damp cloth and cleaned the sweat and their mingled releases from her before changing the sheets.

And now she was still sleeping just as deeply, as Cullen felt his brother enter the back door and move silently through the house.

The twin bond they shared had never waned, even when Graeme had been driven to insanity by the mating hormone in his system and the inhuman experiments of a scientist who enjoyed driving Breeds to the worst depths of a living hell.

When his brother had escaped he'd found Cullen. A monster, maddened by the above-genius-level intelligence he possessed and the animal instincts fighting for dominance. But even as the Primal, Graeme had known a strange sort of empathy, even if he had lacked compassion at the time.

"The mating's strong," Graeme commented, leaning against the wall beside Cullen and crossing his arms over his chest. "As is the animal waking within you."

Cullen's lips curled in contempt at the comment.

The animal was strong, his ass. It was a testosterone-driven snarling beast clawing at his brain and his senses.

He wanted to shoot it.

"You're a stubborn man, Cullen," his brother sighed. "It only stands to reason that the Primal animal that's been sleeping inside you is just as stubborn. So stubborn it remained hidden at a time when you were at your most determined to call it forth."

"Why would I need it, then?" Leaning against the frame of the door, he crossed his arms over his chest and shot his brother a derisive look. "Those instincts weren't there when I wanted them to be, why would I want them now?"

It didn't seem to matter what he wanted, though, because the animal that had remained so still and silent since he was a young boy was coming alive with a vengeance.

"Because now it doesn't just matter to the man, but to the animal as well?" Graeme asked knowingly. "Come on, Cullen, you let her walk away from you even after the first signs of Heat began showing inside both of you. You woke those instincts with your refusal to claim her."

"Bullshit," he muttered.

Stepping forward, he gripped the doorknob and closed the door silently before stalking through Chelsea's house to the kitchen.

"Don't you have better things to do than harass me, Graeme?" he asked, keeping his voice low. "I know I have better things to do than to be harassed."

Graeme's chuckle wasn't as grating as it should have been; he let it pass by him with no more than a grimace of irritation.

"Harassing you is always a favored pastime," Graeme assured him. "My research indicates it has something to do with the fact that we share that twin instinct." For a second a hint of confusion flashed in his expression before he gave a little shake of his head and a dismissive shrug. "Researching that has been almost as interesting as the research I've done on the recessed animal genetics."

"Neither of which you figured out," Cullen pointed out as he pulled open the refrigerator door for a bottle of water. Extracting two, he tossed Graeme the other, uncapped his own and took a long drink.

"I don't have to answer all the questions," Graeme answered with a hint of mockery. "Just some of them."

"Evidently you haven't answered any that could have helped me at any given time," Cullen snorted, rubbing one hand over the back of his neck. "And what the hell makes you think the mating began before she resigned? I wasn't sleeping with her."

"You bit her the morning she resigned," Graeme reminded him. "She told Cat about it. She was quite put out that you didn't kiss her."

Cullen stared back at Graeme blandly. He was definitely going to have to have a talk with Chelsea about sharing confidences with Cat.

Telling Cat was the same as telling Graeme. Even Cullen knew that one.

It didn't change the truth, though. He had nipped her neck that morning. His frustration level had exploded when she'd given him her resignation. He knew now what had happened, though then he hadn't thought to question if his Breed instincts were making an appearance.

As Chelsea had tried to leave the house, the impulse to pull her to him, to mark her neck, had been impossible to control. The animal that had been so silent inside him for so long had awakened that morning with a vengeance. Just long enough for the animal to claim her.

"Usually once the mating begins, there's no going back," Graeme began.

"The glands beneath the tongue," Cullen murmured. "The cinnamon taste when I kiss her." His brow furrowed. "They weren't swollen that morning."

Graeme shrugged again. "Your instincts allowed just enough of the hormone to release that it would ensure no other could take what belonged to you. Especially a Breed. She carried just a hint of the mating scent, just enough that it was detectable. Even I didn't realize what the scent meant at first."

But his brother had eventually realized Chelsea carried the mating scent and hadn't come to him?

"When did you realize it?" He placed the water bottle on the counter carefully.

Graeme sighed heavily as he paced to the table, his fingers curling over the back of a chair.

"The night she was attacked," he finally admitted. "I came to check on her. The scent was stronger, the spike in adrenaline obviously contributing to the strength of it." Graeme frowned as though perplexed. "I'll have to check into that anomaly."

"You can check into it later, Dr. Jekyll," Cullen grunted, knowing how distracted his brother could become when it came to his research. "You should have been looking for a cure all these years instead of playing Mr. Hyde."

Graeme's brow arched mockingly. "There's not a Breed or their mate that's wanted a cure. I'd be wasting my time. You know I hate doing that."

Cullen glared back at him.

"Chelsea will want a cure." How could she not? She'd already tried to escape him once by resigning; she'd told him countless times how she wanted him out of her business. Knowing she was tied to him wouldn't please her.

"Will she?" Graeme mused, watching him a little too closely for comfort. "What do you want?"

What did he want? Pushing his fingers through his hair, Cullen realized he didn't have an answer for his brother. He had no idea what he wanted past keeping Chelsea in his bed and keeping her safe.

"It doesn't seem to matter what either of us wants, does it?" he replied, the feel of yet another growl rising in his throat causing his teeth to clench momentarily. "I gather she's stuck with me, no matter what she wishes."

Graeme simply watched him, saying nothing, his cunning green gaze assessing and far too curious.

"As you're stuck with her," Graeme stated, though there seemed to be a question in his voice. One he didn't ask, thankfully.

"So it would seem." He breathed out roughly. "The question now is how do I keep her safe? There's not a chance in hell she's going let me finish this investigation for her, and the scent of her Heat is going to distract not just me but every Breed in the same vicinity with her. Especially those Council bastards determined to snag a mate."

"Lucky for you, your genius brother just might have something that will help. Not a cure." Graeme grinned wryly. "But definitely something interesting."

"Lucky for you, Cullen." Chelsea stepped into the kitchen, shocking him by her presence, by the scent of the betrayal she felt. "Not a cure, but if you're lucky, maybe you can turn it into one. Right?"

Dammit, his senses were so filled with the scent of her that he hadn't known she had slipped up on them. But Graeme had known. Hell, his brother probably heard the change in her breathing when she woke.

The bastard.

◆　◆　◆

Chelsea stared at the two Breeds, forced back the hurt raging inside her and placed it behind the wall of ice she used whenever she was on patrol. Breed senses could detect fear, lies, any strong emotion.

He hadn't said as much, but she'd heard the tone of his voice, felt his reluctance to admit he didn't want a cure himself.

Of course he wanted a cure. He wouldn't have meant to mate her, just sleep with her. Besides, the first nip to her neck that morning in his home had been done in anger, not arousal. And now his Breed status was making him pay for it.

Joy, joy.

"Now I can truly call you sister," Graeme stated, forcing her to break eye contact with Cullen.

"You can truly kiss my ass," she muttered, resentment surging past that icy shield before she could pull it back. "I didn't marry his mangy ass, and wouldn't have if he begged."

Rather than taking offense, Graeme turned and collected a small black pack he'd placed on her counter and unzipped it efficiently.

She watched him, frowning. Dressed in dark jeans, his black shirt tucked into the belted band, he reminded her of an animal, of the huge cat his genetics had been created from. Self-satisfied, arrogant and superior. She'd never had a cat as a pet simply because of their cool, distant demeanors.

When he pulled two pressure syringes from that pack, she stepped back warily. Cullen shot his brother a disgusted look, but he seemed more resigned than protesting.

"Let me give you a short explanation of Mating Heat and the hormonal therapy I have here." He laid the syringes on the table before crossing his arms over his chest and staring back at her with cold, hard purpose. "Mating Heat will build. It's called Heat for a reason. The need to fuck and be fucked"—he ignored Cullen's disgusted curse—"becomes overwhelming. You can't work for it, you can't socialize for it, the hunger for it obliterates all other needs. And to make things worse"—his smile wasn't a comforting sight—"the scent of it is something you can't hide, even by staying indoors. A Breed driving past the house can detect it." Primitive violence flashed in his eyes. "Especially the Council Breeds searching for a mate to abduct and turn over for experiments. If you're lucky, they don't catch the scent before you conceive, which is the only time the Heat settles. And most felines conceive pretty quickly." He tilted his head and watched her curiously for a second. "I think I'd enjoy being an uncle. I'd be very hands-on with my siblings' cub too . . ."

Chelsea noticed that she and Cullen both extended their arms just as quickly at that observation. The thought of a child was terrifying enough . . . but Uncle Crazy-Ass being hands-on?

"Hmm," he murmured suspiciously, but injected the therapy he said the syringes held.

"Just for your information," Chelsea informed him after he finished and put the syringes away, "I'd never let you be hands-on with my *child*."

His brow lifted. "Bad mommy. Don't you know kids want the very playmate you want to keep them from?" He chuckled at the look of dislike she shot him. "And I'd be around often. Very often."

She could see this turning into a war of words she didn't want to be a part of. Turning to Cullen, she pointed her finger back at him angrily.

"You and I are going to talk, Cullen Maverick. You do not spring things on me after the fact. If you recall, I don't like it at all."

She had to content herself with the wince that crossed his face. If he kept it up, she'd black his eye again.

Maybe.

———

From Graeme's Journal
The Recessed Primal Breed

Mating Heat, an anomaly marked by its anomalies.

In the recessive Bengal Primal, those anomalies and variables of Mating Heat can't be predicted, nor can they be explained. The only certainty is that the Primal exists for a single reason alone: to protect the mate it shares with the Breed. It has no other reason for being, and asks for no other reason—

———

So the tabloid stories were true.

Like cats, the need for sex would become so overwhelming and overpowering that mates couldn't resist each other.

She couldn't blame the Mating Heat for her fascination with Cullen, though, or the arousal. He'd been turning her on since she was at least sixteen or seventeen years old. Just the thought of him then had made all her teenage hormones crazy.

And it hadn't gone away after she left her teens either. In some ways, it had only gotten worse. At some point, Chelsea had even realized that the two lovers she'd had resembled him.

Pacing her bedroom as she waited for Cullen to run his brother off, she looked at the bedside clock, shaking from the inside out.

If he didn't hurry, she'd follow him again and run Graeme's ass off herself.

Mocking, superior prick. Even Cat laughingly called him the same thing. Often.

Chelsea wasn't laughing.

She was furious.

She had half a mind to just call her sister, Isabelle, and demand the answers. But Isabelle would call her father and he'd call her grandfather and the next thing she knew they'd be having another save-Chelsea-from-herself family intervention.

And only God knew how much she hated those. She hated them so much she refused to tell Isabelle anything that would bring one about.

As she glanced at the clock again, she inhaled roughly, nostrils flaring with such irritation she could barely hold it in.

So much for keeping her emotions on ice. They were burning so hot and livid right now that Breeds in neighboring states were probably smelling it.

And her patience was at an end.

Stalking toward the door, she came to a hard stop as it opened and Cullen stepped inside. Closing the door quietly, he watched her so intently for long moments that she finally gave a hard snap of her fingers just to distract him.

"I get it. You're pissed," he said then, his jaw tensing.

She stared back at him, eyes widening in outrage. "Pissed?" She pushed the word past her lips as they tightened furiously. "Oh, Cullen, I am so beyond pissed. You can't even imagine."

She'd never been so furious with him.

With one hand he rubbed at the back of his neck, his gaze wary now.

"Did you know about that mating bullshit?" she demanded, watching his face and seeing the total lack of response. Her ire exploded further. "You knew!" she hissed furiously, completely outraged now. "You knew and you still spread those kisses around like kids spread the common cold. What? Do you have a frickin' harem now?"

Oh, that so wasn't going to work for her. He could just leave right now.

"Dammit, Chelsea, it doesn't work that way." Shooting her an infuriated look, he stomped to the wooden chest at the end of her bed and sat down, jerking one boot off.

"That isn't what I just heard from Graeme," she snapped back, her hands going to her hips. "And you can just put that boot right back on because you are not staying here tonight. God only knows how many women you have waiting to be serviced. Don't let me hold you up."

Damned alley cat.

He wiped his hand over his face, shaking his head as a grimace pulled at his expression.

"Hasn't Isabelle told you anything about her mating with Malachi?" His boots thumped on the floor, irritation flashing in his expression.

"My sister's too busy telling on me to bother telling on anyone else." She gave a hard flip of her hand as she glared at him furiously.

So much for keeping her sister's secrets for her when they were younger.

"Breeds only mate once," he told her then, surprising her. "After they mate they never desire another. It's actually physically impossible for either a Breed or their mate to have another lover."

That stopped her cold. And not necessarily in satisfaction.

"What if you die? Or I kill you?" She arched a brow.

Killing him really wasn't a bad idea at this point.

He shot her a wary look, keeping his gaze on her as she paced to the other side of the room before turning back to him and crossing her arms over her breasts defensively.

She hated feeling this way. Like some damned shrew, completely out of control. But she knew what was coming, she could feel it all the way to the bottom of her soul.

She could feel the cage being assembled as she fought to stay free of it.

"There's not a lot of information on those who have lost their mates," he finally answered, resting his arms on his knees and clasping his hands together as he watched her carefully. "But those who have mated have one thing in common. The touch of anyone besides their mate is highly uncomfortable and in some cases painfully so. The injection Graeme gave us will allow impersonal touches. Shaking hands, social hugs. It will prevent conception for the time being and dilute the mating scent. The demand for sex won't be as extreme, but it will eventually build to the extreme if ignored."

She inhaled deeply. The cage was coming closer.

"No harem," he assured her.

Chelsea shot him a disgusted glare.

"And no cure." She couldn't believe it. She could not be tied this way to a man who didn't love her, or respect her, let alone acknowledge the abilities he knew she had.

"No cure," he agreed softly. "But none of the mates I know are unhappy or dissatisfied, Chelsea."

Then they weren't with a mate who considered himself stuck, as Cullen did.

"I'm sorry, honey." Rising to his feet, he crossed the room, stopping in front of her as she watched him with wary anger.

"Don't you 'honey' me. It was bad enough working with you," she accused him heatedly. "You treated me like a kid who didn't know her own mind. You'll just use this mating thing to try to control me now."

He had her in his arms before she could turn away from him and retreat once again, her head pulled back and his lips slanting over hers in a wild, feral hunger she was helpless to deny.

◆　◆　◆

Fuck, he loved touching Chelsea, and he knew that the pure sensual joy he found in touching her wasn't all Mating Heat.

Mating Heat had nothing to do with how silky her skin was, how soft and warm she felt pressed against him. And it wasn't why the need to touch her over the past years had driven him nearly insane.

She was like a flame in his arms, reaching for him, burning through his soul with the need she gave him in turn.

Her lips parted beneath his, just as wild, just as driven by the over-whelming hunger for him as he was for her.

His tongue pumped into her mouth, spilling the liquid heat of the hormone to both their senses, stronger now, more intense than before.

The taste of it in his mouth had been killing him as she'd stalked out of the kitchen.

He'd waited too long for her, too many years, too many nights needing her. As his kiss ate at hers, his tongue stroked and licked between her lips, and Cullen tore at their clothes, getting rid of them however possible, as quickly as possible.

Tearing his lips from hers long enough to push her to the bed, he nearly lost his breath at the sight of her.

Dark, apricot flesh, her breasts swollen and topped with cherry-ripe nipples. Slender legs, well-toned thighs and the prettiest pussy in the world.

Fuck, he loved her pussy. The fact that she didn't wax or shave fascinated him. Neat, well-trimmed little curls framed the dark pink bud of her clit. Moisture beaded on the curls covering the swollen folds below, her sweet juices a subtle, tempting scent that made him crazy to taste her.

Stripping his jeans off, Cullen watched her with narrowed eyes, his breathing sawing from his lungs as he fought for control. Just enough control to relish the sweet taste of her before the imperative need to take her overwhelmed his desire to just enjoy her.

As he eased onto the bed, spreading her legs and sliding between them, his lips were poised above the little curl-shrouded mound. Watching, he let a finger slide through the slick moisture-laden slit.

"How pretty," he groaned, his voice deeper, darker than before. "So wet and sweet. Just thinking about eating your pussy has me ready to come."

"Stop thinking about it and eat it, then."

The sensual demand had his cock jerking against the blankets and the taste of the mating hormone flooding his mouth. Helpless against that hunger, Cullen lowered his head and with the sweet heat of the hormone spilling from the glands, he drew the sensitive bundle of nerve endings to his mouth.

"Oh God . . . Oh God . . . Cullen," Chelsea cried out, her hips jerking as his hands slid beneath her rear, fingers clasping the rounded flesh as he lifted her closer to his mouth.

◆   ◆   ◆

The most incredible heat and blazing pleasure tore through her clit. It was unlike any sensation she'd ever known. As he sucked the swollen bud, his tongue lashed over it, sending her senses burning with the friction he was creating.

Lifting her knees, she tried to pull herself closer, desperate for more of the extreme heat, more of the agonizing pleasure.

"Oh God, it's so good." As she fisted the blankets in her fingers, wild whimpers fell from her lips. The extremity of the pleasure was tearing through her, burning her and gathering in force.

Shudders worked over her body, through her senses. Her clit was so swollen, so sensitive that each lash of his tongue was like a stroke of ecstasy itself.

She couldn't bear it. The suckling heat of his mouth, the hungry flicks of his tongue and growls of male pleasure added to each lash of sensation until she was fighting to breathe. She was certain she couldn't survive it any longer before orgasming only to have him push her higher.

"Cullen, please," she cried out desperately.

He lifted her closer, and his lips and tongue went lower. Licking forcefully past the entrance to her vagina, he stole her breath.

He licked, stroked. The furious waves of pleasure were sharper, brighter, her inner flesh flexing with increasing strength as her need for orgasm became agonizing.

Just when she was certain she couldn't bear another second of the increasingly fiery bands of sexual tension gripping her, Cullen's lips lifted, wrapped around her clit, and his fingers were tunneling through the rippling tissue of her sex.

The explosion was a cataclysm. Imploding waves of rapture burst through her, forcing a cry past her lips as shudders tore through her body.

Before the first wave had time to ease, Cullen covered her body and the heavy width of his cock began pushing inside her. She couldn't stand it. She was certain she couldn't.

Until her greedy senses made a liar of her.

◆　　◆　　◆

Cullen couldn't restrain the harsh groan that tore from his chest. Working the head of his cock inside the snug depths of her pussy, he let each sensation, each harsh wave of pleasure, wash over his senses.

The absolute need to imprint his possession on her and hers on him was desperate now. As desperate as the need for release.

Pumping fully inside, pushing through the clenching depths of her pussy was almost painful in the pleasure squeezing his cock.

He wasn't going to last.

Writhing beneath him, arching into every thrust, he could feel Chelsea rushing into orgasm again and lost all sense of reality.

His teeth gripped the mark at her shoulder. The cum boiling in his balls exploded from him, the rush ripping through his senses as the barb extended from beneath the head of his cock, locked inside her and heightened every lightning stroke of sensation with dizzying force.

For long seconds he wondered if he'd survived the force of it. The power of his release was like nothing he'd ever experienced before and he knew he'd never have it with another woman.

147

If she was taken from him, it would be more than just his soul that he'd lose. He'd die of grief and he'd do so quickly.

Fighting to catch his breath as the barb slowly retreated, Cullen rolled to his side with his last remaining strength, then pulled her into his arms before dragging the comforter over them both.

Tremors still shook Chelsea. Occasional whimpers escaped her throat. Perspiration soaked both their bodies. He'd get up in a minute, he told himself, and at least clean the drying sweat from them.

Just as soon as he caught his breath.

◆   ◆   ◆

No wonder her sister, Isabelle, rarely left her Breed husband's side, Chelsea thought the next morning. Besides the fact that Isabelle was completely in love with Malachi, there was the most incredible, most explosive sex in existence.

Breeds joked about the tabloid stories. They'd grin or outright laugh when asked about it and claim it was Genetics Council propaganda.

That wasn't propaganda that locked Cullen's cock inside her, and it damned sure wasn't propaganda that had hurled her into a series of orgasms that had melted her mind.

Standing in front of the bathroom mirror after her shower, Chelsea stared at the faint mark on her neck. It wasn't as dark as the one on her sister's neck, it was lighter, but no doubt the same mark the tabloids swore all Breed mates carried.

How had the Heat supposedly started? The stories differed. A kiss, sex, the bite, riding next to a Breed on the bus or breathing the same air. They ranged from far-fetched to ridiculous. There wasn't a doubt now that they were true, though.

Turning away from the mirror, she hurriedly dressed in jeans, a tank top and hiking boots before striding back to the bedroom, grabbing her pack and heading to the kitchen for coffee.

And there sat her very reluctant mate—oh God, had she really thought that?—sprawled in a kitchen chair, one hand resting, fingers fisted, on the table as he scanned the e-tablet propped in front of him. He was dressed in khaki desert gear and beige hiking boots; his dark blond hair fell over his brow in disarray as though his fingers had pushed through it often. He looked far too tempting and, if the look in his eyes when he glanced at her was any indication, far too aroused.

Popping a coffee pod in the machine, she slid a cup under the brewing spout. Seconds later she lifted it free, brought it to her lips and sipped—

No.

It wasn't possible.

Turning back to the coffeemaker, she opened the brewing head and pulled the used pod free and checked the underside for the little green dot that indicated it wasn't worth drinking.

And there it was.

Narrowing her eyes, she turned and met Cullen's gaze. He stared at her with a steady watchfulness that assured her he was behind the switch. Turning back to the cabinet, Chelsea opened the cabinet above her and drew the box of extra pods free, checking each one.

That little green dot indicating a decaf product marred each pod in the box.

Son of a bitch.

She dumped the pods in the trash, emptied the still-full, still-hot cup of coffee in the sink, then grabbed her pack and headed for the front door.

"Where the hell are you going?" The deep, rough growl in his voice reminded her that despite that nifty little injection Graeme had given her the night before, she still ached for him.

As she reached the front door his fingers wrapped around her elbow, pulling her to her a stop as she swung around to face him. She lowered her eyes to where his fingers gripped her firmly, then lifted them to meet his once again.

"You're going to lose those fingers if you keep that up, Cullen," she warned him, fighting against the need to just touch him.

His jaw clenched so tight she wondered if his molars were cracking yet.

"Stop pushing me, Chelsea." He released her, though, slowly, very slowly. The fact that he was restraining himself was readily apparent. "We need to talk."

She laughed at that; she simply couldn't help it as she stared back at him incredulously. "Talk? To you? Without caffeine? What dream world are you living in? And you threw away my coffee."

She still couldn't believe it. He'd replaced her coffee, her caffeine, with some pathetic facsimile of a substandard decaf.

Decaf.

What was the point in drinking coffee if she didn't get her jolt? Besides, decaf just tasted flat. That crap wasn't coffee in any shape or form.

"The injection Graeme gave you last night isn't as effective if you swill that damned coffee like it's water," he argued, his gaze fierce, his body practically humming with tension and no small amount of anger. "Caffeine will lessen its effects."

And God forbid anyone actually know she was his mate—mate. Good God, wasn't nature just having the last laugh on every human who came in contact with the Breeds for the horrors a few had committed.

Propping one hand on her hip, she lifted her chin and glared up at him. "Look, I understand the problems you're having with this, I really do." Like hell she did. "Tied to a woman you don't really want, and the animal coming awake inside you refused to save the woman you loved." She lifted her hand quickly when he would have spoken. "Well, you're not by yourself. Trust me, I want to be tied to someone who doesn't love me just about as much as you want to be tied to someone you don't love. And I'll be damned if I'll give up my coffee for it. Tell your brother to up the dose next time if that's such a problem."

Jerking the door open, she stomped from the house, slamming the panel closed behind her and fighting back the tears that wanted to fall.

She wasn't crying for him.

She wouldn't cry for him ever again.

Swinging herself into her truck, she was moving out of the driveway just as Cullen strode purposefully from the house, the look on his face more than a little put out.

He looked pissed.

And that was just too damned bad. He should be in her shoes right now. She was so damned horny she could barely stand it, she hadn't had her coffee and she'd just spent a sleepless night reliving every word she'd heard in that damned kitchen the night before.

He wanted a cure, did he? Well, she'd give him a damned cure if it killed her. And if she got much hornier, it might do just that.

From Graeme's Journal
The Recessed Primal Breed

The Primal Breed instinct is to protect his mate at all costs. To shield her.
To cover her. To stand between her and the world.

A strong, independent mate is hell to shield. Especially one determined
to stand at her mate's side.

Chelsea was aware of Cullen just behind her during the drive to the
Bureau.

She stopped at the coffeehouse drive-thru first and ordered the
largest cup of coffee they sold and made a mental note to stop at
the grocery on the way home and rebuy her coffee. Graeme would just
have to fix that injection next week to allow for her one and only true

vice. Doing without it endangered everyone she came in contact with otherwise.

Swinging into the entrance of the VIP parking of the Western Division of the Bureau of Breed Affairs, she waved to the Breed on duty before checking her rearview mirror. Cullen drove by slowly, tipped a finger to his forehead and continued on his way. No doubt to the Covert Law Enforcement Agency.

That was definitely where he needed to be, out of her hair and occupied with things that so did not concern her any longer.

Parking her truck in the assigned spot, Chelsea grabbed the coffee from the drink holder and swung out of the vehicle. Bumping the door with her hip to close it, she hit the auto-lock on the key fob and lifted the coffee to her lips.

The first drink was hot, with that faint bitter bite and an assurance that it was not decaf. Not that she'd drink the whole cup. She'd be wired for days. She didn't even intend to drink her normally allotted amount.

She wanted her coffee, but she did not want children for Cullen's crazy brother to influence. At least, not for a while. Not until she could raise her children herself, instead of using a daycare or babysitter.

Pushing through the door leading to the lobby, she sidled up to the security counter and flashed the Breed on duty her normal bright smile.

"Hey, Code," she greeted the Lion Breed cheerily. "Cassie and Ashley are expecting me."

Whiskey-colored eyes were speculative as he stared down at her, his nostrils flaring with the subtle sign that he was drawing her scent in.

She waited, pasted a polite smile on her face and told herself she was going to be really nice about things this morning.

Lifting the coffee cup to her lips, she took a fortifying drink, waited another second or two and then frowned.

"Code. Wake up!" she demanded firmly. "Cassie. Appointment. Can I go up now?"

No one got on the private elevator without first going through Code.

"Sure, Ms. Martinez." He gave her another odd look but input the passcode and hit the floor for the elevator. "Better drink what you can of that coffee before the elevator stops. Ashley has some unique ways of ruining it otherwise."

"Only if she wants to die in a unique way," she snorted, stepping into the cubicle. "Later, Code."

The elevator doors slid closed and moved upward smoothly. Before she could take more than a single, lingering drink of the coffee, they were sliding open again.

Chelsea blinked at the Coyote Breed standing in front of the entrance, sending a sharp, momentary flash of wariness shooting through her.

"Cavalier." She cleared her throat and stepped from the elevator, expecting him to step inside.

When he didn't, she moved to step around him and head down the hall to Cassie's suite.

"Ms. Martinez?" He didn't touch her but stepped slightly in front of her, his black eyes cold, his scarred features emotionless.

Chelsea retreated as he moved, suddenly tense, uncertain as she watched him carefully.

"What?" she finally asked him, tensing when he said nothing more, just stared down at her unblinking.

"Director Breaker asked me to show you to his office before you join Ms. Sinclair." He extended his arm in the opposite direction to indicate Rule's office. "After you, ma'am."

After her, huh?

Taking a deep breath, she turned and walked quickly to Rule's office, stopping at the closed door and stepping aside.

Cavalier knocked firmly on the door, opening it for her when Rule's "Enter" could be heard.

Chelsea stepped into Rule's office and caught his gaze as it flickered to her coffee cup.

"We're not discussing my coffee," Chelsea informed him, taking a seat in front of his desk.

"I'll agree with that," he chuckled before returning to the large leather chair and sitting back comfortably.

"I just got off the phone with Cullen," he said smoothly, his gaze still warm but cautious.

"Really?" she drawled.

That snake.

"He has good reason to be worried," he said, his tone more sympathetic than she liked. "On the whole there are few mated Breeds that we're aware of. Protecting those we have is of the utmost importance."

Chelsea stared back at him suspiciously, feeling the coming letdown.

"Are you getting ready to fire me, Rule?" she asked carefully, pushing back her reaction until she heard him say it.

Understanding flashed in his eyes, though his expression smoothed into determined lines.

"Cullen's call has nothing to do with your assignment," he stated firmly. "Which is why I asked to see you. The mating scent isn't as overwhelming as normal, but it is detectable. Every Breed in the same room with you will pick that scent up. And they will never believe a

Bengal Breed would send his mate out to a bar or club without him at her side." He gave a heavy, disappointed sigh. "And that being said, I think we're both aware how difficult that will make your job."

"Say it," she demanded, her voice scratchy now. "Go ahead and say it, Rule."

He sighed at the demand. "I'm sorry, Chelsea, but I have no choice but to let you go."

She was fired.

Chelsea rose slowly to her feet, the hurt barreling through her. She swallowed, and it took a moment before she could speak.

"Do Cassie and Ashley know?" she asked.

Rule shook his head. "I only made my decision after determining the strength of your scent. They're waiting for you in Cassie's suite."

Chelsea shook her head even as he spoke.

"Please . . ." She swallowed again, the ragged emotions brewing inside her and filling her voice. "Please give them my regrets. I have to go."

"Chelsea, you're still welcome here, always," Rule protested, coming quickly to his feet, a frown creasing his brow.

Chelsea shook her head.

Turning, she hurried from the office, not bothering to close the door behind her, terrified she would slam it instead.

She walked quickly down the hall, her head down, unaware of the door opening down the hall.

"There you are." Ashley's voice was filled with laughter as she met Chelsea at the elevator. "Oh, bad girl. Coffee."

Chelsea pushed the cup into the other girl's hand, ignoring her surprise, and stepped into the elevator.

"Chelsea?" Ashley pushed her hand against the frame, the pressure holding the doors open as confusion and worry filled her normally happy voice and dove gray eyes.

"I have to go." Chelsea forced the words past her lips.

"But we have a girl date, remember?" The faint hurt in the Coyote female's voice had Chelsea forcing back her tears.

"I was fired, Ashley," she whispered, meeting her wide, shocked gaze. "Rule just fired me."

Ashley dropped her hand slowly, allowing the doors to close, still holding the coffee Chelsea had pushed into her hand.

Seconds later the doors slid open again, Code's curious gaze easing away when he saw her. "Everything good?" he asked.

Chelsea only nodded before rushing through the lobby and back into the parking garage. Reaching the relative safety of her truck, she gripped the steering wheel, pressing her forehead tight to her hands as she fought to get her emotions under control.

She had been fired because of that damned scent thing?

She could feel the bars of the invisible cage moving in closer, her knowledge that the Mating Heat just might have given Cullen exactly what he wanted causing her breath to hitch.

Chelsea locked away from life, safe and protected.

And it hurt.

✦　✦　✦

Cassie stepped into Rule's office and closed the door quietly before walking across the soft cream carpeting. She ignored the director's wary look but sat down in a chair across from him and leaned back into her seat slowly.

She didn't make him wait long to learn why she was there. She folded her hands in her lap and met his gaze firmly.

"I'll be returning to Colorado once I've packed. I'll require a heli-jet for the trip."

His expression went from curious to brooding rather quickly, his dark blue eyes narrowing in surprise.

"This is about Chelsea," he finally sighed heavily. "She's a danger to herself as well as the operation . . ."

"Do you think I was unaware of her mated status, Director Breaker?" she asked, trying to force herself to be calm. "I knew even before it became a status. Where have you been for the past sixteen years to ever consider that I was unaware of such a thing?" Her extra-sensory knowledge was well-known to him, and she knew it.

He knew it.

"She's Bengal," he stated softly. "One of the most sought-after mates in our society. She endangers herself as well as you . . ."

"You gave me control of this operation." She could feel her calm beginning to unravel. "Complete control."

"Not in this situation. The risk is too high and you should have known it," he stated firmly. "Reorganize your team. It's not dependent on her."

He sat forward then, dismissing her as he pulled one of his files forward and prepared to open it.

As though he had the final say in the matter.

"That is where you're wrong." She came to her feet quickly, her voice rising with her anger as his head jerked up, surprise gleaming in his eyes. Slapping her hands on the front of his desk, she leaned forward, the surging intensity of her anger refusing to allow her to back down or lower her voice.

"This operation damned well did depend on her as well as her mated status. Reorganize your own goddamned group. You won't get a chance to fire me. I quit," she yelled.

Jerking her hands back from the table, she turned to leave.

"You could have warned me of your parameters, Cassie," he snapped behind her.

"Warned you?" As she swung around, outrage snapped in her tone. "It was my operation," she yelled back at him furiously. "Mine. Your other team leaders don't explain every damned detail to you."

"When it's important, they do," he growled, the sound demanding she back down.

"Like hell they do," she cried furiously. "Trust me, Rule, every damned one of them has an agenda in their little operations that you don't know a damned thing about."

She was shaking, so furious now a haze of red was threatening to mar her gaze.

"Dammit, Cassie, settle down," he ordered, giving a hard shake of his head as he heard the door open.

"Oh, Rule, let him come in," she sneered, enraged now, the scent of the arriving Coyote infuriating her. "Aren't you just so threatened by little ole me?" she laughed mockingly. "I'll be ready to leave in an hour. You can shove this position and you can shove your parameters while you're at it because I'm done here."

"Cassie!" The sharp command in his voice had her pausing. "Why is Chelsea so important to this operation?"

She turned back to him slowly.

"Because I decided she was important to this operation," she bit out between clenched teeth. "And I resent that question, Rule, because we both know you would have never questioned one of your male commanders similarly." She shook her head. She should have known better. "Get that jet ready. I'm done here."

This time when she turned from him she swept from the room,

ignoring the Breeds outside the door, especially those team members she'd more or less tattled on.

She was tired of dealing with their certainty that she would fail and their fear of her. Every one of them. They wouldn't look her in the eye and they stank of their wariness that she'd learn their secrets.

She didn't have to learn them, she already knew them. Each and every one of them. And even more, she knew the holes they were digging for themselves. Holes she could have helped them out of.

If she had stayed.

◆　◆　◆

Cullen's head jerked up from the file he was reading, Chelsea's scent crashing into him. It wasn't the scent of arousal that had a growl rumbling in his throat, though. It was the scent of her anger.

The scent of her pain.

She stormed into his office, the door slamming behind her with enough force to rattle the glass.

Cullen rose slowly to his feet, frowning at the overbright eyes and flushed cheeks, the scent of pain and betrayal sliding around him like icy tendrils.

"Thank you." Her voice was husky as her gaze went around the room, taking in the stacks of files, books lying about that needed replacing on the shelves. "For making a mess of this office." She dropped her pack into the chair in front of his desk, controlled the trembling of her lips and forced a bright smile to her lips. "Saved my position, did you, Cullen?"

He glanced around the room before returning his gaze to her. "The commissioner hasn't approved the stupidity tests yet." He shrugged, then tipped his head curiously. "What's wrong, baby?"

She flashed him a look of pain-filled mockery. "How can you ask that question with a straight face?"

"Because I have no idea what the hell is going on," he answered. "And I can't do anything about it if I don't know what I've done."

All that anger and pain was definitely directed at him, though.

As shocking as it was, he could feel the tears she was holding inside.

"Have I ever asked you to fix anything for me, Cullen?" she demanded then, one hand settling on a cocked hip. "At any time have I asked you to fix any damned thing for me?"

He moved, positioning himself in front of the desk and leaning back against it as he forced himself to be patient.

"You were always welcome to ask," he snapped.

"The only thing I ever wanted from you, you couldn't give me. You wouldn't give me," she cried out, her finger stabbing toward him furiously. "Not only did you refuse to even consider allowing me to do more than these messy damned files for you, but you then destroyed the office I spent years organizing. Were you so desperate to get your menial help back that you just had to have me fired, Cullen? That you couldn't even allow me to work for anyone else?"

Cullen stared back at her in shock.

"Fired?" he questioned her with a growl. "Chelsea, I didn't have you fired. What the hell happened?"

The look she shot him was frankly disbelieving.

"You called Rule," she yelled back at him hoarsely, that sense of hurt and betrayal washing over him like a bitter breeze.

"The hell I did," he snapped. "I never mentioned firing you. I informed him, officially, of my now-active Breed status and of our mating status. Nothing more."

"It was officially none of his business," she cried out, her dark eyes burning with anger. "That was our business alone."

For a woman who knew so many Breeds he often wondered if she had any human friends, her knowledge of the Breed society was shockingly inadequate.

"Chelsea, honey." He gripped the edge of the desk behind him in frustration. "The moment my Breed status went active I was required to alert him because of my position in law enforcement. And all Breeds are required to inform either their alphas or the Bureau when they mate. I have no alpha." And he intended to keep it that way. "So I notified Rule. And that was the extent of our conversation."

"Rule fired me," she whispered, licking her lips before giving a little shrug that looked far too much like defeat. "He said the Mating Heat scent would keep me from getting information." She shot him a bitter smile. "You got what you wanted after all. What did you say? There's no cure?" Her smile was too bright and too filled with hurt. "Congratulations, Cullen. Dad will be overjoyed. Granddad will be proud as hell."

And it hurt her so deep that Cullen wasn't certain he could fix it.

"I'll call Rule . . ."

Chelsea was shaking her head even as he spoke. "Please don't do that, Cullen. I don't want or need that good-ole-boy network to fix a damned thing for me." Her smile was tight and hard. "Look at it this way, all that angst over protecting me just got easier."

Got what he wanted?

"You actually believe I wanted to see you hurt like this?" he demanded, staring at her in disbelief. "For God's sake. If I wanted to get you fired, Chelsea, I could have done it a hell of a lot easier without making myself look like the bad guy. And I sure as hell wouldn't have used our mating to do it. The last thing I want you to do is resent your bond with me."

He rubbed at the back of his neck in irritation as the anger continued to glitter in her eyes.

Before he could say anything more, a hard knock sounded at the door, causing her to flinch slightly before she controlled it.

"What?" he snapped, his irritation growing.

The door eased open and one of the junior agents poked his head in warily. "Sorry, Commander, but Director Breaker from Breed Affairs is out here. He's demanding to speak to Ms. Martinez." The agent flashed her a smile. "Hey there, Chelsea. It's good to see you again."

"Hey, Rylan." She returned the greeting, her smile tight. "Tell Director Breaker to—"

"Go to hell?" Rule stepped into the office and flashed Cullen a glare. "Don't bother, Cassie took care of it for you."

Pinching the bridge of his nose, Cullen bit back a frustrated curse.

"You're damned sure trying to make my life hell," Cullen informed him, staring back at the other Breed with a flat, hard warning. "Keep it up and we're going to have words."

Rule eyed him suspiciously. "You're not crazy enough to be a Bengal. Too damned calm."

"Rule, I'm going to kill you," Cullen stated, restraining a growl threatening to rumble in his chest.

"Well, join the club." Rule grimaced before turning to Chelsea. "Will an apology suffice or must I grovel?"

Moving past Rule, Cullen stomped to the door and closed it in Rylan's far-too-curious face. Son of a bitch, this morning was flat going to hell.

Moving between Rule and Chelsea, he gave in to the imperative demand to go to Chelsea.

He ignored the need to stand between her and the Bureau director, opting to move behind her instead and keep a careful eye on the Breed.

"I'll grovel if I have to." Rule kept the growl from his voice, Cullen noticed in amusement. "Or you can accept my apology and the fact that I'll owe you a hell of a debt and come back to the Bureau; otherwise that tyrant personality Cassie unleashed on me will get on a heli-jet she ordered me to have ready and fly back home. The little wench quit on me. Every Breed I know is going to go nuts on me when they find out I was the Breed who caused her to lose her temper."

◆　◆　◆

Chelsea stared back at Rule, certain she misunderstood. Cassie wouldn't have quit. She had just told her and Ashley how important that job was to her. She wouldn't just walk away.

"Chelsea, I have less than thirty minutes here." Rule breathed out heavily, shoving his hands in the pockets of his dark slacks and so obviously trying not to glare at her. "I'll owe you a really huge debt," he gritted out, his gaze flickering to Cullen as though asking for help.

Cullen could only shrug. He'd damned well love to have that debt owed to him, well aware of the boon Rule was offering.

"Fine," Chelsea finally muttered. "But you owe two debts. One to me and one to Cullen."

Outrage snapped in Rule's expression. "How the hell do I owe him a debt?"

"Because you almost got *him* fired," she stated with obvious irritation. "I think that would suck for a mate. And he was starting to get really worried I was serious too."

Rule wasn't convinced. "You can't fire a mate and he knows it."

"And you're running out of time," she pointed out.

A grimace crossed the director's face, but he gave a short, abrupt nod. "Can we go now?"

Turning to Cullen, she shot him a challenging look before grabbing her pack and moving for the door.

Before Rule could turn away, Cullen gave the Breed a hard warning look. Rule's acknowledging nod had Cullen breathing out a heavy sigh before stepping to the door and watching his mate leave.

Every Breed instinct he possessed demanded he follow her and keep her in sight. If he tried that, no doubt she'd have something to say about it. Something he was sure he wouldn't want to hear.

Having an independent mate was going to be the death of him.

✦　✦　✦

She was making him crazy.

Following behind her pickup in his Dragoon that evening, Cullen stared at the back of her head broodingly. Damn, he could shoot Graeme for not warning him that Chelsea was listening in on their conversation the night before.

His brother's hearing was preternatural; she couldn't have slipped up on him, and from the look on his brother's face, Cullen knew she'd not surprised Graeme in the least.

Graeme had let her hear every word, and Cullen still couldn't figure out why his brother had done so. What did it matter now, the events that happened so many years before. Lauren was dead, the past was dead, and his mating to Chelsea had no bearing on it any more than his feelings on the mating mattered at this point.

She'd misunderstood what she'd heard, though.

There were so many things she didn't understand, and he wasn't a man who did explanations easily. Especially explanations where his marriage and his late wife were concerned. And there were so many things she didn't understand about his feelings for her.

Hell, even he didn't understand his feelings for her, and he'd had the past four years to try to make sense of it. He'd hired her as his assistant just because the pull she exerted him on him whenever she was around confused the hell out of him. And he couldn't blame that one on a mating.

Touching his tongue to a canine, he grimaced at the knowledge that it seemed to have dropped lower from his jaw. His gums ached like a son of a bitch, and knowing that those awakened genetics were going to be impossible to hide irritated the hell out of him.

When had it begun?

He frowned, trying to pinpoint exactly when the changes had begun occurring.

Chelsea's resignation the morning she'd arrived at the house about five weeks ago, he realized. His gums had begun aching just after that. He'd put it down to his habit of gritting his teeth, something else that had begun after her resignation. The cinnamon taste in his mouth at odd times, the unbidden growls that had rumbled in his chest when he was extremely frustrated.

The signs of the awakening genetics had been there, but he'd marked them down to coincidences. After all, it hadn't been the first time that animalistic rumble had built in his throat. The restless irritation and even the flashes of advanced eyesight, hearing and strength had been common over the years.

And he could connect all those flashes distinctly to instances when Chelsea had been around. The Bengal inside him hadn't roused until she'd challenged him, though. Until she'd left and refused to return.

He shouldn't have let her leave the Agency.

He knew that now.

If he'd just let her have a place in Command, she would have stayed. But that would have meant having no chance to escape whatever it was she made him feel whenever he was around her too much.

It was the hunger for her.

His hands clenched on the steering wheel. The physical, aching hunger he hadn't wanted to acknowledge, hadn't wanted to give in to, had roused the beast within him.

He wished he could put the bastard back to sleep.

And if his brother's troublemaking tendencies weren't enough, Rule had decided to add his particular brand of bullshit to it. The least he and Graeme could do was take turns making his life hell instead of trying to drive him insane in one day.

Staying close as Chelsea drove through Window Rock, he followed her first through the drive-thru of a popular coffeehouse, again. The size of the cup of coffee the employee handed out the window had him wincing in acknowledgment of her sheer stubbornness.

The woman could give lessons to a mule on sheer determined pride.

And she had enough pride for a dozen Breeds, let alone one little woman.

That determination could well end up getting her killed if he wasn't careful. The two Breeds trailing them were good, he'd give them that. Draeger and Tobias were about the best security team he'd run across. But even the best made mistakes.

Every instinct Cullen possessed warned him that Chelsea was in a hell of a lot more trouble than any of them suspected.

The Coyote who'd attacked her was a known Genetics Council soldier. He hadn't attempted to abduct her, he'd tried to kill her. The fact that she'd managed to stay alive long enough for the two Wolf Breeds shadowing her to get to her amazed Cullen. No Breed, especially one who still followed the Genetics Council, was that damned sloppy. They were too well trained and too damned fanatical when it came to their orders.

So what the hell was really going on?

As he pondered that question, he drew to a stop directly behind Chelsea at the final traffic light at the end of town, his gaze scanning the area. Draeger and Tobias were two vehicles behind in the beige SUV they were driving that day.

Traffic appeared normal, as did the pedestrians moving along the sidewalks. Nothing seemed unusual. No glints of sunlight on gunsights, nothing to indicate any danger, but his instincts were humming. Hell, they'd been humming since Chelsea had resigned and he'd been too damned distracted to figure out why.

He should have convinced her to ride from the Bureau with him and made Tobias drive her truck, he thought, catching her gaze in the rearview mirror, but she'd argued she could drive the damned thing herself. And he was trying, God knew he was trying to let her have a measure of that independence while still protecting her.

The light turned green.

The second traffic began moving, it happened.

The dark SUV in the turn lane at her left didn't turn, the lighter-colored pickup to her right dropped back and from the side street a heavy panel van raced into the intersection, slamming into the side of Chelsea's truck as the SUV to the left swung around to hem her in, almost cutting Cullen off from her.

The carefully calculated strike moved like slow motion through Cullen's senses as adrenaline spiked through his brain and the animal, normally unresponsive and uncaring, surged awake and took control with a ferocity he couldn't have expected.

Man and tiger merged so seamlessly, it was as though they had never been separate. And hovering just beyond was a madness he didn't stop to consider. Not yet.

Cullen jerked the military-grade automatic weapon he kept secured behind the passenger seat free as the Dragoon rocked to a stop. He was out of the vehicle before the men in the SUV next to her could react.

They hadn't expected resistance, depending on shock and awe to delay Chelsea's security as well as her response to the attack.

A roar tore past his throat.

Lifting the rifle to his shoulder, he fired quickly, laying a spray of bullets along the passenger-side door of the car and taking out two of the would-be attackers. Sprinting for the truck, he aimed and fired on the van, forcing the attackers to take cover as he jerked open the door of the truck and hauled Chelsea from the seat.

The occupants of the lighter-colored SUV rushed from the vehicle when Cullen turned his weapon on them, attempting to help Chelsea from her truck at the same time.

Not that she needed much help, damn her. The second the door came open she all but tumbled out, a snub-nosed automatic personal defense weapon in her hands, her gaze filled with cold, hard determination.

Her hair was mussed, her face pale, a smear of blood on her reddened forehead attesting to a bruise that would be forming quickly, but she was lucid and moving quickly to cover him.

"Stay down," he yelled as horns erupted, the clash of several vehicles colliding behind them a distant sound in his brain as Draeger and Tobias raced to their side.

Automatic gunfire peppered her truck as the men in the van, four in all now, fired back, their plan to attack a single defenseless woman suddenly backfiring.

They'd planned for Draeger and Tobias, but not Cullen. They would have separated her from the two Wolf Breeds trailing her with the deliberate chaos, taken her and been gone before the two Breeds could get to her.

At least, that had been their plan.

Within seconds, though, Draeger and Tobias joined Cullen, and heartbeats later six other Breeds from surrounding vehicles were spreading out, armed and going after the four men in the van.

"Clear the streets." Chelsea pushed at Tobias as he tried to hem her in between himself and Draeger. "Stop worrying about me, dammit, and secure the civilians."

Bullets sprayed the street as frightened cries echoed around him. Cullen worked with the Breeds to contain the shooters, whose plans had suddenly exploded around them. His plan was to stay at Chelsea's side, to cover her while the others contained the shooters. Instead, she stayed at his side as he covered the others, keeping the shooters pinned down while the six enforcers moved on the van and her security team pushed those too frightened to run toward safety.

It took no more than mere minutes before the sound of exploding ammunition and enraged curses from the men facing defeat was over. Three were dead, but there was still one left to question.

And through the entire attack, Chelsea's calm flowed through him, shocking him with his knowledge of it, with her composure and ability to handle the danger.

"Contained," a Coyote Breed Enforcer who'd joined the melee shouted out after a quick look inside the van.

"Nation Police are heading in," another enforcer called out as Cullen strode to the area. "Round them up."

He stared down at the three dead men, their hardened, scarred faces not unknown to him. These weren't Genetics Council soldiers. They weren't Breeds who followed their deranged trainers or known associates. They were hardened criminals and part of a group Cullen and his agents had been tracking for more than a year.

What the hell were they doing here?

"Those are Cerves gang members," Chelsea said softly at his shoulder as she tucked her weapon at the small of her back. "This could be really bad."

"Really bad" didn't even begin to define it. Especially if the Blood Queen was looking to punish Chelsea for not getting her daughter to her in time. "Two of them are Cerves's top lieutenants," he agreed, staring down at her with narrowed eyes. "Did you tell anyone about that night?"

"No way, no how." Chelsea shook her head, keeping her voice low. And he hadn't told anyone, even Graeme. Especially Graeme.

"The surviving attacker likes to talk," Draeger stated as he moved to them, his gaze flashing with savage fury. "The cartel received a contract to kill Chelsea. They were going to kidnap her and ransom her for money to the Genetics Council when they were told she was a Breed mate." His eyes flashed dangerously. "She was considered an easy mark."

An easy mark?

She wasn't an easy mark, and Cerves would learn that one fast enough.

"Let's go." Gripping Chelsea's arm, he tugged her after him, heading for the Dragoon.

"Go where?" The strength in her voice, the demand in her tone drew him to a stop.

He stared down at her, feeling the brutal lust; the adrenaline-laced mating hormone racing through his system had the glands beneath his tongue swelling instantly, the cinnamon taste of it slamming against his tongue and into his system with a wild, furious need nearly painful in its intensity.

Graeme had warned him of this. Warned him that any hard surge of adrenaline would overcome the injection Cullen had taken the night before. That adrenaline was still rushing through him, building despite the fact that the danger was all but over now.

She'd been endangered. If he hadn't been right on her ass those gang members would have taken her and turned her over to the Council, and she would have died.

He would have never gotten to her in time.

"Somewhere else," he snarled, pushing her into the passenger side of the Dragoon. "Anywhere but here."

Anywhere but out in the open, surrounded by other Breeds, by unknown dangers.

He had to get her someplace he knew would be completely secure.

Someplace where danger had no chance of touching her.

· CHAPTER 12 ·

He'd almost lost her.

That thought had every bone and muscle in Cullen's body tightening with fury as he raced from the crime scene, heading for his own home on the other side of town.

If he had been just a single car behind her. If he hadn't followed her. If he hadn't sensed something wrong just before that vehicle had slammed into Chelsea's, then she could have been gone, taken by the criminals, or worse, lying in a pool of blood, dead, in the middle of the street.

For years he'd pushed aside that unnamed something that drew him to her. Even before she'd come to work for him, hell, before his marriage. She'd been a sweet, quiet young girl when he'd first seen her in her father's house the night he, Cat and Honor had been rescued. Peeking from the darkness of another room, her gaze had met his, and he'd known a friend watched him with dark eyes, compassion and a whisper of fear for his safety.

There had been nothing sexual in the fragile bond they'd shared until well after his wife's death. But he knew it for what it was now. The animal waking just enough to ensure he didn't overlook the woman who would one day belong to him.

As he glanced at Chelsea's pale face, the scent of her courage and the sight of the determined tilt of her chin had him rubbing a hand wearily over his face. And he'd thought he could contain her? That he could protect her? It was like trying to contain the wind; she'd slip through his fingers every time.

Realizing that didn't help the adrenaline-laced mating hormone ripping through his system now. It only spurred it. The challenge he glimpsed in her eyes every time he stared into them was the same challenge she silently shouted to the world. She was strong, that glint assured anyone willing to see. She wasn't a victim, and she wouldn't allow herself to become one.

She was his mate.

She was the one woman the creature inside him recognized as the one capable of walking by his side. And the thought of her facing any more danger filled him with fear.

No one was undefeatable. That challenge she stared out at the world with could be silenced with one correctly placed bullet or blade. And she'd just be gone.

If his hands hadn't been gripping the steering wheel with an iron hold, they would have trembled. Fuck, his guts were shaking. It would take him a lifetime to get over what had nearly happened to her.

"Why would the Cerves cartel care what the Council wanted?" she asked, her voice tight with reaction to the attack. "They know it was the Council that ordered Louisa abducted and tortured."

"We'll have more information after the surviving assailant's questioned," he assured her. "Until then, there's no sense in asking questions we can't answer."

He couldn't talk about this. He simply didn't have the control he needed right now to do so with any sort of logic.

"But there's not been so much as a rumor of a coming attack." Confusion filled her voice now. "I'm working every contact I know of as well as their contacts looking for intel on which Breeds are being targeted to be abducted. There's not even a hint that anyone's after me, or that I'm in any kind of danger. Even the Cerveses wouldn't be able to keep that quiet, Cullen."

"They kept this quiet," he snarled. "And my informants are part of the family's main security force."

His informants' heads were going to roll as soon as he contacted them.

"He said a price went on my head," she stated, her voice low. "They don't know I was there that night. This could be just business for them."

"Doesn't matter," he growled. "Whoever put the contract out will pay right along with the Cerveses."

Her worried glance and the smell of her regret slammed into him.

"Look," she breathed out roughly, her hands twisting in her lap as she looked down at them for a moment. "I'm sorry you got dragged into this."

"I didn't get dragged into anything." Where the hell did that from? "I came looking for you, remember?" He shook his head at her statement. "Dammit, Chelsea, you should have come to me the first time you were attacked. I might have fought you over having any part of it, but I would have protected you."

"That's just it, Cullen." She swung around, staring at him, her expression fierce. "I shouldn't have to fight you over it. If you needed my help I'd give it unconditionally. You should do the same or stay the hell out of it."

Incredulity flared through him even as his dick only got harder. Damn her. What would it take to make her understand that he just couldn't do that?

"It doesn't work that way," he gritted out. "You might think it should, you might hope it would, but to actually expect it is illogical, Chelsea."

"You have several female agents working in Covert Ops, Cullen," she pointed out, anger beginning to heat her tone. "Not once have you pulled them back because they might get hurt." Her arms crossed over her breasts and a quick glance at her showed a delicate flush on her features and a battle gleam in her eyes.

"There's a difference." The tension already radiating through him only increased. "You just don't want to see it."

"My training's more advanced than theirs," she argued. "I've trained for ten years with Special Forces and Navy SEALs. I'm a part of the Breed Underground and worked in a covert capacity with them, and all you want me to do is your damned filing."

He could smell her arousal deepening, the scent of her need filling his nostrils and intoxicating his senses.

The adrenaline, he told himself desperately. It was all part of the Mating Heat; Graeme had even warned him about it. An adrenaline surge of any kind amped the need for confrontation and for sex. The female mate needed to assert her own independence and test the strength of her mate. She'd push until his animal pushed back. And he was damned if he couldn't feel the animal demanding that Cullen push back.

"This is the wrong fucking argument to have right now," he told her firmly, shooting her a silencing look.

A hard breath expelled from her lips as she turned and glared straight ahead again, her lips pressed firmly together, and he ached for the hurt he could sense spilling from her. She wanted something he simply didn't know how to give her. It had nothing to do with respect or trust or a certainty of her abilities. It was the certainty that he'd never be the same if anything happened to her.

"Breeds only mate once, Chelsea," he finally sighed as he made the turn onto his street and headed for the end of it where his home was located. "If anything were to happen you I'd never get a second chance—"

He broke off, the sight of the vehicles in his drive pulling the growl he'd been holding back free. It rumbled from his chest, deeper, the sound more predatory than any he'd issued to this point.

"God, I so didn't need this," Chelsea muttered from beside him. "What is it, a frickin' family reunion? Intervention time?"

A family reunion just about described it, along with a healthy dose of the past that he just wasn't in the mood for.

"For God's sake, that's your in-laws," she hissed in disbelief as he pulled the Dragoon to the curb rather than blocking the four vehicles in his driveway and being forced to move to allow them to leave later.

His former in-laws. Arthur and Marsha Holden, Lauren's parents.

"They're your cousins," he pointed out, shooting her a brooding glare.

She shrugged with a roll of her eyes. "Can't choose your family, but you can damned sure choose your in-laws. Your taste sucks, by the way."

Chelsea pushed the passenger door open and forced herself to step from the vehicle. The jolt of her feet against the pavement as she was forced to all but jump from the opening brought a muttered groan from her lips.

"Dammit, can't you wait two seconds?" Cullen cursed as she found herself swung up into his arms and cushioned against his broad chest.

Her arms went around his shoulders instinctively despite the angry look she shot him.

"If I felt like waiting, then that's what I would have done," she informed him, suddenly feeling every ache and bruise in her body.

She didn't feel like dealing with her family, not right now while she was bruised and bloody and her father was staring at her with something akin to agonized horror.

He didn't have a chance to reply. Her sister rushed from her husband's side, concern in her expression as she took Cullen's keys and ran to unlock and open the front door.

He carried Chelsea into the house and laid her on the couch in his plain living room. Couch, two easy chairs, a few tables and a lamp.

It had that unlived-in feel even though he'd lived there since the year after his wife died.

The whole house had an unlived-in feel. She'd noticed that the few times she'd been there. It was a place to sleep when he needed it, a place to hang his clothes and shower and little else.

"I'll get the first-aid kit." Malachi headed through the house, looking around as he went, obviously acquainted with it. "Damn, son, when are you going to hang a picture or two?"

"When you buy them and hang them, I guess," Cullen grunted.

Behind him, Chelsea's father, Terran, her grandfather, Orrin, and Cullen's former in-laws stepped into the house. They looked around the living room and into the kitchen as though confused by the feeling of it. Only her grandfather's expression reflected something other than distaste. He appeared thoughtful, his head tilted, no doubt listening to whatever he could hear in the very air itself.

Chelsea didn't doubt the air in the house was speaking to him, spilling Cullen's secrets, whispering to him of whatever it was that spoke of such loneliness in the place Cullen called home.

"Interesting," Arthur murmured, his heavily lined face still drawn with the same grief she'd seen in it at Lauren's funeral ten years ago.

Tall, reed thin, his facial features rather long and too somber, Arthur Holden wasn't a man to joke and laugh with. His wife had once been much more animated, smiling, her hazel eyes always bright with whatever emotion she felt. They weren't like that any longer. The loss of her only child, her daughter, had stilled that sparkle and taken the animation from her expression.

Marsha stood, appearing uncomfortable, uncertain what to do as Malachi placed the first-aid kit on the coffee table and Isabelle sat on the couch next to Chelsea and stared down at her in sympathy and concern.

"If I close my eyes and wish hard enough, will they all go away?" Chelsea asked, her voice low enough that Isabelle and Malachi were probably the only ones who heard her.

"Doubt it, sis." Isabelle smiled gently, her tone filled with wry amusement. "Not this time."

She blew out a hard breath and closed her eyes anyway.

"What the hell are you involved in, Chelsea?" her father exclaimed from the end of the couch, his voice angry as only a worried father sounds. "An attack in the middle of town? Someone tried to rain a war down on you, dammit, and I want to know why."

A damned war was a good description of it. She was determined to ignore the questions, though, until heat exploded in the cut on her forehead just as the scent of alcohol reached her nose.

"Dammit, Isa." She jerked, her eyes snapping open as she tried to pull away from the fiery burn. "That hurts."

Isabelle lifted a dark brow with false innocence. Dammit, she'd meant for the alcohol to burn.

"Don't ignore Dad, he nearly had a stroke on me," Isabelle hissed down at her.

"I'm not ignoring him." At least she wasn't trying to. "I don't know what happened or why, or I would have given a family report the second I stepped into the door."

"Here." Several damp paper towels dropped into Isabelle's hands as Malachi returned from the kitchen. "Clean the blood from her skin first so we can get a good look at those scratches on her arm. They look pretty deep."

They were pretty deep. Glass had rained around her when her truck took the impact of the collision.

She sat still, silent as her father, her grandfather and Arthur Holden followed Cullen into the kitchen. Marsha stood next to the coffee table, her gaze dropping to the bloodied paper towels as Isabelle dropped them to the table beside the couch.

"Stay still," her sister admonished her as she flinched at the probing of the wounds. "These are almost deep enough to require stitches."

"Almost doesn't count." Chelsea felt like pouting.

She wished they'd just stop fussing over her and let her go take a shower. She'd feel much better if she could stand beneath some warm water. The longer she lay there and endured her sister's inspection of the cuts, the colder she felt.

As Marsha finally drew away and moved to the kitchen with her husband, Isabelle gave Chelsea a sympathetic look before drawing back, her blue eyes flicking to the kitchen again.

"It gets easier," her sister said softly. "The symptoms ease and even out pretty quickly once you and Cullen are more certain of each other."

Certain of each other? She'd be waiting awhile for that one to happen.

"He hates it," Chelsea whispered back. "He wants a cure for it." She rolled her eyes despite how bad that knowledge hurt. "Go figure."

Isabelle shook her head, the cloud of dark hair framing her face swaying with the movement. "I don't believe that, Chelsea. For it to be present at all, then whether he wants to admit it or not, he loves you. The emotions always go both ways when it happens."

It. The mating. Was every Breed who married actually mated to their husband or wife? There weren't a lot of marriages, she knew, but if the tabloids were to be believed, each one was a mating.

Giving her a warning look, Isabelle didn't say anything more. A second later Arthur and Marsha moved back into the room and stepped to the couch once again.

It had been ten years since she'd seen them, but they'd never been close with the rest of the family. Arthur's family had once been quite wealthy and they'd always spent most of the time on their California estate until Lauren became older. They'd been in town less than a year when Lauren and Cullen were introduced. After the Holdens lost their daughter, they'd returned to California and as far she knew, this was their first visit back.

They picked a hell of a time to visit.

"Sorry about all this." She tried to smile as she met Marsha's gaze. "Not exactly what you were looking for when you came to visit, huh?"

"Oh dear, I'm just worried about you." Marsha sighed as though tired. "You always were the rebel in the family, weren't you?"

"The troublemaker," Arthur murmured with an attempt at teasing humor. "No wonder your father's hair is turning gray."

"Yeah, that's what he tells me all the time." Pushing herself up, she swung her legs around and put her feet on the floor, looking up at Marsha.

There was little resemblance to the Martinez family in the other woman. She more closely resembled her mother's side of the family, Boston bluebloods as her father once commented.

"We should be going, dear." Arthur laid his hand against his wife's shoulder with a gentle pat. "Let Terran and Orrin see if they can talk any sense into her." He turned then as Cullen entered the room and held his hand out; the dark blue silk suit he wore, despite its tailoring, made him appear more gaunt than he would have if he'd taken the jacket off. "Maybe we'll see each other again before we head home."

"Arthur." Cullen nodded and accepted the handshake. "It was good to see you again."

No, it wasn't. She could see the subtle signs of Cullen's discomfort, which she was certain mirrored hers. She had a good excuse, though; she'd never been comfortable around them.

Turning back to her, Arthur watched her silently for a long moment before he bent his knees and hunched next to her. She watched him warily, barely able to stifle a wince as he picked up her hand and patted it in what she was certain was meant to be a fatherly manner.

"Take it easy, Chelsea. It's a terrible thing when a father is forced to lose a child," he told her, but the arrogant superiority in his tone grated on her nerves.

"No danger." She slid her hand from his and pushed it through her hair to dispel the feel of his touch. "I'm sure they've already reserved a padded cell for me." She grinned over Arthur's shoulder at her father's frowning countenance. "That or chains."

Arthur chuckled at the comment, rose to his feet, then nodded to the rest of the family. "We'll be going now. Let me know if you need anything."

Placing his hand low on his wife's back, he led her to the door and out of the house. As the door closed, Chelsea noticed the air didn't feel nearly as tense as it had while he was there.

"Cullen," Malachi stated long seconds later. "No offense, but there's not a chance in hell I'd turn my back on that man."

That observation struck Chelsea as a perfect description of the undercurrents of tension she herself had felt.

Orrin shook his gray head, his expression saddened. "He's a man tormented by loss," he said somberly. "And by his own inability to prevent it."

Malachi merely glanced at the other man, obviously not agreeing with him. "As I said." He shrugged. "I wouldn't turn my back on him. He was attempting to put everyone at ease, but I could smell his hatred.

It was there, despite the attempts to appear differently. And it was centered on Cullen."

Chelsea looked up at Cullen. His expression was closed, his gaze cool as he met her father's long look. He wasn't commenting, but she sensed he agreed with Malachi. She knew his Breed senses were coming alive with the mating; he would have caught the scent of hatred coming from Arthur if it was there. And if Malachi said it was there, then it was.

"Arthur never approved of Cullen," Terran stated then, surprising Chelsea with the lack of compassion in his tone. "He and Marsha along with Ray pushed her to him, though." He turned to Cullen with a harsh look. "I'm not a fool and I've been around Breeds long enough to know that the stories about the matings aren't complete falsehoods. And they knew it too." He nodded to the door Arthur and Marsha had used. "They never confirmed it, but I saw the knowledge in their eyes when Lauren was screaming at you from her deathbed."

Cullen flinched. The muscle at his jaw bunched, tightening with the fierce clenching of his teeth before he cursed under his breath.

"Dad, we need to leave." It was Isabelle who hurriedly made the suggestion. Moving to their father, she placed her hand on his shoulder and gave him a warning look. "Come on, now isn't the time for this. Chelsea needs to rest. We know she's okay, and Cullen will watch out for her far better than we can."

"Come, son." Orrin joined Isabelle at his son's side. "Wish your youngest well and we'll see if we can't find a drink to ease the tension of the matter." He patted Terran's shoulder and headed for the door. "Hurry yourselves. It's time we leave."

Chelsea forced herself to her feet.

"I stopped and packed a bag for you before heading here," Isabelle told her. "Malachi put it in the kitchen while I was tending your boo-

boos." She shot Chelsea a teasing grin. "Call me and let me know when you need company."

"I will," Chelsea promised, her gaze moving to her father once again as he stepped to her.

"If either you or Isabelle were taken from me, I wouldn't survive my grief," he whispered at her ear as he gave a quick, fierce hug. "Remember that when you're being so damned reckless."

He turned quickly away then and stalked from the house, the door closing heavily behind him.

While she was being so reckless. Tears threatened to fill her eyes at her father's words. Reckless, foolhardy, senseless. Those were his descriptions of her need to fight the injustices she saw in their world.

"He's scared, Chelsea," Malachi told her, compassion filling his expression as his arm curved around Isabelle's waist and pulled her to him. "You're his daughter, his far-too-courageous child. He was watching the report of the attack as it happened. The nightmares he's having aren't even waiting for him to go to sleep. They're flashing through his mind as we speak."

Chelsea blinked back the tears, the knowledge of her father's pain as well as her own tearing at her. "I know that, Malachi," she retorted painfully as she looked away from him, hating that both he and Cullen no doubt could sense every emotion tearing through her now. "But asking me to be anyone besides who I am is the same as killing me anyway." She shoved her hands into the pockets of her jeans and shook her head, her lips trembling in a flood of emotion she fought to control. "And what hurts the most is that every one of you would change me if you could."

"Wrong," Malachi assured her, his tone firm, though no less gentle. "I wouldn't change you, and neither would your sister, but it won't stop any of us from worrying."

"Or from aching in grief if we lost you," Isabelle told her, her voice thick with the tears she was holding back. Moving to her, her sister gave her a quick hug before taking her husband's hand and leaving the house.

Her grandfather patted her shoulder, his dark gaze as fathomless as the oceans.

"Your courage terrifies your father, just as his sister's once did. It isn't your courage he would change, but the dangers that would harm you." He sighed heavily, patted her back consolingly and smiled with loving strength. "The winds have always called your name, whispering across the lands as they called you to defend those others would harm. Now, allow those you would fight for to do the same."

Yeah, that was her grandfather, a riddle within a puzzle, she thought wearily, watching him leave the house. When the door closed behind him she turned to Cullen, feeling the tension radiating from him.

"No sage advice? You may as well, everyone else is dispensing it," she whispered, fighting to keep her chin from trembling with the realization that there was no way to win this particular battle. Just by being who she was, what she longed to be, she was breaking her family's heart and giving her father waking nightmares. Wasn't that a nice piece of information.

"Let me get over my own sense of terror first," he told her, a growl in his voice. "Your father saw it unfold? I was there. And my guts are still cramped with the memory of it. Maybe I can come up with sage advice later."

"You just do that, Cullen." Her breath hitched as she felt herself losing control of the tears threatening to fill her eyes. "I'm going to shower. Maybe by the time I finish, I can find a way to deal with the fact that there's not a damned person that I care about willing to accept me for who and what I am. Lucky fucking me."

Turning away from him she hurried from the room, swiping at the tear that fell to her cheek. She hated crying. Hated it. Just as she hated the guilt that always came with those tears. For ten years she'd fought to find a way to come to terms with her needs and her family's fears. And she'd failed.

She hadn't demanded a position with Covert Ops in the Agency; she'd actually bargained more often for Command and Logistics. She knew that being in the thick of danger was something her family couldn't handle, and she'd tried to balance her needs with theirs. It hadn't happened, though. Cullen had refused her a job in Command, and her application to the Nation's police force had been rejected by the board, who incidentally were all close friends of her father's. The private security agency she'd applied to had demanded references, and Cullen had refused to give them.

They had made the decision for her; she hadn't made it. Rule Breaker had been willing to take a chance on her, though, and now something or someone was screwing that up for her.

Son of a bitch. It was a simple operation. Information gathering. That was all it was. And she was careful. Damned careful; even Ashley and Cassie had agreed that there was no way she could have given herself away. Yet she'd been attacked twice now and the latest skirmish was more violent than even she was comfortable with.

She could handle someone coming at her with a knife, but drug cartel members and automatic rifles in the middle of Window Rock? The implications of it were terrifying. She didn't want her family's fear, and she didn't want their advice. It would have been extremely nice if just one of them, just one, had realized that her terror went far deeper than theirs and it was rooted in far more than her fear of losing any one person.

Just because she wasn't shaking and wailing in hysteria didn't mean her insides weren't trembling with fear now. They were, and for a moment out there all she'd wanted was someone, just one of them, to realize that she wasn't entirely stupid or without a sense of terror at the thought of what could have happened.

Adjusting the shower water, she stripped and stepped in, almost moaning at the feel of the heated water sliding with silky warmth over her sensitive body. It didn't wash away the fear, it didn't wash away the hurt, but it damned sure eased the aches and pain just a bit.

Just enough that when she closed her eyes and let the tears fall, she didn't have to worry that she appeared weak. There was no one to see the tears. But then, there never was. Even the man who was supposed to be her mate.

As that thought whispered through her mind, a brush of cool air had her eyes jerking open before they widened at the sight of Cullen, naked and furiously aroused as he stepped in the shower.

Instead of pulling her into one of those deep, drugging kisses, though, he just pulled her into his arms. One hand cupped the back of her head, holding her to his chest, as the other wrapped around her back, securing her against him.

"I have you," he whispered, his voice low and heavy with a sense of despair.

There was no holding the tears back now. With his chest beneath her cheek and the water flowing around them, she let them fall. Silently. Painfully.

He might not agree, he might not like it, but for once in her life, she wasn't alone.

And how in God's name had he known she felt that way?

From Graeme's Journal
The Recessed Primal Breed

There is nothing more precious to the Primal Breed than his mate. And he will protect that mate with an unequaled savagery.

Chelsea came awake slowly, aware of Cullen's hard body as he lay beside her, her head resting against his chest.

After the storm of tears had passed that afternoon, he'd washed her gently, dried her, then tucked her into bed and held her against him as she fell asleep. Exhaustion, both emotional and physical, had overwhelmed her as the adrenaline eased from her system.

She hadn't felt fear in the moment of the attempted abduction. Just as she had when she found Louisa and when the Coyote attacked, her mind had stayed clear, her training kicking in as she fought to elimi-nate the threat.

It was after the adrenaline plunged that the waves of terror crashed over her.

The last time, she'd been alone. She'd held herself through the storm, her arms wrapped across her chest as she curled in her lonely bed.

She hadn't been alone this time, though. Cullen had been there with her, and it was his arms that held her, his understanding that brought her through the storm. Now she was surrounded by the warmth of his powerful body, shielded and protected.

There were nights she'd ached for this over the years. Ached for him. Nights when she'd stared into the darkness of her lonely bedroom with a bleak acceptance that it was something she would never know.

Being here now, feeling the power and strength of him as she rested against him, Chelsea still wasn't certain exactly how she was supposed to handle it or if she could believe in it.

Breeds only mated once, he'd told her; if either of them lost the other, then they'd be alone. She'd been alone so long, though, that she didn't know if she knew how to be a part of anyone else, even though she longed to be a part of Cullen.

Waking next to him felt really nice, though. He was warm, pow-erful, and she ached for him. The emotional storm earlier that day had dulled the need, her exhaustion pulling her into sleep.

She was awake now and she wanted him. She needed him. Every cell in her body felt overly sensitive as the building sensual need tightened through her with an ache only Cullen could assuage. And that wasn't just Mating Heat. That need for him had been her reality for years.

She had always known that only Cullen could ease the needs that plagued her.

The heart wants what it wants, her father had once told her, and her heart had always been set on Cullen. From the moment she'd first seen him that night when he'd been brought to the Nation, a part of her had belonged to him.

Lifting her hand from where it lay against his chest, she let her fingers caress the bronzed expanse of tough flesh covering tense muscle.

Heat radiated from his flesh as she stroked him softly. Trailing her fingers over his chest, learning the feel of it, sensing the power contained with it, she felt her breathing and her heart rate accelerate.

The response sweeping through her own body still had the power to shock her. Even before waking her breasts were swollen, her nipples peaked with the need for touch. Between her thighs the folds of her sex were slick and hot, her clit aching and the inner tissue clenched and rippling with hungry need.

"You're finally awake," he whispered, his voice a rasp of hungry, aroused male. "I was wondering how much longer I could wait."

"You were waiting for me, huh?" She couldn't help the grin that curled her lips. "I was wondering where your legendary patience had gone."

An amused quirk of his lips met her gaze as she propped herself on an elbow to stare down at him in the dim light of the room.

His green eyes were heavy lidded, his expression filled with lazy male sensuality.

"My patience went right out the damned window when you left," he said, his gaze turning somber as he reached up with one hand to cup the side of her neck. "I think my agents are ready to revolt on me. Ranger mostly just glares at me now."

"You've been a grouch again?" she asked, remembering his reputation for it before she came to work for him. "And here I thought you were doing so much better."

"You left me, Chelsea," he reminded her, exerting just enough pressure at her neck to draw her lips to his. "You can't do that again. Never again."

His lips whispered over hers, stroking, rubbing, and then his head tilted, his lips parted and he deepened the touch with hungry demand.

The taste of cinnamon infused her senses as his tongue rubbed against hers, encouraging her to taste him deeper. And she did.

She loved the taste of his kiss. That subtle heat, the pleasure that coursed through her senses and the low, rough male groan that rumbled from his chest.

Pulling her head back to catch a breath while she still had enough sense to do it, she stared into the marked, sexual need gleaming in his eyes.

With a drowsy, sensual look she flicked her tongue out to touch her lip suggestively, her hunger for him growing in demand as he pulled her to him once again. Her nipples brushed against his chest, the peaks hardening further, becoming so sensitive it was nearly painful. Blood thundered in her head, through her body, a gasp escaping her as his lips covered hers again with desperate, hungry need.

Capturing his tongue as it pressed inside, Chelsea drew the spicy taste from it, moaning at the incredible pleasure racing through her.

Cullen had one hand buried in her hair and caressed up and down her back with the other, stroking the pleasure and need higher and hotter. It wasn't just his kiss or whatever chemical reaction it caused. It wouldn't matter how he touched her as long as he touched her, let her touch him.

She had yearned for him for years, ached for him.

Let him believe this hunger was some fault of nature, of his genetics, if that was what he wanted to believe. She knew better. She knew it had to be so much more.

He needed her touch just as badly as she needed his. It had to be more than lust. He had to feel more than simple sexual need; otherwise she'd be loving him in vain, and that she couldn't bear.

Forcing herself back from his kiss, she stared down at him, her breathing as rough as his. A brick red flush ran along his cheekbones as he stared back at her, his gaze drowsy and far too sexy.

There was more in his gaze than just lust. She'd seen just lust many times in other men's eyes. There was passion there and something more. Something that connected inside her heart and sent a rush of pleasure sweeping through her.

"Are you going to stare at me all night?" His lips quirked as his brow lifted arrogantly.

Chelsea licked her lips, that need that swept over her impossible to resist.

"Let me touch you, Cullen," she whispered, lowering her lips to his hard jaw, kissing her way to his neck.

She let her tongue taste the strong column of his neck, let her teeth rake over it as he had done to hers.

He tensed beneath her, his muscular body hardening in response to her nibbling caresses and slow, licking tastes.

As she slid down his body, the feel of the perspiration gathering on his skin, his heavy breathing, sent a thrill rushing through her. She gloried in his response to her touch, in the feel of his cock throbbing against her thigh as she moved closer to him.

"However you want to, sweetheart. Anytime you want to," he breathed out, the sound a rough rasp as he buried his fingers in her hair. "I'm all yours."

God, she wished that were true.

Moving her lips to his hard chest, she found the flat hard disc of a male nipple. The salt and male taste of him exploded against her taste buds. His flesh was just as hot and wild as his kiss.

Steel-hard muscles flexed and rippled beneath her lips, lean and powerful. Sweat gleamed on his bronze flesh, giving him a sex-god appearance that threatened to steal her breath.

She lifted her gaze and met his narrowed one, pleasure and hunger gleaming in the green depths. As she watched him, she licked from one hard male nipple to the other before grazing them with her teeth.

Touching him was the hottest, sexiest experience of her life. Her pussy was weeping from the erotic experience. Her juices spilled to the swollen folds, heating her clit until it throbbed with torturous need.

Lifting herself close, she straddled his hard thigh, crying out as her clit swelled further and her juices dampened his flesh.

"Fuck, Chelsea, you're killing me, baby," he growled, the rough sound another stroke against her senses.

She was loving him, giving him with her touch what she knew he would refuse to hear. This was all she had, the only way she could show him the depth of what she felt for him.

As she took her kisses lower, the need to taste him, to love him, to fill her mouth with the hard male heat of him, intensified inside her.

"I love how you taste," she whispered, powerless against the needs rocking through her. "Like the desert. So strong and hot."

She licked over his abdomen, ignoring the thick, pulsing head of his cock as his fingers tugged at her hair.

The little bite of heat against her scalp was exquisite. Tugging and pulling, the heated caress sent flames streaking through her senses as his hips arched, the head of his cock grazing her lips.

She let herself lick over it, drawing a rough, rumbling groan from his chest. She moved lower and stroked her tongue slowly down the shaft to the base, then to the tightly drawn sac just below the stiff flesh.

Cullen jerked beneath her, a grating curse leaving his lips as she licked firmly. Her tongue stroked, caressed. The hot male taste of him was intoxicating. His obvious pleasure at her touch only drove her own need higher.

Her womb spasmed as he growled her name, his voice rougher, huskier than before. Moving higher, Chelsea trailed her tongue up the violently erect shaft, feeling the blood pounding through the heavy veins. His fingers were locked in her hair, his thighs tense and steel hard.

Just above the engorged crest of his cock, a bead of sweat trailed down his tight abdomen as it flexed in response to her touch.

Parting her lips over his cock head, she took it in her mouth slowly. Her gaze lifted again, watched the pleasure and male hunger gleaming in his eyes.

His gaze was locked on her mouth and the engorged crest as it disappeared inside. Sweat beaded on his neck, his hard jaw. His lips drew back in a grimace of pleasure, exposing the canines that appeared a bit longer. His eyes were darker, the jungle green color burning and wild.

"Suck it," he snarled, the hard, graveled demand stroking over her senses. "Damn you. I've dreamed of your lips wrapped around my dick."

The taste of his pre-cum spilling to her lips made her feel drunk on the pleasure racing through her. Her lips tightened around the crest, sucking at it firmly as he filled her mouth.

The feel of the silky, steel-hard head of his cock throbbing furiously as she sucked at it drew a moan from her lips. Flickering her tongue over it, beneath it, she could feel her clit approaching meltdown.

Her pussy was soaked from her need for him, her juices spilling to the sensitive folds and dampening her thighs.

"I won't come in your mouth," he gritted out as the crest flexed warningly at the back of her throat. "You want to make me crazy?" His hands moved from her hair, gripped her head and pulled her up forcibly. "Ride me. Come here, baby, and fuck me until we're both crazy."

She eased up his body, straddled his thighs and whimpered with anticipation as the folds of her pussy parted for the wide, blunt head.

"That's it, Chelsea," he groaned, a grimace of pleasure contorting his face. "Ride my cock with that hot little pussy."

Sensations spasmed through her womb at the explicit demand. Erotic and filled with male pleasure, it reached inside her, increasing the sensuality of the act.

His hands gripped her hips, guiding her as his cock began pushing inside the rippling entrance of her sex. The fiery stretch of her flesh as she impaled herself on the heavy stalk dragged a desperate cry from her lips.

Cullen's hand stroked from her hips to her breasts, his fingers finding her painfully sensitive nipples. He exerted just enough pressure against them to send sensation screaming over her nerve endings.

Her hips jerked, lowered, desperate to fill herself with the hard length of his cock. Her hands flattened against his chest, whimpering cries escaping from her throat.

She knew what she wanted, needed.

Throwing her head back, Chelsea lifted again, taking him deeper with each downward push of her hips. Burning pleasure surged through her, stole her breath.

Streaking fire raced from her nipples as his fingers pressed and tugged at them firmly. Those same flames tore a path to the tight depths of her pussy, the inner tissue spasming around his erection as she finally worked it in to the hilt.

Cullen bucked beneath her, driving his hips upward as his hands moved quickly to her thighs to hold her to him. She could feel his cock throbbing inside her, stretching her, possessing her.

Need swiftly overcame any desire to relish the sensations. Chelsea was burning from the inside out, the need for orgasm quickly stealing her control.

And his.

Cullen thrust upward as she lifted herself, fucking her in hard, driving thrusts. Each impalement, each stroke inside the too-sensitive channel stoked the insanity of a hunger burning through both their control.

Moving with him, riding the brutally hard shaft, she let herself fall into the storm overtaking them.

Her hands moved to his hard biceps, her nails biting into the tense muscles as she felt her body tightening. Her pussy rippled around each driving stroke and the world exploded around her. Her senses ruptured and her body jerked, writhed as each powerful contraction of ecstasy tore through her.

Beneath her, Cullen drove inside her harder, buried to the hilt, growling her name, and a heartbeat later the pulse of his release and hardening length of the feline barb locking inside her pushed her higher, tossing her into a cataclysm that she knew she'd never fully recover from.

◆　◆　◆

Dawn was several hours from breaking when Cullen awoke, his body vibrating with restlessness and a renewed arousal for the woman sleeping at his side. Erect and throbbing, his cock demanded a repeat of the pleasure he'd found with Chelsea.

She was sleeping deeply now, though, lying bonelessly on her stomach, her breathing deep and a sense of peace surrounding her. Hell, she had always had that sense of calm, of peace that filled the air around her. It was one of the reasons he'd tried to keep her in the office. She had a way of keeping the whole team on an even keel, no matter how high the frustration level rose.

Rather than waking her, though, he quietly gathered some clothes and quickly showered. Dressing, he checked in on her again, almost grinning at the fact that she hadn't so much as shifted her position and headed to the kitchen for coffee.

He'd no more than stepped from his bedroom to the short hall leading to the rest of the house when he paused. There wasn't a particular scent per se that alerted him to the intruder. It was that absence of scent that identified the Breed waiting for him. He wasn't surprised when he stepped into the kitchen to find Graeme waiting for him; he'd actually expected his brother the night before.

What did surprise him was the Primal he faced instead. He hadn't seen the monster his brother could become since Graeme had mated the young woman the two of them had raised in the labs they were confined to as boys.

The primal markings bisected Graeme's face, like the stripes of the Bengal across bronzed flesh. Blood-tipped claws had emerged from beneath the very human fingernails, pushing past the flesh, curved and lethally sharp as they rested on the table. Wild, jade green eyes gleamed brilliantly from within the stripes, the glow of color like jade fire in the dimly lit room.

This was the Breed that most who saw him never lived to tell the tale about. This was the insanity of a creature pushed to such preternatural rage that even nature itself had no power over him.

"Graeme?" Cullen greeted him warily as he moved to the coffeemaker and placed two cups beneath the brewing spouts. "Everything okay?"

He didn't fear the monster, but neither was he foolish enough to push its unpredictable temper when he wasn't pissed off himself.

Graeme's fingers flexed against the table, wickedly sharp claws digging deep indents in the wood as the battle to control the monster was reflected on his face.

"We go hunting." The guttural, animalistic voice had the power to send chills up the spines of those facing the rage of this creature.

Cullen had never feared the creature, though. He watched it warily. At one time, he'd feared the destruction it could wreak on others, but he'd never feared it personally.

"What happened?" Only Cat and any risk to her could pull the monster free now that Graeme had secured his mate.

He would have been alerted, though, if anything had happened to Graeme's mate or if any danger threatened her, which left Cullen a little confused as to the reason for the Primal's visit.

Graeme's nails scraped the table again, a low, dangerous growl rumbling in his chest as Cullen waited for an explanation.

Or explosion.

Either was possible.

"We go for Cerves," the monster's voice grated. "Now!"

Surprise caused Cullen to stare at his brother more intently now as bemusement filled him.

"This appearance"—he waved his hand toward his brother to indicate the Primal Graeme had set free—"is because of the Cerves attack?"

That dangerous, rough growl sounded again as an enraged grimace curled at Graeme's lips.

"Attack?" Graeme snarled. "An ambush. Four came to take her. They would have cut you down had the other Breeds not been in the

LORA LEIGH

traffic behind you." That growl sounded again, deeper, filled with greater fury. "I tolerate no attacks against those I claim. Mate. Brother." His gaze moved to the entrance of the hall toward Cullen's room where he'd left Chelsea sleeping. "Sister. Cerves will pay for this, as will who-ever sent that Coyote to knife her."

Meaning Graeme intended to cut a swath of blood and death through the Cerves compound. That was just what he needed, Cullen thought caustically. To have the monster everyone believed had left the States be seen tearing drug cartel members limb from limb.

That was the last thing the Breeds needed right now at a time when both the criminal and noncriminal elements were still fascinated with their presence.

And all because someone had dared to threaten part of his family.

"I'm a big boy, Graeme—" Cullen began to protest.

Before he could finish the thought, Graeme was out of his chair and in Cullen's face, an enraged snarl curling his lips.

"My brother. My sister by mating." Clawed fingers gripped the front of Cullen's shirt imperiously as rage hummed in the air around the creature. "We go now."

Cullen looked down at the hold his brother had on him, then back to the monster's furious gaze.

"Where's Cat, Graeme?" he asked patiently. "Does she know the monster's come out to play this morning?"

Handling Graeme while in this less-than-sane, primal state was never easy. And Cullen wasn't certain how he felt about the monster's belief that he could protect him. He was an adult now, not a kid, and Cerves was his fight.

"I will kill Cerves." The monster smiled, obviously relishing the thought of the cartel leader's blood.

"Because of me?" Cullen questioned the threat dubiously.

"You. Your mate. Their blood is mine," the monster grated out in a serrated voice.

Cullen rubbed at his forehead, fighting for patience as Graeme released his shirt slowly, though his brother still glared at him with demonic green eyes.

"Tell you what. Hide the monster in case Chelsea awakens and leaves the bedroom and we'll discuss it," he offered.

Hell, it was too early for a drink and this side of his brother almost demanded one.

A rumbled growl of warning had Cullen grimacing in irritation. He didn't need this, not right now.

"Dammit, Graeme, I don't need you fighting my battles and I sure as hell don't need your protection," he snapped as he felt the Primal's demand that he submit to its wishes. "Pull the fuck back. I'll deal with Cerves, and if you want to be a part of it, then you'll find your sanity and discuss it rationally."

The Primal's roar exploded from Graeme's chest, exploding with enraged violence and probably waking the whole damned neighborhood.

There was no doubt it woke Chelsea.

Before he could push past Graeme and reach the hall entrance, the bedroom door flew open and Chelsea raced from the room wearing nothing but Cullen's shirt, half-buttoned, the tail of which fell below her thighs. In her hands she carried the black, highly lethal, not to mention illegal, fully automatic snub-nosed PDW she carried in her pack.

"Whoa there." He caught her before she could lift the weapon on the Primal Breed poised to eliminate any threat it encountered.

Snagging the weapon from her hands with one hand, he caught

her around the waist with the other, practically lifting her from the floor before she could attack Graeme.

Once she caught sight of the Primal she stilled in his hold, eyes widening before she blinked in amazement. Cullen wanted to curse in frustration.

"What is it?" she whispered, her gaze locked with Graeme's. "And why aren't we shooting it?"

No fear.

He could smell her shock, her inner demand for fight or flight, but there was no fear.

She was staring at Graeme. First his face, then the claw-tipped hands at his side. Her gaze went over the black shirt and dark pants he wore to the muted black boots, then back to his face as wariness filled her expression.

"I try really hard not to shoot my brother, no matter the mood he's in," he informed her, holding her more firmly against him as she pushed at his arm in an obvious bid for freedom.

"That's Graeme?" She kept her voice at a whisper as suspicion filled it. "You're lying. I've met Graeme. He doesn't look like that."

The Primal smiled with savage, bloodthirsty satisfaction, a growl rumbling in his throat. Shooting him a glare, Cullen wondered if investing in a whip and chair would do any good.

"Why is it smiling?" she asked him, ignoring the snap of teeth and warning snarl Graeme displayed. "Give me my gun back. I think we're going to need it."

He glanced down at her with an irritable frown. "No."

"Really?" she hissed, incredulity filling the low tone of her voice. "Look at it. It's insane. Give me my gun before it decides to bite you. Or me."

Graeme's expression darkened at her statement, the stripes turning a deep, furious black.

"Dammit, Chelsea," Cullen cursed, holding to her as she wiggled against him. "He's not going to bite anyone, and you're not shooting him."

Graeme's lip lifted in a dangerous curl of impending violence, his incisor glinting ominously in the low light.

"Is it sane, do you think?" she whispered, stilling against him as her hands gripped his forearm, her obvious fascination grating at his patience.

Grunting at the question, he shot Graeme a testy look, noticing the offended pride in his brother's expression. "Not even on a good day. And stop calling him 'it.'"

"So what is it?" She ignored the order as Graeme's nostrils flared and the displeasure in his warning growls increased.

"You know I can hear you, right?" he grated, the animalistic tone not quite as grating as moments before.

She shot Cullen a surprised look before staring at Graeme in supposed amazement. "It can talk?"

"Chelsea," he muttered warningly, wondering at what point the Primal would grow tired of the "it" title.

If Graeme's louder, harsher snarl was any indication, he was reaching the end of his patience. The sound was low, deep, a grumble meant to intimidate. It was all Cullen could do not to groan in resignation. Chelsea didn't do intimidated very well.

She stiffened against him and feminine outrage poured from her.

"Maybe it's hungry," she suggested, her voice low but definitely goading now. "Do you keep kitty kibble around?"

Silence snapped in the room.

Graeme's eyes narrowed, the jade green color glittering brighter and flaring with rage as he took a step closer and let loose another of those lethal roars.

She didn't even have the good sense to flinch.

Not that Cullen flinched, but he was used to them by now.

Instead, Chelsea waited until Graeme almost seemed to relax marginally at her supposedly submissive silence.

"I'm calling Cat and reporting its bad behavior," she whispered then, as though it were some secret and Graeme couldn't overhear her. "Maybe she'll come collect it. Do you think?"

Cullen tried to push her behind him as Graeme stepped closer, nostrils flaring, the Primal's eyes flickering with impending retaliation.

"Cat will not be pleased with it," she said then, and surprisingly Graeme paused, frowning again.

"Do not threaten me," the grating voice ordered her in a harsh, guttural command.

"Then get from between me and my coffee. Your rude roars woke me up way too early and no one should expect me to be nice under the circumstances." She pushed at his arm again, and this time Cullen just let her go. "Besides." She finished buttoning the shirt she wore. "Wild animals are supposed to be kept outside, not in the kitchen."

She made the comment so blithely. As though a killer weren't glaring at her, his rage building at the insult. Though at this point, Cullen was fairly confident Graeme wouldn't lay a hand on her. Evidently, she was just as confident.

"Before your mate blinks I could take your throat out." Graeme flexed his claws warningly, but Cullen could actually sense a hint of surprised amusement coming from the Primal, an indication that his brother was gaining control once again.

"I'll be certain to include that threat in my list of complaints when

I call Cat later." She shrugged, then eyed him thoughtfully. "I bet you're a blast at Halloween. Does Cat dress as your circus trainer?"

Cullen barely smothered the amazed laughter that would have escaped. The choking sound he made was a piss-poor disguise, though.

Graeme's primal markings were lighter on his face now, the claws retreating beneath his nails as irritation replaced the rage that had held him in its grip.

"No wonder Cat likes you," Graeme grumbled, his voice sounding more normal now. "You're as much a brat as she is."

"I'm actually better at it." Chelsea smiled as she snagged one of the cups of coffee Cullen had started when he first entered the kitchen. "I taught her well. You can thank me later. After I've had my coffee."

· C H A P T E R 1 4 ·

From Graeme's Journal
The Recessed Primal Breed

Ah, mates! Created with a heart and soul of such proud strength and wis-
dom. They are the Breeds' greatest treasures. For the Primal, they are the
only hope for sanity. The flame warming the icy logic only a monster can
possess—

Cullen almost breathed a sigh of relief when Chelsea finished her coffee, ceased baiting Graeme and declared she was heading for the
shower. He just knew that any moment the subject of the previous
day's attack would come up and Graeme would once again declare his
intention to go after Cerves, the cartel leader.

   And Chelsea was no one's fool. She'd instantly realize there wasn't a chance in hell Cullen was going to let the attack slide without some sort of retaliation as well.

Though his and Graeme's ideas of retaliation strongly differed.

When she left the room Cullen sat silently waiting as he heard the bathroom door close. He stared back at Graeme, then rested an arm on the table and pushed his coffee cup aside. He didn't bother to hide his irritation.

"She should be drinking decaf coffee," Graeme said, his gaze flicking to the coffee cup.

"She informed me yesterday morning that if caffeine was a problem, then up the dose of the injection," he scoffed, his lips coming close to an amused quirk at the memory. "She wasn't happy with either of us at the time either."

A noncommittal hum met the news as Graeme stared back at him knowingly.

"You have something on your mind, Cullen?" his brother finally asked. "I can practically feel your displeasure whipping through the room."

Was it displeasure he felt? He didn't think it was. Graeme had crossed a line this time and if he let it go, Cullen knew his twin would just push harder if the chance arose again.

When Cullen didn't immediately answer him, Graeme finally gave a heavy grimace before settling back in his chair and crossing his arms over his chest to scowl at him.

"Go ahead, little brother," he invited irately. "Get it off your chest."

Well, at least his brother hadn't called him a recessed little snot again.

"You will keep your monster contained where I'm concerned, Graeme." Cullen didn't demand it or make it an order, he made a statement of fact. "I don't need or ask for your retaliation as though defending a child from schoolyard bullies. Are we understood?"

He couldn't remember a single instance in their lives when Graeme had reacted so emotionally as to strike against him.

A grumbled, less-than-pleased growl rose from the other Breed's chest as his lip lifted in an irritated snarl.

"We made a pact long ago to defend each other," Graeme reminded him, his tone a warning grumble. "Have you forgotten that?"

His brother kept forgetting that those deep-throated sounds of dominant demand didn't work with Cullen. That only worked within a pack or pride when the one issuing it faced another, weaker Breed.

Cullen wasn't weaker, he just wasn't as crazy as his brother.

"The pact, if you will recall, was to watch each other's backs. To defend one another, as you pointed out at the time, would mean certain death. As would retaliation," Cullen injected without so much as a flicker in response when Graeme's growl deepened. "And don't pull that alpha shit on me, you know it doesn't work."

The labs beneath the Brandenmore Research Center had been a brutal hell most adults would have never survived, let alone two Breed young. The experiments conducted there had often sent both Graeme and Cullen howling in agony, when they were allowed to howl, when they weren't medically paralyzed from doing so. They'd also begged for death more often than not.

For a moment, Graeme's gaze dropped to the table, one finger smoothing over the deep indents his claws had made earlier. Breaking Cullen's gaze didn't mean he was submitting to his brother's demands in any way, and Cullen knew it. It was more a sign of the memories they shared of a brutal past.

Finally, Graeme gave a heavy, somber sigh.

"I won't try to explain the Primal's emergence, nor will I apologize for it," he finally said as he leveled his gaze back to Cullen. "I was out of town when the attack took place. I saw it on the news service no more than an hour before I arrived here." He gave his head a light shake, a frown furrowing his brow. "I went Primal the moment I saw you attempting to save your mate from Cerves's men." Mocking acknowledgment gleamed in his eyes. "At least I came here first rather than the Cerves compound as I would have in the past."

There was that, Cullen agreed, albeit silently.

"The very fact you did it concerns me more," Cullen admitted, still not certain how he felt about the explanation. "I thought you had control of the Primal since mating Cat."

Graeme had spent far too many years immersed with the insane rage of instincts so primitive they defied any attempts to understand them.

Graeme's lips quirked at the comment. "Well now, that was my belief as well," he said rather mockingly as he rubbed at the side of his face, bemusement flickering in his gaze. "As I said, it just happened. An anomaly, I would guess."

"An anomaly?" Cullen gave a snort of amazed disbelief at the description. "I know what you were doing, Graeme. I don't need to be watched over or protected. As I said, I'm a big boy now. I know how to take my own vengeance, if such is needed."

He'd learned how to kill before he was six, and after that, the creature they honed in those labs had learned how to do so with amazing effectiveness and complete secrecy.

"And if you end up dead because some bastard thinks he can take your mate, or worse, your mate and your child should she conceive?"

Graeme asked with a hint of anger now. "Am I allowed vengeance then?"

Cullen shook his head slowly; the fear of just that had raised its ugly head with Cerves's attack. If something were to happen to him, he didn't want his brother risking his life and his own mate's security for vengeance.

"If that happens, ensure Chelsea's and our child's safety, if she conceives." He blew out a hard breath as the thought of a child had his chest tightening almost painfully. "Vengeance is another matter, Graeme. Trying to place a shield around me won't be tolerated. Don't cross that line again. Especially not as the Primal."

The insanity that creature lived within was more than Cullen could bear the thought of. It was a place Graeme now needed to avoid at all costs. A sighting of the Bengal Primal, as he'd been described when his Primal genetics took over, would mean increased danger not just to Graeme but to his mate, Cat, as well. Breeds and the Council alike had once hunted the monster Graeme had been, and those years had only caused his brother to sink deeper into the insanity that held him in its grip at the time.

"No promises." Graeme shrugged, but Cullen read his twin's realization that it was now unacceptable. Then he leaned forward, bracing his forearms on the table, and glared at Cullen fiercely. "Do we go after Cerves together, or do I make my own plans? Because he and his Blood Queen will be brought to the realization that the continued good health and safety of you and your mate is in their best interests and those of their men. And that will happen with or without your approval or your partnership in the matter."

Because they were brothers, because Cullen and now Chelsea were important to Graeme as well as the Primal lurking within him.

That determined stance Cullen accepted. After all, he'd already made plans to find Cerves himself and secure the assurance that Chelsea would never be threatened by the cartel again.

"We can agree on that." Cullen nodded sharply. "Get your team together. I'll meet you at the caverns after I drop Chelsea off at her meeting at the Bureau. It's best if she—"

"Attends that meeting with you." Chelsea stepped into the kitchen from the corner of the hall, her arms crossing over her breasts as she stared back at him with such defiance he found himself making one of those testy, grating growls Graeme was so fond of.

"Not a good idea." He rose slowly to his feet, wondering the best way to handle the determined challenge in her gaze as well as her eavesdropping tendencies.

"Happening," she stated without anger. If she'd met his denial with anger, he might have been able to succeed in making her back down.

The fact that she wasn't becoming defensive over the matter assured him he was in trouble now that she knew his intentions.

Dammit, the idea was to protect her, not to draw her deeper into whatever danger seemed to be shadowing her.

"Not even on a bet," he promised her, though he didn't feel nearly as confident as he appeared and he knew it.

She was under his skin now. He realized that in a moment of such shocking clarity it was blinding. Under his skin, a part of him, and that weakened him, to the point that he knew rebuilding his defenses might not be very successful.

Chelsea stared back at Cullen, all too aware of Graeme's curious gaze as they squared off.

She had known, known to the soles of her feet that he was silently plotting something when she'd left the room. She could sense it, almost feel his intentions as he waited for her to leave the room.

And now she could feel him silently calculating the best way, exactly what to say, what to do, to ensure that she remained safely out of any vengeance he intended to exact.

As if she was going to stand back on this one. That was two attempts against her, and this time, they'd nearly succeeded. Whatever the hell was going on centered on her, not the operation she'd been working on. Cullen could just unruffle his Breed fur and get over this whole me-Tarzan-you-Jane attitude.

"Just a word of warning," she informed him with a scornful look before he had a chance to come back with an argument guaranteed to piss her off. "I will make certain you regret leaving me behind every miserable day of your existence if you do so."

"Emphasis on the 'miserable' there, bro," Graeme pointed out with less-than-helpful amusement.

A little help from his brother would have been nice, but it wasn't really expected. Though, come to think of it, she had no doubt Graeme's wife, Cat, would be right on his ass when he headed to the Cerves compound. Cat wasn't exactly the sit-at-home-and-be-safe type. And she'd be right by his side with his eager agreement, no doubt.

"Give it up, brother," Graeme advised him somberly as he rose to his feet, ignoring Cullen's glare. "Like Cat, her spirit is far too wild and independent to be caged. Keep her at your side instead, where you'll know she's safe from the trouble she might consider getting into. You'll be happier for it."

And keeping her out of danger was proving to be rather impossible, Cullen realized, not really certain how he felt about the situation. He'd spent so many years trying to protect her that he wasn't certain how to go about just watching her back, let alone allowing her to walk into danger with him.

Hell, it continued to amaze him that she didn't want to be protected or saved from the danger. She wanted to fight her own battles, and he was damned if he knew how to handle all that wild courage.

"Plan to be at the caverns early evening," Graeme stated then. "I'll text you the exact time later. I want to get some intel on Cerves first and see what we're looking at."

Moving to the back door, he shot Cullen a gloating smile. "See you and your mate later."

The door closed quietly behind him and did nothing to drown out his taunting laughter once he was outside.

"I knew you were plotting something devious before I ever left the room," Chelsea snapped as he rubbed at the back of his neck and shot her an implacable look. "I learned not to leave overprotective males alone together before I even hit my teens."

Her father and grandfather had been horrible about secretly trying to protect her. Plotting and calculating, always searching for ways to make certain there were protective eyes on her at all times. Her early teens were an exercise in just finding somewhere to breathe without someone counting each breath.

"Is that when you developed your eavesdropping tendencies?" he shot back, the brooding look on his face hiding more than it revealed. "It might occur to you one of these days that you're not invincible."

"I never imagined I was invincible." She arched her brow back at him smugly as she propped her hand on her hip, refusing to be intimidated by him. "What I am is well trained, and you damned well know it. Giving someone else control of my life isn't going to happen, Cullen. Not now, not ever. Not even you."

His eyes flared with anger then. "I don't want control. I want your safety."

"On your terms," she argued back, determined to remain calm. "On your terms, Cullen, not mine. Some trick of biology or chemistry may have ensured we're tied to each other, and I understand you hate the hell out of it, but I will not sit back and be something or someone I'm not. Even for you."

The chemical reaction wouldn't dictate her life; she'd already made that decision. She could handle being tied to him sexually for the time being, but she wasn't counting on him to stick around because she knew he didn't want to be here to begin with.

"And if you end up dead because of something I could have prevented?" he asked, a haunted, shadowed look crossing his expression. "What then?"

"Then unlike your first wife, I promise not to blame you," she said, knowing the look for what it was. "I never asked you to save me, Cullen. I just wanted to fight beside you. If I can't have that much of you, at least, then what use is a mating or anything else between us? I accept you for the asshole you are; the least you can do is accept me for the woman I am rather than the woman you can't forget."

Lifting her chin with a small amount of pride, she turned on her heel and stalked back to the bedroom, and no doubt the shower, her accusation ringing in his ears.

She thought he wanted Lauren back? That his need to protect her had something to do with whatever he might have once felt for his dead wife? And as much as the accusation stung, as much as he hated it, he wondered if she had a point.

Not so much that he wanted his wife back, because that wasn't the case. Even had a cure for her disease been found, their relationship had ended the day she had flung her knowledge of his Breed status in his face and accused him of not loving her enough to cure her. He'd told her he was a Breed before their wedding, unwilling to go into their marriage with any secrets between them. Just as he'd explained what recessive Breed genetics were. But, he'd realized later, she'd already known.

The tabloid stories had fed her belief that Mating Heat could cure her. The revelation that Chelsea's uncle Ray had been aiding the Genetics Council resulted in the proof that Ray had actually pushed Lauren into believing the stories. Ray had preyed on Lauren's fears and her desperation to live, with the information he'd gained on mating and the mating hormone's ability to reverse diseases most often incurable.

The final year of Lauren's life had been hell on both her and Cullen. She'd been so desperate to live, and he'd understood that desperation. But a Breed didn't control mating; he couldn't call it up or force its retreat. And in her final moments that knowledge had consumed her with rage.

After her death, Cullen had deliberately isolated himself, not because of the overwhelming grief everyone assumed, but because he couldn't forget that he had loved her when they married, only to pay the ultimate price for giving someone that much of himself.

Even here, in the house he'd bought after Lauren's death, he'd kept his life as barren as possible. He'd worked, slept and ate when he needed to. He'd fucked when the urge couldn't be denied, but he hadn't formed relationships.

The sound of the shower was a faint pulse of life in the house and Chelsea's presence a vivid splash of color against the dull shadows of the rooms.

She too was a reminder of his failures, though, in some ways. Because she was his mate, and that wild independence she possessed wasn't going to change. It was such a part of her that she'd never be able to contain it. And because Lauren had known that even though she wasn't his mate, still, she had known his mate was close.

"Who's your mate? I know she's close to you. Do you think I don't feel her stealing my chance to live?" she screamed out in rage, her face twisting with it. *"I won't let you have her, Cullen. I swear to you I'll reach out from the grave and destroy both of you."*

The smell of her desperation, her pain, sank inside him like a bitter breath.

He inhaled wearily; the memory of his hopelessness at that time, of her lost hope and ever-deepening terror as death neared, was a reminder of his failure of his wife.

Of his duty to her.

God knew he had understood her desperation to live, to survive. The spirit would fight for life at all costs in most situations. Even then, despite his own feelings of betrayal, if he could have saved her, then he would have. And every day he'd thanked God that the mating couldn't come alive because of guilt alone.

"I'll never let you have her," Lauren whispered just before she slipped into a drugged sleep. *"Do you hear me, Cullen? I'll never let you have her. All you had to do was mate me. All you had to do was save me from this and I would have let you go."* Hatred gleamed in her eyes before they filled with terror and tears once again. *"You were my only hope."* She'd believed that if he'd just loved her, then that would be all it took.

Nature wasn't nearly that kind, though, was it?

He was a Breed; his life had been filled with the knowledge of his and other Breeds' agony and terrors on a daily basis while in the research facility. What he'd sensed from Lauren in those final weeks before her death was a bleak addition to those memories.

The ringing of his sat phone pulled him from his musings and back to the present. Pulling the device from his back pocket, he slid it open after checking the caller ID and greeted the caller.

"Ranger? What's up?" His second in command had charge of the Agency until Cullen's return.

Whenever that might be.

"We have a problem." Fury filled his second's tone as it came over the line. "Dammit all to hell, Cullen, someone got to Morales, the surviving cartel assailant. They just found him in his cell, his throat cut. We hadn't even had a chance to interrogate him yet."

Cullen stilled, the fingers of his other hand curling into fists as they literally ached to slam into something.

"How the hell did that happen?" he snapped back with brutal fury. "Did you pull security coverage?"

"Techs say it was jammed during the time he was taken out." Ranger's voice shook with his own anger. "We took every precaution and the cartel still got to him."

There was no reason for Cerves to come after his own man and take him out. If the story the assailant had given them at the scene was true, then he didn't have much information to begin with. Cerves would be the one with details, not the muscle he used to get the job done.

"Pull in our contacts, see if there's anything out there about the murder. I want to know why, Ranger, and I want to know now. Let me know as soon as you find out anything."

"How's Chelsea doing?" Disgust still rang in the other man's tone. "And I didn't get a chance to tell you Lauren's parents came by Nation headquarters looking for you yesterday."

"They caught up with me," Cullen grunted. "And Chelsea's doing fine. Bruised and sore, but nothing that won't heal in time." Except the memory of it.

"Yeah," Ranger sighed. "The Holdens showed up at the house, then?"

"They were waiting with Chelsea's family when I pulled in the drive," Cullen told him heavily as he swiped his fingers through his hair and paced to the kitchen window, frowning as he stared into the desert beyond his house. "They stayed for a while."

"Damn," Ranger muttered. "How did they handle Chelsea being with you? You haven't really had a relationship since Lauren's death."

No, he hadn't. The knowledge that Lauren had deceived him so easily had been too fresh for those first years. Afterward, he'd been too busy running from that gut-deep hunger for Chelsea that he couldn't seem to escape.

"We didn't discuss it," Cullen informed him, his words clipped, cold. "Look, I need to go. Find out what the hell happened with Morales, and do it fast. I want to know who's targeted Chelsea, and I want to know why. That's priority." Not Lauren's parents or a past he couldn't change.

"Got it, boss," Ranger sighed. "I'll check in tomorrow one way or the other. You still have her Breed security for backup?"

"Backup's taken care of." Cullen stared outside, wondering what the hell was causing the disquiet inside him as he searched for any movement.

"Good to know. Call if you need me."

The line disconnected.

Absently, Cullen slid the phone closed and returned it to his back pocket, realizing his eyesight was sharpening even as he let it rove over the early-morning landscape.

The sound of the shower pulled his attention from anything that might be outside and back to the woman ripping apart his nerves of steel. Instantly, his cock was hard, throbbing, pressing against his jeans with imperative demand. The scent of her filled his head, the faintest hint of her subtle heat, her arousal, reaching him as his tongue began to itch.

He could feel the awakening of his animal senses as he hadn't before; the stillness of it since he'd arrived at the house with Chelsea the day before was over. There were no great revelations, merely an awareness that when those instincts awakened he was fully merged with them. His senses were stronger with that awakening, more intuitive; answers came to him faster, sight, scent, taste and touch revealing far more than they had before.

Turning, he stalked toward the bedroom; the knowledge that Chelsea was holding back from him was startlingly clear. He'd felt it during each confrontation they'd had, just as he'd felt it before dawn when she took him with such need. The need was physical, hollow, lacking the emotion he knew was there. And the instincts riding him weren't going to allow it to go on.

If he didn't secure her heart, he'd lose her anyway. If he didn't find a way to push past whatever barrier he could feel between them, then neither of them would find any peace in their life together.

He was dominant enough, secure enough in his own sense of self that he knew he'd never be satisfied with this half a mating they seemed to have. Cullen did nothing halfway, and he damned sure wasn't going to start with his mate.

· C H A P T E R   1 5 ·

From Graeme's Journal
Recessed Primal Genetics and Mating Heat

A mate forced to wait is a mate whose retribution can sear with the hottest flames and show the Breed the dangers of ignoring the nature of his beast—

Chelsea was just out of the shower, a towel still wrapped around her damp body, when Cullen stepped into the bedroom, his gaze hooded as he closed the door and watched her silently. She hadn't expected him to be pleased with her determination to participate in his planned visit to the Cerves compound, but this distant silence wasn't expected either.

Nor was it wanted.

He let himself believe she didn't know how he felt about protecting her, but she did. She knew the type of man who held her heart. His sense of honor, his need for justice. He was a loner, too intense at times, arrogant and far too self-confident, but that was his nature. That confidence came from experience, training and the sense of honor that filled him.

"I don't want to argue with you, Cullen." She didn't want to have to feel as though she was a disappointment to him any longer.

"Don't you?" he asked her, the rasp of his voice warning her that a growl was on the horizon.

Breeds and those growls. They seemed to think that was all they had to do to get their way.

She shook her head at the question. "I've never wanted to argue with you." She held her hands out to him for a moment before gripping the front of the towel once again. "We're not going to agree on this." She'd realized that while she was in the shower. A bitter smile tipped her lips. "And do you know what? I can't even figure out why this mating thing even happened with us."

They were so incompatible . . .

Her eyes widened, lips parting nervously as the growling sounds rumbled with such feral warning she couldn't help but take notice this time.

As he stared at her, the simmering arousal that didn't seem to ever completely ease away began to build in her body. The reaction didn't really seem unnatural, it was just a little stronger than it had been over the years anyway.

Gripping the towel tighter, Chelsea stared back at him, watching as his gaze began to burn with lust. Swallowing past the nervousness building in her throat, she licked her suddenly dry lips and tried to control her escalating breathing. It wasn't easy to do, especially when he sat down in the chair next to the door and removed his boots and socks.

Standing once again, he stripped his shirt off, tossed it to the floor and then with swift, economical movements loosened his jeans and shed them as well.

Chelsea completely lost her breath then. She hadn't taken the time to really look at the body that gave her such pleasure, until now.

His chest was broad, his abs flat and muscular. Long, powerful legs were tense, the muscles at his thighs rippling. Between those thighs his erection stood out, thick and heavy. The dark head pulsed with the lust surging through the erect shaft, the heavy veins throbbing in tandem with it.

As her eyes widened, Cullen stepped to her and hauled her into his arms, his lips covering hers in an explosion of pure hunger.

Cinnamon exploded against her taste buds as his tongue surged between her lips. Invading, licking, stroking over hers as flaming need rushed through her senses. Just as quickly he pulled back, ignoring her cry of protest. Instead, his lips brushed over her jaw and moved to her neck, scraping over sensitive nerve endings before moving to the mark he'd left at her shoulder.

There, he actually bit her. Not enough to pierce her skin, just enough to send flashing arcs of pleasure racing through her senses. Before she could process the sensual attack it was gone and she found herself pushed back on the mattress.

He groaned, pushing her legs apart before sliding between them. "I dreamed about eating this sweet little pussy for years, do you know that?"

He had? Chelsea stared down at him dazed, because he'd never given her so much as a look to indicate it.

The thought scattered as his head lowered, his greedy lips and tongue tasting her sex with hungry demand.

A rumbled growl vibrated against her clit and sent a pulse of ecstasy to attack her vagina. Chelsea tangled her hands in his hair, the sudden blistering pleasure difficult to process as his tongue circled the sensitive bud. Licking over it, around it, he toyed with it before drawing it between his lips and sucking firmly.

Her orgasm surged through her with a suddenness that was breathtaking. The detonation rippled to her pussy and convulsed her womb. Her juices spilled from her and just as quickly, he was there.

Licking, lapping at the heated moisture, his tongue pressed inside her entrance, his groan sent a vibration of scalding pleasure against her sensitive flesh as he tongued her with quick, rapid strokes. Each hungry thrust of his tongue had her crying out for more, her senses rioting out of control again.

"Cullen," she sobbed, her hips jerking against his mouth.

Fiery, ecstatic, she climaxed again in surging waves as her hips bucked against each stabbing thrust and hungry lick.

The blinding intensity of pleasure came from more than just the act, though, and Chelsea knew it. It wasn't just the sensual, erotic touch alone unraveling her. It was what he did to her each time he took her. That feeling that each time he took her, he possessed more of her heart had a part of her soul shaking in terror.

"This is all I've thought about, all I've ached for, for years." His voice rasped with a rough, dark hunger that had her trembling at the need in it. "Damn you, you've made me crazy."

Rising between her thighs, he stared down at her, his gaze fiery, sweat-dampened features flushed, lips moist from her juices.

Panting, fighting for air, Chelsea stared up at him, dazed as she watched him fighting for control. Cullen? Fighting for control? Until this moment he had been the most controlled person she had ever known.

Before she could make sense of that change, he moved over her, gripping the heavy shaft of his cock and guiding it to the slick, swollen folds between her thighs. They parted over the broad head, opening for him, embracing him as he pressed the engorged crest between them.

Watching, drunk on the pleasure, she trembled at Cullen's sudden desperate need, and she watched as he began taking her.

"I can't be easy this time." His breaths were sawing in and out of his lungs. "Ah hell, baby, I can't be easy."

Easy wasn't what she wanted, though.

Her head ground into the blankets beneath her as he began pushing inside her. Short, quick thrusts parted the sensitive inner tissue. Flashing pleasure-pain struck at her nerve endings and ricocheted through her system.

"So fucking hot," he bit out between gritted teeth, his expression savage, hewn in lines of fierce male pleasure.

Chelsea's hips bucked into each deeper stroke, crying out at the rapture beginning to whip inside her. Stretching her, filling her, he worked his cock inside the snug channel until he completely filled her, possessing her body and, she feared, her soul.

◆　◆　◆

Ah hell, she was so tight, so hot. It was all he could do to hold back to ensure her pleasure, until he relinquished that final thread of control and lost himself inside her.

She writhed beneath him, perspiration dewing her flushed features, her gaze slitted, staring back at him, dazed with the rushing pleasure he was giving her.

He was buried inside her to the hilt, her sweet flesh gripping and milking his dick, destroying him.

Fuck, what had happened to him? He had more control than this and he knew it. Where had it gone?

His breathing was erratic; flaming pleasure engulfed his senses. It was so extreme he was on the verge of shaking, trembling in her grip as he felt her pussy rippling around his erection.

He was steel hard inside her, his dick so engorged, so fucking hard he had to grit his teeth to keep from pounding inside her like a maniac.

"Fuck, you feel good, Chelsea," he groaned, pulling back, the already snug channel tightening around him further as though to hold him inside her. "All I can think about is fucking you, touching you, tasting you."

Finesse was not happening and he knew it the moment he slammed inside her again, feeling her hips jerk, her pussy grasping him, milking at the tortured length of his cock.

Her expression was drowsy, pleasure-drugged, as he stared down at her, a wave of possessiveness gripping his chest as he paused again, loving the way her pussy flexed and rippled around his cock. The feel of it pulled another groan from his chest as destructive waves of nearing rapture raked through his senses and tightened his balls.

What the hell did she do him? What was she doing to him? Mating Heat was physical, it had nothing to do with emotion; it couldn't, could it? Yet no matter how hard he fought he could feel her pushing at the walls he'd built around his soul.

The tiny glands beneath his tongue were doing more than itching now. They were swollen, inflamed with the mating hormone as he tasted the heated essence of it.

Thrusting inside her, he gritted his teeth as he fought to hold back, to relish each stroke of his cock in her sweet pussy; he knew he couldn't keep from kissing her much longer and sharing the drugging essence of the mating hormone.

One hand grabbed her hip, a snarl of frustration tearing from his chest, Cullen lowered his head as his thrusts became harder, deeper, and brushed his lips over hers.

"Kiss me, baby," he growled, his tongue aching for the warmth of that kiss. "Take all of me."

She moaned against his lips, her hands gripping his biceps, nails pricking his flesh as her lips parted, her tongue meeting his as he stroked past the sweet curves.

The cinnamon taste infusing his senses intensified as his tongue stroked over hers. Then her lips surrounded it, suckled at the taste, once, twice, pulling it free in a rich flood of exquisite heat.

Cullen slanted his lips over hers, his tongue plunging into her mouth as a growl tore from his chest. His hand tightened at her hip as the last thread of control unraveled.

Her knees lifted to clasp his hips as he began stroking inside her hard and deep, furious, desperate strokes as Chelsea writhed beneath him, hips lifting for each lunge of his erection inside the snug depths of her body. Her wild cries of building ecstasy intensified the blistering pleasure tearing through him as he fought to hold back his release. Just another minute. Just a few more strokes—

He wasn't going to last and Cullen knew it. And he wanted it to last. Needed it to last. He wanted the sweet heated depths of her pussy consuming him forever.

Sweat dripped from his forehead, and his balls drew up to the base of his cock as he slammed inside her, over and over. The need to come, to fill her, to mark her senses and her flesh, was suddenly so imperative, filled with such primal demand that as he felt her orgasm exploding through her, his lips tore from hers. He covered the mark at the bend of her shoulder and neck and rather than just gripping it, he felt the longer canines pierce her flesh instead.

The faint coppery taste of her blood was overshadowed by the cinnamon taste of the hormone. His tongue lapped at the wound as he released his grip on her, feeling her jerking, shuddering beneath him.

A second later a snarl tore from him as his release ripped through him with an explosion that shattered his senses to hell and back.

Thrusting deep, he arched his back as a band of pure rapture tightened around his dick. The mating barb extended, the ultrasensitive erection emerging and locking inside the convulsing depths of her vagina as the explosion shook him to the core.

He jerked with each heavy spurt of semen erupting from his cock.

The agonizing pleasure shooting through him was euphoric, his release so deep, so strong he wondered if he'd survive the aftermath. Because in that moment he realized Chelsea might well hold more of his soul than he could safely live without if he lost her.

◆　◆　◆

What the hell happened?

How had it happened?

Trying to process the physical and emotional quagmire he found himself in wasn't easy for Cullen.

Hell, dealing with his emotions had always been something he avoided at all costs. Breeds were stripped of emotions at an early age for the most part, the horrors of their creation and their training teaching them quickly that emotions meant not just the death of one Breed, but littermates as well.

The scientists and trainers had learned early that even if their emotions were suppressed, Breeds were incredibly loyal to littermates. They depended on one another, silently—they learned early to hide it, but those who oversaw them caught on quickly.

Breeds knew that if one of them escaped, then those littermates would pay the price. Any attempts to escape resulted in the young being viciously beaten or tortured to death as the offending Breed was forced to watch.

It was a brutal world they'd been created to be a part of, a world so many hadn't survived. Only the strongest and most cunning of those created lived to see freedom.

Freedom hadn't given Cullen the luxury of learning how to deal with everything he'd been taught to push back and ignore, though.

Less than six months after being brought to the Navajo Nation and given a new identity, a new life, he'd met Lauren and married. The next two years had brutalized the few emotions he'd allowed free. When it was over he had forced it all back and returned to his training feeling the least amount of emotion possible.

And that was why when Chelsea came to work for him at the Covert Law Enforcement Agency, she'd so fascinated him. Because Chelsea seemed to feel everything. She could give him a blank stare and pop off a smart-ass comment while her amusement would reach out to him, stroking against him like the whisper of a summer breeze. Or she could narrow her eyes, those pretty lips thinning, and the summer breeze would turn to a blast of fiery anger.

She didn't wear her emotions on her sleeve, though. Cullen doubted anyone besides a Breed could even detect the subtle scents and signs she gave off unless she wanted them to.

She was a strong woman, didn't take offense easily and watched the world with interest and a desire to live that terrified him.

And she kept her word.

That was one thing Cullen admitted he'd been surprised by when she came to work for him. If she said she would do it, she did it. If she gave him a report, then it was, to the word, an accurate accounting of what happened.

So why the hell was he having such a hard time figuring out what the hell she was feeling now? He'd assumed with the Mating Heat that she loved him, but not once had she mentioned the L word or asked for anything resembling a commitment.

Hell, she was still giving the impression that the mating and Cullen were more an inconvenience in her life than anything else. If it weren't for the pleasure he knew she felt and the fact that she said all she'd asked for was to work and fight beside him, he'd have assumed that nature had finally been fucked in her judgment.

Now, two days later, sitting next to her in a borrowed sedan as she made adjustments to her telephoto sunglasses, he found himself clenching his teeth, again, until his jaw hurt.

She was completely focused on those damned glasses despite the fact that the scent of her arousal in the closed vehicle had him so hard again, his cock so engorged, it was all he could do to stay in a sitting position.

"You want to explain to me why we're sitting outside the police station rather than going in?" he asked, realizing he wasn't hiding his testiness.

And he did feel highly testy.

He still hadn't figured out how she'd talked him into this.

He wanted to keep her safely hidden in the house, with Draeger, Tobias and Graeme's men covering them, watching for any dangers slipping up on them. There, he had his safe egress and means of protecting her that he wouldn't have anywhere else.

"These glasses are on loan from the Bureau." As she turned to him, he met her gaze through the dark lenses.

He was impressed. There was nothing to distinguish them from a regular pair of sunglasses.

"Nice," he answered cautiously. "But you still haven't answered me."

She grinned back at him before focusing on the electronic pad she held on her lap.

"The camera built into the lenses themselves has a camera, video and audio. The experimental nanotechnology will follow my eye movements and record and store everything to the e-pad as long as it's connected." She tapped the e-pad. "I can do what I do without you standing over my shoulder growling. And you can keep an eye on me and assure yourself I'm safe."

Looking from the entrance of the police department then back to her, Cullen gave her a mocking chuckle and shook his head.

"You actually believe I'm letting you go in there alone?" Now, wasn't she just the little optimist? "And stop rolling your eyes at me."

Those sunglasses didn't nearly hide her eyes enough to keep his Breed eyesight from detecting the movement.

"I'm a big girl, Cullen," she drawled. "I can take care of myself. Didn't you say something similar to Graeme this morning when you learned he was trying to protect you?"

The little arch of a brow over the frame of the lens assured him he hadn't misheard the sarcasm in her voice.

Trust her to bite his ass with that lecture he'd given Graeme.

"Chelsea—" He counted to ten.

He made it to five.

"Cullen." She interrupted his count as she said his name in a tone so sweet it could have been candy. "If you go in with me, no one's going to talk to me. You glare at everyone."

He was definitely going to end up cracking a molar, his jaw was so tight.

"And there's not a man in that station who's going to believe I've let you out of my sight long enough to question them about anything after that attack on you the day before yesterday," he tried to point out. "The world saw me trying to pull you out of that mess. And those men know me." He pointed his finger to the department in a stabbing motion. "They'll be suspicious."

Her laugh had his cock jerking in far too much interest at the challenge he heard in the sound.

"I bet they like me much better," she informed him with a smirk. "And they'll be expecting me. Without you." Tilting the glasses down her nose, she peeked at him over the frames, her brown eyes sparkling mischievously. "Why do you think Ranger always sent me to question the investigating officers whenever the two of you needed statements? Hell, Ranger's probably sitting on his ass waiting on me to send him my report so he can call you and give his report. No doubt that's why he hasn't managed to send it to you yet."

He was going to kick Ranger's ass if that actually happened. Not that he doubted Chelsea's word, because he didn't. And he knew the reports from the Navajo police were not nearly as in-depth and detailed as they had been when Chelsea was there.

He rubbed his hand over his face, frustration eating at his insides. He didn't want her going in there alone for several reasons, not the least of which, because he knew most of those men in there too and he knew they were damned perverts.

"So all you have to do is watch the screen while I go do my thing," she suggested.

Every human and Primal instinct inside him reared its head in pure male jealousy.

"While you do what thing?" he bit out, keeping his expression carefully calm.

Even his fingernails were aching, he was so tense.

Feminine outrage filled the car with the scent of her offended pride now.

"Really, Cullen?" she asked him with a little insulting curl of her lip. "Don't worry, I promise to keep my pants on. I'm a little shy like that. Especially in public places."

"Dammit, I didn't mean to say that." Patience. He just needed to hold on to his patience. "That attack was too coordinated. We already know there's a price on your head. The closer I am to you, the more I can help you and keep the third attack from succeeding. You're making me crazy here, Chelsea."

"Of course your craziness is all my fault." She gave a bitter little snort of laughter as she turned forward and breathed in slow and deep. It did nothing to still the scent of her outrage and ire, though.

When she turned back to him and removed the glasses, meeting his gaze with cool brown eyes, in that second he knew that if he went with his instincts and followed her, he would damage a part of the relationship he wanted with her and it might not be repairable.

"I'm walking in there alone," she informed him, her voice clipped. "You can watch or you can go home. Follow me and when you do go home, you'll be returning without me."

Slapping the e-pad on his thigh with enough force to draw an irritated growl from his throat, she stared back at him demandingly.

Chelsea knew how to talk to people, he knew that. More important, she knew how to get them talking, how to get information that even those she was talking to didn't realize was pertinent.

Detectives tended to give Cullen only what they thought he wanted, just as he gave them.

But letting her go in there alone was grating on his instincts like nails over a chalkboard.

"Do you have any idea how much I'll worry?" He tried to make her understand his need to make certain she wasn't harmed.

Her anger eased, but the scent of resigned acceptance replaced it.

"Do you know I worried when you were in the field?" she asked him then, staring back at him as the soft scent of remembered fear reached his nostrils. "But I remained at the office, where you said you needed me. Now I'm telling you, you go in there with me and there's not a chance in hell I'm going to get anyone to talk to me."

In that moment he knew he'd lost this argument.

A grimace tightened his jaw further.

"Stop grinding your teeth," she advised him with a little flip of her hand. "Before you crack a molar."

Pushing the glasses back over her eyes, she left the vehicle, slammed the door behind her and jogged across the street.

Alone.

And he hated it.

From Graeme's Journal
The Recessed Primal Breed

---

*The Primal, once active, will never rest, will never sleep, unless his mate is
close enough to touch . . . Only then is she close enough to always protect.*

Chelsea tried to assure herself that she was handling the situation with
Cullen the best way possible. After all, if they were going to have any
peace in everyday life after the danger was over, then she needed to
establish her independence early in the game.

Cullen had no idea how much she would have preferred to have
him at her back as she jogged across the street and into the police
department. Not to mention being enclosed in the elevator with several
unknown men. But if she let herself think about the danger she was

in, then the fear would creep in. A fear that would leave her in the shower shaking from the inside out again. So she didn't let herself think about it, didn't let herself consider it.

She did what she'd done so many other times as Cullen's assistant and used her friendship with the officers and detectives she knew to get the information she needed.

And everyone was willing to talk to her once they realized she was there.

The detectives for the most part were friends of the family. A few she'd actually grown up with and been friends with most of her life.

The news that the only surviving assailant, Hector Morales, had been killed while in police custody shocked her when Cullen had told her about it. To get to Morales it had to have been an inside job. Someone at the department either had helped the murderer or committed the act themselves.

And she couldn't imagine any of the detectives or officers she knew actually killing a prisoner. She suspected several were on Cerves's payroll. That suspicion was even stronger after talking to them. She didn't get the sense they were involved in killing the prisoner, though.

She'd been there over two hours, the sunglasses hanging from the front of her blouse rather than on top of her head. A few of the braver officers actually copped a look at her breasts. She could just imagine Cullen growling each time it happened.

Unfortunately there weren't many details to be found on Morales's death. It happened sometime after three in the morning. The guard on duty at the security cameras reported a technical problem when the screens filled with static, and when the cameras came back up minutes later, Morales was dead.

He'd had no visitors, made no calls, hadn't had a cell mate and no one had seemed overtly interested in him other than their amazement that Chelsea had been the intended victim. Though he might have scuffled with a few of the officers at some point. Officers who didn't appreciate the fact that Chelsea had been targeted.

"I don't know what to say, Chelsea." Dylan Rowe pushed his fingers through his short black hair, disgust glittering in his dark eyes.

He was several years older than Chelsea, an experienced investigator, and Chelsea had always trusted him in the past. Still handsome, and in good shape if the fit of his jeans and gray dress shirt were any indication. His thick, coarse black hair had a raven's sheen, and his black eyes were invariably filled with amusement.

At this moment, his gaze was somber, though, frustration gleaming in it as he tossed a copy of the report on Morales's death toward her.

"What about forensics?" she asked as she picked up the file, leaned against his desk and opened it, a frown creasing her brow.

There was nothing there, just as he'd said.

"Nada." Leaning back in his chair, hands clasped behind his neck, he shook his head decisively. "The final report isn't in yet, but my sister's a tech at the lab. I talked to her earlier." He shot Chelsea a quick grin, his craggy features filling with amusement. "She says hi, by the way."

Tara had been a hell-raiser in school.

"Tell her she still has my favorite pair of boots," she laughed.

Dylan chuckled at the message. "She said you'd remember those boots." Then he sighed heavily, lowered his arms and shook his head. "I wish I had more."

"What about your informants, Dylan?" she asked him. "What are they telling you?"

"Informants? In the Cerves cartel?" His eyes widened. "Really, Chelsea?"

She snorted at the false innocence.

"Tell that to someone who doesn't know how you work," she suggested knowingly. "Come on, Dylan, I know you have them."

He grimaced at the statement before glancing to the door. When he turned back to her, speculation lit his gaze.

"From what I understand, hell hath no fury like Samara Cerves since her daughter Louisa's death. Even my informants were surprised when Morales and his men tried to abduct you. The Blood Queen and her family have been completely focused on finding the girl who snatched her kid from those Coyotes. Samara hasn't cared about contracts coming in no matter how much money's attached to them. All she wants is to find that girl and kill as many Council soldiers and Breeds as possible," he snorted. "She's racking up numbers there."

Chelsea stared down at the file, making certain her expression didn't show a reaction. "She ever find out who rescued the little girl?"

"Whoever that chick was, she's a fucking ghost," he stated with a short sniff of laughter. "Crashed the gates and the minute Samara and her men turned their backs, she was gone like the wind. All anyone knows is that the vehicle carried the Breed Underground insignia." He gave a short little shake of his head and another snort of laughter as he glanced up at her, that laughter gleaming in his eyes. "Has the locals spouting tales about the Unknown again, though. So at least the crazies are being kept busy with something."

She had to laugh at that. The Unknown weren't the legends everyone believed they were, but she didn't care one bit to have them taking the credit for Louisa's rescue.

They were indeed like ghosts, though. So much a part of the land that they were almost invisible.

"It was a shame about that baby, though," Dylan sighed, compassion filling his expression. "Whoever the girl is, she deserves a medal, not the fury Samara Cerves is exploding with in her search for her. She's crazy enough to kill her if she gets her hands on her, though."

"Why?" Chelsea asked, laying the file on his desk and distracting his attention from her face.

"Because the kid died." He scratched at his cheek, bemusement flickering over his face. "I guess she's getting the heat for that, same as the Council Breeds the Blood Queen's rounding up. Anyway." He breathed out roughly as he leaned back in his chair again and gave her a heavy look. "I find out anything else, Chelsea, you'll be the first to know. But that's all I can give you right now."

That promise was all she was going to get today, and Chelsea knew it.

"Thanks, Dylan, I appreciate it," she told him as he rose to his feet.

Lifting her hand in farewell, Chelsea left the office, frustration eating at her as she started down the hall to the bank of elevators.

Someone had to have seen something or someone where Hector Morales was concerned, yet if they had, they weren't telling the tale.

"Hey, Chelsea, hold up." A familiar male voice calling out behind her had her stopping and turning quickly.

She smiled at the dark-haired, lanky agent heading up the hall toward her. Cute in a studious kind of way, usually too quiet and rarely in a hurry, Ranger shot her a quick grin.

"Ranger. Are you here to get Cullen's report?" She smiled at Cullen's second in command.

He strode toward her, looking comfortable in his relaxed jeans, scuffed boots and nicely pressed white shirt, the sleeves rolled back along his forearms.

"Me?" His brows lifted and despite the teasing tone she could see a glimmer of seriousness in his gaze. "Hell, I was hoping you'd have already taken care of that. I just dropped in to see if Marcy wanted to have dinner this evening."

Marcy was his longtime girlfriend. Very longtime.

"Not this time, my friend," she answered, very well aware Cullen was listening to every word. "If I write one I'll send you a copy, though," she teased, knowing how badly he hated getting those reports.

"I'll expect it in a few hours." He wasn't teasing. "You're killing me with this resignation thing. I spend more time here than I do in the office now, and the officers here don't like me near as much as they like you."

Ranger hated getting intel for Cullen out of the detectives.

"Grow boobs," she snickered. "That's all they require. Their brains stop and their mouths start. They're really kind of cute when it happens." And those officers made a running joke of it.

Ranger grimaced good-naturedly. "I told Cullen he made a mistake letting you go. I was hoping this thing you two are doing meant you'd come back."

This thing they were doing?

"I wouldn't bet on it. And I better be going, Ranger." She laughed, determined to leave before he managed to piss her totally off with his comments about her and Cullen's "thing."

"You heading down, then?" He gestured to the end of the hall.

"Yeah, I have a few more things I need to get done today," she told him. "You?"

"I'm still waiting for Marcy." He frowned thoughtfully. "Can we talk for a minute?"

That probably wasn't a good idea, but she had no idea how to get out of it without offending him.

"Sure." She shrugged, pasting a smile on her face. "Is everything okay?"

For a second indecision flushed across his handsome face before it cleared, his features settling into determined lines.

"I know you're staying with Cullen," he finally said, his tone heavy with concern.

Uh-oh, this so was not a good idea.

"Ranger—" She tried to protest.

"Listen to me for a minute, Chelsea." He reached out as though to stop her before pulling his hand back. "Look, there's things you don't know, honey, and I don't want you getting your heart broken over him." Oh God, she didn't want to do this. This was Cullen's friend. He was probably Cullen's only true friend.

"You're making a mistake, Ranger. Let's not discuss this right now, okay?" She tried to warn him. "Your concerns are noted and I promise I'll be just fine."

"You're so damned stubborn." He grimaced. "But you're my friend and I don't want to see you hurt. Okay?"

"I won't get hurt . . ."

"I know you think you love him." He sighed, talking over her as he stared down at her imploringly. "And I know you think he can love you, but it won't happen, honey. Losing Lauren broke something inside Cullen. You'll always be second best and you deserve more than that. You know you do."

Now, this was bad. Cullen was not going to appreciate this advice coming from his friend. He was going to be pissed. Hell, he was probably already pissed.

"Stop, Ranger. We're not doing this." She turned to rush to the elevators, determined to stop the train wreck.

"Wait, Chelsea, please." He stepped in front of her, blocking her way, his face creasing in regret. "He's a hard man . . ."

"And he's your friend, he wouldn't appreciate this and I don't want to hear it." Tightening her grip on the strap of her pack, she fought to hold on to her temper. "And it won't make a difference. I do what I want to do. Period. Now good-bye."

"Come on, Chelsea, you really believe that? You're Lauren's cousin, and he loved her. That's why he brought you into the office, that reminder of her. You're a stand-in for her, nothing more." The shocking statement had her pausing.

"I look nothing like her." She pushed out the words between gritted teeth. "I am nothing like her. That has to be one of the most ridiculous things I have ever heard come out of your mouth. It's right up there with accusing me of wanting your job when Cullen first hired me. It's idiotic."

Working with Ranger had never been easy, but he'd never gone this far before either.

"You're so stubborn." Ranger shook his head in disappointment. "You know, he and Lauren knew about that little crush you had on him when you were a teenager. They laughed about it then. How pathetic you were watching him with those puppy dog eyes all the time. You're just as pathetic now."

She wasn't listening to any more of this. She couldn't. Pushing past him, Chelsea strode quickly to the elevators, intent on catching the one slowly sliding open.

As the doors revealed the interior of the cubicle, she froze in shock as Cullen stepped out, gripped her arm and pulled her inside without saying a word.

And he was furious.

His eyes were flat and hard, the green darker, the amber flecks more pronounced. And she swore he looked taller, broader as he stood beside her after punching the key for the first floor.

Chelsea restrained a groan of pure frustration. She'd actually forgotten about those damned glasses as Ranger kept running his mouth. Geez, she'd known he was a moron for years, but he'd really outdone himself this time.

But despite the hurtful words, she knew, in his own way, he was just trying to protect her.

Sort of.

Like the detectives and officers at the department, she'd known him all her life. And like her family he had a tendency to be overprotective and a little too free with his advice.

Whether she wanted it or not.

Whether she could handle it or not.

Reaching the first floor, Cullen led her firmly from the elevator and through the lobby, ignoring the greetings called out to him from several of the officers and lawyers he passed.

He was more furious than she'd ever seen him. But she really wasn't so happy herself. Not with him or with Ranger.

Reaching the car, Cullen pulled open the passenger door, and once she was inside he closed it with enough force that she winced.

The drive back to his house was anything but comfortable. The tension sizzled around him, heavy enough that a weaker-willed woman would have drowned in it.

Pulling in behind the house, he shut off the vehicle, and rather than waiting for him to open her door she let herself out of the car, ignoring his dark look.

As they entered the house he closed that door loudly behind them as well.

Wow, she'd never heard him slam doors before.

"Graeme canceled the meeting again," he told her, his tone a dangerous rasp of fury. "Cerves won't be at his compound for several more days and Graeme wants to gather more intel before we talk."

"A wise decision," she murmured, watching him carefully.

His expression tightened further and she knew that cracked molar was coming soon.

He shifted, his feet planted firmly on the floor, legs slightly parted, and the prepared stance had a frown flickering on her brow.

"What, Cullen?" She crossed her arms over her breasts and stared back at him with a glare. "Are you going to try to blame me for Ranger's diarrhea of the mouth? Not my fault. That's between you and Ranger."

"Do you want him to die?" The hard, flat look in his eyes had her swallowing tightly at the question.

He wouldn't really kill Ranger, she assured herself.

"Look, I know he's your friend . . ."

"He lied to you, Chelsea," he suddenly snarled, his fingers curling into fists for a moment before he pushed them restlessly through his hair. "At no time did I ever hint that you were at the fucking office as a reminder of Lauren. And I damned sure, not at any time, *never* made fun of our friendship when you were a teenager." His jaw clenched and unclenched with furious motions as he glared down at her, his gaze probing. "I would never have done such a thing."

Anger vibrated in the air around him, frustration and maybe resentment. Maybe he hadn't told Ranger she was a Lauren stand-in of some sort, but it wasn't completely illogical either.

"But I *am* your mate now," she pointed out quietly, that knowledge settling heavy in her heart as she watched him. Perhaps the recessed genetics really were the reason he hadn't mated his wife then. When his Breed instincts began waking, he'd mated her because she was the closest he could get to having his wife back.

"Again, not your fault," he growled, heated lust flashing in his eyes. "And not something I regret for a moment, so don't even go there."

"Why do you think this happened now, then?" she asked suspiciously. "You had four years to make this mating start or to even show me you wanted me. Why now? Why did it just happen now?"

He prowled farther into the room, coming nearer, not stopping until she stepped several feet in the opposite direction.

"Answer me," she demanded, despite the lust in his eyes and her own growing heat. As though the confrontation only made the need to touch, to taste, more extreme. "Why now?"

He inhaled sharply, a grimace contorting his expression. "It actually began the morning you gave me your resignation," he told her, his expression hardening. "The recessed Breed instincts hadn't become active enough, though, to strengthen the mating hormone until I learned you'd been attacked."

She knew how it worked. Graeme had explained it to her. When a Breed was faced with the woman the animal instinct recognized as its mate, then small glands beneath the Breed's tongue filled with a liquid hormone that bound them together physically. According to Graeme, her resignation had caused the inner animal instincts to jerk in response and begin awakening. She was leaving him, and the strength of the animal's refusal to allow that had activated his Breed instincts. Or, she wondered, had the man's refusal to lose his only reminder of his lost wife started the mating instead?

"When I kissed you after learning of the attack, it was stronger. It's only gotten more so since," Cullen concluded. "This had nothing to do with Lauren, and nothing to do some fucking insane view Ranger has of how I feel. For God's sake, she's been dead ten years," he snarled. "He's the one with the problem here, Chelsea. Not me."

"Tell me why it happened now, Cullen," she demanded, needing to understand what was happening to them, and why it was happening now. "What made now different? I had threatened to leave dozens of times and you didn't mate me then."

"Because I was losing you and I knew it," he snapped, his expression filling with frustration as he raked his fingers restlessly through his hair. "I felt it when you drew that damned piece of paper from your jacket. You were leaving me."

And she had been. She nodded heavily, refusing to hide from it.

"I was actually getting ready to leave the Nation," she admitted, watching his eyes flare with pending fury. "It was Ashley and Cassie who convinced me to wait to see if I could get on with the Bureau. And after what happened with Louisa . . ." She gave a heavy shrug. "I changed my mind."

She stared around the kitchen, her body so sensitive now, her need to touch him, to be touched by him, only growing.

"You were going to completely leave me?" he bit out, moving closer again as she shifted farther around the table. "Do you really think I wouldn't have come looking for you?"

Did she?

She shook her head slowly.

"No, I don't think you would have," she admitted, her voice sharper, confused as to why he'd believe she'd even give it a thought. "I think you would have let me go. If I had left as I meant to, the attack by that

Coyote wouldn't have happened and you wouldn't have come looking for me. Then the mating wouldn't have started, and your friend wouldn't give a damn who you were sleeping with."

That smile that curled at his lips wasn't comforting and had nothing to do with amusement.

"Is that what you think?" His eyes narrowed then, tension tightening the muscles at his jaw. "I'll deal with Ranger soon, don't doubt it. But I cannot believe you'd even consider a reality where I wouldn't have come for you."

"It's what I know," she informed him heatedly, the knowledge of it hurting far more than she wanted to admit to herself. "You had four years to decide you wanted me," she pointed out furiously. "We were together almost daily and you didn't want me then. So why the hell should it matter if I left now?"

"And you really believe that? Oh baby, you are so fucking wrong." He was on her before she could evade him, his voice part growl, part incredulous anger.

Before she could stop him, he pulled her hand to the erection beneath his jeans and held her palm in place.

"I've been like iron since the night you showed up at that damned Breed Underground meeting with Steven Fields when you were no more than eighteen fucking years old, and it's only gotten worse since."

She'd been so desperate to see him that she'd all but begged Steven to let her go with him.

"And you want me to believe you've waited all these years for a woman you say you've stayed hard for?" She jerked her hand out of his grip, but the feeling of heat remained. "Really, Cullen? Do you think I don't know exactly who your lovers were over the years? You're telling me you didn't want the women you fucked?"

That memory was enough to piss her off and remind her of the jealousy that ate at her during those times.

"That actually about sums it up." Disgust filled his voice and flashed across his expression. "But I knew myself, Chelsea. I wanted to give you time to grow up first; instead all I did was give you time to find ways to get yourself killed."

"No, Cullen, I figured out how to protect myself and others if I have to. And I'll be damned if I'll feel as though that's a weakness of some kind," she argued fiercely. "Mating me will not change who I am, so don't even imagine it will."

She was not Lauren. She didn't need him to shadow her every move. All she needed was a partner, not some damned grieving widower living in the past . . .

Before the thought could finish she was in Cullen's arms, his lips covering hers, the heated spice in his kiss stronger, more intense than it had been at any other time, and it hit her senses faster, deeper.

The arousal already overheating her senses flared into a conflagration and burned through thought, protest and shadows. Fear receded beneath the feelings that rose when she was in his arms. It wasn't security she was searching for, but she found security in his arms.

The resentment, anger and confusion were swept away by the incredible pleasure and need.

She cried out, her lips parted, her tongue meeting his, arms gripping his shoulders as she held tight to him.

Cullen was ravenous, his need for her as desperate as hers for him.

His head tilted, his lips slanting over hers as he consumed her kiss. Lips and tongues met, melded, and control became a thing of the past.

Chelsea didn't want control, she didn't want to be logical or realistic. In this moment she just wanted to be Cullen's.

"That's it," he groaned before nipping at her lips. "Burn for me."

Burn for him? She was already burning past reason.

Reaching up, she buried her fingers in his hair, nipped his lips as he tried to pull back again before licking her tongue over them.

His mouth slammed down on hers, a groan rumbling in his chest as her lips closed on his tongue, drawing the addictive, heated taste free. An overwhelming rush of sensation and fiery need tore through her senses, clenching the inner flesh of her sex and spasming through her womb.

She didn't have to think; all she had to do was give herself to the need storming through her now. And after his kiss was the need to feel his flesh against hers, skin to skin. She was desperate for it, needing it with the same out-of-control hunger that demanded his kiss.

Chelsea tore at his shirt, needing it off him now. She might have felt a few buttons pop too before he was jerking the material free of his body.

Her blouse was next, buttons tearing free before Cullen managed to release them all. She thought she might have heard material rip.

It took precious moments to shed boots, shoes and clothes, to get to bare skin and the incredible pleasure to be found in the contact.

Chelsea's breath caught as he lifted her in his arms, her nipples raking over his chest, the caress exciting and heating the sensitive peaks. As she lifted her knees to his hips, the feel of the engorged crest of his cock against her lower stomach drew a desperate cry from her.

Her juices wept from her vagina, the inner tissue clenching and rippling with the need for him inside her.

She needed him now. She didn't want to wait, didn't need foreplay. She needed him inside her.

"Now, Cullen," she whispered, gripping his hips with her knees and lifting against him to get the broad crest to the entrance of her sex. "Please. Now."

She was dying for him, her breathing harsh and ragged, nails biting into his shoulders.

Suddenly, her back met the wall. Gripping her thighs, Cullen lifted her, holding her in place as his cock began pressing against the narrow entrance.

"Look at me," he snarled.

Heated pressure flared in her pussy as Chelsea forced her eyes open, staring up at him, dazed pleasure drugging her senses now.

"I need you," she whispered. "Please. Now."

"You were fucking eighteen." His breathing hard, ragged. "A weapon strapped to your thigh and all I could think about was this."

The pressure increased, the stretching, heated sensations as he began pushing inside her pulling a cry from her lips.

Slowly, by increments, his gaze holding hers despite the need to close them, his hips rocked against her, working the hard crest inside the hungry depths of her sex.

"You're mine," he gritted out, his thighs bunching between hers, his eyes flaring with wild lust as she felt that overwhelming, desperate need rushing through her.

A second later, blinding, incredible pleasure tore through her senses. She cried out his name, losing her breath as sensation blazed through her.

Steady, hard thrusts impaled her, driving his cock deeper with each stroke. Pleasure-pain streaked through her senses even as her body demanded more.

She needed more of him. She needed all of him.

Moving against him as he thrust inside her, whimpering cries falling from her, Chelsea felt the rising pleasure beginning to burn through her determination to hold a part of herself back. To keep from becoming lost in the whipping emotions she felt rising in the storm tearing through her.

The need to become lost in him was strong, though. It was becoming stronger each time he took her and taking more and more willpower to hold a part of herself back.

Her arms tightened around him as her head fell to his shoulder, the feel of him laying a burning trail of kisses down her neck. She could feel her climax building, rushing through her.

His hands gripped her hips, his cock shafting furiously inside her now.

Brilliant, white-hot sensation suddenly exploded through her. The rush of ecstasy stole her mind, drawing a shattering cry from her as his teeth gripped the mark at her shoulder, his tongue rasping as his cock plunged deep.

A desperate, breathless cry was torn from her as she felt the barb extend, locking him in place as his release began spurting inside her. Explosions of ecstasy shuddered through her again, the lightning-bright rush of sensation and emotion terrifying in its strength.

She'd been desperate to hold a part of herself back, but in that moment she wondered if Cullen hadn't already slipped inside her soul.

· C H A P T E R   1 7 ·

From Graeme's Journal
Recessed Primal Genetics and Mating Heat

Research into recessed Breed genetics, especially those of the recessed Primal instincts, has been woefully lacking and nearsighted.

The Primal senses what even the Breed himself cannot pick up. And in regard to his mate, there are few secrets she can keep from the feral creature determined to claim her—

Hours later, his body curled around Chelsea's, Cullen stared into the darkened room, a frown furrowing his brow. Despite the excessive sexual play, Chelsea was still awake. She was exhausted, yet for some reason she still hadn't slipped into sleep.

"You're not sleeping," he finally pointed out softly. "I can feel you thinking."

And he knew Chelsea. Thinking was sometimes her worst enemy.

"I didn't come to the Agency wanting Ranger's job," she said quietly then. "I just wanted to be close to you."

He flipped her over quickly, one hand covering her lips as he stared down at her fiercely.

"I know that, Chelsea," he told her firmly, seeing the uncertainty and regret in her eyes. "Ranger has his own issues with the past, and he tends to hold on to things way too long. But that's not your fault. He knows that."

Lifting his hand, he let his fingertips brush down her cheek, loving the silken feel of her skin and the warmth that went far deeper than just flesh.

"I don't want his job," she said without anger then. "But no matter what the mating demands in our relationship, I won't be happy filing your papers for you and waiting for you in the office. I'd be miserable."

He knew that now. He'd already accepted that the time for that was over, and that he'd have to make peace with his fears and over-protective tendencies.

"Chelsea, we'll straighten all this out between us so we're both happy once the threat against you is over," he promised her. "If I stay with the Agency I promise you won't be in the office filing papers unless I'm filing them with you."

A hint of amusement sparkled in her eyes then as he felt her hand at his hip, caressing, warm. "You're not allowed to do filing. Remember?"

Now probably wasn't the time to tell her he'd already made a mess of any organization she'd ever had going in that office. He could tell her that later.

She settled against him, though, and drifted into sleep, leaving him awake and staring into the darkness of the room.

The friendship he'd believed was set in steel was over forever now.

Ranger was going to have to be dealt with, and soon. Rising from the bed and leaving the warmth of his mate's relaxed body, Cullen stared down at her for a moment, the sight of her in his bed filling him with a satisfaction he couldn't explain.

His head lifted, the faint sound of his phone pinging from where he'd left his jeans tossed to the kitchen floor, drawing him from the room. Finding the article of clothing, he pulled the phone free and stared down at the text displayed.

Is she okay?

If he didn't answer it, no doubt Graeme would arrive on his doorstep and make the situation worse.

He keyed in the speed dial to his brother's number, and the call was answered before the first ring finished.

"Do you know what happened at the police department?" Graeme asked, his tone so icy Cullen wondered if he was talking to Graeme or his Primal.

There were times he envied his brother's arrogance and knowledge of his own inner madness. Shades of gray didn't concern his brother, just right and wrong, what was just and what wasn't.

"I know. She was wired. I heard every word."

Silence filled the line for long moments.

"And Ranger still lives," his brother mused with dangerous softness. "Interesting."

That softness was an indication that his brother felt he needed to make the hard decisions for him as he'd tried to do for most of their lives.

"Stay away from him, Graeme. I'll deal with him," Cullen ordered. He was actually able to take care of things himself.

"I misjudged that man, it would appear," Graeme commented. "I'll have to rectify that."

"You'll have to let me deal with this," Cullen reminded him. "Don't push me, Graeme, I'm not in the mood for it."

A mocking snort came across the line. "When are you going to grow tired of others striking against your mate?" Graeme asked then, the curiosity in his voice only pissing Cullen off further.

"We can't all call up a monster that enjoys shedding blood when we want to," Cullen snorted with a bitter fury born of the pain wrapped around his senses. "I'll take care of Ranger, and when the time comes I'll take care of Cerves and whoever put that fucking price on her head. But I won't leave a trail of body parts doing it."

Rather than hanging up on him, enraged, as he had in the past, Graeme laughed with mocking amusement. "Ah, brother, how you do enjoy lying to yourself. I think I'll be rather amused when you're forced to face the truth."

"If you don't stop talking in riddles and tell me something constructive, then I'm going to find something better to do," Cullen warned his brother.

"The Cerveses were in Mexico City when the attack occurred. They were scheduled to be there for several weeks still to allow Samara to deal with their daughter's death. They're flying back in tonight and have ordered all the top lieutenants to be waiting for them. No word yet on what has them returning so soon."

Cullen knew Juan Cerves, though he knew the cartel leader's brother, Esteban, much better.

"Juan's temper is unpredictable, but if Esteban is with him, he'll be calmer. If he didn't order the hit as Morales said, then he could just be intent on reestablishing his hold on his organization," Cullen said thoughtfully.

"Hmm," Graeme murmured. "We'll see, I guess." A heavy sigh came over the line now. "What's Chelsea doing now?"

Cullen glanced over his shoulder before rubbing wearily at the back of his neck. "She's sleeping. She's trying to pretend that what Ranger said didn't bother her, but I know her. It was painful."

Silence filled the line for long moments.

"What are your instincts telling you about Ranger, Cullen?" Graeme asked then. "Not your head. Your instincts."

What were his instincts telling him? Some of those instincts were so new, the information they sensed, the scents, so new . . .

"Don't think about it, just answer me." The growl in his brother's voice was a guttural rasp.

"I'm not sure." Cullen blew out a hard breath as he paced the kitchen and picked up the discarded clothes, tossing them into the attached laundry room.

"Were you recording while she was wired?" Graeme questioned him curiously.

He had been.

"It was recorded," Cullen said, impatient now to replay her confrontation with Ranger.

"Send me the file," Graeme urged him then. "Perhaps I'll sense something you haven't."

Cullen disconnected the call without answering. Going into his cloud files, he forwarded the file to his brother. Perhaps there was something in the confrontation that he hadn't seen at the time.

He'd heard every word Ranger said to her and had listened in disbelief to the other man's deliberate attempts to hurt Chelsea and drive her away from Cullen.

Pacing to the back door, he stepped outside, the early-evening sunlight bearing down with heavy heat. Making his way to the shaded corner of the house, he leaned against it, extracted the single, slim cigar he kept tucked in his front pocket and, bringing it to his lips, lit it with a flick of the lighter he pulled from the pocket of his jeans.

Relishing the flavorful bite of the tobacco as he inhaled deeply, he tried to make sense of events he'd worked hard to forget. And to push aside the unreasonable fear that those events just might have something to do with the danger Chelsea was in now.

CHAPTER 18

From Graeme's Journal
The Recessed Primal Breed

Mating Heat in the recessed Primal Breed will often begin with more subtle signs physically, but with much more dramatic psychological results—

She was in serious trouble.

The next morning Chelsea fully admitted she was involved in emotional quicksand that she was totally unprepared to navigate. She still had no idea what had enraged Cullen as she talked to Ranger the day before.

She could see being angry over Ranger's words; she was angry herself. But Cullen had been furious.

Stepping into the kitchen after her shower, wearing cutoff denim shorts, a tank and bare feet, she finished cleaning up the dishes from breakfast and acknowledged that the emotional situation was becoming chaos.

She'd been certain that what she felt for him was love during the years she worked for him, but in the time she'd spent with him in the past weeks, she realized she'd really had no true concept of love.

The depth of what she felt for him now was terrifying. It wasn't just the explosive, hotter-than-hell sex or the fact that she knew the man he was, admired him, despite his arrogance, and knew to the soles of her feet that she'd never have to worry about him straying to other women.

It was that undefined, ever-deepening certainty that they'd clash often, challenge each other daily, but she knew she'd never regret living her life with him.

But if she ever learned for certain that he regretted not mating Lauren, and resented mating with her instead, then it would devastate her.

He'd loved his first wife. She remembered seeing that in his expression as Lauren walked down the aisle at their wedding. If it weren't for the mating and the fact that if he'd mated Lauren he could have saved her, then the thought wouldn't torment her. And she wondered, if he had the choice to make, would he go back and give Lauren the mating Chelsea claimed now?

When he'd told Graeme that she was the one who would want a cure for the mating that first morning, she'd heard the dark undertone in his voice and she'd had a terrible fear it was Cullen who wanted the cure instead. Maybe it wasn't the cure but the regret that the mating had come with someone other than his dead wife.

What if Ranger was right? What if she was just a stand-in for Lauren?

Drawing in a deep breath, she pushed those thoughts away, determined to not let herself go there. She'd be damned if she'd be jealous of a memory. She didn't have time for it.

Putting away the last of the dishes, she turned in surprise when the kitchen door opened and Draeger stepped just inside the entrance.

"Cullen around?" he asked, his gaze sweeping the kitchen and living room.

She shook her head, watching him curiously as she dried her hands on a dish towel. "I think he's in the garage or basement. Should I go find him?"

"Company," the Breed answered. "His second, Ranger. He said it was important."

Great. Just what she needed this morning.

"That's not a good idea," she hissed, staring back into the kitchen, just knowing Cullen was going to walk in at any minute.

Behind him, the door was suddenly pushed open and Ranger barged in, his expression furious. Flushed, fists clenched, his gaze glittering with suppressed violence as Draeger moved quickly between him and Chelsea with a growl of warning.

"Call off these fucking guard dogs of yours," he ordered, the violence in his gaze shocking. "Or are you such a coward that you can't talk to me now?"

She had a feeling he really didn't want to talk. He was staring at her like he wanted to kill her.

"Let him talk, Draeger," she ordered the Wolf Breed quietly.

Cullen must have talked to him, she guessed. He deserved to be angry if he believed Chelsea had betrayed his attempt to protect her. God, she wished she could have warned him the day before—

"I was wrong about you," he bit out, and she was shocked by the pure hatred in his voice now. "You're nothing but a little whore determined to make certain no one stands in your way with Cullen, aren't you? Not a wife's memory. Or a friend."

She flinched at the insult, her eyes widening as she glimpsed Draeger gripping the weapon strapped to his thigh.

"Ranger, you need to leave," she said painfully. "Before Cullen comes in here and hears this . . ."

"Why did you do it, Chelsea?" he whispered, lifting a hand out beseechingly. "What did you say to him? For God's sake, I thought we were friends."

"Now isn't a good time for this, Ranger." She shook her head, trying to find something to say that would calm him down, that would get him out of the house before Cullen heard him.

Lifting her gaze back to him, she watched his face slowly leach of color, his eyes going to her neck for a moment, right there where Cullen had left the mating mark. When his eyes jerked back to her, his face flushed, rage glittering in his eyes.

"'Now isn't a good time for this,'" he sneered, that hatred deepening in his eyes. "When's a good time, bitch? After you've completely brainwashed him?"

This was so beyond not good that it wasn't even funny. The words hurt, but Chelsea knew that if Cullen caught him here and heard the insults he'd go ballistic on the other man.

"Get him out of here, Draeger," she ordered the Wolf Breed, suddenly frantic. "Before Cullen comes in here."

Ranger's gaze went to her neck again, such incredible pain flashing in his eyes that for a moment, compassion nearly overwhelmed her.

"Too late." Cullen stepped into the room from the hall, his voice so devoid of emotion that Chelsea felt a flash of fear surge through her.

Evidently, Draeger felt the innate threat as well. Tension pervaded the room, the suffocating feeling causing her heart to rush with panic as she watched rage flash in his flat green eyes.

A promise of retribution filled Ranger's face as Cullen stepped to her silently, obviously determined to deflect any threat toward her.

"Chelsea." He gripped her arm, his voice low as both Ranger and Draeger watched him carefully now. "Would you go to the other room for a few moments?"

She wasn't about to—

"Like hell," Ranger burst out, taking a step toward her.

Cullen's reaction was immediate. A feline snarl of enraged warning burst from his chest, stopping Ranger in his tracks.

Chelsea didn't blame him; she was just as shocked. The canines Cullen flashed at the side of his mouth were definitely longer, looked sharper. He appeared broader, the muscles rippling beneath his T-shirt, his biceps bulging. She'd never seen anything or anyone with the potential to jump into a killing fury that Cullen had now.

"What did she do to you, Cullen?" Ranger asked, his voice horrified. "Look at you." A shudder swept through him.

Chelsea could feel her heart racing, fear sweeping through her as a growl rumbled in Cullen's chest.

"Listen to you, Cullen." Confusion swept over the other man's face. "You're like a monster, unable to control yourself. You've never been like this. What did she do to you?"

"What have you done?" Cullen snarled. "Chelsea didn't say anything to me about you. And I don't recall mentioning her name when I talked to the commissioner."

The commissioner? He was the only person who wielded more power than Cullen in the Agency.

"Don't lie to me, Cullen." Misery filled Ranger's voice as he lifted his hand again, only to let it fall to his side immediately as he turned to Chelsea, contempt flashing in his eyes then. "I see her at the police department and a few hours later, not only is my position as co-command rescinded but I've been fired without just cause simply because you decided you can't work with me? By God, I'll sue . . ."

"Read the agreement you signed when you came to the Agency," Cullen reminded him, the ice in his voice deepening. "The loss of trust in you is just cause. And I don't have to justify the loss of it."

Ranger gave a furious, bitter laugh, his nostrils flaring, disgust echoing in the sound.

"That's bullshit." His fists were clenching and unclenching at his sides, rage and pain contorting his features. "At least tell me what she said. I'm sure the other agents would love to know how she finally managed to get rid of me. We all know she's been after my job for years."

Chelsea shook her head, blinking back at him in shock.

"That's not true," she protested.

"Oh, so fucking innocent," Ranger sneered. "You." He stabbed his finger at her accusingly. "You've been after my job ever since you walked into that damned office. You've done nothing but connive . . ."

"Enough." Silence filled the kitchen at the guttural sound of Cullen's voice, the echo of animalistic fury shocking in its depth.

Ranger stared at him in shock as Chelsea glanced up at him, then to Draeger as he watched with wary tension. She could feel the tension boiling now, threatening to explode with repercussions she didn't want Cullen or Ranger to face.

"Cullen . . ." Ranger tried again, his voice, his expression turning, pleading.

"Chelsea didn't have to tell me anything." Cullen silenced him instantly. "She was wired with strict orders not to reveal the wire. I heard every word, every lie for myself. And I do recall her trying to silence you more than once. You deliberately tried to hurt her, and you lied to do it." He inhaled deeply, obviously trying to pull in a measure of calm. "My decision's been made. I'm on leave for the moment, but the commissioner has my duties until my return. That should give you time to clear your stuff from the office."

Ranger's gaze flickered to her neck again before he turned back to Cullen.

"Lauren was right all along," he sneered spitefully. "You didn't really love her. You let her die. How does it make you feel to know you traded your wife's life to have her?"

Pain shattered her heart at the accusation as she felt Cullen's arm tense further beneath her hand, the fury building in him. The cruel words were designed to hurt and they had.

"Draeger, get him out of here," Cullen ordered, his voice softening. "If I have to do it, I may end up killing him."

Ranger sneered back at her then, cruel amusement curving his lips. "How does it feel?" He was shaking with fury now. "How does it feel, fucking your cousin's little pet, you stupid cunt? That's what she called him, you know?"

Draeger grabbed Ranger, jerking him back as Chelsea jumped in front of Cullen as he made to move to rush the other man. Deep, primal growls were erupting from Cullen's throat as Draeger hauled Ranger out the door, the sounds grating and filled with fury.

The accusation had sliced her painfully, Chelsea admitted, because she knew it had hurt Cullen. She'd seen his face, seen the misery that flashed across it just before he started to jump for the man he'd called friend since those first weeks when he arrived in the Nation.

She inhaled slowly, trying to stop the shaking she could feel in her hands, her body. Turning away from Cullen slowly, she fought to accept the fact that because of her, Cullen had just made an enemy of one of the few friends he'd allowed himself to have.

"Why did you have him fired?" she asked, confused as she turned back to him. He stood in the same place, his gaze locked on the door Draeger had forced Ranger through. "If it was because of me, then you made a mistake, Cullen. That wasn't what I wanted."

Cullen's gaze sliced to her, the icy expression on his face causing her to swallow nervously.

"He lied to you," he finally stated harshly. "He was trying to hurt you."

She shook her head in denial, pain-filled regret exploding her mind. "He was just being a stupid man." Tears filled her voice and dampened her eyes. "He was trying to tell me not to get my heart broken. That's all."

This was all her fault. Because she couldn't hide the glasses, because she hated male superiority, because she'd never imagined Ranger would speak against Cullen. It was her fault, and she hated it.

"So he lied to you?" His brows arched as his gaze filled with disgust. "That's why he told you I blamed you? That you were no more than a stand-in for Lauren? That we laughed at you while we were married?" A cold smile shaped his lips. "Oh no, baby, I watched that video more than once. I saw what you didn't want to see. He wanted to hurt you and drive you away from me, knowing there's every chance you'll be dead within days if you do so. That was pure maliciousness in his eyes as he told you about Lauren, and I'll be damned if I'll even try to work with him knowing how easily he betrayed our friendship and tried to endanger you."

Had it been? She shook her head, wondering if Cullen had seen something in Ranger that she hadn't the day before. And it was possible she'd missed it. The hatred in Ranger's eyes moments ago and the sneering disgust in his words had been so virulent, filled with such depth, that surely it hadn't come into being overnight.

"Cullen . . ." She licked her lips nervously, wondering exactly what had gone on in his marriage, needing to know now when she'd tried to avoid it because of her fear of the potential truth.

"We're heading to Graeme's," he told her before she could say anything more. "Get ready and get what you need for a few days' stay. Cerves is back in the States and I think I'm ready for a few answers now."

Without waiting for an answer he strode to the door, flung it open and stalked outside. Before the door closed behind him she saw him jerk free one of the slim cigars he kept tucked in his shirt pocket.

Two cigars in as many days; he was on a roll now, she thought painfully. If only she had a vice of her own to find comfort in.

◆　◆　◆

He could feel her confusion and her pain.

Holding the cigar between his teeth, Cullen lit it with a heavy drag of the fragrant tobacco and fought to push the scent of her distress from his mind. It had exploded through his senses at Ranger's final words, stabbing into him and sending the need for violence rushing through him. He would have killed Ranger if he could have gotten his hands on him. Because what he'd had to say to Chelsea was nothing compared to the insults against her Cullen had learned the other man was spreading at the Agency.

For some unknown reason Ranger had been infuriated with Cullen's leave of absence, blaming Chelsea and her supposed possessiveness for it rather than the fact that she was in danger. The other man had even gone so far as to state it wouldn't surprise him that she'd arranged the danger herself to ensure Cullen's attention.

As he drew on the tobacco again, the sharp bite had him grimacing as he relished the sensation. It was a terrible habit, he knew. One he'd picked up several years before, courtesy of Dane Vanderale.

Dane swore by the cigars and every month like clockwork, Cullen received a box of thirty from Africa, courtesy of the Vanderale heir.

Now, leaning against the shaded column of the portico, he stared at the cylindrically rolled tobacco and fought to get his fury under control. There was still a part of him that wanted to wait until darkness fell and stalk the man he had once called friend. And when he found him, he wanted blood.

Perhaps that was the part that had him feeling so off balance. Ranger hadn't done anything to deserve death, but telling his instincts that was impossible.

Sliding his gaze to the side of the house, he watched as Draeger stepped beneath the shaded patio, his expression faintly curious as he stared back at Cullen.

"That didn't take long," Cullen said between gritted teeth, still forced to restrain animal instincts that felt far too unfamiliar.

Draeger gave a short nod of his dark head.

"I'd watch my back if I were you," the Wolf suggested. "He's out for your blood."

Maybe, Cullen thought wearily, though he'd never considered Ranger a stupid man until the other day.

"Don't let him back in," he warned the Breed. "I didn't think he'd show up here or I'd have already given you a heads-up."

"I figured," Draeger acknowledged, producing his own cigar from the pocket at the side of his black mission pants and lighting up.

"Vanderale gets around," Cullen grunted, glancing at his own cigar and using it as an excuse to check the burning tips of his fingers.

"Yeah. True." Draeger gave a short, amused chuckle. "Thing about Vanderale, though? He gets around more than anyone realizes. That laid-back-playboy persona of his actually fools most people and Breeds alike. Before you realize it, he knows everything there is to know about you. Even things you don't know yourself. Then there are those little spies of his that no one can ever identify but who just love filling his ears with valuable little tidbits of gossip."

Cullen turned and stared at the Wolf, waiting.

Leaning back against the other column, Draeger drew on the cigar and stared out at the desert for several moments.

"Some of us have actually learned from him," the other Breed informed him.

"And what have you learned, Draeger?" Cullen asked, not really too worried about whatever information he had.

Draeger inhaled the tobacco deeply before releasing the smoke in a slow, heavy breath.

"You know Ranger was your wife's lover," Draeger said then. "Yet you've allowed him to ride your coattails all the way to your second in command." Curiosity filled the other Breed's voice. "Why did you trust him, knowing he couldn't be trusted?"

Fuck. Now how the hell had anyone figured that one out? To his knowledge only he, Ranger and Lauren had known.

"I knew, even then," he admitted; remembering those days wasn't always comfortable. "They'd been in love before I arrived in Window Rock. They resumed about a year after we married, but not without my knowledge of it."

"You're a better Breed than I am." Draeger slid him an assessing look. "Or are you just dumber?"

Cullen actually grinned at the insult. It was damned hard to take offense at the wry curiosity in the Wolf's voice.

"Ask me how I'd handle it if one of Chelsea's ex-lovers came around," he grunted, then blew out a hard breath. "I realized why she married me not long into the marriage. She knew I was a Breed before I told her. Either she guessed that the tabloid stories about Mating Heat were true, or Ray Martinez told her. Hell if I know." And it hadn't mattered for a very long time. "I could smell death on her. I wasn't going to deny her what she'd given up in her desperation to live. Ranger tried to stay away, but the sicker she got, the more they needed each other. And any love I'd felt for her was nothing more than compassion at that point."

And why couldn't he tell Chelsea that? Talking to her about those days was just about impossible for him. Pride? he wondered. To admit his desperation for some connection, for some kind of roots in those days was humiliating in a way.

Draeger nodded at the explanation. "Just because you're trained by death doesn't mean that dying makes it any easier."

Cullen flicked him a glance and realized the lessons they'd learned, in different places, from different monsters, weren't so dissimilar.

"Pretty much," Cullen agreed. "The friendship was something I'd believed had endured." He shrugged, feeling the loss of something that hadn't even existed except in his own mind. "I was wrong."

"Might have been, until he realized you were actually beginning a relationship with someone else. You moved on, he's still living in the past. And seeing that mating mark on Chelsea's neck didn't help matters much. He's going to become a problem."

Cullen gave a short bark of laughter. "Don't start trying to make me feel better, Wolf. I thought you might know me better than that."

Draeger pursed his lips before giving Cullen a knowing look. "Lauren married you hoping the kitty's love meant a feline mating, huh? An instant cure for the disease killing her." There was compassion in the Breed's voice but not an overabundance of it.

"That about sums it up," Cullen agreed, hating the fact that he hadn't realized that truth at the time.

"And now Ranger can't accept that you'd actually give that mating to someone else. Let alone Lauren's little cousin." Draeger pointed this out as though in concession of what he'd already known. "What are you going to do when he strikes out again? And you know he will."

"Hell if I know," he bit out roughly. "Let's pray Ranger lets it go at this point. He can hate me till hell freezes over and I won't regret it. What I sensed from him today didn't just start. I was just too damned stupid to realize it all these years."

And the animal instincts had been sleeping, refusing to come out and play and allow Cullen to sense the truth.

"Well, take this for what it's worth." Draeger snapped the fire from his half-smoked cigar before tucking it back into the pocket on his mission pants. "That buddy of yours hasn't considered you a friend for a long time, if he ever did. The sense I got was a hatred well aged. He's gunning for you, but even more to the point, he's gunning for your mate."

Cullen watched the other Breed, feeling the truth of the statement.

"He better not even consider placing his finger on the trigger, then," he stated softly. "He makes that mistake, then he'll die. And that's a fact."

And it was probably a good idea to put one of his own spies on Ranger's ass, just to be sure. Because like Draeger, Cullen had sensed not just the fury but also the hatred. The kind of hatred known to make even smart men have their moments of stupid.

Cullen would hate to have to kill a man he'd once known as a friend, but if that former friend thought to strike against his mate, Cullen would kill him before he gave it a moment's thought.

And without a moment's regret.

· CHAPTER 19 ·

From Graeme's Journal
Recessed Primal Genetics and Mating Heat

Whether recessed or active, the vast intelligence, incredible cunning and iron resolve of a Primal is an ever-deepening, ever-reaching invitation into madness and the thirst for blood.

She could have sworn Cullen said they were meeting at Graeme's to discuss a little trip to visit the Cerves family. Instead, after arriving at Graeme and Cat's seemingly deserted house, Cullen led her into a basement entrance and then through a concealed doorway into an underground tunnel.

He motioned her into a golf cart of all things and, to her amazement, drove her through the network of steel-reinforced, well-lit passages.

"It's just about a mile to the main cavern," he told her as he drove with a casual confidence that betrayed the fact that he did it often.

"How did the tunnels get here?" She stared around them as he traveled between thick stone walls.

The tunnel was easily twice the width of the cart, with other passageways branching off occasionally in other directions.

"Mining, several centuries ago, I believe." A smile quirked at his lips. "Graeme swears he found a vein of gold in one of the offshoot tunnels, but I haven't convinced him to show it to me yet."

Before long, Cullen turned the cart into a slightly narrower tunnel before pulling to a stop behind a matching cart.

"The main cavern's through there." He nodded to a wide, arched entrance as they stepped from the cart and Chelsea followed behind him.

From one surprise to another—the cavern they entered was easily the square footage of a modest home and at least two stories high. On one side, a curved metal staircase extended up to a landing that held a large, heavy wood door. On the opposite side, it appeared Graeme had set up a well-equipped medical lab. There were at least a dozen varying types of computerized processing units and a computer set up with no less than half a dozen monitors.

State-of-the-art and well lit, and obviously used often.

"Mad scientist much?" she muttered suspiciously as they neared the work area.

"Dr. Jekyll's lab is more like it." Cullen glanced at her over his shoulder, a small grin edging at his lips. "You met Mr. Hyde yesterday."

"No way." She could not stop a spurt of laughter. "You actually call it that?"

"You call him 'it,'" he pointed out, shooting her a mocking frown. "Trust me, he likes 'Dr. Jekyll and Mr. Hyde' far better."

Graeme chose that moment to enter the main cavern from a separate entrance on the other side of the lab area wearing a white lab coat, white shirt, jeans and leather sneakers. Behind him, Ashley strutted, her slight form swallowed by a matching lab coat as she seemed to be admiring the far-too-large fit. Cat followed behind them, dressed in jeans, a black T-shirt and sandals, shaking her head at them, obviously on the verge of laughing.

"There you two are," Graeme announced in a distracted, mad-scientist sort of way. "Good. We can get started."

"Madhouse," Cullen muttered beside her. "Come on, let's get it over with."

"Get what over with?" she asked suspiciously, eyeing the lab equipment.

She had a feeling Cerves wasn't the only reason they were visiting Dr. Jekyll's lab.

"Here's the thing about Graeme," Cullen stated softly with a flash of brotherly patience. "Sometimes, it's just easier to give in and let him get things out of his system than to argue with him. That way, Mr. Hyde isn't nearly the nuisance he could be."

"What kind of things?" Maybe she should escape now while she could still possibly get away with it.

"Scared?" He slid her an amused glance as he moved to the computer monitors, activating the screens and reading what appeared to be an extensive analysis of some blood sample. "You'll face down cartel assailants and Coyote soldiers but balk at the sight of Graeme in a lab coat?"

"I'm not allowed to shoot Graeme," she hissed, glancing to where the other Breed and his wife had stopped at one of the far counters where Graeme was checking information on another, smaller computer. "Not so with cartel assailants and Coyote soldiers."

"Yeah, Cat would get a little put out," he agreed. "But if we don't play nice, then he might refuse to tell us whatever he's learned about Cerves."

As a bribe, or a threat, it would probably work, Chelsea thought with a sigh.

"Leave my equipment alone, Ash," Graeme demanded as he and Cat headed toward Cullen. Behind him, Ashley had paused next to a large cabinet lined with long, narrow drawers. "Your alpha should keep you locked up for the sanity of everyone who knows you."

"Not to mention those who don't," Cat laughed teasingly as she shot Chelsea a subtle wink.

"Oh, they are so unimportant if I have yet to meet them," Ashley assured them as she moved closer and perched on one of the cots that sat against the stone wall, her gray eyes twinkling merrily. "Cullen, you are looking so well mated," she drawled teasingly, her Russian accent still very apparent despite the years since she'd left the country. She turned and winked at Chelsea then. "Way to go, girlfriend."

The Coyote female wagged her brows then and blew Cullen a kiss as Graeme moved to her, carrying a small plastic tray with several vials and needles lying atop it.

Pushing up the sleeve of the overlarge coat, Ashley extended her arm and Graeme quickly and efficiently extracted several vials of blood.

"Graeme is a secret vampire," the younger woman grinned as Chelsea watched dubiously.

"Mad scientist is more like it," Cullen grumbled as he turned back to face them, his arms crossing over his chest as he leaned against the heavy table holding the array of computers.

"Katya, our Coyote specialist, is so jealous of him." Ashley gave a quick little roll of her eyes. "She thinks he knows more about Coyotes than she does."

"I do," Graeme stated absently as he carried the tray and the vials over to a work center that held several smaller machines.

"Okay, Chelsea." Ashley jumped from the cot, her chin jerking toward it. "Your turn, chickie."

"Whoa." Chelsea stepped back quickly, straight into Cullen's chest. "Not in this lifetime. I'm sure he has enough of your blood to entertain him for a while."

Cat snickered at the comment.

"Don't worry, I'll protect you from Dr. Jekyll," Cullen assured her, the amusement in his tone causing her to shoot him a look of promised retribution. "I'll take care of you myself."

Gripping her waist, he lifted her to the cot as Graeme placed another tray containing the vials and extracting kit on it.

"Why does he need my blood?" She flicked the items a frown before eyeing Cullen suspiciously.

"Because," Graeme answered for his brother, "I based your hormonal therapy on Cullen's blood samples since I didn't have yours. Your blood and DNA sample will give me a much more accurate baseline to work from."

Graeme was inputting information into one of the machines as he spoke. "There's a reason why you're able to go about a normal routine without a few quickies every couple of hours."

A flush heated her face as he looked over his shoulder at her and shot her a teasing grin.

"Graeme, stop," Cullen warned his brother as Chelsea extended her forearm to him warily.

Graeme gave a mocking little snort of amusement.

"Also," he continued, turning back to the machine. "If you're going to continue moving about in public, then a stronger scent blocker would probably help. It will keep the Council's Breeds from detecting the mating scent." He frowned. "They've been skulking around a bit more than normal lately."

She looked up at Cullen, wondering what the hell he was getting her into.

"Don't forget the DNA swab." Graeme stretched his arm out behind him, a sterile swab gripped between his fingers.

Taking the swab as he laid aside the vials now containing her blood, Cullen broke the seal, and when Chelsea opened her mouth he quickly rasped the insides of her cheeks with it.

"This is highly weird," she informed him.

"And wanting to do the nasty like rabbits a dozen times a day isn't?" Ashley teased, her gray eyes dancing with laughter.

"Not as weird as this. And definitely more fun," Chelsea assured her, watching as Cullen moved to the machines, his voice low as he asked his brother something about the baseline and the DNA. It was more science than she wanted to understand.

"Graeme's been bitching because Cullen hasn't been in the lab working with him lately." Cat moved to the cot and sat next to Chelsea as Ashley wandered off and began inspecting equipment and drawers curiously. "He gets distracted when I come down here to play assistant."

Her cousin's scientific smarts had arrived in her late teens, and her proficiency in it had shocked her teachers. Cat—Claire, as she'd been called then—had changed a lot that summer and even more so over the years.

"Yeah, he gets all kitty frisky on her," Ashley drawled as she examined an array of scalpels she'd found in a drawer.

"Ashley, leave them alone," Graeme growled as Ashley lifted her hand to pick up one of the sharp instruments.

Ashley shot him a pouting look but closed the drawer.

"You know," Graeme said then. "I believe Khileen had some new polishes and shoes arrive from Paris today; she said . . ."

An excited little squeal cut through the rest of the sentence and Ashley shed her lab coat quickly, tossed it over the back of a stool and ran for the staircase, racing up it, the heavy door at the top closing with a bang.

"Last time she was here, my favorite scalpel disappeared with her," Graeme sighed as he shot a fond look toward the stairs. "She's like a little pack rat."

"Coyote hoarder," Cat corrected him, laughter filling her voice. "Her Coya, Anya, is threatening an intervention."

"Someone should keep her closer to the Coyote stronghold," Graeme grumbled then, concern apparent in his tone. "It's getting harder to keep her tagged without rousing her suspicions."

Chelsea gave Cat a questioning look.

"Graeme believes Ashley's been targeted by a stalker or the Council."

"Knows," Graeme corrected his wife, the statement filled with confidence. And he was completely serious. "There's a difference between knowledge and belief."

"So he tags her how?" she asked her cousin.

"I've convinced her she's in danger of developing allergies and needs a biweekly injection," Graeme answered as he turned back to the blood samples he was working with. "I inject a small tracking device in her arm. Her alpha refused to authorize a permanent one, so I have to settle for a temporary. They degrade fairly quickly, though. But if she disappears, then I'll know exactly where to find her."

Cat turned back to Chelsea, grinning. "He's evil, huh?"

"That's one word for it, I guess." She could come up with a few more accurate terms.

"Come on, there's drinks and sandwiches I keep in the other room. We'll chat while they do their thing." Sliding from the cot, Chelsea moved to follow Cat. As she neared Cullen he reached out, snagged her wrist and dropped a quick kiss to the top of her head, though his gaze remained on whatever experiment they were running.

Graeme wasn't the only brother with mad scientist tendencies, it seemed.

◆   ◆   ◆

Making certain Chelsea was out of earshot, Cullen watched the hormonal readings as they slowly began to display on a monitor, a frown working at his brow.

"We had company before we left the house," he told his brother quietly.

"Ranger?" Graeme guessed, a rumble of displeasure in his voice. "Was he put out that you had him fired?"

The rage Ranger had displayed concerned him more than he wanted to admit. The scent of hatred coming from the man he'd called friend had shocked him with its depth. Hatred that strong had to have been brewing for a while.

"Draeger pulled him out before I could get hold of him." He breathed out roughly before relating the incident to his brother.

Cullen shook his head when he finished, still trying to make sense of it. "I could feel his need to hurt her, Graeme. I believe he's attempting to justify blaming Chelsea for the fact that I didn't mate Lauren."

Silence descended but for the beeps of the machines and the low whirring of their fans as he and Graeme continued to run the blood and DNA samples.

"I suspect Lauren knew Chelsea was your mate." Graeme shocked him with the statement.

Turning to his brother, Cullen watched him suspiciously now.

"How do you figure? Hell, even I didn't know. God, Graeme, she was like thirteen or something when I married Lauren."

Graeme stilled then, a distant look coming over his expression for long moments before he shook his head as though in reply to some inner dialogue. His brother could be amazingly good at talking to himself too.

"I believe Lauren may have had some psychic ability. Weak, but still present enough that she might have picked up on something you were unaware of at the time," he revealed. "Just as I believe your mate has a stronger gift, perhaps one similar to her grandfather's or her cousin's."

Orrin Martinez was a Wind Listener, able to hear secrets in the wind, he'd told Cullen once. Chelsea's cousin Megan Arness had such a strong empathic ability that until her mating with a Lion Breed, Braden Arness, she'd been forced to keep herself mostly isolated.

"And you know this how?" Cullen questioned him doubtfully.

"I'm really not certain how I *knew*." Graeme stressed the past tense. "When I found you it was right after her death, I believe. I broke into the clinic treating her and stole several blood and urine samples that were taken just before her death." He flashed Cullen a satisfied look. "Specialists such as hers keep those for various tests after the death of a patient."

"Thief," Cullen muttered, watching his brother warily.

"Whatever works," Graeme stated. "I've tested those samples extensively over the past ten years," he explained then as he input commands on the keyboard and another monitor flared to life, filling the screen with a series of multicolored, complicated genetic strand sequences.

"Orrin Martinez." He pointed to the upper strand. "Lauren's, and Chelsea's." He identified the lower strands. "Lauren's is similar to her grandfather's, though the exact makeup of it is much weaker and was far harder to find. While your mate's appears far stronger, but the makeup of it is entirely different. The research I've done indicates Lauren may have held a slight sensitivity I believe to be in the 'reading' category. Possibly the ability to sense bonds and connections. I'm still working on it, though. I'm certain I'll have a clearer picture of it soon enough."

Cullen could only shake his head in amazement. Graeme could read genetic code with an instinctive, terrifying ability. His intelligence and instincts where genetics were concerned were growing at an astounding rate after his mating.

In some cases, his brother had revealed, he no longer needed to be in Primal form to sense genetic as well as emotional bonds and had even begun to recognize certain genetic markers by scent.

"How do you keep what little sanity you possess?" he asked his brother. The amount of information Graeme could sense would drive even the strongest minds into never-ending madness.

"What sanity?" Graeme murmured, completely serious now. "Never doubt the madness, brother. I simply control it, rather than it controlling me now. For the most part anyway. Now, as for your mate," he continued, shooting Cullen a sharp look. "She's amazingly healthy. I can smell the changes occurring in her genetic code; it's adapting, though slowly, which indicates a much stronger mating. It's in line with the Primal genetics I've always suspected you possessed. Though I'll know more once I've processed her samples."

Primal genetics, or the madness his brother called his greatest strength and the monster that lived inside him. Graeme had been trying to convince Cullen for years that he carried the same monster inside him, merely waiting for the proper trigger to set it free.

"Once I have all her readings I can create a treatment that will be much more effective and enable the two of you to adapt to the mating much more comfortably than most," he informed Cullen.

The process of putting the hormone therapy together could take several days, though. And that therapy was imperative at this point.

"By the way, I tagged you and your mate last week with the injections I brought," Graeme informed him blithely. "You can decide if she's made aware of it or not. I wasn't going to do it, but the madness overcame my hesitancy."

"One of these days I'm going to stop being so patient when you decide after the fact to inform me of the crap you inject into my body." Cullen sighed, glad his brother's madness wasn't homicidal.

"If you say so." His brother obviously wasn't bothered by the threat as he began coding information into the computer again. "This should be ready in about forty-eight hours," he predicted. "I'd like more blood after the injections, though, just to be certain I have everything coded properly."

"I'll take care of it." Cullen nodded.

"By the way," Graeme said then, his head lifting as though just remembering some bit of information. "Are you ready to talk to Cerves? He's waiting upstairs along with his wife and brother. Lobo's playing reluctant host as they wait for us."

Cullen's brows lifted in surprise. "You had them grabbed?"

"Actually, no." Graeme's brow creased with bemusement. "They showed up several hours ago at Lobo's gate, requesting to meet with him. It seems they're certain there may be a misunderstanding with the commander of Covert Law Enforcement, who they've learned may be a hidden Breed." As he flashed his canines, his gaze gleamed with the wild awareness of the feral creature within. "They've asked Lobo, as the resident alpha leader, to mediate for them." The feral promise of savagery grew stronger in his gaze then. "I believe Juan was a bit concerned when the Primal informed him that you weren't his only problem. He controlled his bladder much better than his lieutenant did. The poor man pissed himself."

Cullen smothered a spurt of laughter as he eyed his brother with mock disappointment. "They just don't have any fortitude anymore, do they?"

"Ball-less," Graeme amended with a sigh of regret. "They just take the fun out of torturing them, don't they?"

A chuckle escaped despite Cullen's best attempt to hold it in. That was his brother's favorite complaint. They just weren't fun to torture anymore.

Cullen gave a heavy breath then, turning back to his brother.

"Before we go up, there's something you should know first."

Graeme stared back at him curiously.

"It was Chelsea who rescued their daughter from the Coyotes that night. I was there, undercover at the time on another operation. I managed to get her out of the Runner she crashed through the gates, get her into mine and out of there before anyone could really identify her. My contact there was able to wipe the security discs and further ensure that Chelsea's identity wasn't compromised. There's a chance Samara might recognize her, though. Before Chelsea revealed Louisa buried under a blanket and strapped into her seat with her, Samara had her gun in Chelsea's face, ready to fire. And that woman has a memory like an elephant."

Graeme was silent, his only reaction the slight widening of his eyes in surprise.

"Now, why didn't I see that one coming?" Graeme pursed his lips, staring back at his brother thoughtfully. "Interesting. Very interesting."

· C H A P T E R   2 0 ·

From Graeme's Journal
The Recessed Primal Breed

The world will rarely acknowledge what only a Primal can accept.
  The Breed believes there are only two types of life, predator and prey.
  The Primal believes in three; predator, prey and Primal.
  And the Primal sits silently at the top of the food chain.

There was something so surreal about stepping into Lobo Reever's opulent study and coming face-to-face with the woman who had held a gun in her face less than two months before.

The woman who stood there, along with the two men, wasn't the woman whose face was spread across tabloids and newspapers before the death of her daughter. The piercing blue eyes and heavy mass of white-blond hair were the same, but the face wasn't nearly as perfect and icily serene.

The Blood Queen she was called, because of the blood she and her family spilled in their battle to maintain control of the powerful criminal organization she'd inherited at the tender age of twenty-one.

The woman standing next to her husband, his arm wrapped protectively her, was a grieving mother. Deep grooves were carved beside her lips, dark shadows marred the skin beneath her eyes and she hadn't even tried to use makeup to hide the effect of the loss of her child.

Samara was dressed simply in black. The tasteful sheath fell below her knees and covered her arms to her elbows. Paired with the dress were expensive black heels and a matching clutch. The fact that she hadn't bothered to adhere to her normal standard of presentation was telling.

Standing next to her were her husband, Juan, and her brother-in-law, Esteban Cerves. The two men were tall, broad and physically fit, but not exactly handsome. They had black hair, black eyes and swarthy complexions, but the cold, emotionless looks they were said to have weren't in evidence any more than Samara's.

Lobo made the introductions, ensured everyone had a drink, then invited them to sit in the large seating area on the other side of the room.

Sitting back in the comfortable leather sofa next to Cullen, across from the longer matching couch the three Cerves family members sat in, Chelsea glanced around the seating area. Graeme and Cat were in the chairs next to the sofa at Cullen's side while Lobo and his head of security, Devril Black, sat likewise on the opposite side of the couch.

Looking down at her hands in her lap, she felt as though all eyes were on her now. It reminded her of family intervention night in the Martinez household.

"We've made the formal introductions," Lobo stated, his deep voice just a little rough but still a pleasant, masculine sound. "We can now address the reason for it."

"Pardon us, Alpha Reever," Samara stated, the soft, silky cadence actually quite pleasant. That slight hint of a Spanish accent lent it an exotic quality. "I believe we're waiting for the reason for this meeting to actually raise her eyes and look at us."

The gentle prod wasn't lost on Chelsea, but she chose to ignore it. The habit of tucking her emotions behind a veil of ice wasn't working. She needed it to work. She needed desperately to find a way to push everything back. Especially the anger.

Because of this woman's determination to hold on to a criminal empire, that sweet, precious baby had suffered a horrible nightmare before dying.

"I think I blame myself most for what happened to my Louisa," Samara stated when Chelsea didn't speak, her voice thick with emotion. "Were I not the Blood Queen, then those monsters would have had no reason to steal my baby from her bed and cause her such pain. Is this not correct, Ms. Martinez?" There was nothing but pain and remorse in the woman's voice.

And still, Chelsea fought the anger burning through her like wild-fire as she felt Cullen's arm tighten around her.

He didn't make excuses for her or try to explain her silence to anyone. He just held her, allowing her to lean on him.

Chelsea hadn't realized until she entered the study and saw Samara's grief how very angry she'd been at this woman. Had it not been for the Cerveses' criminal activities, then as Samara said, her child would have never been targeted and never suffered that horrific night.

Logically, she knew better, though. The Council had targeted other children as well in retaliation against their parents. And the same brutality had been used. Except those children had died alone within such horrible nightmares.

Breathing in deeply, she forced herself to lift her head slowly, her eyes meeting Samara's.

"I'm sorry," she whispered, her emotions still so torn she had no idea how to deal with them. "No matter what parents may or may not have done, no child deserves to be hurt. Especially with such cruelty."

Samara's lips trembled for a moment before she managed to control it.

"I had wished to thank you," the other woman whispered then, holding tight to her husband's hands. "And to apologize. There was such rage that night inside me. When you crashed through our gates I did not imagine it could be more than another attack of some sort. We believed the property we were using there to be a secret none were aware of but our private security. I did not expect deception from Louisa's tutor. She had been with us since my daughter was first born and I believed her to be just as devoted to her." Hoarse. Ragged with tears, her voice broke and it took several moments before she could continue. "I wanted to thank you but had not been able to learn your identity to do so."

Chelsea shook her head. "I failed. Why would you want to thank me?"

Samara's eyes widened. "And how did you fail? Because Louisa passed?" she asked.

Chelsea could only nod painfully.

"You brought my baby home to pass, in loving arms, held by her momma and poppa." Tears slipped from Samara's eyes unashamedly. "She woke for us and we could tell her of our love. She was warm, and tucked safely in her own bed. She did not die . . ." Her shoulders trembled, the naked misery in her eyes breaking Chelsea's heart. "She did not die alone in a nightmare."

Juan winced at his wife's words, pain creasing the dark features as he pulled her closer to him, a tear escaping the corner of his eye as his brother, Esteban, looked away, blinking back the moisture in his own eyes.

"Here, baby." Cullen pressed tissues into her hand, and only then was Chelsea aware of the tears falling down her face.

Finally, Samara gained control of her weeping. Taking the tissues her husband pressed into her hands as well, she dried her face, sniffing delicately before whispering her thanks to a man who appeared to be more a gentle giant at her side than a criminal cartel leader.

"Louisa said it was your voice in the dark, speaking of her momma, that led her through the darkness," Esteban told her then. "That you whispered her momma was awaiting her, to just come to you." His fingers formed into a fist until his knuckles turned white as it lay against the arm of the couch. "You took much personal risk to yourself to rescue her and then to race through the night to return her to us. Whatever we have"—one hand flattened against his chest firmly—"it is yours. You have only to ask."

"Carte blanche," Graeme murmured. "How very interesting."

"Graeme," his wife warned softly. She said nothing more, but evidently he was willing to listen to her for the time being.

Juan breathed out heavily, glancing to Graeme and his wife before turning back to stare at Chelsea.

"There was a time when I believed only the promise of violence would protect us and those we cared for," he said roughly. "Esteban and I knew very little of gentleness as boys. We knew only the lessons that the strong survive. Only those willing to break the rules were feared." His black eyes were bottomless with hollow rage and grief.

"Until Louisa was born, Esteban, Samara and I knew so very little of the true depths of love. She taught this to us . . ."

"She was our miracle," Samara whispered, seeming almost dazed now with the pain she was feeling. "Then, the night she was taken, when we were certain we would never see her sweet face again, an angel brought her home to us so we could whisper our good-byes. So we could surround her with our love. And for that, there is no thanks great enough."

As Samara spoke, Chelsea couldn't help the tears that fell, couldn't stop the ragged hitching of her own breath as she fought back the sobs that wanted to be free.

"I did it for Louisa," she told them, barely able to talk. "Not for any sort of payment or favors. There's nothing I want."

"But if there were . . ." Graeme spoke up, his voice hard. "Sending your men to abduct her and sell her to the bastards who killed your daughter seems in rather poor taste to me."

"Graeme," Cullen growled warningly.

"No, he is correct." Esteban lifted his hand at Cullen's warning. "Were we to have ordered such a thing, then we would be no more than the monsters who hurt the niece I so treasured. Unfortunately, we were in seclusion when this attack was made. We were made aware of it when one of the Breeds in our employ managed to track us down and inform us of what had occurred."

"We returned as quickly as we could." Samara leaned forward imperatively for a moment before sitting back and once again clasping her husband's hands desperately. "The Cerves family does not accept contracts to assassinate, nor do we kidnap for ransoms. We definitely do not strike against young women who are not part of the shadows we exist within."

"Who offered the contract?" Cullen asked, his voice harsh. "I want that name."

Esteban wiped his hand over his face wearily. "Who offered it, we do not know. Fidel Sanchez, he was in charge in our absence." Esteban's voice hardened. "He did not know the identity of the person who offered the contract, but the man spoke to Morales and he was certain he had recognized the voice. He told Fidel he would make sure, then reveal the identity. The contract was for Ms. Martinez's death, and he indicated the hit was personal. Fidel said there was hatred in the man's voice. But when Fidel began putting the plan together he learned that her association with a rumored Breed was possibly that which is reported as a mating, and there was much more to be made for giving a mate to the Genetics Council."

"Bastards!" Samara cried out then, rage burning in her face as a shudder tore through her. "Fidel knew who took my baby and what they did to her." The grief-laden sound was heartbreaking, as was the sight of the mother leaning forward, fighting to get control of her emotions as silent sobs shook her. "To even consider such a thing—"

Juan brought her back to his arms, pulling her head to his chest as he stared at the floor, the pain in his face reflecting that of his wife's soft sobs.

"Fidel Sanchez has already arrived at your Bureau of Breed Affairs," Juan stated when he could look at them once again. "I spoke to Director Breaker myself when my men arrived. He will be tried by Breed Law. And they will punish him for this attempt. He is being questioned by their interrogators. Perhaps he will tell them more than he told us."

Esteban handed his brother more tissues, his expression weary and filled with pain at the sight of his sister-in-law so torn with grief.

"Whoever offered the contract also killed Morales," the brother revealed then. "He contacted Fidel just after doing so and demanded he finish the job and kill Ms. Martinez. Fidel was meeting with a shooter when Juan and I arrived unannounced."

"And now all our people know the dangers of attempting to follow Fidel's examples and accepting contracts we do not approve ourselves. But even more, they now know the hazards of doing any business with the Genetics Council." Juan's smile was one of icy vengeance.

"And we still don't know who's behind it," Cullen bit out. "Did he say anything else about the person offering it?"

Esteban, Juan and Samara all shook their heads in denial.

"I had his testicles in a very painful vise as well." Samara's smile was pure Blood Queen. "I believe had he known anything more he would have told us."

No doubt. Chelsea was still struggling with the reminder that these grieving parents were also murderous.

"I'm curious," Graeme asked, his tone somber.

The three Cerveses looked over at him inquisitively.

"Exactly how do you get them to the point where they're aware you're placing the vise on their testicles? I find they piss themselves within moments, and keeping them conscious becomes more a chore than anything else." The seriousness of the question had Chelsea blinking back at him in shock.

"The trick to sustaining consciousness is to not overly shock their little minds or their bodies," Samara answered, her tone equally serious. "Don't use a sledgehammer when a rubber mallet will suffice. You work your way up to the sledgehammer."

"Graeme, please." It was Cat who protested the turn of the conversation. "Save the blood and gore for a later discussion."

"Forgive me, Ms. Parker." True regret flashed in Samara's gaze. "This is not the proper time or place for such things. I hope you will accept my apologies."

"But *he* asked the question," Chelsea pointed out. "Let *him* beg forgiveness." She threw Cullen's brother a heavy frown, to which he just smiled back complacently.

"There are rules, Chelsea, to everything," Samara stated, her gaze still shadowed with grief, though Chelsea could glimpse the chill of logic and cold hard reason as well. "Strong, independent women fight such rules in their youth, but we learn, eventually, the way of such things."

Evidently she had no intention of learning the way of things then. She'd be damned if she'd apologize to *it* when a stupid question popped out of his mouth.

Cullen shifted beside her and cleared his throat.

Looking up at him, she was surprised to see the amusement flickering in his gaze.

"The look on your face was quite extraordinary," Samara said with a soft smile. "Perhaps he knows the way of your thoughts."

Not hardly. The only thing he'd cared to learn about her was how to make her orgasm. Though he was quite good at that.

"Maybe." She shrugged, not revealing what she thought of that.

Samara sighed heavily then, the momentary amusement she felt drifting away beneath the grief once again. Meeting Chelsea's gaze, she gave her a sad, wistful smile. "Perhaps one day you would allow me to tell you of the little girl you brought home to her momma and the many ways she changed a woman who held no belief in mercy or compassion before the evening I felt the first faint movement of her within my body. And I would tell you how she spoke of you." Tears glittered in her eyes once again. "I would love to share my memories of her with you."

And strangely, Chelsea knew she wanted to know those memories.

She nodded back to the mother hesitantly. "I'd like that," she whispered. "I'd like that very much."

✦   ✦   ✦

Cullen heard the hunger in Chelsea's voice to hear the memories of the little girl she'd brought home to her parents, and in that second he realized something he knew he'd been hiding from for far too long.

He loved her.

His proud, courageous Chelsea, so determined to watch his back rather than accept the protection he would have given her. He wouldn't have been happy with that, though, he realized. She was his mate, and the danger to her would never completely go away. Better she be able to fight by his side. He knew several instances when it had meant the difference between other Breed mates' life or death.

And nothing meant more to him than ensuring she lived. Unless it was ensuring she lived happily.

Sitting here, seeing the utter devastation in this family at the loss of the child they loved, he knew he never wanted to face life without Chelsea. And trying to lock her away from living just to protect her would smother her.

He didn't want Chelsea smothered.

He wanted her loving him as he loved her. The rest, he realized, they could work out as they went.

✦   ✦   ✦

Stepping into the house later that night, in the soft glow of the light Chelsea had left on earlier, he realized the house actually looked warmer than before. More welcoming, maybe.

Locking the door behind him, he turned back to her, watching as she sat down on the couch, her expression so damned sad it broke his heart.

"She's a murderer," Chelsea whispered. "All of them are. They traffic in drugs, people and anything else they can get their hands on, and I felt so sorry for her." She looked up at him, her expression filled with guilt and regret. "I wanted so bad to hate her and all I could do was cry for her and Louisa."

His chest actually tightened at the knowledge of her pain, her own sense of grief.

"It's not in you to hate, baby," he sighed, sitting down beside her and pulling her close to him. "And it wasn't her you felt so much pain for. It was Louisa." He kissed the top of her head, feeling her against him, a warm, sweet weight. "She must have been a very special little girl. One of those sweet souls that visit us for a minute to teach us the true meaning of love."

They had so much to talk about, he realized. There were so many things unsaid between them.

"You were what? Twelve?" he asked. "The night we showed up at your father's home?"

Curled against him, she nodded against his chest.

"The Underground had just snatched us from the grip of Council Breeds after months of running. The girls I'd been trying to protect, Honor and Fawn, were exhausted and terrified. I knew I couldn't protect them if the ones who rescued us turned on us." He buried his fingers in her hair, his mind on the past. "And there I stood, frantically trying to decide if the girls were safe or if I should try to plan to escape." They'd even been too terrified to eat. "Then I glanced into the dark room next to the kitchen and saw you." He couldn't help but smile at the memory. "Big brown eyes and dark hair. Then you grinned and winked." A little laugh vibrated against his chest. "Your father had been trying to convince us to eat some soup."

"His vegetable soup is so good," she reminded him with remembered relish.

"We were terrified to eat, though," he told her somberly. "The Council scientists sometimes drugged our food or drink. And there we were, smelling the most incredible scent of food. I'd never smelled vegetable soup in my life, let alone eaten it. My mouth was watering, the girls' stomachs were growling and we hadn't eaten in days. About the moment you winked, your dad offered soup and milk again, trying to convince us to eat. And I refused again." He had to chuckle at the memory. "And I heard you say, 'Oh, that's so dumb. Soup. Yummy.'"

"I said that?" she asked in surprise. "I could have sworn I just thought it."

"But I heard you," he told her softly. "And I knew in that moment that I could trust you. When I could never be sure of anyone else, I could be sure of the little girl watching me from the dark." He paused, remembering that little girl Chelsea had been. So full of laughter and life. "I hadn't known my animal instincts before then, so I didn't understand that in that moment something so unique had happened. Those instincts had awakened for just a moment. Just long enough to recognize what a nineteen-year-old Breed had no idea how to understand. The animal inside me recognized you. Those instincts knew you were my mate."

She was silent for long moments.

"You don't have to say that . . ." she whispered, but he could sense her need to believe him.

Cullen snorted mockingly.

"At my wedding?" he asked, amused now when he hadn't been then. He'd been damned confused. "I clearly heard you call me a dummy."

Her head jerked up, shock rounding her eyes, parting her lips.

"And, Chelsea," he told her gently. "I do know far more about you than just how to make you orgasm."

Her lips parted as she licked the curves nervously, and he could see her need to understand how he'd known what she was thinking.

Just when he thought he'd found a way to explain it, his phone rang demandingly, the programmed ring tone one he couldn't ignore.

"Dammit," he cursed.

Amusement and lingering questions warmed her eyes as she rose from the couch and waved to the phone. "I'll wait for you in bed."

"And I'll hurry," he promised. "You can bet on it."

Flipping the phone open, he brought it to his ear. "Commissioner Jenkins, how can I help you . . . ?"

· C H A P T E R   2 1 ·

From Graeme's Journal
Recessed Primal Genetics and Mating Heat

The Primal, whether recessed or active, lives within a world of shadows, beckoning madness and brutal strength.

The Primal is not of emotion, gentle and enduring, but icy logic and steely resolve formed by the vast reaches of an intelligence of which even he does not fully comprehend the true depths. And it is this creature whose struggle will be the most difficult to navigate within an emotion formed in chaos, rather than cold hard fact.

That emotion called love . . .

They were going to have to talk.

At least, he was going to have to talk, Cullen told himself the next evening as he listened to Chelsea while she worked at the kitchen table.

It wasn't Chelsea who had a problem talking or expressing herself. Everything she felt for him had always been there in her eyes, in her expression. Besides that, the ambrosia scent of pure chaos was a delicate, subtle presence around her at all times now. The provocative, highly arousing scent of her love for him lingered in the air around her and infused his own unique scent.

As he paced through the kitchen and into the living room, the restless frustration pushed at him. The need to clear up so many misunderstandings, to explain actions that even he didn't fully understand, rode his back like a malevolent demon.

And that demon was clawing at his chest viciously.

Staring through the privacy glass of the front door, he let his gaze rove over the house across the street. Someone had moved in a few months ago. He'd been uncomfortable with the house being empty. Anyone could have used it to watch his home. Knowing it was occupied now made it seem less a threat.

Glancing down the street, he saw the SUV Tobias sat in. Draeger had been watching the back of the house earlier. The two Wolves were damned good. There had been a few times that it had taken even Cullen a few minutes to locate the two Breeds.

Turning from the front door, he made his way through the softly lit house back to the kitchen and the back door. The house was rarely dark anymore. Chelsea kept a lamp on here and there and made it a point to illuminate whichever room she was in.

She wasn't frightened of the dark, she'd assured him the night before when he questioned her about the habit. She simply enjoyed the light and the feeling that nothing was hidden.

Chelsea didn't like subterfuge in her personal life; he'd already known that. She didn't like secrets when it came to her relationships with others and made it a point not to keep secrets that would damage those relationships.

Leaning a hip against the counter, he watched as she worked on her laptop and talked on the phone at the same time. She was still trying to chase down leads on who had taken that contract out on her life, just as Cullen had for the better part of the day. She'd spent every spare moment running down any information or whisper of a lead she could find, as Ashley and her sister Emma made any necessary trips to chase down names or contacts.

"Cullen has several agents working on it," she said into her phone as Cassie Sinclair listened on the other end. "I know that a few of the enforcers we've been working with have some contacts that go much deeper in this game than I've been able to make so far. I contacted them earlier and I'm waiting for word back."

One leg was crossed over the other, her foot rocking rhythmically as she glared down at the video she and Cullen had both gone over more than once.

"There's no word yet if anyone else picked up the contract or even if it went back out. I'm confident no one within the Cerves organization will be picking it up, though," Chelsea replied to Cassie's query on the current status of the contract.

Cassie was silent for several moments, and Cullen picked up the sound of a heavy sigh before she said, "Call me then if you learn anything new, and we'll do the same. Though so far, Fidel hasn't given us any information that the Cerveses didn't include in what they sent to us. I'll update Rule and get back to you soon."

Disconnecting the call, Chelsea laid the phone on the table, closed the laptop, then rose and walked into the living room, where she plopped down on the couch and activated the e-pad with a muttered "Dammit."

The frustration had been building in her through the day, just as the restlessness was building in him. And he couldn't blame it on Mating Heat; he'd already had her twice, and all before dinner.

"Graeme has a line on an informant who has ties to the police department," he told her, following her into the living room. "He sent one of Lobo's Breeds to track him down. He's hoping to have some information soon."

She raised her head, her gaze lifting to him as her fingers tightened on the device. Finally, she rolled her eyes in exasperation.

"Graeme is so full of shit," she told him with mocking disgust. "His informant is Esteban Cerves, with Juan and Samara's blessing, and we both know it. He hit it off with them like they're old, familiar friends. He should be ashamed of himself."

"That's basically Cat's opinion," he chuckled, realizing the soft light of the lamp next to her caused lighter brown highlights to shine beneath its glow.

Dressed in cutoffs and a figure-hugging tank, her feet bare, her toes painted an outrageous shade of brilliant blue, courtesy of Ashley, she looked like the teenager he remembered her being rather than the far-too-courageous, too-stubborn young warrior he knew her to be.

"Doesn't listen to her, though, does he?" She watched him knowingly. "He's going to use this fascination they have for him to suck them of information while he completely mind-fucks them." She gave a little wave of one hand to emphasize her opinion. "What's so damned hilarious is that Cat and I actually warned Samara it was going to happen and she just smiled, as though we were children telling tales. He's a menace, Cullen."

He smiled at the exclamation, realizing how often he smiled now.

"So I've told him often," he assured her. "He just ignores me too."

"He needs his own pride, or a house full of screaming kids." Pure mischievous pleasure filled her expression before it fell dismally. "Geez, I couldn't do that to a kid."

Scheming little wench.

"However he gets the information on the identity of Morales's killer or whoever put out that contract, the closer we'll be to learning who's trying to kill you. And ultimately, that's all that matters to me."

Laying the e-pad aside, she sat back into the couch, rubbing her arms as though chilled, a frown brewing at her brow.

"That brother of yours is so devious he probably already knows who offered that contract and he's just waiting to strike. Before long the poor guy will be locked in Graeme's lair, spilling his secrets as well as those of everyone he knows."

"I wouldn't put it past him," he agreed.

"Why would anyone even want me dead?" she mused, turning her gaze back to him and tapping a fingernail against the arm of the couch. "It doesn't make sense."

No, it didn't make sense, and no matter which way he turned in the investigation he kept running against a brick wall.

"Ex-lovers?" he asked, though he'd already had that angle checked.

Sliding him a sideways glance, she smirked back at him. "Yeah, all two of them, right? Besides." She scratched at her ear with a grimace. "They're both married and living on different ends of the East Coast now." She flashed him a teasing smile. "I'm actually very well liked, you know?"

Yes, she was. She was one of those people who drew friends and loyalties no matter where she went.

As he watched her a shadow passed over her expression, a thought that obviously caused her some discomfort.

"What?" he asked her, watching her closely.

She stared down at the device on her lap for a long moment.

"I had some messages earlier. One of them was from Dad." That discomfort had her shifting in her seat.

"And?" Cullen probed, wondering what her father could have told her.

Somber regret touched her expression before she frowned up at the ceiling.

"Dad said if I don't tell you, he's going to. He's a little pissed." Her lips tightened, obviously not happy with her father's demand.

Cullen waited silently, her reluctance to tell him causing his suspicion to grow by the second.

Lifting her head, she stared back at him, her dark gaze filled with regret. "Ranger came to see him. He tried to convince him I was trying to steal his job and asked for his help to convince Commissioner Jenkins to reinstate him."

Cullen stayed perfectly still, feeling a wild, icy need for retaliation brewing in him at the scent of Chelsea's humiliation.

She lowered her head again, fiddling with the e-pad though he doubted she was actually working on anything.

Cullen clenched his teeth before fighting to relax his jaw. Moving to the couch, he sat on the other end and blew out a heavy breath as he turned his head to stare back at her.

"Graeme suspects Lauren had some small ability to sense bondings or emotional connections," he told her carefully, seeing the frown that touched her brow when she lifted her gaze back to his. "The more I think about it, the more I believe he could be right. And I believe she sensed a bond between the two of us and guessed that once you were older, you'd be my mate." He gave a weary sigh. "I knew she married me hoping for a mating to cure her," he admitted. "Just as I learned she and Ranger were in love. That last year, before her death, she and Ranger were actually together a lot. I assume she told him that Ray had confirmed the truth of Mating Heat and the fact that I hadn't mated her."

Chelsea shook her head in confusion. "I was so young when you married. Even Granddad didn't foresee this."

"Don't fool yourself," Cullen snorted. "Your granddad sensed far more than you realize. He might not have said anything to you, but I believe he was aware of it."

She looked down at the e-pad for a moment, then back to him. "Do you regret it, Cullen?" she asked, her voice low. "That you couldn't mate Lauren?"

And only Chelsea could ask that question without anger or resentment and that quiet sense of understanding he could feel flowing from her. She wouldn't hate him if he felt that way, but the damage to her heart would be catastrophic.

"I have no regrets in who my mate is," he promised her, unable to stop the gentleness that flowed through him or the soft curve of a smile. "What happened then, or now, isn't your fault. If fault has to be laid, then I'll take it. I should have paid attention to the signs of Lauren's deception. Just as I should have paid attention to those I sensed from Ranger." The signs had been there, and his animal instincts hadn't been completely asleep. Just rather lazy and disinterested until his mate came of age. "During our marriage, Lauren's antagonism toward you

increased, though. Little comments she would make, her fury whenever she saw you. I believe she sensed that bond somehow. Knowing
the gifts your family's shown in the past, I can't discount it."

"If she had such an ability, I would have thought she'd have told
everyone who would listen." She frowned thoughtfully. "But Granddad
mentioned something similar just before Lauren's death about her
knowing things she shouldn't." She gave a little shake of her head. "I
can't remember why he said it, though."

"What about you?" he asked then. "What psychic ability do you
have besides projection?"

Amusement filled her eyes as a little laugh left her lips. "Oh, I have
mad skills. Haven't you seen the floating silverware?" She was obviously restraining her laughter.

"Smart-ass," he retorted. Her sense of humor had always lit up the
Underground offices of the Agency when she was there. God, how he'd
missed it. "And I'm being serious. The Genetics Council targeted your
aunt because of the predominance for psychic gifts on both sides of
the family. I believe Orrin once said something about your grandmother having certain gifts."

Remembrance stole across her expression, and her love for her
deceased grandparent clearly showed in her eyes.

"Grandmother could dream-walk," she remembered fondly. "But
only with young children. She used it to soothe their nightmares and
bring them sweet dreams instead. Isabelle has some small ability with
that as well. I had no idea of my ability to do any kind of projection,
though. No one's complained but you." Her smile was wickedly teasing.

"What exactly is dream-walking? How does it work?" he asked.

Chelsea shrugged at the question. "You'll have to ask Isabelle. She
doesn't really talk about it. As for Lauren?" She laid the e-pad aside

and gave a small sigh. "She wasn't close to the rest of the family. If she'd had such an ability we wouldn't have known about it unless it came to us through family gossip."

"Did your grandfather tell you Lauren had cancer before we married?" he asked, watching her carefully.

She shrugged in discomfort, dropping her gaze to her fingers. Evidently she had known. Just as she had known he was a Breed. He remembered seeing her the night the Breed Underground had brought him, Honor and Cat to Terran Martinez's home. She'd peeked at him from the darkness of the other room as he stood in the kitchen, determined to protect the girls. Those eyes had been filled with warmth and curiosity.

"Look at me," he demanded softly. "Just for a minute."

Lifting her eyes, she stared back at him silently, terrified of what might be coming, knowing he could shatter her heart. Cullen could feel that knowledge between them, just as he felt her love wrapping around him.

"When I came here I was desperate for roots, for a sense of belonging," he said sadly. "The phrase 'young and dumb' can apply to Breeds as well."

She nodded, licking her lips nervously. "I can understand that need. Anyone can."

He moved closer to her, reached out and touched her lips with a whisper of a caress.

"Lauren was beautiful and so desperate to live. I was young and my Breed senses nonexistent. Most Breeds can smell a lie, no matter their age. And I didn't have that ability. What I had was a hunger to feel normal." Picking up her hand, he ran a finger over the back of it and sighed heavily before staring back at her once again in regret.

"Cullen, I wasn't jealous like that," she whispered. "We were friends, and suddenly you just weren't a part of my life anymore. It hurt, but I don't resent you or Lauren in any way."

"You're not listening." His jaw tightened furiously, the need to explain, to find the words to explain, filling him with frustration. "I was desperate to believe lust was love and so eager for those roots that I fell into the whole fantasy of it." He shook his head at the memory. "And I was too young, too dumb and desperate for that fantasy to realize that Raymond's fondness for Lauren and his knowledge of my Breed status was a dangerous combination. They thought young lust and desperation was all it took to create a mating, and that a mating would heal her." He laid his finger against her lips when she would have spoken. "I don't hate her for it. I don't even blame her for the attempt. I never have. But I couldn't have mated her. It wasn't possible."

"Because you were recessed . . ." She nodded.

"That's not why. Mating Heat will awaken Breed instincts and they can become active in a second," he explained. "That wasn't why."

Confusion had her staring back at him helplessly. "Then why? I know you loved her . . ."

"You're not listening," he reproved gently. "Lust and a need for roots cannot create a mating. Just because I wanted to believe I loved her at the time doesn't count. Subconsciously, I knew better. And if I didn't, then my Breed instincts sure as hell did."

Chelsea licked her lips nervously, her heart suddenly racing, hope beginning to explode through her despite her best effort to contain it.

"There, you're getting a clue now, aren't you?" The soft approval in his voice had a tremor racing through her.

He couldn't be telling her what she was so desperate to hear.

Could he?

"Chelsea, I love you," he whispered, his voice deeper, rougher. "That's why the Mating Heat flared when I knew you were leaving the Agency and me. That's why, when Graeme told me of your attack, there was no way I couldn't have come to you, and the Heat was stronger when I did. I was going crazy without your laughter, your smart-ass remarks and the warmth that's so much a part of you. I love you. I even loved you when you were a bratty twelve-year-old who winked at me and decided I was crazy for turning down her father's soup. Some part of my instincts demanded I give you a chance to mature, though, as you became older. To grow in who you were, not who I wanted you to be."

Chelsea was shaking by time he finished, joy exploding inside her like fireworks as his eyes seemed to glow with a warmth she realized had always been there, just tamped back. Tamed.

And it was hers.

A laugh spilled from her and she threw her arms around his neck. Falling back to the cushions, he dragged her over him, the strength of his arms enfolding her.

He was hers.

"I love you, Cullen," she cried, finally able to give voice to the feelings that had only grown inside her over the years. "I love you so much."

He pushed her hair back from her face, his touch incredibly gentle, his expression filled with everything she'd dreamed of, even when she'd been convinced he'd break her heart. Yet she'd still given him that heart to shatter if that was what he wanted to do with it.

"Come here, baby," he growled, hunger filling his eyes, his expression. "Come here, my love."

He undressed her first, then himself, the lamp's glow washing over the sun-loved color of his flesh, emphasizing his powerful chest, hard muscular abs and lean thighs and the thick length of his cock.

As he moved over her, his kisses sent hungry flames of need licking through her senses, pleasure pulsing through her veins like adrenaline as he pushed between her thighs, one knee pressed into the cushion of the couch and the other braced on the floor.

His deep, rough growl as her knees lifted, clasping his hips, had her breath hitching in her throat. The signs of his pleasure made her feel more feminine, sexier than before. With one hand he guided the crest of his erection to the aching flesh between her thighs, tucked it against the slick opening, then began pushing inside her.

The sensual, stretching heat battered her senses as he worked the stiff shaft inside her, impaling her with a rush of brilliant sensation.

"That's it, baby," he groaned at her ear, his voice rough, his touch, his kiss, demanding. "So fucking sweet. God help me, I love you. Love you so much, sweet Chelsea."

As he thrust to the hilt inside her then, she lost her breath. The sound of his vow, the heat of his body, his possession overwhelmed her.

He had all of her, but now, she held all of him. Heart and soul and everything in between.

With his lips loving hers, tongue parting them and thrusting inside, he spilled the heated spice she'd grown addicted to as the sensations built to a critical level.

She loved him. She loved this. Loved the waves of exquisite pleasure that rushed through her when he touched her, when he stole her sanity with each hard thrust inside her body.

"I dreamed of this," he groaned, each sturdy, powerful thrust rasping and caressing tissue growing more sensitive with each drag of his cock through the snug depths.

Breathing heavy, their gasps filling the silence of the house, she cried out as those bands of sensual, erotic tension tightened, pushing her higher, closer to the edge of the maelstrom. With each thrust that storm inside her became more powerful, binding her heart ever deeper to him.

"Fuck. Yes," he groaned at her ear when the storm overtook her.

She arched into his thrusts, feeling his hand clasp her hip, his hips moving faster, stroking flames through her senses that overtook her in the next breath.

The explosion was fiery, waves of pure ecstasy battering at her senses now. When he followed her, the barb locked him inside her. The eruption of violent sensation detonated again, quaking through every cell of her body as his release followed hers.

"I love you," she cried out, sobbing with the pleasure, knowing nothing could ever be more perfect than this. "Oh God, Cullen, I love you."

◆　◆　◆

Shock filled him.

His father's heart was breaking at the words he heard through the listening device he'd managed to place in Cullen's home.

He'd actually been willing to let Chelsea live after all. The risks in killing her himself were too high, just as putting out another contract risked having the Cerves family coming after him. From all appearances and everything he heard, he was beginning to believe that if Cullen no longer thought someone wanted to kill Chelsea, his affair with her would pass. Just as the others had, those whores whose bed Cullen had shared.

Even Ranger's certainty that she carried the mating mark was in doubt. After all, it could have just been a love bite.

As the sounds of animal lust began, he hurriedly switched off the device, Cullen's declaration to Chelsea causing his stomach to pitch with sickening disgust.

He'd lost his daughter, the only bright spot in his life. Her loss had broken him, just as it had broken Marsha. As long as Cullen stayed away from the woman Lauren had sensed her husband was bound to, then Arthur had let things be.

Then Ranger had warned him Cullen had become obsessed when Chelsea resigned from the Agency. Pacing, snapping, having Ranger check on her every few days, Arthur had sensed what was coming.

He'd been certain that hiring that Coyote was the answer, but the bastard just had to try to use a blade rather than a bullet. Chelsea had lived and the Coyote had died.

Moving to the window, he stared out across the street at Cullen's house. The soft glow of the living room lamp, the occasional flash of a shadow against the curtains was something he'd not seen there until Cullen had brought Chelsea to his home.

Before, the house had always been dark, not even a porch light burning. Cullen left for work before daylight and returned well after dark, and he'd never brought a woman to the house, preferring to do whatever he did with them, then return to his own bed.

And it wasn't like that anymore.

His daughter was gone, and the man who could have saved her felt it was okay that he hadn't.

A tear escaped the corner of his eye at the memory of the hope that had been stolen from them.

Raymond had been certain Lauren could be saved when he came to Arthur with the plan. All Lauren had to do was convince the Breed to fall in love with her; that was all it took for the Mating Heat to begin.

Then Lauren would be cured. They were certain that soon, she'd be healthy again.

Until Lauren had called while on her honeymoon. The very day after her marriage. She'd been sobbing, swearing she'd sensed Chelsea's thoughts with her new husband. She swore she remembered the feeling from her youth, when she'd met another member of the family whose thoughts of her had been incredibly distasteful. She'd been upset for days.

Hysterical, inconsolable, she swore Chelsea had called to Cullen's recessed animal for that split second, and that animal was bonded to her.

Lauren's gift hadn't been strong enough to read whatever the thoughts were; she hadn't been strong enough to be healthy or strong enough to ensure that Cullen mated her so she'd live.

Chelsea had taken it all.

She'd taken Lauren's ability to read projected thoughts, her health, her strength, but worst of all, she'd taken Lauren's mate, leaving her to die.

Did Cullen really think that bitch would be allowed to live?

Chelsea had to pay for letting Lauren die, just as Cullen had to pay.

Hell, no one would have cared if Cullen took the little whore to his bed if he'd just healed Lauren. Lauren's dreams had been to marry Ranger, to give him children and live her life with him. A healthy life.

They hadn't asked Cullen for that much. All they had asked was that he heal the wife he had sworn to protect.

"Do you believe me now?" Ranger asked from the darkness behind him. "What are we going to do, Arthur?"

Arthur sighed wearily. "Did you take care of the custodian who let you into Morales's cell?" he asked, watching the light and shadows from the house across the street.

"He's dead," Ranger assured him. "I put the bullet in his head myself."

"Then we're safe," Arthur said softly. "And we can make Cullen and Chelsea both pay for allowing our Lauren to die. Now they'll both have to suffer for what was taken away from us, Ranger."

Both of them.

CHAPTER 22

From Graeme's Journal
The Recessed Primal Breed

—*Ever vigilant*

—*Always searching*

Each sight, each sound, every scent that touches its senses is a piece of information, an instinctive puzzle the Primal pieces together. He's always searching, always waiting, existing for but one reason.

The survival of his mate . . .

The next night Cullen eased from the bed, the restlessness plaguing him, refusing to rest. Next to him Chelsea slept deeply, her breathing slow and even. Physical and emotional satisfaction surrounded her, as did peace. She wasn't just calm, she was at peace, and sensing that filled him with pride. Now, if only he could still the deepening sense of something not quite right, that warning energy that he couldn't find a cause for.

Rising from the bed and retrieving the clothes and boots he'd shed earlier, Cullen dressed quickly, silently, before making his way from the house.

Darkness closed around him, shielding his presence. The dark clothing he wore blended into the shadows, hiding him from normal eyesight and ensuring that he blended into the dark. As he freed the Primal senses, the scents surrounding him flooded his mind. And there were so many scents.

This was why so few Breeds lived within cities, he knew. There were too many scents. It made it difficult to distinguish individual smells unless the Breed knew what to look for or had already scented the prey.

Tracking through the night, he made his way around the block, house to house, finding nothing to trigger suspicion or that primal warning again. Until he reached the ravine at the back of his property. There, he caught a smell he knew shouldn't be there.

Ranger.

The other man had been watching the back of the house. There was a faint scent of a Desert Runner, no doubt what the man had used to travel through the desert. Now why the hell was his former co-commander watching his home?

His eyes narrowed as his gaze swept over the ravine, his Breed sight picking up the slightest details right down to the impression of a body as it lay just out of sight, enabling the watcher to peek over the rise and watch the back of the house. And he was armed. That faint metallic scent drifted to his nostrils as a grimace pulled at his lips. Ranger needed to clean his rifle again. He was amazingly lax when it came to keeping his weapon in peak condition.

There had been a time that Cullen had automatically cleaned Ranger's weapon at the office when he'd cleaned his own. That had stopped years ago when Ranger had just dropped the gun to his desk one day with an absent order to clean it for him.

Cullen hadn't cleaned the gun. He'd all but thrown it back at Ranger, his reaction so quick, so explosive it hadn't just shocked Ranger. It had shocked Cullen as well.

Years of what he'd believed was friendship flashed through his mind. There were so many instances when he should have known that the friendship was deliberately cultivated and the many ways Ranger had used it.

Some humans had an almost animalistic sense, an instinctive cunning for how to best use others. They could subconsciously size up strengths, weaknesses and the others' potential to benefit their lives or goals. Ranger had that instinct; Cullen simply hadn't wanted to admit that the man he called friend used it as he did.

Jumping lightly into the ravine, he came to a crouch, drawing in the scents carefully, lifting the cover just a bit to a well of such vast knowledge and impulses that he found himself keeping it carefully contained.

The well was chaos, supercharged, and he was pretty damned certain that it was best to keep it tightly closed, just as he often cautioned his brother to do with the Primal.

That small bit he allowed free was like a drug rush, though. Suddenly, his senses were so sharp, so clear that for a brief second, it was dizzying. The impulse to throw the cover open flared briefly through his head, only to be instantly denied.

He'd found the calm within his mind after coming to the Nation, after staring into a twelve-year-old girl's dark gaze and instinctively becoming locked within the calm that was such a part of her. She'd shared her sense of security, her sense of place within the world, he realized. The moment he'd felt her shock that he refused the food, the animal instinct inside him had instantly recognized the child for what she would be, latched on and drawn that serenity she carried deep inside him.

And it had all been done so seamlessly, without Cullen ever realizing that his Breed genetics were awake within him but simply refusing to react until ready. Not when Cullen wanted it to awaken or react, but when the animal deemed the time had arrived.

Now, drawing on that powerful, inner darkness waiting at the edges of awareness, he identified the scents the ravine carried, and the essence of the man who had been hiding there.

Hatred was the strongest scent, acrid and bitter, like bile against the back of the tongue. It was the strongest of the emotions left behind. Beneath it was confidence, deception. He was certain that whatever his goal was would be achieved. That certainty had its own scent, its own bitter dregs that Cullen's senses found distasteful.

Beneath it all—the hatred, confidence and deception—was the scent of madness. And Cullen knew that scent well; it was similar to the scent Graeme sometimes carried. But whereas the scent Graeme carried was a quick, hard assault to the senses, it didn't carry the dark undertones of blood, no matter how much blood his brother shed.

Graeme believed death was the only way to rid the world of monsters. Let them live and they might breed, and some freak of genetics might well breed another monster. He didn't believe in mercy. Justice was justice, he would often say, and unaccepted acts required what the world viewed as unacceptable reactions.

This scent of madness, rather than a sharp, shocking burst, was just an assault to the senses, despite the faintness of it. And it lingered in a way that had a sudden rumble of a growl threatening to escape his throat.

A second later, he stilled, another scent reaching his senses as it crept up behind him. The Wolf was making just enough noise to alert Cullen that he was there.

Rising from his crouched position, Cullen caught sight of the Breed moving through the shadows, the dangerous wariness he used to stalk the night almost hidden, yet Cullen recognized it instantly.

Remaining crouched, he waited, drawing in Draeger's scent and realizing the Wolf wasn't there because he'd sensed Cullen's presence. It wasn't a scent he was stalking, but the feeling that something far too dangerous lurked in the night.

Animal senses could be amazingly perceptive with or without scent.

Releasing a soft, growling alert of his presence, more a welcome than a warning, he saw the Wolf tense before immediately relaxing. In the next breath he dropped into the ravine, then crouched a good ten feet from where Cullen relaxed back on his haunches.

"Aren't you a surprise," Draeger muttered, his voice pitched low enough that Cullen was certain it went no farther than them. "I couldn't smell you out here, but I damned sure felt that burst of whatever the hell you released. Had the hairs on the back of my neck standing straight up."

Wonderful. He'd end up having to tell Graeme about this, simply to see if it was something his brother had experienced and if accessing those darker senses could be hidden.

"Hmm," Cullen murmured, meeting the Wolf Breed's look. "Tell me, have you caught his scent?"

He didn't have to say who.

"I found it about half an hour ago," Draeger told him as he neared

Cullen. "I was canvassing the area to make certain it went no farther. So far, it's confined here, but his scent is off some way. Has my instincts bristling."

"Yeah, yours and mine both," he admitted, rising slowly and moving closer to where Ranger had positioned himself. "He had his weapon with him. I know because I recognize the scent of it. He doesn't keep it cleaned. It has a distinct scent from the ammunition he uses."

"Damn, son, that's a hell of a nose you have," Draeger commented, surprised. "I caught the scent of a weapon, but that was about it. I couldn't pin it down." Rising to his feet, he came nearer, drawing in the scent at the location Ranger had rested. "That's still all I catch." Cullen could feel his intense gaze flickering back to him again. "Why did you slip around me? You could have let me know you were out here."

Cullen shrugged. "I didn't slip around you. I was restless and decided to check the area myself. I caught his scent as I neared the ravine and decided to check it out."

"As you neared the ravine?" Draeger asked with a bit of surprise. "I was in the ravine and almost at this position before I caught the scent."

Propping his hands on his hips, Cullen let his gaze sweep through the night as he ignored Draeger's comment.

"This is downwind of the house," Draeger pointed out, resting one hand on the sidearm at his thigh. "Would have been easy to hide here, it's farther out than we patrol." He breathed out heavily. "Bastard."

"Where's Tobias?" Cullen asked him.

Draeger tapped his ear, indicating the small communications device he and Tobias used. "He said to tell you the dinner smells coming from your house every evening are killing him."

Cullen let a grin edge at his lips. He'd end up gaining weight at this rate.

He looked around once again, asking himself what the hell Ranger was doing watching his home.

Home.

It had always just been "the house" before; now, because of Chelsea, it was home. It was the soft glow of lamps lighting the room, the smell of something she was cooking drifting through the house, the scent of lemon furniture polish after she straightened each room and now, the faint glow of the kitchen night-light she'd plugged in at the counter, a welcoming invitation of warmth.

It was also a perfect tool used by predators to detect movement in the house.

"Let's get back to the house." Cullen turned and headed back the way Draeger had moved in.

Concentrating on Chelsea with that little edge of power he'd released, he realized he could sense her. She was still sleeping, a deep, heavy sleep that she rarely slipped into.

Sliding beneath the arch of the covered patio, he eased behind one of the stucco columns, drew two of the cigars he carried in his pocket free and handed one to Draeger.

"'Preciate it." The Wolf nodded. "Fucking Tobias found my stash and I haven't had a chance to replace them yet."

"He's still alive?" Cullen asked, his voice low but amused as he lit his own cigar before extending the lighter to the other Breed.

Lighting the rolled tobacco, Draeger gave the lighter back to Cullen.

"I fucking hate Dane for getting me started on these," he growled.

Cullen shot Draeger a wry look. "His family makes these damned things in Africa, just for the Breeds. The blend was specially created so it doesn't block our senses or linger in them once we're finished. All the pleasure, none of the pain," he drawled.

"Hmm." Draeger made an agreeable sound. "This is some good stuff, though. I can be madder than hell and ready to rip someone's head off. Smoke one of these fuckers and I'll consider letting them live for a while longer."

Holding the slender cigar between two fingers, Cullen considered it for long moments. Maybe he should have Graeme check them out. Lifting it to his lips, he drew in the fragrant smoke once again. Hell, he'd been smoking them this long, a few more days wouldn't hurt.

"You know, Tobias and I were at the Cerves compound meeting with a contact when Chelsea busted through those gates with that little girl of Samara's." He leaned back against the column beside him, facing Cullen. "We saw you rush her out of there as fast as hell, before Samara came looking for her. I was terrified that kid would be dead before they got her to the doctors waiting in the estate and certain Samara would kill Chelsea if that happened." Compassion flashed in his expression. "Instead, she's spent weeks since searching for the woman who rescued her little girl and gave her those final days with her."

"Doesn't sound like the stories of the Blood Queen, does it?" Cullen remarked. "I didn't see you there. You were keeping yourselves well hidden."

"We were there for intel and stayed in the shadows," he sighed. "You know they took the kid because the Cerveses refused to use their informants to keep the Council apprised of Breed movements in the area." A bitter smile touched the Wolf's expression. "See, little Louisa loved all things Breed. And if Louisa loved it, then there wasn't a chance in hell they were touching it. So those Coyotes took her daughter instead. She's childless and looking for a daughter. I have a feeling, after that little meeting you told me about at Lobo Reever's, Samara Cerves thinks she's found a daughter."

Cullen hadn't missed Samara's affection for Chelsea before they'd left the Reever estate. The other woman, though grief stricken, had remarked that she'd always imagined Louisa would have the same gentle soul Chelsea had, as well as the same reckless courage.

"Not as long as she's a criminal." Cullen shook his head. "Chelsea won't have it."

Draeger chuckled at the observation.

"When Chelsea was attacked by that Coyote I wondered if that had something to do with her rescue of Louisa," the Breed admitted then. "Then came the Morales hit and I was sure of it. So I did a little checking and finally found the Coyote's partner. Tobias and I had a little talk with him earlier today. It seems the one who attacked Chelsea told him the hit came not because of anything she'd done." He paused, watching Cullen carefully.

"It was because of me," Cullen guessed then. "Someone guessed I was getting ready to take her as my lover."

Draeger nodded with a short, abrupt movement before inhaling from the cigar, then lowering it to his thigh.

"The partner didn't know who it was. It was information he was supposed to get later, but didn't, because I killed his little friend. But if it's because of you, after the shit Ranger was spouting and now his presence in the ravine, I'm guessing it was him."

That wasn't the man he'd known, Cullen thought bitterly. The man he'd known had been a friend and a confidant. But the hatred Cullen had glimpsed in Ranger's eyes now made him a very dangerous stranger.

Drawing on the cigar he frowned, that restlessness and sense of wild fury clawing at him again. Lowering the cigar to his thigh, he drew in the scents of the night and still couldn't place what was bothering him so deeply.

Just to be sure, he directed his senses to the Wolf Breed. What he sensed from the Wolf was the same as it had always been. That core of animalistic honor, human will and Breed fury. A silent, soul-deep fury they all felt, but fought to hide even from themselves, Cullen knew.

At least, until they mated.

"Whoever it is," Cullen said softly, the knowledge of it a certainty that filled his head, "they'll try again. I can feel it coming. I've felt it for days now."

His gaze swept the night beyond the patio and still couldn't detect anything, but he could feel it. Like a tendril of sullen fury reaching out to him, he could sense it.

"Yeah," Draeger agreed, a hiss of sound that would have done any feline proud. "I can feel it like a breath at the back of my neck. Tobias has been itchy too. Tonight that feeling's particularly irritating, ya know?"

Yeah, he knew exactly what the Wolf was talking about. That feeling had his nerves on edge.

"You should get her out of here, Cullen," Draeger told him quietly. "Get her to Graeme's. She'd be safer there."

Yes, she would be. Hell, he should have stayed there instead of bringing her back.

Maybe he should move her tonight.

A faint sound from Draeger had his head jerking around, his gaze finding the Wolf.

He was slumped against the post he'd been leaning on, his eyes open, panicked as he slowly slid to the ground.

Aware but unable to move. Helpless.

Stunned by the paralytic the Council had created to hold Breeds' bodies completely still, muscles relaxed, no matter how much pain the scientists inflicted.

Even as his gaze found Draeger, Cullen was jumping for the back door, desperate to get to Chelsea. And it was already too late.

He felt the dart bite into his neck, the instant, burning, paralyzing effects sweeping through his body as the wild fury he'd sensed trapped inside him broke the bonds containing it.

His mate was defenseless.

Graeme's estate

The report in his hand fluttered to the metal table as Graeme froze, becoming completely still, the Primal jerking awake. Instantly the twin bond he shared with Cullen snapped into place; everything his brother sensed or felt in that moment, Graeme knew with crystal-clear awareness.

The absolute fury and maddened rage of Cullen's Primal struggled against the paralytic, fully awake now and pushing past Breed resistance.

There was no time to warn his mate.

Bengal markings burned over Graeme's skin, claws ripping through the tips of his fingers as strength surged through his body and a roar echoed through the caverns.

Within seconds a powerful black motorcycle shot into the night, the creature riding it enraged and out for blood. And it knew the faces of its victims and the scent of their malevolence.

Hell, he should have killed Ranger and Arthur Holden when he'd wanted to, years ago.

· CHAPTER 23 ·

From Graeme's Journal
The Recessed Primal Breed

Once called to protect his mate, and given freedom by the Breed pushed to the last edge of hope, the Primal will know no mercy.
Nor will the Breed—

Chelsea came awake instantly, her eyes flaring open, an overwhelming sense of panic causing her to roll off the bed and drop soundlessly to the carpeted floor.

The black silk shirt Cullen had worn earlier still lay crumpled on the floor next to the nightstand and her pack. Pulling the compact automatic weapon from the side pocket of the pack, she laid it beside her and hurriedly pulled the shirt on, quickly buttoning it. Thankfully it was a short-sleeved shirt and she didn't have to take time to roll the sleeves up. She grabbed the wrinkled sweatpants that lay half under the bed and jerked them on quickly, her gaze moving around the darkness, searching for whatever had brought her awake.

The automatic, icy containment of all emotions, especially fear or panic, kept her heartbeat regular, or kind of regular, allowing her to hear every sound rather than her racing heartbeat.

Unfortunately, there was nothing to hear.

The house was quiet. And dark.

The soft glow of the kitchen night-light was absent, the partially open bedroom door showing nothing but darkness beyond. And she knew Cullen would have never turned that light out.

He wasn't in the bed with her either. She peeked over the edge of the mattress, just to be certain, and there was definitely no Cullen.

The knowledge that whatever woke her was dangerous crawled over her flesh. That sensation assured her that danger was in the house with her.

Holding her weapon carefully at the side of her thigh, she crept silently to the partially open door and let her gaze slide to what she could see of the hall.

Where was Cullen? Why wasn't he in the bed with her?

He wouldn't have left her alone and gone anywhere without her. He was too protective, too possessive.

So where was he?

Staying completely silent and allowing her gaze to adjust to the darkness, Chelsea lowered herself closer to the floor before sliding through the narrow opening between the door and the frame. Any movement of the door would alert an intruder that she was awake, and she wanted to make certain she saw them first.

Once in the hall, she remained low to the floor, watching the darkness carefully.

There were no odd shadows or shapes that she could glimpse, nothing to indicate why the lights were out or what had brought her so quickly awake.

She could only see part of the kitchen and living room, and she debated the best way to slide from the hallway. The living room door was closer, but something kept drawing her gaze to the kitchen. A sensation or overwhelming impulse.

Moving her gaze around the darkness again, she noticed that everything looked normal. If there was danger, and she was certain there was, then it was just out of sight. But which way?

Rather than moving, she stayed completely still and waited.

Watched.

Part of her training for the Breed Underground had been just this. Remaining still and silent, unmoving while she tried to outwait her trainers.

In this case she wasn't trying to outwait anyone as nice as her trainers.

She could feel the tension slowly gathering inside her, an assurance that whoever was out there was waiting as well.

Where are you, Cullen?

The ice around her emotions threatened to crack when she couldn't sense him, couldn't feel him. Whatever she felt in that moment sent a chill up her spine, and panic threatened to break through the ice.

She felt maddened violence unchained. What the hell could that be?

Where was Cullen?

Even as that thought passed through her, the suddenness of the attack, when it came, shocked her.

The blow to her head wasn't enough to knock her out. Instead she was thrown to the floor, her weapon falling from her hand as she fought to remain conscious.

A second later, harsh fingers gripped the hair at the back of her neck, dragging her to her feet as she cried out at the pain.

"There you are, pretty girl," a dark, sinister voice crooned, his curved canines flashing in the dark as black eyes gleamed with malicious pleasure. "Wanna be my chew toy?"

"Not yet." The voice that came out of the dark sent a searing surge of bitter betrayal tearing through her.

The Coyote quickly jerked her around to face the man who spoke: Arthur Holden. But standing beside him was Theodore Ranger, and in their eyes she saw the promise of pain.

"Let's go," Ranger ordered, nodding to the back door. "Before we're seen."

Pain exploded in her head then, stealing consciousness and hope. Her last thought . . .

What happened to Cullen . . . ?

◆　◆　◆

Cullen felt Chelsea's sudden silence. It wasn't like sleep where he could sense her peace or her calm. She was suddenly just gone.

Minutes later the back door opened, the scents of the three passing mingled with Chelsea's. The fury already raging through him exploded with greater force at the scents he identified. Arthur and Ranger and with them a Coyote Breed whose malignant scent and stench of old blood marked him as a Council Breed.

As they passed, carrying his mate, strength surged through him, Primal power and strength erupting beneath his flesh. Claws tore through the tips of his fingers, stripes burned across his flesh and a consuming, insane rage pushed the last of the effects of the paralytic from his body.

Distantly, he realized the shock Draeger experienced as Cullen flipped to his feet and into a crouch. He heard the sound of a heli-jet that had landed just after he went down and was powering up, preparing to lift off.

Launching himself toward the black craft, he ran across the property behind his house, a roar ripping from his throat. The heli-jet lifted from the ground as he neared it, gaining altitude even as he pushed himself up, springing toward the aircraft with another enraged roar.

He almost managed to secure a fingerhold.

Almost.

A feline scream shattered the night as he hit the ground and the heli-jet shot through the night sky, taking his mate with it.

With his teeth bared, the furious guttural sound tore from his throat, echoing through the night as his twin appeared beside him.

They'd taken his mate.

"Get the Runner," Graeme snarled. "She has a tag under her skin and I have the tracker. We'll find her, Cullen. I promise you, we'll find her."

◆　◆　◆

Chelsea came awake slowly, fighting the nauseating pain in her head. Arthur and Ranger hadn't given a damn about damage, had they? She could feel her eye already swelling, throbbing horribly right along with her head.

Concussion maybe. Several deep bruises, nothing broken, and she was fucking cold. Of course, she wasn't exactly dressed for strolling through the desert night.

"Our little chew toy's awake." A sinister chuckle sent a chill racing up her spine. "We'll get to play soon."

Forcing back a shiver, she told herself Cullen would be there soon. He'd come for her as soon as he realized she was gone.

"Open your eyes, bitch." A kick to her thigh, hard enough to pull an involuntary cry from her lips that was met with a low chuckle.

Chelsea glared through the tangle of hair that fell over her eyes. The longer they waited to kill her, the better her chances of survival.

The other two Coyotes weren't alone at the low fire—drinking coffee, and that coffee smelled almost good; sitting with them were Arthur and Ranger.

"Look how angry those eyes are," Arthur sighed. "As though she has a right to that anger."

She had a right to her anger. Of course, she wasn't the crazy one.

"You made all this incredibly easy, Chelsea," Arthur told her, regret filling his tone and his expression. "Though I had actually decided to let you live, to let my anger go. Until Cullen mated you."

The two Coyotes sitting at the fire watched her with cold, unblinking eyes.

"Cullen will kill you, Arthur," she told him, her voice bleak. "You'll never get away with it."

"Why do you think that?" The taunting smile on his face was actually scary.

Carefully taking in everything around her, Chelsea began quickly formulating the best way to escape. Her options were actually rather limited, though.

Arthur stood next to the Runner parked just behind them; Ranger sat on the hood, his booted feet propped on the metal brush guards as he watched her with hard, hate-filled eyes. To his side was another

Runner, the running lights at the sides of the vehicle actually lit and glowing dimly in the darkness of the night.

There were two Coyotes hunched next to the fire, sipping coffee silently, their gazes hooded as they watched her. The third Coyote stood by the Runner, anticipation gleaming in black eyes, his scarred face highlighted by the flickering flames.

"You didn't answer me, Chelsea," Arthur snapped, frowning at her as he walked toward her, the hatred in his face causing her stomach to sink. "What makes you think Cullen will kill me? Do you think he knows either Ranger or I was there?" His smile was triumphant. "Word will reach Cullen in a few days that you were taken by the dogs that killed the Cerves brat. And your body will never be found. But he can sense you, can't he?" His look was filled with pleasure now. "And he'll know the hell you're experiencing. A hell even these dirty dogs can't compare to."

Arthur missed the looks the two Coyotes slid his way at the insult. She had a feeling they might end up killing him before Cullen ever managed to arrive, if the looks the two Breeds shared were any indication.

"He'll smell you," she told him wearily. "You and Ranger both."

"Not so." Arthur smiled, the flickering firelight throwing a reddened hue over his expression as he stood above her. "We used a scent blocker ourselves. His animalism may be active now, but it's distinctively weak. Otherwise, he would have caught the fact that I've been staying in the house across from him for months."

The bastard was crazy and it was obvious neither he nor Ranger knew anything about Breeds or how their instincts worked.

And those Coyotes sure as hell weren't helping them out.

"You can give up hoping for a rescue," Ranger called out to her then. "Cullen has no idea where you are or who took you. And by the time the effects of the paralytic he was shot up with wear off, you'll be long gone."

Oh God. The paralytic was one of the most horrifying drugs created to use on the Breeds while they were in captivity.

"She's figuring it out now," Arthur said quietly. "She's not as stupid as we thought she was."

That paralytic could last up to eight hours, in some cases longer. She could be dead by the time he found her. Or what he said? Long gone?

She wasn't going to make it easy for them. She would have her chance, she promised herself, and the longer they fucked around, the greater her chances of actually managing to get away.

It wouldn't be easy, but she'd take whatever she could get.

"He'll kill you the hardest, Ranger," she warned him. "Cullen trusted you."

"Of course he did." Ranger shrugged, unaffected. "I made sure of it when your uncle Ray told us what he was. If his Breed status changed, then we needed to know so Council soldiers could reacquire him."

There was no way she could hide her surprise.

"Yes, the Genetics Council." Arthur smiled cruelly at her look. "Covering our tracks when Ray died wasn't easy. Do you really think he was the only one watching those bastards? Your Breed Underground is good, but the Council is better, and they've been at it far longer. You could never guess the men and women you meet almost every day who are part of a very organized network to keep track of those fucking animals and the dumbasses who support them."

The Coyotes glanced at each other, their expressions flickering with distaste. They didn't like being called animals. Go figure.

"With you gone, his mind tormented by that little gift you have to communicate with him, especially while you're screaming in agony I bet, then we'll have our revenge. When we're tired of tormenting him, then we'll take him out. Or the Council will come for him." Ranger grinned, the thought of it evidently giving him a large measure of satisfaction.

"Lauren really didn't want Cullen hurt." Arthur sighed, his voice saddened as he stared down at her. "She had a good heart despite his betrayal. He could have saved her, though, but he let her die instead. He has to pay for that."

Chelsea shook her head desperately. "He would have saved her if he could."

Fury instantly transformed Arthur's face. "How could he save her when you refused to allow him to do so?" he burst out, enraged.

Before she could avoid the blow, he backhanded her with enough force to throw her to the side, her mouth filling with blood as waves of dizziness began washing through her.

"She knew you were the reason he wouldn't mate her. She knew you were his mate."

"I was twelve," she gasped, weakly spitting out blood and trying to breathe through the pain.

Oh God, that hurt. That hurt so bad.

"You were and still are nothing but a fucking whore," Arthur screamed. "She knew every time he could sense you. You wouldn't let him go. Not even long enough for him to save her."

His foot connected with her hip, and the agony that streaked through her pulled a hoarse cry from her throat. The pain shattered her senses, causing her stomach to heave sickeningly.

"Enough, Arthur," Ranger ordered. "Leave something for your dogs to chew on later or they'll feel cheated."

"She deserves to pay." His breath heaved in and out of his chest. "If she had left him alone, Lauren would have lived."

Chelsea fought to keep from passing out. Dark waves of agony kept rolling through her senses, making her wonder if he'd broken her hip.

"Breeds never mate children," one of the Coyotes sneered. "The animal won't respond to a female who's physically incapable of enduring the Heat."

"Lauren knew he would mate her . . ."

"That sounds like a personal problem to me." The other Coyote laughed. "I don't care what the bitch did, I just want make sure she still has a little fight in her when it's time for us to play."

"And you wonder why I call them dogs, Ranger," Arthur sneered, moving away from her.

"I didn't say I wondered why." Ranger laughed. "I said one day one of them will end up killing you for it."

She wished they'd kill him now.

Where was Cullen? He really needed to hurry and rescue her now. If he didn't hurry, then she might not survive the night.

What were they waiting for anyway?

Chelsea fought the shudders threatening to tear through her body. She was too cold to restrain the deep tremors, and that made it harder to push back the pain. Cullen's shirt and her thin cotton sweats weren't much protection.

"What time is it?" Arthur snapped from where he paced by the fire. "Have they contacted yet?"

They. The Genetics Council. She had to find a way to get away from them; she didn't have much time left.

"Not yet," the third Coyote answered. "They shouldn't be much longer. They had to make a stop first."

Cullen had told her the Genetics Council would love to get their hands on a Bengal Breed mate. And it looked like Arthur intended to give them one.

"You won't get away with this, Arthur." She had to swallow back the need to vomit. "Cullen will make certain of it."

"Cullen will be too busy grieving for his mate." He laughed gleefully. "This is actually much better than having you killed as I first planned. This way, Cullen suffers as Ranger suffered. Terran knows the hell I've lived, and you get to pay for Lauren's death. It works out beautifully. Once the Council scientist who's arriving confirms the mating, you'll be taken to one of their facilities. That's your punishment and Cullen's for letting my daughter die."

He was crazy.

Chelsea stared back at him in shock.

"Arthur, don't do this." She couldn't believe the horrible evil spilling from his mouth. "Lauren wouldn't have wanted you to do this."

"Lauren's dead, Chelsea," he stated brutally. "She's been dead for a very long time and I've waited long enough to make certain Cullen pays for it."

There was no convincing him. She could see the insanity gleaming in his eyes.

I love you, Cullen. Closing her eyes, Chelsea sent the thought out, hoping he was right about sensing the strongest of her emotions.

She turned her head to look at the stones behind her when she realized the boulders she'd been resting against before Arthur's blow held darker, deeper shadows stretching out behind them. Her eyes narrowed, realizing that behind the rocks there was actually what appeared to be a small entrance into the wall of the shallow canyon they'd brought her to.

Dragging herself back to a sitting position against the rocks, she had to keep from blacking out as pain shot from her hip, exploding in it as she struggled to pull herself up.

Resting back against the rocks, she lowered her head and drew in a deep breath, watching them from beneath her lashes.

If she got lucky, really lucky, maybe it was deep enough that she could slip inside it and the narrowness of the entrance could hide her scent. Graeme had said the hormonal therapy he injected her with had an added scent blocker, that it wouldn't completely hide her scent, but it wouldn't carry as far.

She just needed them to be distracted for a minute, that was all.

Instead of becoming distracted, though, the quieter of the three Coyotes never took his eyes off her. Each time she let her gaze drift to the fire and the coffeepot sitting on the rocks next to it, she realized he was watching her.

The other Coyote had leaned back against a boulder, eyes closed; the third stood with Ranger. Arthur paced or stood with his back to her and talked to Ranger as the younger man rested back against the windshield of the Runner.

Her gaze moved to the coffee again. It was smelling better by the minute, and the scent was drifting to her, teasing her with the knowledge of the warmth it would hold.

It was then she realized she was actually downwind of them. If she did manage to slide behind the rocks behind her and into the hidden entrance extending into the wall, then her scent might actually be hidden enough that she could get away with it.

Sliding her gaze to the fire once again, she saw the tallest of the Coyotes fill his coffee cup, then bump his buddy's shoulder with some laughing comment. The other gave a low, approving laugh as the Coyote strode away from the fire toward her.

Arthur and Ranger glanced at the movement, then turned back to their conversation.

Of the three Coyotes, the one nearing her was by far the most dangerous. Tall, corded muscles shifted beneath his khaki-colored pants and shirt, and his gaze was piercing. His eyes weren't black, she didn't believe, but she doubted they contained any mercy either.

"Hey, man, give her some for me," the Coyote with Ranger called out, laughing. "I'll give her some for you later."

Oh God.

Stopping next to her, the Coyote hunched on his knees, the steaming coffee held between his hands.

"You look cold." He extended the cup, the metal rim touching her lips as she watched him warily.

He gave a slight nod toward the cup. "Go on, before they get suspicious and Holden decides to come over and see what we're doing."

He pressed the cup a little more firmly against the seam of her lips and tilted it as they parted. The heated liquid dribbled over her lips and to her tongue. The moist heat flowed from the cup, and as she swallowed she swore she felt the heat sinking to her body.

Pausing briefly, he would wait, tip the cup to her lips again, and give her more, letting her sip at it greedily until she didn't care that she could taste the decaf. She was so cold she didn't give a damn if it was decaf or not, she needed the heat.

"Come on, Dog, make the show interesting, man," the other Coyote called out. "I know how shy you can be."

Hard lips quirked at the snicker from behind him.

"Can you run?" he asked, his tone so low she could barely hear him, and the question shocked her.

She pulled the surprise back and pushed it behind the ice. She was downwind of the other Coyote, but it was better not to take chances.

"The hip," she muttered. "I won't be fast."

"Bastard." The curse was a quiet, insulting hiss.

"Who are you?" she asked, glancing to the fire as the Coyote stood with Ranger and Arthur now, obviously regaling them with some story.

"Don't worry about who I am. Now here's how we're going to do this." He kept his gaze on hers, intent, demanding. "And you have to do exactly as I say."

"Why help me? You killed Louisa," she accused him painfully. "Why help me and not her?"

"Not me or my partner." Something cold and vicious flashed in his gaze. "But they don't know that. If you want to live, shut up and pay attention."

She shut right up.

✦ CHAPTER 24 ✦

From Graeme's Journal
The Recessed Primal Breed

Once free, the Primal will track his mate or his enemy, to the ends of the Earth if he must. And God help the enemy if he's found with the Primal's mate—

Cullen could sense his mate. She was alive, reaching out to him and preparing to run. He swore he could feel her plotting, though he could also sense her certainty that he would come to her. She knew he would, but she was determined to help herself as well, believing that if she could manage to get away, then the danger to him would be lessened.

Wild courage and soul-deep independence. That was his mate. And he was coming for her. When he reached her, when he knew her safety was ensured, then both Arthur and Ranger would die.

Leaving them alive wasn't an option. Alive, they'd always search for a way to escape. The risk that they'd find a way to hire out another attempt on Chelsea's life was too high. Come dawn, their blood would stain the desert, and their hatred would be stilled. Their threat to his mate would never exist again.

Crawling on their stomachs, he and Graeme eased to the top of the shallow canyon, surprised at the area where the Coyotes had chosen to camp for the night. Their campfire sent flickering shadows through the ragged cut formed into the Earth. The Coyotes along with Arthur and Ranger were positioned at the wide mouth of the canyon while Chelsea sat inside it, too far away from the fire to feel its warmth, and the night was far too cold to allow her to maintain her body heat.

Forcing his gaze from his shivering mate, Cullen slid his attention back to the Coyotes as they sat around the fire. Neither of the two at the fire had been the one who'd aided the abduction of his mate. The smell of dark malevolence and old blood wasn't drifting on the breeze as it eased from the canyon. The scents he picked up assured him that he recognized the two who waited with all apparent laziness, for whatever reason they were there. The third, next to Ranger, was another story.

"What are they doing here?" Graeme hissed, a low hiss of savage, impending danger as he too recognized the scents of the Coyotes below. "Son of a bitch. Someone needs to kill them and their master."

"They're no doubt manipulating the situation," Cullen growled. "They can live as long as they don't endanger my mate or stand between us."

He was taking her out of there. He'd only paused at the top of the canyon long enough to get a look at the situation and determine the best way to go in. He could slide over the canyon wall; the strength that filled his muscles and hardened his bones now ensured that he could take the high drop easily. A good thing, because to stay out of sight of the sniper rifle Ranger kept carefully in his hands, it wouldn't be possible to climb down the more slanted entrance.

And their time was limited. From the conversation minutes before, he knew the heli-jet carrying the Council scientist sent for Chelsea would be arriving soon, along with a team of Council Breeds. A team was normally composed of a dozen of the best the Council had trained and whose loyalties were considered solid.

As he watched, the Coyote he'd recognized first, a powerful, smart-ass bastard, filled a metal cup with coffee from the pot at the fire before strolling across the distance to where Chelsea was propped against the canyon wall.

"Hey, man, give her some for me." The sound of lust and amusement was called out as the Coyote approached Chelsea. "I'll give her some for you later."

Ranger and Arthur both laughed, their gazes cruelly satisfied as they watched the Coyote move toward Chelsea. Before he reached her, the one next to the fire rose and stepped to the Runner, his laughter drawing their attention as he began to regale them with some story of blood and mayhem.

Keeping his gaze on the Coyote approaching Chelsea, Cullen watched as he crouched next to her, placed the cup against her lips and allowed her to drink the steaming liquid. The small amount of confidence the warmth returned to her would ensure mercy if by some chance Cullen had to kill him.

"Can you run?" The Coyote's words were too faint to hear, but

Cullen's better-than-normal night vision picked up the carefully formed words on the Breed's lips.

He didn't hear her response, but he knew it. Hell, he didn't even need to acknowledge what he sensed; he knew Chelsea. She would have to be unconscious to not attempt to escape. She was too damned stubborn to stay in place and wait to be rescued.

"We've got to move," Graeme hissed. "That heli-jet due in will become a problem if you don't have Chelsea secured first. I may need your help taking that scientist."

"I'm not here for a scientist." Cullen's gaze snapped to his brother, but just for a second.

"Fine, get your mate out of here and I'll take the scientist myself." The harsh rasp of the Primal's voice wasn't in the least worried about going against a dozen Council Breeds on his own.

"From a team of armed, brainwashed Breeds?" Cullen asked dubiously.

"The scientist is damned important or she wouldn't be traveling with her own security team. Besides, one less scientist they have in their possession is one less monster running amok in the world."

His brother just couldn't let this be easy, could he? He never failed to find a way to make things more difficult. As though the situation weren't dangerous enough.

"Cat will be pissed if you get yourself killed," Cullen warned him, the words a reminder of what could happen, nothing more.

"She'll be pissed anyway because I didn't bring her with me." Graeme glanced to the sky just as Cullen felt what was coming.

The heli-jet was still miles out but coming in fast and covert. The danger to his mate was increasing with unacceptable speed.

At the same time, the Coyote next to Chelsea gave a hard burst of laughter as Chelsea screamed into the night. She rolled from the Breed, struggling to her feet, obviously having a difficult time staying upright.

She was hurt, unable to run.

"Go on," the Breed laughed. "Run, little rabbit. You have two minutes to hide."

That was all Cullen needed.

In a fast roll he went over the edge of the canyon, dropping to the ground in a silent crouch. The Primal surged closer to the surface.

Between one heartbeat and the next he could feel the additional strength, his senses opening to such vast perception that it would have been painful if the additional adrenaline weren't surging through him.

Graeme would do as he wanted no matter Cullen's objections, and he knew it. It was far better to secure his mate first, then help Graeme.

If any help was needed.

◆　　◆　　◆

"If I don't live through this, and if the women on the heli-jet that's arriving aren't rescued, then you contact Dash Sinclair," the Coyote warned her. "You tell him Jonas's suspicions are true. Do you understand?"

"I understand," she assured him.

"Now, I'm going to start laughing. I want you to scream, get to your feet as fast as possible and get to the back of the canyon. There's a cave there. I've ensured that it will hide your scent. Get there, all the way to the back, and you'll find hidden fissures running down the wall. Slide into one of those and remain silent. Enforcers will be here before dawn and their commander will know to check those caves, just in case."

"What's going on?" she hissed, feeling the sense of danger rising even as she sat there. "And who are you?"

"I'm just a dog," he told her quietly. "That's all. Now, are you ready?"

He didn't give her time to answer. His laugh was suddenly dark with depravity, his expression turning cruel and filled with purpose.

Chelsea screamed, putting all the horror and fear she could into it.

She could sense Cullen coming closer in the minutes the Coyote had sat there. She could feel him, his warmth beckoning to her. The oddness of the sensation, the certainty of it, gave her strength as she struggled to her feet. The pain at her hip was slicing, almost putting her back on the ground, but she managed to find her balance and suck in a hard breath to control the dizzying reaction to it.

"Go on, run, little rabbit," he suggested with brutal savagery. "You have a two-minute head start."

Run to the back of the canyon.

Turning, Chelsea cried out in agony as her hip threatened to go out on her, but she managed to move, limping as quickly as possible into the heavy darkness of the canyon stretching out behind her and heading to the far end.

A cave. *Hide in a fissure,* she reminded herself, pain and the icy cold of the night making her clumsy, stealing too much of her strength. But she managed to push past the low boulders and keep going despite the rocks that bit into the soles of her feet and the agony vibrating in her hip.

One second she was gasping, her breaths almost cries as she pushed herself to follow the orders the Coyote had given her; in the next, she was swept up into Cullen's arms, the heat of his body sinking instantly into her as she tried to smother her shocked cry.

He didn't speak. With a speed she could have never imagined, he ran the length of the canyon, keeping her securely clasped against his chest until she found herself in the cave the Coyote had told her was there.

Easing her down to a smooth, flat boulder, he gripped her shoulders, his eyes glowing green and gold in the dark as she stared up at him in shock.

"You have to wait on me, baby." He pushed her pack into her hands. "Your weapon's in there, but I don't know what else you had packed. Stay here."

He gripped her shoulders again, his fingers just short of bruising as those eyes held her transfixed.

"Promise me you will, Chelsea. Promise me you'll stay safe," he demanded.

She had her weapon, a Thinsulate jacket and a pair of sneakers in her pack. She would be safe.

"I promise," she gasped, drawing in hard, desperate breaths. "I'll stay safe."

His lips ground down on hers then, his tongue thrusting between her lips as the shock of the blazing heat of cinnamon, combined with a taste that reminded her of the desert at midday, slammed into her.

The mating taste whipped through her senses, drowning the screaming pain and erasing the dizziness in her head as her body came alive for him.

As he pulled back, those brilliant eyes blinked, the startling glow of them suddenly dark, only the glitter of life staring down at her in the pitch black of the cave.

"Stay put, no matter what," he rasped, the growling sound of his voice not his normal roughened tone, but there wasn't time to question.

She could hear the low hum of a heli-jet coming in on stealth mode and coming in low. The vibrations of the powerful motor trembled through the cave as Chelsea hurriedly dug into her pack and dragged on the night vision glasses she kept there.

Instantly she could see. Not as well as she could if she were outside, but she could see to find the cushioned socks she wore with the thin sneakers that folded easily into her pack. The jacket she pulled around her arms as quickly as possible, zipping it up to her neck.

Her weapon had been pushed into the side pocket, still loaded and locked in readiness to fire. There were pain pills at the bottom of the pack, but she left them in place. She still hurt, but the pain wasn't slicing ribbons tearing into her ability to think. And she could walk, if not gracefully, at least not with the staggering weakness that the pain caused.

Seconds later she was slipping from the mouth of the cave just as the first enraged roar of a tiger screamed through the night, followed quickly by the second.

The night lit up like fireworks exploding too low to the ground. Automatic weapons shattered the peaceful quiet, lighting up the entrance to the cave with rapid flashes of light that had Chelsea rushing to get closer.

There was plenty of cover to stay behind, she assured herself, but she was not letting Cullen and Graeme have all the fun by themselves. Now dammit, that was just uncalled for.

At that thought, the violence that exploded through the night shook the ground with the thunder of powerful Runners suddenly shooting out of nowhere, along with the explosions of automatic weapons discharging enough ammunition to supply a small war. Which was what it sounded like was going on. The night had erupted into a war, and they were leaving her out of it.

Dammit.

◆　◆　◆

Cullen glimpsed Ranger and Arthur running for the outcropping of boulders and rock opposite the canyon entrance when the cartel soldiers swept in from the night, Graeme's wife, Cat, leading the fray with the roar of a Bengal that should have done her mate proud.

Ranger tossed his spent rifle to the dust, scampering away and leaving Arthur to rush after him, his aging body unable to keep up though he gave it a valiant effort.

Graeme was in the thick of the Breed soldiers who spilled from the heli-jet. Twelve hard-eyed, savage beasts intent on nothing but success. Their intent and Graeme's Primal were at odds, though, and as usual, Graeme ended the fight with a victorious feline scream that echoed through the night.

It might have taken him longer than usual, and Cullen was pretty certain he took at least one bullet.

He'd glimpsed Chelsea, still limping but safe, covered by several of Samara Cerves's soldiers as she stepped from the mouth of the canyon. Safe. Thank God, his mate was safe. Though she was at present searching for him.

He had a little matter to take care of first.

He moved lazily through the night, following the scent of panic and fear, a snarl pulling at his lips. And as he expected, he faced Ranger first. Obstinate, his eyes filled with hatred, he tried to jump from the dark in a surprise attack.

His arm went around Cullen's neck, trying to twist him from his feet as he stood still, patient, until the other man dropped to the ground, his legs folding under him. Turning, Cullen stared down at him. The blood he'd scented on Ranger was a bright, vivid splash at his right shoulder and across his left side.

He could live through the wounds, Cullen knew, but he still had another wound to contend with.

"I loved her," Ranger suddenly screamed. "She was mine first. Mine. You don't deserve to be happy, you let her die."

"I didn't let her die," Cullen stated simply, the Primal bite to his voice and his more savage appearance causing Ranger to flinch. "I simply refused to mate a woman I didn't love, and one who sought only to use me to live. Lauren came to peace with that before she died, and I believed you had."

Ranger shook his head, sobbing. "I won't forget that you let her die. I won't. You and that bitch . . ."

Breaking his neck was a simple matter.

Cullen did it without emotion, without remorse, though he had no doubt that when he saw it through Chelsea's eyes, he'd know remorse. He'd know remorse, but he'd also know his mate would be forever safe from the man's unreasonable hatred.

As he stepped back from the body, his gaze lifted. Arthur stepped from behind one of the larger outcroppings of rock, the thin light of a half moon gleaming on the barrel of the weapon he held in both hands.

"Look at you!" Awe and terror mixed with the hatred and psychotic impulses raging through his former father-in-law. "You're a monster."

Cullen growled, a low, savage sound that widened Arthur's eyes and had him trembling.

"You're the monster," he assured the other man. "I'm your executioner."

As the gun fired, Cullen flowed to the side and launched himself at the older man. The bullet flew by harmlessly. Before it struck the rock Cullen had stood next to, the other man dropped to his knees, his gaze sightless now, the deep gouge across his neck severing life before his knees hit the dirt.

Cullen swung around in the crouch he landed in, watching dispassionately as the broken, lifeless form fell to the ground on its side, blood seeping slowly into the dirt beneath it. Then he raised his gaze and met the compassionate, loving eyes of his mate.

Her weapon lowered to her side and a heavy sigh whispered past her lips as she stared at the two men, their bodies still in death, their threat forever silenced.

"They would have ensured we were never safe," she told him without regret, though the sweet scent of her compassion flowed over him, wiping the taint of death from his senses. "Maybe they're at peace now."

He didn't really care if they were or not. They were no longer a threat.

"Graeme and Cat are hissing at each other again because she wanted to fight one of the Coyotes," she told him, limping toward him slowly. "He wouldn't let her and now she's pissed. We should get out there. I think she's going to bite him."

Cullen jumped for her and swung her into his arms as in the darkness his lips touched hers, the rage finally easing from his mind, the burning stripes he'd felt over his body cooling, fading away as her arms clung tight around his neck, her lips meeting his and her love wrapping around his senses.

He was home, he thought. Finally, irrevocably, he had found home.

◆　◆　◆

The Cerves cartel members did the cleanup in the clearing at the entrance of the canyon, their hard eyes, harder faces intent as Graeme and Cullen tossed the bodies of Ranger and Arthur next to the dead Council Breeds who had met the enraged Bengal with a surfeit of confidence but a severe lack of strength and sheer cunning to match.

Just outside the center of commotion, the black stealthy heli-jet sat, ominously quiet. The pilot lay half in, half out of the cockpit, his blood staining the dirt below him. On the other side, the copilot still sat in his seat, a gunshot wound in the center of his forehead.

From the opposite side of the commotion Samara, Juan and Esteban moved quickly into position, weapons held ready, as Esteban gripped the handle to the door and quickly jerked it open.

Samara stared into the heli-jet, something inside her twisting with so much pain it was all she could do to hold back a scream of agonized rage.

The girl—child really, she couldn't be older than five or six—was bound hand and foot, naked, long black hair tangled around her too-thin face, her brilliant green eyes filled with panic and staring back at them with dazed shock. With her, the scientist Graeme had demanded possession of was unconscious, but alive, slumped against the side of the seat she sat in.

The girl, though, was wide-awake, and filled with such fear that her eyes broke Samara's heart.

Snatching a folded blanket she glimpsed beneath the seat, Samara quickly checked for any watching eyes before hurriedly wrapping it around the child, lifting her in her arms and then turning to Esteban.

"They took my baby," she hissed, determined, the fierce protectiveness she couldn't control surging through her. "This is my child. Take her now, and make certain no one sees her."

"Samara." Compassion filled his voice, but she could see the doubt beginning to cloud his eyes.

"Now!" she demanded. "No one can know from where she came. Take her now."

The voice of the Blood Queen; she'd perfected that voice when she was but a child herself.

"Go," Juan ordered him firmly, his tone brooking no refusal.

Looking down at the girl, Esteban felt her shuddering, hard, vicious tremors, her beautiful eyes filled with such fear he couldn't bear it.

Nodding abruptly, he turned and rushed to the Runner he'd driven in, strapped her into the passenger seat and then, activating the stealth mode and sliding the night vision glasses over his face, pulled soundlessly into the waiting night and headed for the compound.

Staring at the scientist, her gaze hard and cold, Samara debated killing the bitch but knew she could be a bargaining tool as well. They'd need someone who understood the unique physiology of Breeds to ensure that the child remained healthy, and Graeme wanted this woman.

There would be no way to hide the child from him, but she had a feeling Graeme didn't exactly think with the same rationale as other Breeds did, even his brother.

If she couldn't bargain with him, she'd just make certain the girl disappeared.

But this woman didn't look like a scientist, she thought, finally giving the unconscious form a closer look. She didn't look more than twenty. Actually, she looked very familiar.

Far, far too familiar.

The world knew this young woman, this Breed who shouldn't have been here in this heli-jet.

"Sweet God," she whispered, brushing aside the multitude of heavy black curls and peering into the girl's pale face.

"Get Graeme," she snapped as two of her soldiers rounded the side of the heli-jet. "Get him now."

The soldier rushed away as Samara felt a heavy, dark foreboding sweep over her.

This was no scientist.

Delicate, quite fragile, and like the child, her hands bound behind her.

"Samara?" Graeme strode around the craft, his wife at his side as Cullen joined him, aiding Chelsea as she limped next to him.

They moved to the entrance of the jet as Samara moved aside.

"This is the only woman here," Samara informed him, shock still filling her. "Tell me this is not who I believe it to be."

◆　　◆　　◆

Cullen moved to the door of the heli-jet and stepped next to his brother, shock resounding through him.

It wasn't possible.

He drew in her scent quickly and knew it was. How in the hell had Council soldiers managed to abduct this woman?

"Cassie?" Chelsea's suddenly panicked voice ricocheted through the night as she struggled to climb into the interior of the heli-jet. "Oh my God, Cullen, let me in there. Cassie?"

Cassie Sinclair?

He glanced at his brother, seeing the narrowed eyes, the flaring of his nostrils.

"Get her out of there," Graeme suddenly growled. "Get Chelsea out now."

Cullen didn't wait for questions; he simply gripped her waist and dragged her back despite her struggles, holding her against him as Graeme moved closer to the unconscious young woman.

Her scent was Cassie, with only the slightest, subtle difference.

"Graeme?" Cullen questioned him softly, suspicion suddenly flaring inside him.

Graeme shook his head, his gaze turning back to Cullen.

"That's not Cassie," he stated.

Chelsea froze beside him. "Of course it's Cassie," she snapped. "Who else could it be?"

Who indeed? Graeme thought warily, but it was not who it appeared to be.

"That is not Cassie Sinclair," Graeme stated again, nodding toward the unconscious woman. "That's her twin."

As he made the announcement the ground rumbled with sound as three stealth heli-jets hovered over the area.

"This is Director Breaker, Western Breed Affairs. Stand down for landing. I repeat. This is Director Breaker, Western Breed Affairs, stand down for landing."

The announcement had Cullen's eyes narrowing, a growl rumbling in Graeme's throat and Samara Cerves cursing a blue streak.

"I'm going to rip his head off," Graeme snarled. "And stuff it up his ass."

Turning, they watched as the crafts landed. Doors opened, spilling out three dozen enforcers and the director of the Window Rock Breed Affairs office.

Striding toward them, Rule, Lawe and surprisingly their mates rushed to the heli-jet.

"I hear we have a scientist to collect," Rule announced his, eyes narrowed as he took in Graeme's expression.

"Actually," Graeme growled. "You don't."

"Come on, Graeme." Rule smiled consolingly. "You know I can't let you keep her. We had a report they were flying close and we've been searching for them all night."

"There's no scientist," he snarled.

"Dammit, Graeme, I'm not in the mood to fight you . . ."

"Fuck you, you mangy damned cat." Graeme stepped aside, the frustration in his tone unmistakable. "There's no fucking scientist."

Rule and Lawe stepped to the entrance of the heli-jet, then froze.

"I just left her at the offices." Shock roughened his voice. "How the fuck . . ." He turned back to the enforcers trailing him. "Contact Jonas. Now!" Turning back, he stared at the unconscious young woman. "There was no report of attack . . ."

"It's not Cassie, Rule." Chelsea gripped his arm hard. "That's not Cassie."

"That is Cassie," Lawe snapped. "You know . . ."

"It's her twin, dammit," Graeme growled, a rough, savage sound filled with impatience. "The witch has a twin . . ."

Rule stepped closer. Easing into the interior cautiously, he reached out and carefully brushed aside the long, lush curls that spilled around her pale face.

"She smells like her," he protested, his voice shocked.

"There's a difference." Graeme's querulous tone was followed by a vicious curse. "Trust me, it's there."

Lawe joined his brother and crouched in front of the girl, staring at her, their expressions disbelieving.

"Get the medic over here," Rule said to his brother, never taking his eyes off the girl's face. "Contact Jonas yourself. Send all the enforcers back but your four most trusted. I want a lid on this." He turned to stare at Samara with piercing, ice blue eyes.

She shook her head. "None have seen this but those standing here now," she told him quietly. "The heli-jet was empty but for the Council soldiers. There was no scientist. I swear this to you."

He stared at her for several more long moments before nodding abruptly, his gaze flicking to his brother, Lawe, as he suddenly jumped from the interior and hurried to the waiting enforcers.

"Fuck." Rule turned back to the girl, moving farther inside the comfortable interior as both Diane Justice and Gypsy Breaker climbed in beside him.

"I second that," Diane murmured. "Get ready for the explosion. We're going to get to see Dash Sinclair erupt and Jonas melt down. It's not going to be pretty."

It wasn't going to be pretty indeed.

Wrapping his arms around his mate, Cullen moved from the heli-jet; the desire to get her someplace secure, someplace safe, was a driving need he couldn't ignore any longer.

"Come on," Graeme snarled. "Let these bastards clean up. We'll return to the estate. You can have your suite in the house or the one in the caverns. Take your pick."

Cullen shot him an amused glance. He was in big brother mode again.

"Deal with it," Graeme snapped. "I'm not in the mood for your I'm-a-big-boy crap tonight. Let's roll."

"Take our Runner, there's four seats." Juan nodded to the vehicle still sitting where they'd left it between them and the Bureau heli-jets. "We'll collect it later, I'm certain."

It would be much later, Cullen thought, swinging his mate in his arms, holding her tight until he reached the Runner.

Graeme's estate was closer, he thought.

That would work.

It would work perfectly.

· E P Í L O G U E ·

From Graeme's Journal
The Recessed Primal Breed

Brother, when your Primal has emerged, I pray your mate has come through whatever danger has stalked her. With the mating, a Bengal's Primal cannot remain caged. Recessive or active, the Primal will surge back to its place beneath the skin.

With your Primal free, your mate by your side, know that even in Primal form, even at my most brutal, still the thought of my mate was not the only one that drove me. The thought of the brother who sacrificed the solace of his animal for so many years for me, was always a knowledge I held close to me as well.

She was his life.

Holding his mate close later that day as he came awake, Cullen felt a sense of relief that was euphoric. This was his woman, his mate. Because of her and the connection they'd shared since that first night at her father's, he'd controlled the Primal as it emerged.

The extraordinary strength and cunning it possessed had ensured his ability to protect her, but her bond to him and his knowledge that she lived had kept the feral madness from overtaking him.

Now, looking back at the knowledge he'd sensed as the Primal, Cullen knew that connection was the reason he'd also maintained his calm over the years.

Until Chelsea had tried to leave him and resign from the Agency.

Running his hand up her bruised hip in a whisper of a caress, he let the miracle of her sink inside him, warming parts of his soul he'd never known were cold. Those hidden places were now warm and comforted and filled with the love that flowed from his mate.

Brushing his lips against her neck and licking over the mating mark, he felt her come awake. Languidly, lazily, she stretched against him. Her hum of pleasure was a gentle sigh against his arm where she rested her head.

"Good morning," she murmured, her rear flexing against his hard-on.

"You feel so good this morning."

"Just this morning?" she asked, a smile filling her voice.

"Every morning." He nipped her ear, then licked over the little wound.

Her breath caught as he sensed her pleasure and her need beginning to fill the air around him.

"Hip hurt?" he asked, smoothing his hand over her rear, determined he wouldn't hurt her.

"No pain." She sounded surprised. "Whatever Graeme put in that injection absolutely rocks."

He had to grin at that. Graeme's mad-genius mind occasionally came up with a miracle. That injection, Cullen often thought, was just that, a miracle. A painkiller as well as a powerful aid to the Breed's already strong ability to heal.

"Feel good, do you?" he chuckled.

"What does he put in that? He could make millions." She was stretching cautiously again, easing into moving, testing the area of her body that had been abused.

"It only works for Breeds and their mates," he assured her. "The few humans he tested it on didn't react real well."

Violent heaving for the better part of an hour had resulted.

"From the appearance of his lab, money's no object anyway," she sighed as his lips brushed over her shoulder. "That feels so good, Cullen."

His fingers trailed over her thigh.

"You have to rest or the medication in the injection won't do what it's supposed to," he warned her. "So you just lie right there and I'll take care of everything."

"Will you?" Laughter bubbled in her throat. "I think I could probably handle that."

Sliding his hand between her thighs, he lifted her leg, easing it over his as he tucked the head of his cock between the slick, swollen folds he found there.

A little moan fell from her lips as he began working inside her. Slow, easy thrusts, taking her by increments, loving the heated, flexing caress of her snug pussy around the ultrasensitive, engorged head of his cock. So sweet and hot and so much pleasure that he was amazed by it every time she took him.

"I love you," he groaned at her ear. "With all of me, sweet Chelsea, I love you."

Chelsea felt her heart melt, the incredible pleasure rushing through her, burning brighter, sharper as she felt the emotion flowing from him. The commitment, the promise, had always been between them.

She had never realized he was always a part of her. He had been a part of her since she sensed he was too terrified to eat because he feared the soup was drugged.

There was so much she knew now, things she sensed. He was a part of her soul, not just a part of her body.

Though the pleasure rushing her as he became a part of her body was so incredible, so sensual, that she knew she'd never find anything this good anywhere but in his arms.

"Kiss me, Chelsea," he groaned, pushing completely inside her, the iron-hard length of his erection buried to the hilt.

As she turned her head to him, his lips came over hers, covering them and caressing them with hungry demand. Chelsea felt the drugging, drowsy pleasure rushing through her. His kiss was wildfire, cinnamon and spice and the wild taste of the desert air. And she loved it.

She loved him.

That taste marked him as hers only. Her heart and her mate and every dream she'd ever had.

She moaned when his lips slid over her jaw, her neck, his hips moving with strong, sure strokes as he pumped his shaft inside her. Sensitive tissue parted to each heavy thrust, clenching around his erection with each retreat and return.

Impaling her with each rocking movement of his hips, he caressed and stroked the slick inner flesh even as his hands and lips moved over her shoulders, neck and breasts.

His fingers gripped her tender nipples, hands cupped and molded her swollen breasts. Hungry lips moved over her shoulder, the base of her neck, his teeth rasping over the flesh and sending sharp, vibrant flashes of sensation streaking to her womb.

"I love you," she gasped, feeling the tension increasing in bands of impending ecstasy.

That tension, the pleasure, it raged through her, chaotic and whipping with a storm of such sensation she felt herself becoming lost within it.

The heavy, heated thrusts became faster and harder, stroking inside her with driving intensity. The storm raged, it built and in a flash of blinding, destructive ecstasy, it exploded through her senses. On the heels of her orgasm she felt Cullen thrust deep, hard.

The mating barb emerged, locked him inside her, increasing the storm and the explosions tearing through both of them.

His release spilled inside her, pulsing hot and brilliant in continuing waves of blinding pleasure.

When the storm eased, Chelsea found herself collapsing boneless to the bed, wasted from the pleasure and ready for another nap.

Still, a protesting moan fell from her lips when he pulled free of her, his breathing heavy as he curled himself around her.

"I love you, wild woman," he whispered, his voice drowsy and rough with emotion.

"I love you, tiger man," she answered, feeling his arms wrapped around her, a kiss pressing to the mating mark.

They had so much to talk about, so much to figure out. But they had time for that. Time to make everything work and to find the compromises that would them both happy.

WESTERN DIVISION OF THE BUREAU OF BREED AFFAIRS

A lifetime of running was over, and that wasn't a good thing.

Running hadn't been so bad. She'd been free, able to feel the breeze against her skin whenever she wanted to, able to run in the wild, to taste the falling rain or feel the sunlight against her skin. She'd just had to be careful whenever she did it.

Running had been fraught with fear, with uncertainty, but if she was running, then she had a chance at a future, a chance to live.

She was very much afraid those chances were a thing of the past now.

Kenzi Deacon paced the opulent suite she was confined to, bare feet sinking into the thick, expensive carpet. She preferred the feel of grass beneath her feet, she thought wearily. The wind against her face, the sound of the forest filling her ears. She didn't like being here; she didn't want to be here. But there was no way to escape either.

The silver toe ring she wore flashed at the ragged edge of her jeans, drawing her attention for a heartbeat of time and clenching her chest with pain. The ring was the last gift from her parents. It was the only piece of jewelry they'd ever given her, for any reason, and she'd been so surprised, so pleased by it. And no more than days later, they were gone. Murdered.

They'd tried so hard to protect her, fought to keep her hidden. They'd been so certain they would be safe, buried in the Cascade mountains, when they'd made the harrowing trip there years ago. *The last refuge*, her father had called it, his studious, somber expression showing none of the concern she knew he'd felt.

They'd been found, though. Her parents were murdered in front of her eyes, her father's desperate attempt to shield her mother so heartbreakingly hopeless. Even as he'd thrown himself in front of his wife, that knowledge had been in his eyes, that the running was over.

Now here she was, one of the two places they'd fought to keep her free of. And one of the two places Kenzi had sworn she would never allow herself to be. She'd been so certain she could keep this from happening, so certain . . . And she'd been so wrong.

Pushing her fingers through her short mop of black hair, she shot a disgusted look at the wig that the Council Breeds had so carefully fitted to her head before taking her from the cabin she'd lived in with her parents. The riotous curls spilled from the seat of the chair she'd tossed it to, tumbled to the floor and reminded her of the reason she'd been hunted for so many years: her genetic tie to the young woman the Council was offering a fortune for.

She hated it, and she hated the knowledge that those Breeds had planned to pass her off as the woman she looked so much like to collect a bounty they were so greedy for. They weren't even part of the Council. They were no more than mercenaries, despite their appearance.

She hadn't even been able to fight them as they put that monstrosity on her. Whatever they'd had in that dart they shot in her neck, it had taken her down instantly, paralyzing her, though she'd been awake, able to feel everything. To see everything.

To watch as the mercenaries fired on her parents, bullets ripping into her father's body and slamming into her mother's. The fear, the smell of their blood, the horrifying realization that nothing would ever be the same again.

Stalking to the wide windows overlooking the desert, she stared out at the rising hills and vastness of a land she'd once longed to see. She'd never been to the desert before. The heavy forests of the mountains were easier to hide in, her parents had always insisted. She had a feeling it wouldn't have mattered where they hid; they would have still been found. They were destined to be found. They should have done as she'd suggested years ago and deserted her, saved themselves while they still could.

The sound of the door opening behind her had her swinging around. At the first glimpse of the Breed that entered the suite, her heart began pounding out of control before she could force back the terror rising inside her.

Rhyzan Brannigan.

Celtic green eyes, long pitch-black hair falling between his shoulders from the leather thong that held it low at his nape. Six and a half feet tall, he towered over her short five feet four.

He was dressed in dark, obviously expensive dress slacks and a white dress shirt, the sleeves rolled to the elbows, but the veneer of civilization did nothing to hide the animal beneath. Pure power and primal awareness filled his gaze as well as his expression. Those green eyes flicked over her, from her feet to her short hair, before turning from her as though she was insignificant. She didn't matter; only the reason for her existence, the threat she might pose to the woman she shared the features of her face with, mattered.

As an individual, as a person in her own right, she meant nothing. He simply didn't give a damn if she survived or not.

Those brilliant green eyes flicked to the wig, then back to her before he strode to the table at the side of the room.

"Would you sit down, please." He extended a hand to the chair across from him, his expression forbidding as he watched her.

Crossing her arms over her breasts, she stared back at him mutinously. "I know how to stand and talk. I can even walk and chew gum at the same time."

His brow arched, the bland expression devoid of emotion.

"Aren't you multitalented," he murmured before those hard green eyes became chips of ice. "Now sit your ass down before I have you tied to the fucking chair."

The clipped order, delivered with crystal-clear demand, assured her that he wouldn't hesitate to carry out the threat.

Great. The son of a bitch was just as hard as her father had said he was. And likely just as cruel.

Watching him warily, she moved to the chair, pulled it out and sat down.

Kenzi remained silent as he followed suit. Once settled at the table, he placed the electronic pad he carried in front of him and activated it with precise, controlled movements.

Once he had a file pulled up, he went over it for a moment before lifting his gaze back to hers.

"There was no file found with any information on you in the heli-jet you were on, nor on any of the Breeds flying with you. Those we have in custody claim they captured you in the mountains and were picking up another young woman in the desert before flying to Argentina. Is this correct?"

Kenzi shrugged. Did he really expect her to cooperate that easily? She was terrified of him, but she was even more terrified of being forced to stay there.

After a few seconds the Coyote Breed laid the stylus he held on the table, folding his hands over the e-pad, and gave her another of those icy stares.

"Because of the young woman you look so much like, I'm willing to make this an interview rather than the interrogation I would personally prefer. Now, a few ground rules." Ice dripped from his voice. "Shrugs are not answers. You will answer me. Lie to me and I will know it. Attempt any deception and I will know it. Now, shall we start again?"

She waited until she thought he was ready to ask the question again.

"What's the difference between this and an interrogation?" she demanded, her one weakness, her temper, coming out to play.

He blinked. Once.

"No truth serum, no pain, and no cell where every time you go to take a piss other prisoners are watching and trying to jack off at the thought of catching a glimpse of your bare ass. Do you have any further questions?" The answer had her swallowing tightly, but she did have one more question.

"If I cooperate, will you let me leave?" she asked. "Today. Can I just walk out?"

His expression gave nothing away. Whatever he was thinking, there was no reading it. And that could be very bad for her.

"Answer every question honestly and provide me with what I need, and after that, I don't give a damn where you go," he assured her. "But I will have the answers I want first."

Kenzi nodded hesitantly, praying he wasn't lying to her.

"Your previous information was correct, then. The Breeds transporting me in the heli-jet had no information on me. I know they weren't Council, though. They were mercenaries. They intended to collect a bounty being paid for the woman I look like, just as they intended to collect a fee for the woman they were picking up in the desert."

He made a quick note on the pad before lifting his gaze back to her.

"What is your name? Your full name," he asked her without emotion, without any sort of interest really.

She inhaled slowly, deeply. She hated questions.

"Mackenzie Elizabeth Deacon." And she knew the questions would just become harder to answer.

"Birth parents?" he asked.

She glared at him, hating him, hating the questions.

"I didn't ask to come here," she reminded him. "Your people brought me here against my volition."

"Shall I ask the question again?" He stared at her again, green eyes surrounded by heavy, thick lashes, his tone so cold she'd probably get frostbite.

"Dane and Elizabeth Colder," she answered, fighting to push back the resentment and pain at the thought of them.

"Known siblings?" Rhyzan asked in that hard, brutally cold tone.

"Cassandra and Kenton Sinclair." She stared over his shoulder now, concentrating on the mirror behind it, trying to distance herself from the "interview."

"Known genetic status?"

Known genetic status. Human or Breed, and if Breed what designation. She knew what that question meant.

Her lips thinned. "Coyote."

Her interrogator paused then. "You mean Coyote and Wolf."

She turned her gaze back to him. "No, Mr. Brannigan, I mean Coyote. My genetics weren't mixed, only Cassie's. I'm the throwaway child. The one they didn't want." What had happened to the Wolf child, though?

He said nothing for a long moment, then placed the stylus on the table and watched her clinically.

"Answer this one question and you can walk out of here now, and just disappear if that's what you want," he told her then. "The moment I confirm the answer and have what I want, then you can leave."

Kenzi nodded hesitantly.

There were strings attached. She knew there were. Freedom could never be that easy.

"Where is your sister, Cassandra Sinclair?"

She blinked back at him, not certain what he meant. Confused, she gave a short, quick shake of her head.

"What do you mean?" she asked, frowning at the flash of retribution in his gaze.

"I mean, Cassie disappeared just before your arrival here, in this building. Tell me where she is, and you can go." His expression didn't shift an iota, but his voice had a terrifying harshness to it that had her heart jumping in fear. "If you don't tell me, then I'll throw you in the deepest, darkest fucking cell I can find."

Cassie was gone?

Kenzi could feel the fear beginning to tear through her, panic surging past her fragile control as her heart began racing, pushing the adrenaline-laced terror straight to her mind and freezing her with the implications of what he'd just said.

"I don't . . ."

"Tell me you don't know, and I'll drag you to that cell right now," he growled, and she believed him. She could see it in his face, see his desire to do it, hear it in his voice.

Kenzi jumped from the chair, the panic rioting through her making her sick to her stomach, threatening to make her heave on the beautiful carpet.

"But I don't," she whispered. "I don't know . . ."

He rose to his feet, picked up the pad and stared down at her with chilling disregard. "I'll give you some time to think about it, Mackenzie," he offered coldly. "Have an answer when I come back, or I'll send you to that cell."

He walked out. Not a backward glance, not another chance to answer his question or another threat. The door closed behind him, the sound of the lock clicking ominous in the silence of the room.

She didn't know . . .

And it wouldn't matter.

Now she was really fucked . . .

CERVES COMPOUND

Samara was there when her baby opened pretty green eyes and blinked up at her.

In the child's eyes, there was a flash of confusion, of fear that she should have never felt, never known.

"There's Momma's baby," Samara whispered, her voice hoarse, love suddenly flooding her, swelling inside her soul as she touched the child's cheek.

"Momma?" the child asked, the uncertainty in her voice bringing tears to Samara's eyes. "Are you my momma?"

Samara brushed back the tangled curls, her lips trembling as she held back her tears.

"Yes, baby," she whispered. "I'm your momma. Do you remember your name?"

Little lips trembled and tears filled her eyes, distress darkening the emerald hue.

"It's okay, sweetheart," Samara promised. "I think you must have had a nasty fall. Your name is Lily, for the beautiful flowers I love. Lily Cerves. Do you like that name?"

Lily nodded, the tears drying, though the confusion remained. "Why don't I remember my name, Momma?"

Samara inhaled, her breathing hitching at the wash of emotion and fragile hope building inside her.

"I think you fell and bumped your head, baby." Samara eased her fears. "But Momma has you now and I won't let you be hurt ever again."

Her heart melted, already loving this child, determined to protect her from anyone who would harm her.

"Rest now, my Lily. Momma is right here with you," she promised the baby, her Lily. She brushed her fingers over the child's flushed cheeks.

Lily's eyes closed, fluttering against baby cheeks before sleep settled over her again.

It was then that the Breed, Graeme, stepped from the shadowed corner of the room, his gaze heavy as he stared at the child.

"Get out of the business, Samara," he growled. "And hide her. Hide her well."

Samara nodded faintly, brushing back the dark hair next to Lily's cheek.

"We were doing so for Louisa before she was taken," she told him quietly. "We wanted only for her to be proud of her momma and poppa. We will continue to do so now. We will remain here, on this estate. Where her uncle Graeme can help us care for her."

It was a risk bringing him there, letting him see the child, but they'd been unable to wake her. And she would need someone who understood her Breed physiology, in case she became ill or hurt.

"We can take care of her, Graeme," she whispered, desperate now. "Juan, Esteban and I, and you." She had nothing but hope at this point. "If we take her to the Breeds, then the Council will not stop hunting her. This way, no one knows what happened to her. Perhaps even the soldiers lied and she was not there."

Staring at Lily, Graeme restrained a sigh. It wasn't quite that simple, but only a few of the soldiers were left living and they wouldn't be living for long. He'd have to make certain of that.

It seemed the Council was still playing with genetics. This child was proof of that.

This beautiful, innocent child was even more unique than Samara knew. The only way to protect her was to indeed hide her. From Council and Breeds alike.

How very interesting, he thought.

It might be time to start a new journal.

✦ BREED TERMS ✦

Breeds: Creatures of genetic engineering both before and after conception, with the genetics of the predators of the Earth such as the lion, tiger, wolf, coyote and even the eagle added to the human sperm and ova. They were created to become a super army and the new lab rats for scientific experimentation.

The Genetics Council: A group of twelve shadowy figures who funded the labs and research into bioengineering and genetic mutation to create a living being of both human and animal DNA, though references to the Genetics Council also refer to affiliated political, military and Breed individuals and groups.

Rogue Breeds: Breeds who have declared no known loyalties and exist as mercenaries following the highest bidder.

Council Breeds: Breeds whose loyalties are still with the scientists and soldiers who created and trained them. Unwilling or unable for whatever reason to break the conditioning instilled in them from birth. Mostly Coyote Breeds whose human genetics are far more dominant than in most Breeds.

Council Soldiers: Mostly human, though sometimes Breeds, soldiers who willingly give their loyalty to the Council because of their ideals or belief in the project and their belief that Breeds lack true humanity.

Bureau of Breed Affairs: Created to oversee the growing Breed population and to ensure that the mandates of Breed Law are fully upheld by law enforcement agencies, the courts and the Breed communities. The Bureau oversees all funds that are paid by the United States as well as other countries whose political leaders were involved with the Genetics Council or any labs in their countries. They also investigate species discrimination and hate crimes against Breeds and track down scientists, trainers and lab directors who have escaped Breed justice.

Director of the Bureau of Breed Affairs: The position has been held for the past ten years by Jonas Wyatt, a conniving, calculating and manipulating Lion Breed who ensures that Breed Law is upheld and all Breeds are given a chance to be free to find mates who will ensure future generations of the Breed species.

Breed Ruling Cabinet: Composed of an equal number of feline, Wolf and Coyote Breeds as well as human political leaders. It governs and enforces the mandates of Breed Law and oversees Breed Law where the separate Breed communities are concerned.

Purists and Supremacists and Their Various Groups: Groups of individuals who for reasons of religion, fear or just personal feelings believe that the Breeds are not human, but no more than puppets created in man's image. They're determined to destroy first the Breeds' public standing, then their lives. They dream of a world where Breed genetics have no hope, no chance and no threat of ever infecting the human population.

Their species discrimination against the Breeds includes but is not confined to the following: capturing Breeds and Breed-mated couples for further scientific study of how to weaken them or create a drug that will prevent the conception of hybrid children; guerrilla attacks against Breeds and Breed facilities; public outcries and protests against Breeds, Breed-funded and -hosted events and/or charities; bombings of Breed offices, attempts to kill key Breed political figures and general harassment whenever possible.

Nano-nit: A tiny microscopic robotic device that can be attached to a video or audio bug. Once in the proper location, it can be activated remotely, when it then detaches and finds the closest electrical source, where it will burrow inside and then follow the current to a designated electrical impulse for cameras, computers, televisions or any audio/video or computerized component, and then begins uploading specifically programmed information. Once the internal hard drive is filled, the nit then detaches and follows the electrical currents once again, to a point away from the original location, where it then finds a device, any device with Internet or uploading capabilities, and then transmits the information to a location that cannot be determined unless the nit is found during the upload process, after initial activation.

Named a nano-nit because of its size and similarity to the parasitic louse egg, or nit.

There is no known security to detect a nit specifically, and once activated, it's impossible to find, detect or exterminate. To find out, the host device must first be detected, then placed in a static-free, airtight shell, where a nit reader is plugged into the host device. The nit is then activated and makes its way from the host to search for an electrical source. It moves then to the nit reader's signature using the attached nit cord, which is an open-ended electrical cord that simulates the source the nit requires. Once there, a tiny probe locks the nit in place, allowing the reader to decode the programming and determine its original commands.

Nits have very little encryption. Because of their size and the requirements for upload space, programming is confined to what to upload and where to dump.

Because of their specific technology, a host device can be only an audio or video transmitter or bug. The nit is unable to function independently when attached to any other device.

Mating Heat: A chemical, biological, pheromonal reaction between a Breed and the male or female Breed or human that nature and emotion have selected as their one mate. Believed to be able to only mate once— though as Breed scientists have noted concerning other anomalies within the Breeds, nature is playing with the rules of the Breed species. To this point, general information on Mating Heat has been contained. Tabloids and gossip columns write about it, but no proof has been found to verify the rumor of it. Yet.

Mating Heat Symptoms: (Breed) A swelling of the small glands beneath the tongue and a taste, often different from Breed to Breed, that could be spicy, sweet or a combination of both. Heightened arousal. The need to touch and be touched by the mate often. A heightened need for sex that results in a sensitivity to each touch and release that heightens the pleasure as well.

(Mate) An almost addictive need for the taste of the mating hormone secreted from the glands beneath the Breed's tongue. A sensitivity along the body and heightened need for sex that can become extremely painful for the female, whether human or Breed. Heightened emotions, an inability to refrain from touching or needing to be touched by the other.

Desert Dragoon: A vehicle built with independent suspension to traverse the rough, rocky and often uneven terrains of the desert. Built wide, for power rather than speed, blocky and capable of ramming through obstacles and carrying mounted weapons. Equipped with stealth technology, real-time GPS, satellite communications and laser- and bullet-resistant force fields that operate for short periods of time and act as theft deterrents.

Breed Ruling Cabinet: A cabinet of six high-ranking Breeds of each species and six humans of prominence and/or power that makes decisions for the Breed community as a whole.

Breed Law: The laws that govern every legal, contractual, criminal or enterprise endeavor involving any Breed or Breed affiliate, including but not limited to wives, children, siblings, parents, lovers, intended spouses or the same of mates involved, and how the various governments of participating countries must deal with them.

Law of Self-Warrant: Any Breed can, one time only, accept punishment or death for any criminal act that would cause their mate, child, parent or other associated relative to face a punishment the Breed believes would cause his mate or child more harm than the loss of the Breed would cause.

Hybrid/Breed Hybrid: A child conceived naturally of a mated couple or of a Breed-human couple, whether mated or through artificial insemination.

4/17

7 × 12/17 (8/18)
4 × 12/18 (8/19)(12/21)(4/24)